A Virtual Affair

# TRACIE PODGER

Copyright © 2016
Tracie Podger
All Rights Reserved.

This book is a work of fiction. Characters, places, events and incidents are a product of the author's imagination. Any resemblance to real persons, living or dead, is purely coincidental. By purchasing this material, you agree not to share content to anyone or organisation without prior permission from the author. You agree not to sell, trade, copy or cause to copy, pirate or cause to pirate, scan, replicate or contribute to the replication of any portion of this publication. You also agree to abide by the Digital Management Rights Act.
If you have not purchased A Virtual Affair by Tracie Podger, or it was not purchased for you, please return it to the seller and purchase your own copy.

You can contact Tracie via email to tpodger@hotmail.com if you have any questions or concerns.

# The Serenity Poem

*Grant me the serenity*
*to accept the things I cannot change;*
*courage to change the things I can;*
*and wisdom to know the difference.*

*Living one day at a time;*
*enjoying one moment at a time;*
*accepting hardships as the pathway to peace;*
*taking this world*
*as it is, not as I would have it;*
*trusting that all things will be made right*
*if I surrender;*
*that I may be reasonably happy in this life;*
*and supremely happy*
*forever in the next.*

# Prologue

Do you know what hope smells like? Let me tell you...

First, I have to explain where I am. At the bottom of my small garden is a gate. A plain wooden gate that needs one hinge fixed. Beyond the gate are a few steps carved into a grassy bank. It's down those steps that you can reach the beach.

The Atlantic Ocean pounds the centuries old cliffs, the rugged shards of black rock snake their way into the sea, and the coarse yellow sand whips around my feet. I breathe in deeply. The smell of exposed seaweed and salty air fill my senses. That is what hope smells likes.

For a long time there had been no hope. I was at the bottom of a well, in the worst place I could be. I couldn't see the light at the end of the proverbial tunnel. I felt nothing but sorrow and sadness—and pain, so much pain. It has been a long journey, but I need to take you back a couple of years, not quite to the beginning but to a pivotal point in my life. A time when I thought everything was going to be okay, when I thought my life was turning around. A time when I had plans and believed I had the future I longed for. But I was wrong. It's only now that I have hope.

What am I hoping for? A reply to an email I have just sent.

# Chapter One

It was on a cold, blustery, and wet January day in 2014 when my best friend, Carla, asked me a question that was to change my life.

"Please, Jayne, think about it. Or rather, don't think about it. Let's just do this. I need it. Can I use emotional blackmail? That's okay, isn't it? Because we *are* lifelong friends, and lifelong friends do this kind of thing."

She smiled at me in a silly kind of way, and batted her very long fake eyelashes.

We were in the local coffeehouse, The Blue Cow, when she landed her grand plan on me. When I say coffeehouse, it doubled up as an art gallery. The walls were adorned with paintings, some hideous, and several of my photographs.

"Jayne? If emotional blackmail isn't going to work, then can we try pleading, begging, perhaps? You're going to be forty-five this year; that's halfway through your life. It's my present to you."

"I wasn't listening, what did you ask? And that's more than halfway through my life," I smirked at her.

She sat back with a scowl, folded her arms over her chest, careful not to crease the cream Chanel lambswool and whatever cardigan. I think it was the over description of her latest purchase that had me tuned out.

"I'm kidding. I heard you. You want me to run the risk of unbelievable anguish, the wrath of him indoors; the arguments that will lead up to and after a holiday with you."

I rested back in my chair and folded my arms over the ten-year-old blue knitted cardigan, probably from a charity shop, with mismatched buttons. I batted my short, stubby eyelashes, a result of not removing the previous day's mascara, at her.

"Yes," she simply answered.

"Okay."

"Okay?"

"Okay."

"Fuck, you gave in way easier than I expected. I spent a fortune on this bribe as well," she smiled and laughed, then handed me a lovely decorated paper bag with red ribbon handles.

"A gift? I should have held out a little longer."

"Open it." Carla clapped her hands and bounced on her chair a little.

I deliberately pulled the ribbon bow open slowly. Carla was a 'rip it open and throw the wrapper on the floor' type of woman, I liked to tease her. I heard her sigh but she wasn't going to bite that time. I opened the bag and peered inside. Whatever the gift was, it was wrapped in red tissue paper. I reached in and pulled it out. A Victoria's Secret sticker held the tissue paper closed.

"If this is underwear, I'm not opening it here," I said.

"It's not. Now open the bloody thing."

I ripped through the tissue paper to see red material. My cheeks coloured the same shade as I held up one of the items. A scrap of material that had two plaited ties on the edges masqueraded as bikini bottoms.

"My arse won't fit in that," I said.

Carla laughed. "It's your size, and it's not supposed to cover your whole arse, which is not large at all."

"That will just about cover one cheek." I picked up the top. "And that will cover just a nipple," I said with a laugh. The bikini was gorgeous, there was no denying that, but the last time I'd worn such an item I was a preteen.

I placed the items back in the bag and sighed. "Thank you, but you need to stop buying me things. You're making me feel like a charity case."

"Jayne, I've known you my whole life. I want to do this for you. I want you to get away from him, if only for a couple of weeks."

Him: the wonderful, best friend to everyone but his wife, the adulterer, the cold-hearted-didn't-care-took-every-moment-to-humiliate-me husband that went by the name of Michael.

I looked through the steamed up window and out over the village green. People were scurrying to and fro, going about their day, and visiting the local shops. I'd lived in the village for almost twenty years and loved everything about it; the gossipy old women that sat on tables near us to the kindly old man who ran the pharmacy. Although everyone knew everyone's business, there was something comforting about the village.

"He's going to burst a blood vessel over this," I said quietly.

"And do you really care?"

I thought for a moment. I'd never done any of the things I'd planned when I was younger. Michael wouldn't allow it. I did care though; that was the point. Michael would make my life hell, from the moment I told him to the point of leaving, but I needed the holiday. Carla needed the holiday.

It had been two months since her divorce had been finalised, two years of battling her ex-husband after discovering his affair. I remembered the day Carla had called me. She was sobbing and it was hard to understand her. It was only that her name showed on my phone, otherwise I would not have recognised the caller. I jumped in the car and drove straight to her house. Thankfully I had a key; she was in no state to even make it to the front door. I found her curled in a ball and crying on her bed.

It seemed Charles, who worked with Michael, had decided to spice up his already perfect life with a little secretary sex—clichéd but true.

The secretary had decided she wanted more and deliberately got pregnant. Outcome? One miserable secretary, one screaming baby, and Charles much lighter in the pocket and property portfolio, thanks to a wonderful female judge.

Carla had forgone her career. For as long as I could remember she had wanted to be an architect. Yet she'd done nothing but dead-end jobs, such as shelf stacking in the local supermarket at night, to help support Charles while he trained in the money markets. His affair had devastated her, but the fact that he had fathered a child had destroyed her. Carla couldn't have children and the thought that Charles was to become a parent, the one thing she so desperately wanted, tore her heart apart.

"So?"

I turned back to face my best friend. "Let's do it."

We left the coffeehouse and walked the few paces to the travel agency. Ten minutes later, we were flicking through brochures for the holiday Carla had in mind.

"That's it," she said, pointing to a page.

"I can't afford that," I replied.

"You're not paying, I am. Or rather shithead is," she said with a smile.

"I can't let you pay for that. It's the Maldives, that's bloody expensive."

"I know, and I am." She turned to the assistant. "Can you book that please?"

"Carla, we need…" She cut me off with a raised hand.

A half hour later, our holiday was booked and paid for. We were to leave in two weeks. I panicked.

Wrapped up in our coats, hats, and scarves, we started the short walk back to my house. Although Michael wouldn't be there, my stomach always knotted the closer I got to home. It did a triple knot on that day.

I loved my home. I'd fought and, for only the one time, won the battle to live in that house. Prior to that, Michael and I had lived in a sterile apartment in London, but when our second child came, we had no choice but to move. Kent, close to a motorway and train station, was a compromise I'd fought hard for.

As we reached the front gate, Carla gave me a hug and made promises to call me that evening before climbing in her car and heading home herself. I walked the path to the front door.

Before I'd even managed to close the door, I was assaulted. Twelve stone of muscle leapt at me, tongue licking and tail wagging. Houdini was the only one that was always pleased to see me. I knelt to give my dog a hug and thanked my lucky stars I had my coat on. His slobber was everywhere.

"Did you miss your mum?" I said, burying my face into his

black fur.

He followed me to the kitchen. I shrugged out of my coat and put the kettle on. The wind howled, rattling the single pane windows in their rickety frames. The house was listed, and we couldn't replace them with the plastic double-glazed ones Michael had wanted, thankfully.

I sat at the kitchen table with my cup of tea and opened my laptop. I Googled the Four Seasons in the Maldives. They owned two islands, ours, Landaa Giraavaru, was the more exclusive. A bubble of excitement started to chase that knot away.

"Guess what? I'm going to the Maldives," I told the dog.

I had many conversations with Dini; he was my second best friend and disliked Michael about much as Carla. Dini and Carla got along famously as long as he didn't go near her. Slobber and Prada never seemed to mix well. I sat for ages looking at the pristine beach, the beautiful azure-coloured sea, and read everything I could about the island. Then panicked again.

I had nothing to wear. I had the red bikini, of course, but not one item in my wardrobe suitable for a five-star island. And absolutely no way of purchasing new clothes for a holiday I knew Michael was going to disapprove of.

Each month I had to produce a set of fucking accounts, every purchase I'd made had to be accounted for. He'd question every item from the amount of panty liners—he didn't think they were necessary—to the bag of dog food; he didn't think the food or the dog were necessary.

As I passed the telephone in the hallway to make my way upstairs, I noticed the red light blinking; I had messages.

"Mum, your phone is never on, I really don't know why you

have one. Anyway, I won't be home this weekend; some friends have invited me to the South of France. I'll tap Dad for some money and see you in a week's time. Can you collect my laundry for me?"

Casey, my daughter and most definitely a clone of her father, had left the message. I sighed. She was in university, thoroughly spoilt by her father, who believed her to be his protégé, and as much as I loved her, a rather stuck up young lady. I had no intention of collecting her laundry. I blamed his parents for her attitude. Whether or not they truly were the upper class they portrayed themselves as, it was rubbing off on their granddaughter. They favoured her over my son, Ben, and that irked me.

I headed for my bedroom. Dini climbed on the bed while I pulled clothes from the back of drawers and storage boxes hidden in the wardrobe. There had to be something suitable among them.

I didn't care about the black hairs that would be left on the duvet; it was my bedroom. Michael had taken himself off to the spare room a year ago, citing my insomnia as his reason. After an hour of rifling through old clothes, I sat heavily on the bed. Dini laid his head on my lap, his dark brown, sorrowful eyes looked up at me.

"I know," I said. "It's all shit."

Michael thought nothing of spending over a thousand pounds on a handmade suit. Yet my bedroom floor was covered in clothes more than ten years old, and mostly charity shop finds. I'd managed to unearth two sundresses, a couple of pairs of shorts and some vest tops. From my knickers drawer, I dragged out a swimsuit so threadbare the white of the elastic could be seen through the black material. I wanted to cry.

I lay down on the bed and snuggled against Dini. How the fuck had my life ended up that way?

Michael and I had only married because I was pregnant. He'd spent a month berating me, trying to convince me that an abortion was the only option. He was an up and coming money trader, he didn't have the time for a child, he'd told me. But he did what he thought was the decent thing and we married, lying to everyone that Ben was born premature when he arrived seven months later.

I loved my son from the minute I found out I was pregnant and threw myself into being a stay at home mum. Michael wanted a nanny, wanted as little disruption to his life as possible. Over time, I became all the things he wanted—the cook, the cleaner, and the nanny. Somewhere along the way, I lost myself.

I wallowed in my self-pity for an hour or so, before reaching for my nightstand and taking out my journal. I'd kept a diary for years; it was always the one thing I looked forward to at Christmas time. My parents, my wonderful, loving, working-class parents, always bought me a new diary for Christmas and it would be the first gift I'd open. I smiled when I thought of my parents. They lived nearby in Crinkly Bottom as they called it. It was a complex for the elderly. Each had their own little bungalow and a community hall where they played cards one night a week.

They were the best grandparents as well. When I found myself pregnant for a second time, I sobbed on my mum's shoulder. For whatever strange reason, I stayed loyal to Michael and never burdened them with my troubles. But my mother knew. She knew my husband didn't love me, he never had.

We were both in a relationship we didn't want, yet neither had the courage to do anything about it. Many times over the twenty-five years we had been married, I'd wanted to leave, but I could never bring myself to do it, and I knew why. I was scared of being alone. My self-esteem wasn't just on the floor—it was digging its way to Australia. For years, from day one I guessed, Michael had chipped away at it. I was never good enough. I didn't cook as well as his mother. I couldn't socialise with his colleagues and their wives because I wasn't as intelligent. I remember the words that killed any feelings I'd had for him.

"You can take the girl out of the gutter, but not the gutter out of the girl," he'd said.

Michael believed, by marrying me, he'd done me a favour. He'd dragged me up from my working-class roots and spent years trying to mould me into the trophy wife he wanted. For a while, I complied. I did the lunch with his colleague's wives thing, but there was only so much talk of shoes and handbags I could stomach. They were great for walking in, for carrying the keys in, but an hour discussing the merits of the new Prada over the Louis Vuitton bored me shitless.

"This isn't getting us anywhere, Dini boy. Time for a walk," I said, sliding my legs over the side of the bed and sitting up.

The word 'walk' had Dini in a frenzy. He chased his tail and narrowly missed knocking me down the stairs as he rushed past. I grabbed his lead, pulled on my Wellingtons and coat, and opened the back door.

The house sat behind a farm and woods. We had a little gate that led straight into the field, although I never needed to put Dini on a lead, I slung it around my neck anyway.

The wind had died a little but the cold stung my face as I pulled my hood up. I walked and thought, planned, and even spoke out loud, the conversation I would have with Michael when he returned home—if he returned home.

Many times he would stay in London; where, I had no idea. Well, I did but refused to acknowledge it. He had early meetings, he would tell me. 'Early meetings' seemed to have become code for staying with the slut he was currently fucking. I giggled as I spoke the swear words out loud. I knew her, of course. Her husband had left her and Michael was the shoulder she used to cry on. She was his golfing partner, a typical, middle class, cling to anything with money type. She was welcome to him. As much as Michael didn't love me, I didn't love him either. It had saddened me when I'd first realised.

I walked my normal route, calling to Dini when he ran from my vision and headed home. I kicked off my Wellingtons, caked with mud, before entering the back door. Dini ran into the kitchen and straight to his bed in front of the Aga, the warmest place in the house.

I checked the mobile I'd left on the kitchen counter and noticed some missed calls. One from Casey, who had left a message telling me she'd call me another time, and one from Ben. After making tea and settling at the kitchen table, I called Ben back.

"Hey, Mum, been for a walk?" he asked once he'd answered.

"I have, sorry I missed your call. What are you up to?"

Ben told me about his latest landscaping project. I listened, loving to hear the enthusiasm in his voice as he spoke. He'd dropped out of college. Like me, he wasn't academic but loved to be outdoors. He'd started his own landscaping business, initially just helping the locals with their gardens. He'd asked Michael for a loan. Michael refused, of course. Casey could have what she wanted because she was still in education; Ben had to beg. Aunty Carla came to the rescue and helped him get his business off the ground.

"I have news," I said once he'd finished telling about a wonderful garden he was planning. "I'm going on holiday to the Maldives with Carla."

"Wow, that sounds amazing. When?"

"Two week's time, and I have a favour to ask. Can you look after Dini?"

"Of course. And two week's time? Blimey, Mum, you don't hang about. How did you get that past the old man?"

Ben rarely referred to Michael as Dad. No matter how hard I tried to protect him, he'd always felt the distance from Michael.

"I haven't told him yet," I said with a giggle.

"How do you think he'll take the news?"

"Oh, I'm sure he'll be thrilled for me," I said with a snort.

"Fuck him. You go, Mum. If you need some money, I have some saved."

Was it wrong of me to never chastise my son for swearing? He only ever did when he talked about his father. Ben was twenty-five years old, a grown man, and one I was extremely proud of. He lived with Kerry, the most beautiful and kindest young woman I'd ever met. Casey and Michael disliked her, of course; she wasn't from the county set.

"Thank you, darling, but I won't take your money."

We chatted a little longer. I asked how Kerry was. Ben was a little concerned that she had been poorly of late, but we ended our conversation with promises to speak the following day. Ben called me every single day. Casey I heard from once a month, if I was lucky—unless she wanted something.

I hadn't heard from Michael and was reluctant to call him. He was always cross when I rang him at work, but the evening was drawing in and I wanted to prepare dinner. I decided to send him a text.

*Can you let me know what time you'll be home? I want to get dinner on.*

I hesitated before pressing send, not really knowing why. Any form of communication with Michael was difficult. His reply was quick to arrive and curt, as usual.

*Won't be. Staying in London.*

I slammed the phone on the table. I wanted to ask if he was staying with her. I wanted to call him all the names under the sun, show him how far from the gutter my vocabulary had—or rather hadn't—risen. But I did none of that. I did what I always did—I ignored it.

He must have known that I knew. Although nothing had ever been said, I'd washed his shirts, stinking of her sickly, overpowering perfume. I'd scrubbed the lipstick stains from his collar and laughed, bitterly, at how corny that was. I wanted to confront him; it would be the ideal opportunity for us to separate. But I wasn't confident I'd walk out of our marriage with enough to live on.

I hated that I felt that way. I hated that I was only staying for the security. It made me feel weak. I hadn't worked the whole time we had been married and I was unsure what I could do. I'd been a secretary for a lovely old gentleman in his accountancy practice before getting married. My typing skills were still up to speed;

18

maybe I should start to look for a job. Maybe I could actually start that plan I'd written down years ago—Get Jayne A Life plan.

I had a plan, a very detailed list of things to do before I died. I'd just never started it. I'd had dreams and hopes from childhood for an exciting future; I hadn't fulfilled any of them. Instead I was stuck in a marriage of convenience, with a man who didn't like me, and was too scared to do anything about it.

# Chapter Two

"Good morning, how did he take the news?" Carla said, as soon as I picked up her call.

"He didn't come home."

"With the slut?"

"I imagine so," I replied.

"Oh, Jayne. Please do something about this. Kick him out, anything."

We had the same conversation on a regular basis. What Carla didn't understand was that she was a much stronger character than I was, and for all of Charles' faults, he didn't argue that much when he'd received the division of property and the payment he had to make. I believed Michael would fight me to the bitter end. He'd deliberately wear me down. He would make sure I was dragged through court, and he'd have the backing of his wealthy parents, not that Michael didn't earn well himself.

"Why don't I come over? We can plan," she said.

"Plan for what? But come on over anyway. I'll put the kettle on."

I loved Carla; we had known one another from birth. Our parents were friends and had lived next door to each other, in our small terrace houses in South East London, but sometimes she didn't 'get me.' She didn't understand my fears, she didn't see the forced smile I planted on my face every single day, when all I wanted to do was curl up in a ball and cry over my pitiful existence.

I just wanted a husband who loved me, children who respected me, and to have a life I could be proud of. I felt guilty all the time. I was living a lie and it was becoming harder to conceal my sadness from everyone.

I heard a car pull on the drive. Dini ran to the door, growling. He was a Neapolitan Mastiff, a dog I'd found a couple of years ago tied to a tree in the middle of winter and rescued, much to Michael's disgust.

Carla had a key and while I poured hot water into the teapot, she let herself in. I chuckled as I heard her try to stop Dini greet her.

"No. Down. This is Prada, not fucking Primark," she said.

"Dini," I called for him. "Leave the Prada alone."

"Remind me to visit in sweats next time," Carla said, as she placed her new handbag on the kitchen table.

"Like?" she asked, sweeping her hand over the pale blue leather.

"It's a bag."

"It's a lovely Michael Kors bag."

Carla wasn't materialistic, but she did enjoy spending her divorce settlement on nice things. I didn't begrudge her at all. She appreciated what she had, she didn't take anything for granted, and was way too generous with her friends.

"Tea?"

"Mmm, please. So, we need a plan, an exit plan," she said.

I sighed as I sat and placed the teapot, mugs, and a jug of milk on the table.

"Carla, can we do this another time?"

She looked at me. "Of course. You look tired."

I hadn't gotten much sleep the previous evening. I wasn't getting much sleep any evening. My body ached from tiredness. Tears formed in my eyes and she took my hands in hers.

"It's okay. We'll get you through this, I promise."

"I'm tired, Carla, not upset. But I can't deal with Michael right now. I don't care if he spent the night with her, I really don't. I know I have to face it at some point, but I'm too tired right now to do that."

"But it must hurt," she said gently.

"Of course it hurts, and maybe I'm lying to myself when I say I don't care. Maybe that's my defence mechanism to stop it hurting as much as it should, but I don't love him, he doesn't love me. Why neither of us can just walk away is beyond me."

"He won't leave because he thinks it's going to cost him too much. He told Charles that ages ago. He wants to wear you down enough so that you leave. And you know what? It makes no difference in court. He's been having affairs since the day you met him."

As blunt as she could be, Carla wasn't telling me anything I didn't already know. I appreciated her brutal honesty, most times.

"I have to prove it though, don't I?"

"You know her, you know her name and bloody address, Jayne. It's not hard and I don't believe she would want the scandal.

She's played the poor wife of an adulterer herself for long enough. Who knows, maybe that's why her husband left her for someone else, maybe he knew."

"I love you, you're my best friend, but let's talk about this after the holiday."

I felt badgered. She meant well, but when Carla was on a mission it was difficult to stop her.

"Okay, but please, promise me this. You will think about it. I can pay for the lawyer. You will walk away with something, I can guarantee you of that."

It all boiled down to money. I felt like a money-grabbing bitch. I hadn't worked. I hadn't contributed financially to our home, to the bills, to anything. All I wanted was to be able to feel secure. I didn't want half of what he had, just enough to keep me going until I got on my feet, and even that made me feel shallow. I had wanted to be a stay at home mum. No one had forced me to give up a career, not that I had one, really. I wanted to make a nice home for my family.

"Have you packed yet?" Carla asked, jolting me from my thoughts.

"I started to have a look. It was depressing."

"Come on, let's see what you've got."

We headed up the stairs to my bedroom. I'd made a small pile of things I thought suitable. They were waiting to have a run through the washing machine.

"Is that it?" she asked as she held up the pink sundress I'd found.

"I like that dress. And yes, that is the pile I have, at the moment, of course."

"It stinks."

"It won't once I've washed it." I snatched the sundress from her. There was the distinct smell of plastic from the storage bag the dress had been living in.

Carla opened my wardrobe and began to rifle through. "Do you have anything else of colour?" she asked.

I stood beside her. "No, doesn't appear so."

My wardrobe consisted of black, grey, blue, and drab brown attire. I hadn't realised just how depressing it all looked.

"I'll bring over some things tomorrow," she said, as she closed the door and moved to the chest of drawers.

"Yeah, right. You're what, a size eight? I'm a fourteen, if I suck my belly in."

She was ignoring me. "This is nice," she said and she turned and held up a white silk camisole top with red poppies.

I took the top from her and looked at the label. "That's not mine," I said quietly.

"What do you mean it's not... Surely, it's not hers?"

"I don't know. It's too big for Kerry and too small for me." I sat heavily on the bed.

"You don't remember washing it?"

"No, maybe Kerry did. She uses the washing machine because theirs is broken."

Carla sat on the bed next to me.

"He's had her in my home," I whispered.

For once, she kept quiet. I took the top from her and folded it. Why I folded it so neatly, I had no idea, but I placed it on the top of the chest of drawers.

"Let's go through the other drawers," I said.

I wanted a distraction, wanted to find some nice clothes to take on a holiday I was determined to enjoy. I clenched my jaw closed and emptied the contents of the drawer on the bed.

Michael came home unannounced late that afternoon. He took me by surprise; I couldn't recall a time he'd arrived home before seven o'clock. I had arrived back from walking the dog when I heard a noise upstairs. The floorboards creaked above my head as I shrugged off my coat in the kitchen. I stilled and listened. As I crept to the bottom of the stairs, I could hear his muffled voice. Remembering which step to avoid for fear of giving myself away on the loose treads, I climbed the stairs.

"I know, I will. I'll discuss it with her tonight. For now I have to find some clean clothes. Is it that hard to have clean shirts available for me?" he said.

*Clean shirts*? He had a wardrobe full of them. I paused on the landing.

"I have to do everything myself, what with working all the bloody hours. Honestly, this move is going to be wonderful."

*Do everything myself? Move?*

I moved closer to the bedroom door, thanking myself for insisting on a deep pile carpet for the upstairs. His door was ajar; I could see him on his mobile pacing the room.

"I know, baby," he whispered.

I'd heard enough. At no point in the whole time we had been together had he called me anything other than Jayne. Or dumb, that was a word he used a lot. I forced a cough and watched him freeze, shut off the phone, and then he surprised me by putting it in his underwear drawer.

I marched on the spot for a few seconds before pushing open his bedroom door.

"Oh, it's you. I didn't know who was up here," I said.

"Unlike you to be brave enough to confront an intruder, Jayne. Why didn't you send up that useless dog?"

"Mmm, I wonder what would have happened if I'd set my useless dog on you. Who were you talking to?"

"No one. I may have been mumbling to myself, rehearsing a rather important pitch I have tomorrow, but since you've never been interested in my work, I won't bore you with the details. I doubt you'd understand anyway."

*Pompous prick*, I thought.

"Before you rush off again, I have some news. Carla invited me on holiday with her."

I held my breath. "I hope you turned down her offer," he said.

"No, I said I'd go."

He turned to face me. "And how do you think you'll pay for this *holiday?*"

"It's my birthday gift," I said. My voice grew quieter.

He laughed. "Gosh, I bet you feel like the poor relation. We don't accept charity, Jayne. Tell her you can't possibly go."

He stared at me with his arms crossed over his chest.

"You know what? Yes, I do feel like the poor relation, thanks to you and your fucking budgets. I haven't had a holiday since the kids were small, and even then, I was the one to ferry them from activity to activity while you sat and recuperated on the beach."

"I work, Jayne, fifty hours a week or more. If anyone needs a holiday, it's me. And if you can't have a conversation with me without using foul language, we'll continue this when you've grown up. I have a dinner to attend."

He turned his back and headed to his wardrobe. I stood with my stomach in knots and a mouthful of expletives that I kept locked in.

*Fuck you, fucking prick, dickhead, twat,* ran through my mind.

"It's not right, what she's doing. You should see poor Charles..."

Before he finished his sentence I verbally launched at him.

"What was *not right* was *poor* Charles fucking his secretary. I mean, how clichéd can you get."

I walked away.

I was sitting in the back garden, wrapped up against the biting wind, when Michael left the house. No words of goodbye were said, just the slam of the front door, and the spray of gravel against the sidewall of the house as he sped from the drive, I guessed.

I raised the hand containing the one cigarette I had a day, waving it at him in defiance of his no smoking rules. And then the tears fell. Why couldn't I stand up to him? Why couldn't I tell him how he made me feel? He belittled in such a subtle way it wasn't noticeable to anyone but me. He made me feel worthless. Being a stay at home mum wasn't a *job*; it was a vocation for me. I didn't envy the women that had to work and bring up their children. I didn't envy those that chose to work. I did what I thought best for our children. I kept house, I was a mum, there was a dinner on the table each evening, clean clothes in the wardrobe every day, and a tidy house.

A thought hit me. I stubbed out the cigarette and made my way back up the stairs. The phone I'd seen him throw in his drawer was gone. He'd obviously been speaking to her. I sat on his bed and thought about what I'd heard.

He'd said, *'this move,'* What had he meant by that? Although I had no reason to, I opened his wardrobe to confirm to myself. A row of neatly starched and pressed white shirts greeted me. So he had no clean shirts? I wondered just how dumb she was to believe him.

Michael ignored me for the remainder of the week. He hardly came home and when he did, he took himself off to the living room to read his paper and have a glass of whiskey each evening, only forcing himself to be in my company at meal times. I wasn't sure why I was bothering to cook him a meal. We'd sit at the table in silence, and he would spread papers alongside his plate, no doubt to avoid having to speak to me.

I spent the week making meals for the freezer, washing and ironing my holiday clothes, and writing lists of how things worked, which button to press on the washing machine, where the iron was, the Hoover. Not that I thought for one moment he'd use any of it.

Carla came over almost daily and we spent ages looking at the Four Seasons website, planning on what spa treatments to have, how many books to take, whether to go sunset sailing, or just sit with cocktails. I got excited and terrified as the week wore on. I hadn't mentioned to her what I'd seen or the conversation I'd had with Michael. I found myself not confiding in her as much, for fear of her taking action; action that needed to be taken but that I didn't want to confront.

I didn't sleep well the night before the holiday. I tossed and turned and woke in the early hours. I took myself downstairs to make a cup of tea and have a cigarette. My one a day habit was slowly creeping up to five. Michael hated that I smoked, he hated that I drank wine, and judging by the bottles in the recycling bin, that habit was increasing too.

Dini joined me in the garden as I shivered just outside the back door. I could hear the crunch of his footsteps on the frozen lawn but being black, couldn't see where he had gone. Dini never barked, but would emit a low growl. A growl that rumbled from his chest and at night, in the dark, raised the hairs on my arms. I shuddered and called him inside.

Ben would collect him at lunchtime and I'd made sure to have his bed and food packed and placed in the hallway, alongside my case. Michael had ten shirts washed and ironed in his wardrobe, alongside five suits and ten meals in the freezer. There was nothing that I hadn't thought of. I'd left a message for Casey, but she never returned my call.

I took my tea back to bed and picked up my journal. I wrote about how excited I was, and how upset at the lack of enthusiasm from Michael and Casey I'd been. Ben was thrilled for me, and Kerry rang or messaged with snippets of information she'd found about the Maldives on a daily basis. She was still poorly and I'd urged her to contact her doctor. Although slim, she'd lost a little more weight over the past week or so, and I was concerned for her.

It was the crash as someone fell over my plastic suitcase that woke me a little later; I must have dozed off. I heard a curse and the slide of the suitcase as it was shoved across the wooden floor then the bang of the front door being slammed shut. I rose and looked out the bedroom window to see Michael walk down the garden path. He hadn't said a word, no, 'goodbye' or 'have fun' the previous evening.

I showered and dressed then walked around the house with my cup of tea to make sure I had left it spotless. I walked to the sideboard in the living room and picked up a family photograph. It was years old. Casey was in a pram but we were smiling, and I think it might have been the last time we did.

As much as Michael was indifferent to Ben, I believed he blamed that pregnancy on him *having* to marry me, the moment Casey was born he doted on her. He never changed a nappy or got up for the midnight feed, but that girl could do no wrong. A pang of something I tried desperately to swallow down hit me. I was jealous of her in one way. I loved her, I loved her spirit and independence, but I was also jealous that he could love her and not me. The guilt that followed was often overwhelming.

I treated my children equally. As selfish as Casey could be, I'd never let her feel that I favoured Ben over her. Unlike Michael. The ringing of the telephone interrupted my thoughts.

"Hey, baby girl, I'm just ringing to wish you a happy holiday," my father said once I'd picked up the phone.

"Hi, Dad. Thank you. I'm looking forward to it."

"Your mum says to be careful. Don't drink the tap water."

I laughed. "I won't. Now, how are you both?"

Dad had been suffering with a cough for a while and I'd nagged him to visit the doctor. He had been a docker in his younger years; a tough, big, burly man with calloused hands that were so gentle when he'd stroked my hair each night after putting me to bed.

"Your mum made a cake yesterday. I ate it, of course, but it was awful. Took out a tooth, I did."

"You never?"

"No, but it was still awful."

I had the most wonderful relationship with my dad. He was a storyteller. As a child I would sit on his lap for hours on end while he told me of foreign lands with pirates and unicorns. He'd travelled the world, in his mind. It was only in my teens that I found out he'd never left England. "Too many bloody foreigners," he'd say with a laugh.

Our call was brief but it left me with a smile.

As I waited for Carla to arrive, I checked and rechecked my bag. I had my passport, my keys, and a little money. Not that I was allowed to take from the joint account but unbeknown to Michael, I had a small savings account with a few hundred pounds in it, a rainy day account. I'd taken out £200, hoping that would be enough.

I had no idea what my husband earned. He was senior to Charles, and I knew Carla had been awarded a little over half a million pounds, a flat in London, and the house in Kent. Charles had invested the huge bonuses money traders were awarded in the eighties and nineties in property. Bearing in mind how astute Michael was; I believed he would have done the same. It was on my list of things to do when I returned; investigate just what my husband earned and owned. I was sick of having to justify every purchase.

Dini ran to the front door long before I heard a car pull up outside and the clip-clop of heels on the path. I took one last look around the kitchen, left the note to Michael on the table, and picked up my bag.

"Oh, I am so excited," Carla said as I opened the front door.

"So am I. Take my bag while I grab my case," I said, handing her my oversized handbag.

I bent down to give Dini a cuddle, whispering that I'd miss him before taking the handle of my case and closing the front door behind me.

We chatted the whole way. Thankfully, the motorway was clear and the journey took the hour we had expected. I'd texted Ben and Kerry, left another voicemail for Casey and then turned my phone to airplane mode.

There was no queuing; Carla strode straight to the Business Class check-in desk and we were given our passes to the Emirates lounge. Before heading to the lounge, we took a quick tour of the shops. Carla just had to have a new pair of sunglasses. While she tried on black pair after an identical black pair, I browsed. I wouldn't waste my money on perfume or accessories, although a nice sarong took my fancy; it was something to wear on the beach instead of having to pull on a sundress. With purchases made, we headed to the lounge.

I felt a total fraud sitting in the plush leather seats, being handed champagne and coffee, told where to help myself to snacks.

Carla lapped it up. Despite coming from the same background, I'd always told her she was born into the wrong class. She suited the Business Class lounge, she'd suit the First Class one. I was conscious of my unruly, brown curly hair that stayed in a permanent ponytail, of the cheap clothes, and fake handbag.

"Do we need to go to the gate yet?" I asked, disturbing Carla from her magazine.

"No, they'll call us when it's time."

"But it says a gate number," I replied, pointing to the screen on the wall.

"They'll call us, stop panicking," she said with a laugh.

I settled back and waited. I checked my phone regularly. I wondered whether I'd receive a message from Michael. Although he knew I was visiting the Maldives, he had no idea what island. I rested my head back, closed my eyes and started to think.

The breakdown of my marriage had been a gradual process. If I had to be honest, we should never have married in the first place; we were so incompatible. We met at Carla and Charles' engagement party, something she tells me she regrets. I guess I was enamoured by him. I remembered that I had seen him across the room; it was as if he was holding court. I wasn't as frumpy back then but I wasn't a beauty either… I was just plain Jayne.

He blamed me for falling pregnant. I had been on the pill but unwell and didn't know it would affect it working. The shock when I realised had been overwhelming. I'd sat on the information for nearly a month, hiding the morning, afternoon, and evening sickness I'd suffered until Michael confronted me leaning over the toilet and retching. He stomped around, shouted, and cried. Not for me, not for our child, but for himself. It was a couple of days later that he announced we were to book our wedding at the local registry office for the next available date. I wore a simple dress, the cheapest I could find, Carla and Charles were our witnesses and our guests extended no further than immediate family. It wasn't the wedding of my dreams, and I remembered my dad telling me that I didn't have to go through with it; we could walk away.

I guess I was embarrassed, ashamed even. Michael didn't even smile at me as I walked up the aisle; he kept his gaze firmly fixed on the wall above the registrar's head. And that was it. Once the formality was over, our guests left, and we went back to the apartment he owned.

"Stop thinking," I heard. I opened my eyes to see Carla looking at me.

"I'm not."

"You are. When you think of that prick your jaw works from side to side."

"He hasn't spoken to me for nearly two weeks, no goodbye this morning, nothing."

She didn't respond but it was hard not to notice the pity that clouded her eyes. I didn't want her to feel sorry for me; I was in a mess partly by my own doing.

"Come on, let's go board the plane," she said, as she stood and held out her hand.

We linked arms and wandered to the gate. We were shown to our seats and offered yet another glass of champagne. We clinked our glasses and toasted ourselves.

"To a fabulous holiday," Carla said.

I smiled. No more thinking, no more wishing for something I was never going to have, no more Michael—at least for a couple of

34

weeks.

After a short stopover in Dubai, we arrived and taxied to the airport. The doors were opened and we were allowed to disembark. The heat as I walked down the steps to the tarmac immediately had my shirt sticking to my back. Because we had flown Business Class, our luggage was first around the carousel. We made our way through the airport to a concrete area outside and looked around. Carla spotted a man holding a plaque with the Four Seasons logo; we made our way over.

"Welcome. Can I take your names, please?" he said, checking his clipboard. "Your boat is ready. Let me take those bags for you," he added.

We were shown to a small white minibus and handed cold, wet facecloths as we boarded. I was thankful the air conditioning was on full blast. It was less than a minute drive before we pulled up alongside a concrete jetty and shown to a waiting speedboat.

Yet another cold facecloth was handed to us, along with a bottle of water. A crewmember held out his hand to help me board, and as he did, I stumbled a little. Immediately one of the two occupants of the boat rose to help me. I grabbed onto his shirt, feeling solid muscle underneath. I mumbled my thanks before looking up and into the most amazing blue eyes. I made a conscious effort to close my mouth. He was smiling at me, and he was gorgeous. He had dirty blond hair, but it was those eyes that had me captivated.

"Ahem," I heard from behind.

My face immediately coloured. "I'm sorry, and thank you," I mumbled again before sliding into a seat.

"You're welcome," he replied in an accent I was unfamiliar with.

Carla sat beside me; she looked and raised her eyebrows at me before leaning in close.

"Wow, did you see his eyes?"

"I know, they're the same colour as the sea."

The captain, if that's what the driver of a small speedboat was called, was giving a safety brief; I wasn't listening. I was mesmerised by the man. He sat with another across the aisle and one row up. All I could see was a side profile as he angled his head to listen to the captain's brief. I felt a nudge in my side.

"Stop staring and listen. If we sink, I'm not saving your arse because you don't know where the life jacket is."

I giggled. I felt like a teenager who had just been caught out. I straightened myself in my seat and concentrated. Just a few minutes later we were on our way. The boat whipped across a sea as still as a millpond. Flying fish raced us; it was exhilarating. I looked out across the clear sea, a beautiful blue, to see small, white sand islands with lone palm trees and sandbanks.

"This is unbelievable," I said.

"I know, look at those fish."

It was a short, too short, journey before the boat slowed and we moored alongside a dark wooden jetty, lined with impeccably turned out staff. The two guys stood and he smiled; slightly plump lips framed perfect white teeth. I blinked rapidly. He gestured with his arm for us to climb from the boat first. Hands were extended from the jetty and, without stumbling that time, I found myself on

36

solid ground.

"Wow," was about the only word I could use to describe the scene in front of me.

The long jetty led to a wooden building with a thatched roof. The sand was so white the sun reflected from it and I had to squint. Palm trees lined the island, some bent so low their leaves ghosted the water.

"It's certainly better than the brochure," Carla said. She had taken two drinks from a young girl dressed in, what I assumed, was traditional clothing.

We were asked to follow the guy that had met us at the airport to the reception area. I kicked off my shoes and followed, hopping from one foot to the other as the soles of my feet met the heat of the wood.

We were led into an open-sided reception; my feet sank into the cool sand floor, and we sat on sofas while we waited for our paperwork to be completed. The two guys sat opposite us.

"Have you been here before?" he asked. He had a soft, quiet voice.

I looked up, unsure at first whether he was addressing me.

"Erm, no. First time. You?"

"Yeah, not to this island, though. I'm Stefan, by the way. My friend, Morton."

He held out his hand for a formal shake.

"Jayne, and this is Carla."

The receptionist interrupted introductions as we were handed keys and instructed that a golf buggy would take us to our villa.

"Maybe we'll see you again," Stefan said as Carla and I stood.

I smiled and nodded, a little tongue-tied. For a moment, his piercing blue eyes held me captive; I felt my face flush.

A nudge to my ribs brought me out of my semi-trance.

"Me thinks you have the fanny tingle," Carla whispered, as we made our way to the waiting buggy. I stopped in my tracks, staring at her open-mouthed.

"The what?"

"The fanny tingle. He is gorgeous, so I don't blame you."

I went to speak, then shook my head before laughing.

"He's just being polite."

"Polite or not, I could dive into those blue eyes and never need to surface for breath."

The buggy came to a stop beside a blue gate in a white stone wall. We'd driven along a sand path that centred the island, passing staff that stopped to welcome us. The gate was opened and we stepped into a private garden attached to the side of our villa. It was simply amazing. Palm trees lined a path to the beach; there was a plunge pool on one side and a wooden deck on the other. Sunbeds with cream cushions sat facing the pool along with a small table and chairs.

We were shown through the door to the villa and, at first, I stopped in my tracks. It was a simple wooden construction but beautifully laid out. I placed my handbag on one of the large beds with crisp, white linen and took a walk around. French doors opened up into the garden, just a few steps from the pool. Behind the beds was a wall that spanned three quarters the length of the room. Behind that was the bathroom. Two sinks were moulded in a stone countertop, a white bath sat on silver claw feet, and through a gap in the wall was an outdoor shower. Thankfully that white wall curved around it for privacy.

By the time I'd done my tour, our guide had left us and Carla was already unpacking her case.

"Did you see outside? It's amazing," I said.

"I know. And look, a welcome bottle of champagne," she replied.

On top of a unit of drawers sat a silver ice bucket with a bottle of Billecart-Salmon Rosé champagne. The name meant nothing to me but Carla seemed to be impressed.

"I think we need an hour or two on the beach, recover from the journey," she said.

"Absolutely."

While she changed into the skimpiest bikini I'd ever seen, I unpacked. On our walk from the speedboat, along the jetty, I hadn't seen anyone on the beach so decided to be brave and opt for the red bikini Carla had bought me.

Carla scrunched her long blonde hair into a bun; the messy style looked like a hairdresser had spent hours creating it. She sprayed herself with her factor ten sunblock and grabbed her book.

"Go grab some sunbeds, I'll be there in a minute," I said, as I shrugged off my shirt, having finally unpacked and put everything away.

I stripped and peeled on the bikini bottoms, having to loosen the side ties a little. I wasn't overweight as such. I was in proportion but had those childbearing hips my mother always told me were a bonus and stretch marks across a slightly flabby stomach, where children had nestled for nine months each.

The only part of my body I didn't mind was my boobs. Still firm, I covered them with the flimsy bikini top and took at look at myself in the mirror. Red was definitely not my colour. I was too pale skinned and even paler by the time I slathered on my factor fifty. My brown unruly curls had already started to frizz in the humidity as I redid my ponytail. I tucked away a couple of tendrils of hair protruding from the bottom of my bikini. Maybe I should have taken Carla up on her offer of a trip to the beauty parlour. Feminine matters had not been top of my list for a long time. Michael and I had given up on sex many years ago, and there never seemed any point in making my bits look tidy just for me.

Grabbing my sunglasses, a bargain find from the local charity shop, and my book, I walked through the French doors and followed the path to the beach. The flower border opened up onto a pristine, near-white sand beach. Carla was already stretched out on one of the two double wooden sunbeds.

"Wow," I said.

"Wow, indeed. I'd literally just plonked my arse down when a waiter appeared with a menu and took a drinks order."

"Look at the colour of that sea."

Close to the shore it was as if God had taken a glass of glacial water and dripped one drop of blue dye in it. As I approached the water's edge, I could see through the water to every ripple of fine sand. I waded in. The water was warm, small fish darted past my legs, the deeper I went. In the distance I could see the edge of the reef and the colour changed to a deep blue, the same blue as Stefan's eyes.

I made my way back to the sunbed.

"The water is so warm," I said.

"Maybe we'll get some snorkelling stuff," Carla replied.

Carla was reading through the island brochure; she detailed the spa treatments on offer and a list of activities.

"Sure beats Cornwall," I said with a laugh.

Every year of our childhood, the whole street would pack up their cars and drive the seven or so hours it took back then to Cornwall. Days were spent on the beach, getting sunburned, and evenings in the clubhouse on site. Our parents would rent little wooden chalets, the same ones year after year.

"Do you remember the body boards?" Carla said.

"God, yes. I also remember the splinters and grazes."

We had wooden body boards that we'd tried to surf on, and by the end of our week, all the kids had splinters in their feet and grazes on their knees.

My favourite memory of those holidays was being carried to bed each night by my dad, salty hair all tangled and skin peeling. Those were the best holidays I'd ever had.

"We had so much fun back then, didn't we?" she said.

"Do you remember our life plan?" I asked.

One evening, I think we were teens at that point; we'd sat on the beach with our friends, none of whom we saw anymore, and wrote our life plan. I wanted to travel the world, to help rebuild communities in poverty-stricken regions, photograph wildlife in Africa, and rescue the children of Ethiopia. I wanted to leave a legacy. I hadn't done any of it. Sadness swept over me. Instead, I'd left school, went to college, worked for a few years before meeting Michael, and any thoughts of a life plan were squashed.

"There's still time," Carla said quietly. I looked over to her. "There's still time to do some of those things. I can see what you're thinking."

I smiled. "One day," I said.

We settled back as the waiter appeared with cold drinks and read our books. We could chat or we could sit in silence; just being with my best friend in the place the word *paradise* was invented was a joy.

# Chapter Three

Before we dressed for dinner, I rubbed moisturiser on my already pink skin. Freckles covered my arms and across my nose. I'd hated my freckles when I was a child, wishing them gone. My dad had told me they were left there by my soul each evening. It would leave my body when I slept to party, pinching me before it did so it could recognise me on its return. I'd believed that for years. As I grew older, I began to love my freckles. It was only when they joined up that my skin coloured, gave the illusion of a tan.

"I do believe it's cocktail hour, so will you hurry up," Carla said.

The island was an hour ahead from the rest of the Maldives; cocktail hour was as the sun set. We opted to walk to the end of the island, along the shore, and to the bar that jutted out into the sea. It was another open-sided building with soft sofas placed around small wooden tables. We chose to sit opposite each other on sofas placed on the veranda.

As a waiter came to take our order, I noticed Stefan and Morton enter, he caught my eye and both strode over.

"Do you mind if we join you?" he asked.

"Of course not. Have you settled in?" Carla replied.

Stefan took the seat next to me. He stretched his arm along the back of the sofa and although nowhere near me, I felt a tingle across the back of my neck. My stomach knotted and I felt the blush creep up my cheeks at his proximity.

"You said you've been to the Maldives before. When was that?" I asked.

He shuffled so he faced me.

"We come here for the scuba diving. Last time was a couple of years ago, now."

"Scuba diving, wow! We might go snorkelling but I don't think I could do that."

I was rambling, mumbling into my drink; I wasn't used to having a conversation with a man. In fact, other than the kids, Carla, and the dog, I don't remember the last time I said anything more than a passing 'good morning' or to ask for goods in one of the local shops.

"Where are you from?" I asked. I'd struggled to place his accent.

"Denmark. Aalborg. It's a beautiful place, coastal."

The conversation flowed. We talked about his diving, my dog, our children but neither mentioned partners. He was easy to talk to and I found myself comfortable in his presence. A second round of drinks was ordered and, although such a small thing, it pleased me to hear him ask for the same drink I'd had before. Just the fact he'd remembered made me smile. Every now and again Carla caught my eye. Her eyebrows were slightly raised and she smiled.

"Would you like to join us for dinner?" Carla asked. I could have kissed and kicked her equally.

"That would be great," Morton replied.

We stood and walked the short distance, along the beach, to one of the three restaurants on the island. Having the menu in front of me gave me the shield I needed. As much as I'd enjoyed talking with Stefan in the bar, I was feeling confused. He took the chair opposite and turned his head to speak to his friend. I studied his profile. His hair fell over his forehead and my fingers twitched with the desire to brush it from his eyes. His jawline was chiselled to perfection, and I watched the way his mouth moved as he spoke, the way his tongue ran over his lower lip occasionally, and a thought flashed through my mind—I wanted to bite that lip. I blinked rapidly to rid myself of such thoughts.

My hands shook slightly as I held the menu up to cover my face. I saw his fingers grip the top of my menu and he gently pulled it away, turned it the correct way up, and handed it back with a smile.

"That might work better," he said. I sank in my chair to hide.

With orders placed and the menu removed, I had nothing to hide behind. As much as the conversation had been easy in the bar, as the evening wore on, I was feeling more and more conflicted. I enjoyed spending time with him; I wanted to spend more time just talking. He did something I wasn't used to; he listened. He found what I told him interesting, but it felt wrong. The thoughts running through my mind felt wrong, the feelings coursing through my body felt wrong. Everything felt wrong.

Stefan, Morton and Carla chatted through dinner. I picked at my meal, pushing most of it around the plate. It was delicious, although Indian was not a particular favourite of mine, but I'd lost my appetite. When the meal was done and the plates cleared away, I looked up from my lap and caught Stefan smiling at me.

"Time difference caught up with you?" he asked.

"I think so. I'm sorry I'm a little quiet. I guess I'm tired."

"No need to apologise. How about a coffee?"

"Why don't we all head back to the bar?" Carla added.

I nodded, although heading to bed was more of a temptation. Once bills were signed for, we rose from the table, and I tensed as Stefan placed his hand on my lower back to guide me through the neighbouring tables. His touch had caused an electrical pulse to shoot through me, ending between my thighs.

Carla and I made our way to the same sofas we'd sat on earlier while the guys went to the bar with our orders.

"Are you okay?" she asked.

"No. Talk about it later?"

She nodded but I saw the concern flash through her eyes.

"I think I'm jet lagged, nothing to worry about," I added.

My latte was placed on the small table in front of me and Stefan sat opposite. I'd made a point of sitting next to Carla. He lounged back; one foot rested on the opposite knee and sipped his coffee.

"What are your plans tomorrow?" he asked.

"Sunbathe and explore the island, I think. Carla wants to spend some time in the spa. You?"

"We're diving in the morning. I'm looking forward to it."

"Tell me about your diving?"

He leaned forwards slightly; his face became animated as he spoke. He told me about the many countries he'd visited, the seas he'd dived in and the underwater photographs he'd taken. Photography was a hobby of mine and I felt more comfortable as the evening went on. We had something in common. It seemed there were two conversations happening, Stefan and me, Morton and Carla. I detected a little spark between those two. Both guys were good-looking, tall, athletic in build and fit. Being the shortest, with the darkest hair and the fairest skin, I felt dowdy sitting amongst them.

Stefan yawned; he stretched his arms above his head and his white t-shirt rose, showing defined abs and a trail of soft blond hair on an already tanned stomach, leading to the top of his jeans. Again, my face flushed as I stared.

"I think it's time we headed to bed. We'll see you tomorrow, maybe?" he said.

I nodded as he rose.

"Goodnight, ladies," Morton said, giving Carla a wink. The guys left.

"Phew!" I heard.

"Phew, indeed. You seem to be getting along with Morton."

"No talk about me. What is going on with you, Miss Adams? I've never heard you talk as much."

Carla never referred to me by my married name; it was her way of not acknowledging Michael.

"He's easy to talk to, I guess." I blushed, yet again.

She smirked at me. "Mmm, you have the feels?"

"Will you stop with all your 'feels' and 'fancy tingles'? He's a nice guy being polite, I imagine. He's not interested in me."

"I beg to differ. Do you like him?"

"If I was a teenager, yes. I'm forty-five and married. I don't 'like' other men."

"We are on a beautiful island with two beautiful men. It's okay to have a little fun."

"I'm married, Carla."

"Yes, to an arsehole who's probably fucking the slut as we

speak."

I winced, pain ripped through me and tears sprang to my eyes. Carla covered her mouth.

"Oh, God. I'm so sorry. I didn't mean that. Jayne, I'm truly sorry. I'd blame the wine if it was true, I just have a big mouth and no filter sometimes."

"It's okay. Probably true but doesn't mean I'm about to do the same."

"I'm not suggesting you jump into bed with him. Just let yourself have fun. Let someone like you, want to spend time with you, show you that you're worth the effort. Because you are."

I took her hand in mine and gave her a smile.

"Now, Morton? Strange name though."

We giggled. "He's rather nice, I think."

"Would you..."

"Would I what?"

"You know," I stammered.

Carla laughed. "Of course not, however, a little flirting is great for the confidence. You should try it."

I often forgot how devastated she had been by Charles' affair. As much as my confidence was on the floor, I guessed hers was, too. I raised my coffee cup.

"To flirting," I said.

We woke late the following morning; it was the knocking on the door by the cleaner that finally had us struggle out of bed.

"What do you want to do today?" I asked.

"Let's grab something to eat and then check out the spa. We can book some treatments. And I really want to do that sunset cruise thing. They take us to a deserted island for a glass of champagne."

"Sounds good."

We dressed and left the villa for what turned out to be brunch.

The spa was a haven of tranquillity. We found it on the other side of the island, an island that only took twenty minutes or so to walk around. It was accessed via a wooden jetty. We sat in reception, browsing the selection of treatments, and decided the following day was spa day. After booking we headed back to our villa and our sunbeds on the beach.

A large umbrella had already been erected between the two beds and cold towels were hidden under a metal container. I pulled off the sundress I'd worn over the red bikini and settled down in the shade. Carla pulled her bed out and into the sun.

The great thing about sunglasses is that the recipient of my lustful gaze was totally unaware. I was propped on my elbows watching Stefan walk down the jetty, having just arrived back from his dive. He wore board shorts that hung on his hips, and even from where I sat, I could see the muscles defined on his stomach. I squinted; sure I could see a tattoo just above the waistband of the shorts.

"Stop staring," I heard, then a chuckle.

"I'm not staring, and you couldn't possibly know what I'm looking at," I replied.

Carla leaned up.

"How about two gorgeous Danes?"

"Where?" I feigned innocence.

She chuckled some more and relaxed back down on her sunbed. I did the same.

"You quite like him, don't you?" she said.

"He's a nice guy, I've said that before, but I'm not sure what you mean."

"I have to confess, I don't think I've come across such politeness in men. Maybe it's their culture. Whatever it is, we're about to experience more. They're coming this way."

Oh no! I stretched out on the bed to flatten my stomach a little while trying to reach under to find my sarong.

"Hi, did you have a good dive?" Carla asked.

"Great, got some fantastic photographs," Morton answered.

"Let me see," she said.

Morton sat on the end of her bed and angled his camera so she could see. Stefan stood awkwardly. I was going to have to move and offer him a seat. I sat up, still holding in my stomach. He smiled and once I'd removed my sandy feet, perched on the end of the bed.

I casually laid the sundress across my lap.

"What did you see?" I asked.

"Sharks, manta rays; it was a great dive. Want to see?"

I nodded and he shuffled up the bed to sit alongside me. He held out his camera in front of him and I had no choice but to get closer. His tanned body was salt encrusted, but it was his hands that I'd stared at the most. Strong hands with fingers that I wanted to strum over my body. My stomach flipped as he leaned a little closer to me. Our arms touched as he showed me the screen in the back of his camera.

He flicked through his pictures, detailing each shot. His gentle voice felt like wisps of a breeze licking over my skin as he looked over my shoulder. I was sorry when he'd come to the end of his pictures and moved away.

One of the many staff that patrolled the beach asked if we'd like refreshments. Morton placed an order for two sunbeds. It seemed the guys were to join us. Beds and a small table were soon dragged into place, cold wet towels and drinks were handed over and we settled back to sunbathe. I refused to close my eyes; terrified I would let out a snore if I fell asleep.

"How about a swim?" Stefan said. We'd been silently reading or dozing for an hour or so.

I was sweating. I had been wanting a dip in the sea for ages but was too scared to move. Too scared to have Stefan see my wobbly bits as I walked to the water's edge.

He stood along with Morton and Carla, and all looked at me. Oh fuck!

"Sure," I said. I stood, clutching the sundress to me and hoped they'd walk off before I let it drop.

I had no such luck. I placed the sundress on the bed with my sunglasses and braved it out. Thankfully, as we reached the sea, Stefan continued to stride in and dived under a gentle wave. He surfaced some way away and swam to the edge of the reef. Carla and I did our gentle breaststrokes until we were in deeper water.

Stefan trod water a little way out and beckoned to me. I shook my head. I wasn't comfortable in water where I couldn't see the bottom. He laughed before sinking under. Just as I'd turned to head back to the beach, I felt a hand snake around my waist; Stefan had surfaced behind me. He pulled me back against his chest.

"Trust me, I've got you," he said, as he gently dragged me back to where I'd last seen him.

Although I couldn't reach the bottom, I could see it until he took me over the edge of the reef. I held onto his arm.

"See there?" he pointed.

I looked down; a baby shark was cruising alongside the reef.

"Oh, shit, take me back," I said. He laughed.

"It's not going to hurt you."

"I don't like when I can't see the bottom."

"It's okay, I've got you," he repeated.

He was strong enough to tread water and keep us both afloat. His arm was still around my waist, his hand splayed on my stomach and I relaxed a little. I could feel his chest against my back and his breath caress my neck, not that I thought that was his intention.

"Ready to swim back?" he asked. I nodded.

I wasn't. I wanted to stay in his embrace but those feelings of guilt, of wrongdoing, flooded my mind. Reluctantly, I let go of his arm, he let go of me and we began to swim for the shore.

"We're doing the sunset cruise later," I said as we walked back to the sunbeds. I grabbed my towel and dried my face.

"Sounds good, can we join you?" Morton said. He and Carla had made it back to shore before us.

"Sure, why not."

The guys left to book the cruise and Carla and I headed back to the villa. A dip in the fresh water pool was in order. My pinked skin needed respite from the heat and salty water.

"Morton wants to keep in touch when we leave," Carla said.

We had our elbows resting on the side of the pool and our bodies floating in the cool water.

"Wow, are you going to?"

"I might. It would be nice to have a male friend."

"Do you think you could have a relationship with him?"

"I doubt that, but he's fun company."

We fell silent until it was time for a shower.

We arrived in reception to find the guys already waiting. One of the staff from the water sports centre met us and escorted us along the jetty to a waiting catamaran. Having never been on a catamaran before, I was unsure how to climb aboard. Two hulls were connected with what was basically rope netting. There was no graceful way to do it so Carla and I crawled, much to the amusement of everyone else.

It was the most thrilling thing I'd done. The boat glided across the Indian Ocean, rising on one hull as the wind picked up. I clung on, laughing out loud. My heart pounded with excitement and my smile spread the faster we went. I couldn't remember the last time I'd laughed so much.

We eventually arrived at a sandbank. The pilot—I'd been told off for calling him captain—helped me from the boat, and hitching my sundress to my thighs, I waded to the shore. We sat as a glass of champagne was handed to us and watched the sun set. It was probably one of the most beautiful sights I'd seen. As the sun lowered, its orange glow spread across the calm water.

Stefan had decided to sit beside me. As he placed his hand on the sand to lean back, his fingers brushed against mine. I looked down at them and his thumb swept over my wedding band.

"Are you happily married?" he asked quietly.

I couldn't speak. I looked up at him. His dark blue eyes were staring intently at me and I felt tears pool in mine. I gently shook my head.

"I guess neither of us would be sitting here if we were."

It was the only conversation we had about our lives outside of the fantasy the island had surrounded us in. Sadness washed over me. I thought on his words. Were we both so miserable? More importantly, were we only drawn to each other because of our miserable lives? I think that would have been worse.

As the sun dipped below the horizon, we made our way back to the boat. It was a calmer sail back to the island, and once back on land we walked to the Italian restaurant.

Something had changed. Although I still found Stefan easy to talk to, we chatted and laughed through dinner, there was an undercurrent of tension. Perhaps it was in my mind. Carla, who was normally so in tune with me, hadn't indicated she felt anything different.

The evening ended, as usual, back at the bar for a drink before the guys left. Their dives each morning started early.

And so it went on. Carla and I spent each day on the beach or in the spa; the guys joined us in the afternoon and for dinner. As the holiday wore on, I became more comfortable with Stefan but that undercurrent of tension got greater. At night, I longed for him, for his touch. The guilt intensified.

# Chapter Four

Our last evening had been spent with the guys dancing to a local band in the bar. Stefan had held me close as the band played their last song; he'd sung quietly along with the lyrics.

Their departure was later than ours the following morning, but they came to reception to see us off. It was awkward; both Stefan and I were quieter than normal. Carla and Morton exchanged details and I watched, envious of their budding friendship. A porter came to take our luggage, and we followed along the wooden jetty to the waiting speedboat.

"Jayne," Stefan said.

I turned to face him. "If you want to, I'd like to stay in touch," he said.

He reached out holding a business card. I took it from him, my fingers gently swept over his name printed in the centre of the card.

"I'd like that, too."

He took a step towards me and placed his hands on my shoulders, his thumbs just caressing the side of my neck. I looked up at him as he leaned his head closer to mine and his lips brushed against my cheek.

He stood straight, smiled and nodded, then walked away.

I watched his retreating back until Carla gently took my arm.

We climbed aboard the boat and took a seat.

"Are you okay?"

I sighed. "I don't want to go home. Thank you so much for this holiday."

She placed her arm around my shoulder and we made the journey to the capital in silence.

The flight home was torture. My cheek tingled where Stefan had placed his lips for hours after. My stomach knotted as we made the exchange in Dubai, knowing the next stop would be Heathrow. Dread set in and mixed with the guilt I felt for the feelings I'd developed towards Stefan.

"You have nothing to feel guilty for. You know that, don't you? You did nothing wrong," Carla said as we exited Heathrow and headed for our taxi.

"I don't know about that," I replied.

"Nothing happened, you just made a friend."

I hadn't told Carla about the feelings coursing through my body. I hadn't told her about the ache in my stomach each night and the heat of desire that spread between my thighs every time Stefan had touched me. Nor about the spark of electricity I'd felt wherever he'd place his hand.

The house was cold when I opened the front door. It felt bleak. Carla waved from the taxi as it reversed from the drive to take her home. I walked from room to room, noticing it was exactly as I had left it two weeks prior. The note to Michael was still on the kitchen table. I opened the freezer, not one meal had been used. I walked around the house and to his bedroom. I opened the wardrobe, ten shirts were missing, they weren't in the laundry room either, and I knew he hadn't even been home

Nothing had changed in the house but me. I wasn't the same plain Jayne that had left it. Whether it had been meeting Stefan, whether it had been standing up to Michael and taking that holiday, I'd changed. I was determined to keep in contact with Stefan; I wanted a friendship. In my mind I wasn't doing anything wrong.

I unpacked my case and loaded the washing machine; I took a meal from the freezer and settled down to listen to the answer machine. I'd received a call from my mother-in-law, enquiring whether Michael and I would be attending lunch that weekend. There was a call from Casey, excitedly telling me about a ski trip she'd been invited on and one from Ben to welcome me home. He'd obviously held the phone to Dini and encouraged him to bark, he didn't, of course, but I smiled at the gesture.

The house was silent except for the hum of the fridge. I retrieved my cigarettes from the empty biscuit tin, their usual hiding place, and opened the back door. I shivered. February in Kent was a million miles away from February in the Maldives. I sat at the garden table and inhaled the evil nicotine for the first time in two weeks.

As I leaned back and exhaled slowly, I thought of him. I could see his blue eyes in my mind, the slightly lopsided wicked grin he saved for me, and the blond hair that flopped over his forehead and was always messy. I pictured his salt encrusted body, but all of that paled into insignificance when I thought of the greatest thing he'd given me—his time and undivided attention.

I headed back indoors and turned up the heating. It had been set low and I wondered if Michael had forgotten I was due home that day. It was as if the house had been closed up, vacant. I collected my laptop from the study and settled at the kitchen table by the Aga, thankful that he hadn't turned that off.

Taking Stefan's card from my purse, I studied it. He owned his own business in Denmark, a marketing agency it appeared. He hadn't given me his personal contact details but his business ones. I opened up my email account.

*To: Stefan*

*From: Jayne*

*Date: 17 February 2014*

*Subject: Freezing from the UK*

*Hi, I'm home, it's cold and miserable here. I'm already missing the sun and the feel of sand beneath my feet. I hope you made it home okay and wish you well on your return to work. I downloaded some of the pictures from my camera; I have some nice ones and great memories.*

*Jayne x*

I deleted the X, and then retyped it. I didn't want him to think I was sending kisses but just leaving my name seemed so formal.

I checked through my emails, deleting every one. No one emailed me, other than foreigners to tell me I had won a million pounds in some lotto, or a relative I'd no knowledge of had died and if I handed over my bank account details, they'd transfer an inheritance, or Viagra. I'd often wondered who sent those emails to someone with the name 'Jayne.'

I closed down the laptop and smiled. I'd made a new friend, the first since I'd married Michael.

A blast of cold air wafted down the hallway when the front door opened and Michael trudged in carrying a holdall. He dumped it in the kitchen.

"The trains are a bloody nightmare. You'd think South Eastern would get their act together. We have this every winter."

No, 'Hello'. No, 'did you have a great holiday?' No mention that I'd just returned from two weeks away.

"Oh, I need a dress shirt for tomorrow evening. I have some bloody boring function in the city. God forbid I should miss it."

I sat in stunned silence as he shrugged off his suit jacket, left it hanging over a kitchen chair, and took himself off to the lounge with his paper. I heard the chink of glass as he poured his usual shot of whiskey.

I picked up my car keys, my purse, and walked to the hallway. I retrieved my coat from the hook, and as I opened the front door, I heard him call out.

"Did you hear? I need a dress shirt. The one with the black buttons."

I slammed the front door behind me.

My hands shook as I inserted the key in the ignition. Tears blurred my eyes as I backed out the drive; I angrily brushed them away.

Not one fucking word of kindness. Not one fucking word about my holiday. Not one fucking hint that he'd missed me.

"Prick! Fucking douchebag, twat!" I shouted, making up as many swearwords as I could.

I slammed my hand on the steering wheel as I drove, catching the eye of the driver in a neighbouring car.

"Oh, fuck off," I said through gritted teeth.

I must have looked quite mad. The only time I ever spoke my mind, let out the screaming in my head, was when I was alone in the car. I drove to Ben's.

"Hey, Mum, are you okay? I wasn't expecting you until tomorrow. I could have dropped Dini off, you know," he said once he'd opened the front door.

"I'm great, jet-lagged for sure. I missed my baby, wanted to collect him and see you both."

"Aw, that's nice. Missed me or the dog?" he teased.

"The dog, of course." I whistled for him.

Dini came bounding towards me and gave me the welcome home I'd wished for from my husband. He leapt, placed his paws on my shoulders, and licked my face. Okay, I hadn't wanted Michael to lick my face, but a hug or even a smile would have been nice.

"Jayne, did you have a good time? Come and tell us all about it," Kerry said.

The willowy, tall blonde with a permanent smile walked towards me. She had rosy cheeks and looked far healthier than she had just two weeks prior.

"You're obviously feeling better, I'm glad," I said.

She looked from me to Ben; her smiled widened. She bit down on her lower lip and patted her belly while raising her eyebrows.

"You're not? Oh my God, how?"

"Well, there are these birds and some bees..." Ben said. I swatted the back of his head.

I pushed the dog off me and pulled her into a hug.

"I am so pleased for you both. When did you find out?"

"This morning, we haven't told anyone yet. I'm only a month gone so I want to keep it quiet for a little while, but I'm just so excited," she said.

"I'm going to be a grandmother!"

I squealed a little, Kerry cried, and Ben hugged us both.

"Now, tell us about this holiday. I'll put the kettle on," she said.

Ben and Kerry rented a tiny modern house on one of the new estates that were springing up on the outskirts of the village. They hated it, but it was all they could afford. The one bedroom wouldn't last them long with a baby on the way. You could barely swing the proverbial cat in their bedroom, let alone fit a cot.

We sat and drank our tea. Our conversation alternated between my holiday and the pregnancy. Before I'd realised, an hour had passed.

"I need to get back. Your father is waiting on his dinner, no doubt," I said as I stood.

I hugged Kerry, grabbed Dini's bed, food, and lead, and headed for the car. Ben walked me out.

"Have you told Dad or Casey?" I asked.

"No, you can if you want, but other than that, we'd like to keep it to ourselves for a little longer."

I nodded, hugged, and kissed him, loaded the dog on the backseat, then drove home.

I tensed as I got closer to home, and my stomach knotted. I pulled onto the drive and sat in my car for a few minutes before taking a deep breath and opening the door. Dini bounded over the driver's seat and followed me out. He sniffed before cocking his leg against the umbrella Michael had left by the front door. I clasped my hand over my mouth to quieten the giggle.

The smell of Thai food wafted from the kitchen. As I walked through I noticed empty tin foil containers on the counter. Michael had obviously ordered himself a takeaway but there was nothing left for me. He could shove his dress shirt up his tight arse.

I uncorked a bottle of white wine, plated some cheese and biscuits, and sat in the kitchen with my laptop and a memory card. I downloaded the rest of my holiday snaps as I ate and drank.

Once the download was complete, I flicked through them; stopping at the only one I had taken of Stefan. He was standing at the water's edge, side to the camera and looking out to sea. My finger trailed over the screen and across his body. I quickly clicked to the next picture when I heard Michael walk from the living room.

"I'm going out," he said, his voice brusque.

"Oh, before you go, can you take this?" I ran up the stairs and grabbed the camisole top I'd found from my dresser.

He was at the front door when I rammed it into his chest.

"I don't do that tart's washing," I said, then walked away.

I heard his sigh of exasperation and it infuriated me. As the door slammed behind him, I sat and tears of anger fell. What a great welcome home. I shut down the laptop and headed upstairs. I was tired; I needed a shower and to curl up in the warmth of my bed.

I didn't sleep. I tossed and turned and was awake when I heard Michael return. The clock on my bedside table showed two in the morning. He didn't try to creep but stomped up the stairs to his bedroom. I turned on my side and cried again.

My marriage had been in tatters for years. It had gone downhill right after our wedding. I wasn't the wife he wanted. In the beginning, I'd managed. I'd gone to the office parties and met his clients. Although it had never been me, it was Scarlet.

Scarlet was my inner person, the woman I wanted to be. She was beautiful and confident, could hold a conversation, and everyone wanted to be her friend. The reality was so far removed that only a glass or two, or three, would bring Scarlet to the surface. But after a while, even she had deserted me.

I must have fallen asleep, as the closing of the front door jolted me awake at seven o'clock. I lay for a while, disorientated and disturbed. I'd dreamt that I was sinking. I could still feel the sensation in my body. I was sinking into an abyss where the darkness was sucking me slowly in and I couldn't climb out. I was screaming for help, my mouth was open but no sound emerged. The screaming was all in mind. Whether I'd screamed out for real or not, I had no idea, but my throat was sore and my cheeks damp.

My limbs felt heavy as I climbed from the bed. Tiredness swept over me, despite the fact I'd slept on and off for over ten hours. I stood in the shower, hoping the water would revive me.

Once dressed in my usual jeans and a sweater, I made my way downstairs. The kitchen remained in the same state it had the previous evening. I cleared the takeaway containers away and washed the dirty plate left next to the sink. While I waited for the kettle to boil, I let Dini out in to the garden.

With a cup of tea to warm my hands, I sat and opened my laptop. I wanted to look through my holiday pictures properly. My heart fluttered in my chest when I saw a notification that I had received an email. I opened my account and smiled.

*To: Jayne*

*From: Stefan*

*Date: 17 February 2014*

*Subject: Cold also.*

*Hey, thank you for your email; it was a nice surprise this morning. I came into work early to catch up. It's also cold here in Denmark and you will have to forgive my message. I have to change my keyboard from Danish to English to speak with you. Do you remember the song we danced to? It was playing on the radio as I drove in; gave me good memories too. Send over any nice pics. :)*

*Stefan x*

My smile got broader as I read, then reread. He'd added a kiss after his name too. That small thing meant more than the fact that he'd responded. His spoken English was better than his written and once I'd closed down the email, I Googled a Danish translation app. I thought it might be nice to converse in his own dialect. I'd listened to him and Morton talk and there was no way, despite their teaching, I could speak his language. I'd ended up spitting over him.

"Dini, my baby. We need a walk," I said to the sleeping dog.

Immediately, his ears twitched. He jumped to his paws and ran for the back door, claws scratching against the tiled floor.

I had a spring in my step as I walked through the brown turned field to the woods beyond. I smiled as I recalled Stefan's email; all traces of my earlier tiredness and anxiety were gone. I even sang, out of tune, of course. Dini bounded ahead, sniffing his way from tree to tree, chasing imaginary squirrels and frequently ran back, panting, to check on me. The trill of my phone in my pocket was the only sound to be heard.

"Hi, did you sleep? I didn't, not one wink. I feel exhausted," Carla said after I'd greeted her.

"Same. It feels odd having shoes on. I'm walking the dog at the moment. The signal might go."

"I can't believe how chilly it is. How was Michael when you got home?"

"He didn't say a word, other to complain about the trains and demand a dress shirt for this evening. I walked out and went to pick up Dini. And guess what? I'm going to be a granny."

Although Ben and Kerry had wanted their pregnancy to be kept quiet, I had no doubt they wouldn't mind Carla knowing; she was like family to them. I heard a scream down the phone. I laughed.

"No way! How amazing! Tell me all."

We chatted for a few minutes longer before the phone lost signal and I headed back the way we had come. The kitchen had warmed up overnight, or perhaps it was the bitterness outside that made the house feel cosy. I shrugged off my coat, having deposited my Wellingtons in the laundry room, and switched the kettle on to boil. With another cup of tea in my hands, I called Carla back.

We chatted for an hour about the pregnancy, Michael's indifference, and the holiday. There was no mention of the guys and I hadn't told her of the email I'd sent nor the one I'd received. I wasn't entirely sure why but I hadn't wanted to share him. I wanted to languish in the fantasy for a little longer before a comment, or a warning, burst my bubble.

Michael didn't come home that evening; I wasn't expecting him to. If he had a function, he would stay in town. I never asked where. I guessed I hadn't needed to—I knew. I found, for the first time, I enjoyed him being away. I'd always been comfortable with my own company and it gave me time to email.

After a simple pasta dinner, I scanned my photographs, selecting the better ones of me, the island, the guys, and Carla, before copying them to a file. I opened my emails, and without needing to think of what to say, I typed.

*To: Stefan*

*From: Jayne*

*Date: 16 February 2014*

*Subject: Holiday Pics*

*Hi, I hope you had a great first day back at work. I've put together a selection of photographs. I hope you like them. I found out yesterday I'm going to be a grandmother. Me! I'm so excited. My son, Ben, and his partner, Kerry, are expecting. I'm so thrilled for them. I've already decided the baby can't call me granny; it makes me sound so old. I'll have to think of a suitable name. So, how are things? Is work busy? I hope my email isn't disturbing you. Let me know what you think of the photos, although they're not to your standard ha ha.*

*Your friend, Jayne x*

Less than an hour later, I received a reply. I wasn't expecting to, as it was early evening.

*To: Jayne*

*From: Stefan*

*Date: 16 February 2014*

*Subject: Re: Holiday Pics*

*Hey yourself :) Great pics and you're a good photographer. Remind me to teach you about exposure! A granny, wow. You don't look old enough but I'm pleased for you. I'm working late before meeting my sons after football practice. Morton said to say hello. He's going to email Carla soon. Work is super busy. I have a new contract, a big one, and I'm excited about it. And you'll never disturb me. I look forward to hearing from you. I have some nice pictures of my own. I'll send them.*

*Take care, my friend. S x*

I read, and as before, reread the email many times. I loved that he signed off with just his initial. It was as if some intimacy had crept in.

I went to bed that night with a huge smile on my face and slept right through until the following morning. It was the ring of the telephone that had woken me. I reached over to answer it.

"Good morning, Jayne. I trust I didn't wake you," Francis said.

I held in the groan as I recognised my mother-in-law's voice and glanced at the clock. I had slept in later than normal; it was close to nine.

"I wanted to catch Michael before he left for work to congratulate him."

"He leaves about seven, Francis, but I'm afraid he stayed in London last night after a function. I'm sure you can catch him at work."

She knew he wouldn't be around at that time of the morning.

"I don't like to disturb him. I know how hard he works to provide for you."

Her barbed comments had long since failed to hit their target.

"What did you want to congratulate him on?" I asked. I knew she was baiting me, and for once, I was curious.

"His new contract, of course. It's extremely exciting. I was telling the ladies at the Women's Institute yesterday. The Colonel is extremely proud."

The Colonel, her husband, Albert—and why the fuck she didn't just use his name, I had no idea—had never been proud of his son. Albert, obviously, had been in the military and was bitterly disappointed his only child had not followed in his footsteps. I wondered what Francis' game was.

"I'll be sure to let Michael know when he finally returns home," I snapped.

"Please do. Am I to assume you'll be attending luncheon on Sunday?"

"Michael may be. I'm afraid I have plans."

I'd never missed her formal luncheon before. Every other Sunday Michael dragged a reluctant family with him to sit, stiff-backed and in fear of damaging her best crockery. It was a ritual I intended to finally break.

Francis and Albert were a wealthy couple. They'd travelled the world while putting their son in boarding school. But I had to thank them for one thing—they had set up trust funds for both my children. Ben had accessed his for the rent deposit on his and Kerry's house. Casey had been forbidden access until she finished university. Francis loved the control over my children the fund gave her, I imagined. Ben had often remarked that he'd celebrate with the remainder of his when they died.

I replaced the telephone in its cradle and made my way to the shower. Not even Francis would spoil my mood.

With just a towel wrapped around me, I stood in front of the mirror. My hair was in need of a cut and maybe a colour to cover the grey roots. I dropped the towel. I'd never looked at myself, I mean, *really* looked at myself. I'd never taken care of my body, and maybe that's what turned Michael off. The tart was slim and toned, tanned from days on the golf course with manicured nails and glossy hair. She hadn't brought two children up single-handed; she didn't clean and cook every day, ironed endless amounts of shirts, and gardened. She had a cleaner, I imagined.

I grabbed the handful of fat around my midriff, inspected the silver lines that crisscrossed my stomach and hips and sighed. With a shake of my head, I dressed. Until that holiday, I hadn't thought about how I looked. I had no desire to have regular haircuts or paint my nails. I had no one I wanted to do that for.

I rifled through my cosmetics drawer and found an old bottle of red nail varnish. Sitting on the edge of the bed, I painted my nails. I couldn't remember the last time I had.

With the dog walked and the house cleaned, I decided to take a walk into the village. As I passed the post office, I stopped to look at the notice board; occasionally there would be mention of a concert or a play being performed locally. My gaze came to rest on an advertisement for a job. A secretary was required part-time in a local school. I patted my pocket for a pen and piece of paper, knowing full well I wouldn't find one.

Mrs. Oliver, the florist, came out of the post office door. She smiled and bade me a good morning, whilst holding the door expecting me to enter. I did. The old post master, whose name I never knew, greeted me from his counter.

"There's an advert in the window, can I get the details?" I asked.

He wandered over.

"That one? I should have taken that down ages ago. That job's been taken. Old Mrs. Preston got that," he said.

"Okay, not to worry."

"If you're looking for work, maybe try the pub. I know that young girl walked out recently."

"Thank you, I may do that."

I left the post office with no intention of visiting the White Horse. Not only would Michael throw a fit if I took a job as a barmaid, it really wasn't something I'd want for myself either. But after seeing that notice, I'd made a decision. I wanted to go back to work. I wanted to earn my own money and not have to account for what I did with it.

My cheeks prickled with the cold but I felt refreshed. I was huffing a little by the time I made it home, forgetting my house was deceivingly uphill all the way back.

Dini greeted me with his usual enthusiasm as I entered the house. It took an age to get out of my coat and kick off my shoes. I decided to take a tour around the Internet and see if there were any job agencies locally.

My notifications indicated that I had an email. I was pleased to see Stefan had sent a file with some photographs.

*To: Jayne*

*From: Stefan*

*Date: 17 February 2014*

*Subject: More Holiday Pics*

*Hey, J, some pics. And yes, that one is my favourite. No time today but will speak soon.*

*S xx*

Two kisses! I beamed and quickly opened the attached file. Stefan had sent some underwater ones mixed in with land shots. There was the most amazing photo of a palm tree that hung over the water's edge, with the leaves brushing the surface of the water. The sun was setting in the background and he'd captured the orange hues over the surface of the water perfectly. I earmarked it as one to print off. It would look lovely in a frame.

I caught my breath at the next picture. It was of me. A close up headshot as I was looking out to sea. I looked so sad; whatever I had been thinking about had brought tears to my eyes. I had no recollection of the photo being taken. The evening breeze had caught my hair, which fanned slightly out behind me. I must have been wearing my black strapless sundress, as all that could be seen were bare shoulders.

My eyes were bright with my tears, the green almost emerald. I rose and looked in the hallway mirror. Were my eyes truly that colour? Why had I never noticed just how vibrant they were?

I minimised the file and pulled up the last photographs I'd taken, one prior to my holiday. I was always snapping away and often Ben would grab my camera and take selfies of us both together. I found a photo of us. We were laughing but my eyes, although green, were dull.

Maybe it was the contrast against my slightly tanned face that had made my eyes so bright. A thought ran through my mind, an unexpected one.

My eyes were bright because for the first time in years, despite whatever had caused those tears, I felt free.

I focused on that thought. Being away from Michael had felt liberating. I hadn't realised how stifled my life was, how controlled and where each moment was accounted for until I'd studied that photograph. I brought it back up again. Despite the fact I was looking at myself, I loved the image. There was perfect clarity and focus.

It was the only picture of me and I hoped it was the one Stefan was referring to when he'd said, '...that is my favourite.'

# Chapter Five

For the first month, Stefan and I emailed every day. Often it was just general chitchat, what we had done during the day, what the dog or our children had been up to. Neither mentioned our partners. As winter moved into spring, our emails lessened. Instead of daily, we wrote once or twice a week. Stefan would often email after working hours, and I wondered if he stayed late especially to do that. Another thing that had changed was the tone of the emails.

*To: Stefan*

*From: Jayne*

*Date: 20 March 2014*

*Subject: Angels and dreams*

*Hey, S, hope you're well. It's sunny here for a change. I might sit in the garden. I saw a program on Denmark the other night; there's an artist, somewhere in the North who made little silver angles. They looked wonderful. I have tried Googling the artist but I can't find anything about him, can you try? Anyway, had a nice dream about you last night. ;)*

*J xxx*

*To: Jayne*

*From: Stefan*

*Date: 20 March 2014*

*Subject: Angels and Dreams – what a mix!*

*J, I don't know anything about the artist but I will look, and tell me about the dream. ;)*

*S xx*


*To: Stefan*

*From: Jayne*

*Date: 20 March 2014*

*Subject: Angels and Dreams – it was!*

*:) Don't think so, that one was all for me! However, it was rather good!*

*Hugs and stuff*

*J xx*


*To: Jayne*

*From: Stefan*

*Date 20 March 2014*

*Subject: Angels and Dreams — sulks*

*J, that's not fair. Tell me about "stuff" too.*

*S xx*


*To: Stefan*

*From: Jayne*

*Date: 20 March 2014*

*Subject: Sulks are for children*

*You would love to know what "stuff" was, but that's my secret!*

*J xx*

I had a theory. Whenever I painted my nails red, and I suspected it was nothing more than symbolic, Scarlet made an appearance. I welcomed her. I'd missed her. For some reason, I had all the confidence in the world when I was sending those emails. I could be anyone I wanted to be. I could be flirty and say the kind of things I wouldn't dream of saying face-to-face. Often it wasn't the words that had formed in my mind, but hers as they travelled down to my fingertips. I wondered if I had a split personality, not that I would voice that concern to anyone.

The dream I had half told him about stayed with me for days. I had woken in the middle of the night, aroused and desperate for some relief. We had been on that sandbank back in the Maldives, alone. It was my perfect *From Here To Eternity* moment. I lay underneath Stefan on the shoreline as waves lapped around our bodies. His kiss was deep and fierce; he'd held my head between his hands and ground his pelvis into mine. I recalled how I'd wrapped my legs around his and scraped my nails down his bare back.

I'd woken to a throbbing between my thighs, a dampness that took me by surprise. I'd reached down with my hand and gently touched the cotton of my knickers before pulling my hand away, in shock at the wetness I'd found. I'd never pleasured myself, I wouldn't know how. It left me frustrated and full of longing. It left me sad.

"Are you off to the gym today?" I asked Carla after she'd answered her phone.

"I am, why?"

"I might come with you." I didn't get a reply, just silence.

Carla had wanted me to join the gym and accompany her on her weekly visits. I'd never been one for exercise, other than walking the dog.

"Are you sure? I mean, I'd love for you to come with me. I'll pick you up on the way."

"Great, see you later."

I rushed upstairs to find something to wear. Then panicked because I wasn't sure I even owned a pair of trainers. After rummaging through my wardrobe, I found an old pair of leggings, a t-shirt long enough to cover my backside, and a pair of trainers. I packed them in a bag and waited.

"Well, that's a smile I haven't seen in a long time," Carla said as I walked to her car.

I'd seen her pull up outside the house and climbed in the passenger seat.

"I'm happy today."

She furrowed her brow but said no more. I'd been to the gym some month's prior for an induction. In fact, if I thought hard enough, it was probably a year ago, but I never returned. I'd woken that morning with a plan, a secret desire to get fit, to look the best I could, to put my 'Let's Get Jayne A Life' plan finally into action.

"I think Michael has something up his sleeve," I said as we changed into our workout clothes.

"Huh?"

"His mum rang a little while ago, wanting to congratulate him on his new contract, she never said what it was and I never asked. Then he received a letter from a bank in Japan."

"Have you asked him?"

"No, we don't really talk anymore. We sit in different parts of the house on the odd occasions he's actually home."

"You need to. I'd have opened the letter."

"I'm not interested, to be honest. I haven't been to Francis' for *luncheon* for ages either. Maybe I should go Sunday and see what's going on."

"I'm surprised she didn't tell you, the nasty old witch."

"I think she was waiting for me to ask, which I wasn't going to do."

As we walked into the gym, we chatted about the kids. Casey was due home that weekend and I looked forward to seeing her. She hadn't been home since Christmas. But her coming home posed one problem. Michael and I would have to communicate, put on the pretence that we actually spent time together. I decided to head to the running machine, or walking machine as I'd renamed it; I didn't run. Carla took the one next to me, popped on her headphones and jogged. It baffled me that people took to a running machine to jog. We lived in a beautiful part of Kent; the Downs were on our doorstep, yet guys ran on a grey metal machine watching MTV on the TVs bracketed to the wall. They could be running across the fields, along the footpaths, dodging sheep shit, puddles, and potholes. I chuckled as I upped the speed to a brisk walk.

We spent an hour moving from machine to machine before heading for a shower and then a welcomed coffee. I was dressed with wet hair tied up in a bun before Carla had finished reapplying her makeup.

"I'll get the coffees," I said, heading for the changing room door.

As I waited, I took out my phone and connected to my email account. I hadn't heard from Stefan after our fun exchange about 'stuff' but scrolled through and reread all his messages. I did that often. Whenever I felt down, I read them. They brought a smile to my lips and I felt good. At no time did I think anything was wrong, he was my friend—my secret friend—and he made me feel happy.

With coffees drunk, we headed home. Carla dropped me off in the village; she had an appointment in town and I was getting a haircut. I'd made the appointment the previous day. While I was there, I decided to invest in a manicure. Might as well push the boat out a little.

It felt strange to walk home with loose hair; wisps of soft silky strands would whip around my face in the breeze. As I arrived home and held the key to the lock, I looked at my nails, painted a vivid red. I decided that was going to be my signature colour.

I settled at the kitchen table with my laptop.

*To: Stefan*

*From: Jayne*

*Date: 10 April 2014*

*Subject: Gym!*

*Hey, S. I went to the gym today. I know, the gym! I've decided to get fit, lose a few pounds. I got a haircut too. How boring am I, telling you this ha ha. So, what's happening in the world of marketing?*

*J xx*

While I waited for his reply I made myself some lunch, tuna on crispbread, boring but slimming. I was determined. I wanted a job, I wanted to lose weight, and I wanted to look good. Somewhere in the back of my mind, to a place I pushed thoughts I didn't want to confront, I was hoping that I'd see Stefan again. I was doing this so I looked good when that happened.

I sat drumming my fingers on the kitchen table waiting for a reply; I didn't want to leave in case I missed it. I didn't think of the rationale on that. His email would be there when I returned but I looked forward to his replies. I checked the clock on the wall trying to work out what he would be doing right at the moment. Perhaps he was out to lunch.

A key in the front door startled me. I hastily closed the lid of the laptop. Michael walked into the kitchen.

"You're home early," I said, annoyed that he was.

"Yes." He slowly removed his jacket and hung it over the back of the chair.

He seemed hesitant to leave the room and I wondered why.

"Do you want tea, coffee?" I asked, more so to break the dense atmosphere that had suddenly filled the room.

"Coffee would be good." He took a seat at the table.

"You look different," he added. His comment took me by surprise.

"Nothing different about me, maybe you just haven't looked lately."

He sighed at my retort. "I see you most days," he said.

I placed his coffee cup on the table in front of him. "No, Michael. You haven't *seen* me in years."

I picked up my cigarettes and headed for the garden. By the time I'd arrived back in the house, Michael was in the study on his computer. I took my laptop and headed upstairs. I wanted the privacy of my bedroom to see if Stefan had replied. He hadn't. I did the next best thing—I brought up his company website. I'd looked at it many times, not understanding anything as it was written in Danish, but there were photos of Aalborg. I wondered what it would be like to visit one day.

For the rest of the day, I got on with chores. Washing, ironing, and cleaning the house filled the afternoon. Michael hadn't left the study. I'd heard him on the phone and it surprised me to hear him speak in a foreign language. He stumbled over his words and laughed but it seemed a strange thing to do. I knew he dealt with foreign banks and other traders, but he'd never worked from home before. I was itching to ask why.

That evening we ate our meal in silence before he retired to the living room and I stayed put in the kitchen. It was the warmest room in the house. Michael wouldn't invest in a new heating system. His answer to anyone who complained of the chill in the rooms was to put a sweater on. Many a time I'd gone through the drawers of the desk in the study looking for any financial information. Maybe we weren't as well off as I assumed. Maybe we needed to budget, or maybe he was just tight.

"I'm heading to the pub for a drink," Michael said, surprising me. He never visited the pub.

"Okay," I replied, half expecting him to ask me to join him. He didn't.

Something was definitely off. I racked my brain trying to remember the last time he'd arrived home early from work. Once he had left, I sat at his computer. It was password protected, and after trying all our dates of birth, I gave up. I flicked through paperwork on the desk. Not much made any sense to me, it was mainly figures, projections, investments—but whose?

I felt my anxiety levels begin to rise. I had no doubt he was up to something. Perhaps he was preparing to finally move in with the tart. Maybe he was paving the way to leave me penniless. I took myself back to the one place in the house I felt the most comfortable and did the one thing I always did when anxiety threatened to overwhelm me—I poured a glass of wine and emailed Stefan. I'd drunk the first glass while I read through previous messages. I poured another.

*To: Stefan*
*From: Jayne*
*Date: 10 April 2014*
*Subject: Fantasies?*
*Hey, S. If I told you my fantasy would you tell me yours?*
*J xx*

I'd giggled as I pressed send and waited. Although he hadn't replied to my earlier email, he did to that one.

*To: Jayne*
*From: Stefan*
*Date: 10 April 2014*
*Subject: Intrigued*
*I think perhaps I'll stay at work for another hour. Tell me…*

*S xx*


*To: Stefan*

*From: Jayne*

*Date: 10 April 2014*

*Subject: Are you ready?*

*I'm standing in my bedroom in front of a full-length mirror. I'm naked after my shower and my body is wet. You stand behind me. You look at my reflection in the glass and wrap one arm around my shoulders. Your other hand splays on my stomach. Gently, you slide it down. I rest my head back on your shoulder and you whisper words I don't understand in my ear. You tease me with your fingers, making me come. My body feels alive, on fire. Your lips ghost the skin on my neck, up to my ear and you continue to whisper. I can feel your erection, hard against my back as you pull me against you. And I want to feel you inside me…*

*J xx*


I'd pressed the send button before reading what I'd typed. When I went back to the email my mouth fell open. Holy shit! I covered my mouth with my hand and panicked. Where the fuck had those words come from. That wasn't me. Scarlet had made an appearance without me knowing. I giggled as I drained the second glass of wine and poured another. I raised my glass to her, catching sight of my red painted nails. Good old Scarlet.


*To: Jayne*

*From: Stefan*

*Date: 10 April 2014*

*Subject: Continue?*

*I wouldn't be a good lover if I left it there. Tell me more...*

*S xx*


*To: Stefan*

*From: Jayne*

*Date: 10 April 2014*

*Subject: Lover?*

*How good a lover are you? Tell me your fantasy...*

*J xx*


*To: Jayne*

*From: Stefan*

*Date: 10 April 2014*

*Subject: The best*

*My English is not so good, so I'd rather show you.*

*S xx*


I dropped the glass I was holding, thankful it was a heavy cut crystal and didn't break. When? When would he show me? My heart hammered in my chest. I fought with Scarlet to ask the question. She'd have replied with a date and time, a location and exactly what she wanted him to show. I needed some fresh air. I called for Dini and grabbed my coat. Stepping out in the garden, I took in a lungful of cold air. It burnt my chest but I needed the cold to dampen the heat that coursed through my body. Excitement bubbled in the pit of my stomach. Did Stefan mean he wanted to meet? I closed my eyes at the thought just as reality crashed through me. I slumped into the garden chair and held my head in my hands.

What the fuck was I doing? I was married; he was married. It was wrong. What I had done, what I had written, was so wrong. But I couldn't stop myself. I refused to entertain the idea that I was living a fantasy because real life was unbearable; I pushed that thought to the back of my mind. I was just having some fun, I was making myself happy, and no one would get hurt.

*To: Stefan*
*From: Jayne*
*Date: 10 April 2014*
*Subject: Really?*
*I guess showing is better than telling. ;) Perhaps I'll dream about that fantasy and let you know what happens next.*
*J xx*

*To: Jayne*
*From: Stefan*
*Date: 10 April 2014*
*Subject: I'll show…*
*Oh, it is! And I'm an expert at showing…*
*S xx*

*To: Stefan*
*From: Jayne*
*Date 10 April 2014*

*Subject: Please do*

*I'll look forward to experiencing your expertise. ;)*

*J xx*

I waited for his reply; it didn't come. I checked my watch and noticed how late it was. The pub would be closing shortly, real life would return. I headed up to bed before that happened.

It was early; the sun hadn't risen when I woke to the sound of Dini growling. He often growled at the wildlife rustling in the garden, perhaps he had spotted a fox. I climbed out of bed and wrapped a dressing gown around me to ward off the chill. I winced at the snores that resounded around the upstairs hallway; Michael had left his bedroom door open. I'd been glad when he'd used the excuse of my insomnia to take to the spare room. It was his snoring that kept me awake night after night.

I made a cup of tea and let Dini out into the garden, he could chase off whatever was lurking. I picked up my mobile and opened the emails. In the cold light of day, or early hours of the morning as was the case; I wished I could have taken those emails back. I seemed to become a different person when I typed, all my thoughts, feelings, and in that case, fantasies poured from my fingertips. I'd always had Scarlet. I remembered back to childhood, those firsts. The first day at school, I would pretend to be her: confident and sassy. My first date with Michael, I'd tossed my hair, twirled a strand between my finger, and probably pouted as well. The first time I met his boss, Scarlet had been on top form that evening, telling smutty jokes and laughing. Michael had been furious; he'd dragged me to the car once the evening was over by my arm and bruised my skin. I'd tried to explain, but how could I?

Scarlet was the me I wanted to be. The one who appeared as if by magic when I needed courage, when I needed a voice to speak words plain Jayne never had the confidence to. With her blonde hair and perfect figure, everyone loved her. Maybe I was going mad, maybe I'd always been.

It was Saturday afternoon and I was expecting Casey. Michael had taken my car to collect her from the train station. Although it was within walking distance, the weather was foul. She rushed through the front door, leaving it open so the elements could chill the house further, dumped her bags on the floor, and ran to give me a hug.

"Mum, it's so good to see you. I'm starving and I have a stack of washing," she said.

"It's good to see you too, darling. How was the ski trip?" I ignored the 'stack of washing' comment.

She shrugged off her coat, letting it fall to the floor in the hallway before heading to the kitchen. I picked up the coat and hung it on a hook.

Casey talked a hundred words a second as she reeled off her adventures. I listened, I was interested but I also wanted to know how she funded all her trips. She'd been to the South of France, skiing in Austria, and was about to take a trip to America. I smiled as I listened, loving her enthusiasm for life. Michael came and sat next to her.

"Isn't it amazing, Mum, about Dad's new job? You will get me on an internship, won't you? I mean, Japan, sheesh, how unbelievable is that. When do you leave? I can come in August, I think. I love the apartment; it has three bedrooms, doesn't it? I want to be able to invite friends." Casey rattled on and on, gushing about her father's new job in Japan. I stared at him; he stared back but then had the grace to lower his eyes after a minute.

"So, Mum, what will you do about the dog?"

I looked at her, blinking. "Nothing, the dog will stay with me, of course."

"But you can't take the dog to Japan. Well, I guess you could but…"

"I'm not going to Japan. In fact, this is the first I've heard of it."

Her mouth gaped open; she looked between Michael and me.

"I'm not going anywhere, because I want to stay here for the baby."

"Baby?" Michael said.

"Yes, oh, didn't I tell you? You're going to be a grandfather. How silly of me to have forgotten something as important as that." I stood, grabbed my cigarettes and headed to the garden.

I cursed myself. I'd spoilt Ben and Kerry's surprise. A plan had been made that they would visit that evening, I was to cook a meal and they would make their big announcement over dinner.

"Mum?" Casey closed the kitchen door behind her, she handed me a jacket as she took a seat beside me.

"I'm sorry, I didn't know," she said.

I took her hand in mine. "It's not your fault, darling."

"Why didn't he tell you? I knew a couple of weeks ago."

That comment made me feel a hell of a lot better. "I don't know."

I stubbed out my cigarette and we made our way back into the kitchen. Michael was nowhere to be seen. I texted Ben an apology that I'd stolen his moment and set about to prepare the evening meal.

Despite the strained atmosphere, we had an enjoyable evening and thankfully, Ben and Kerry were not upset that I'd told everyone about the baby. Inside I was in turmoil. I went through the motions. I smiled, I responded when necessary, but I also kept myself busy clearing plates, serving dessert, and tidying up once everyone had retired to the living room.

"Are you okay?" I heard. I had been leaning over the sink trying to calm my racing heart when Kerry walked into the kitchen.

"I'm fine. I think I've got a little heartburn," I said.

The sense that I was about to have a panic attack seemed to be hitting me frequently of late. It was something I'd never experienced before. I'd feel my face heat up, my heartbeat increase, and my hands would start to shake. I'd feel sick, my vision blurred, and noise became just a hum around me. I'd managed to swallow down the panic and continued to wash up.

"Let me help," she said. She picked up a tea towel and dried the pots that didn't fit in the dishwasher.

"How are you feeling?" I asked.

"Okay, the sickness has gone, thank God. I have an appointment on Monday. Ben is really excited."

"Aw, that's nice to hear. You two are going to make the most wonderful parents."

Kerry came from a large, raucous family. They rowed and fought but there was a lot of love. Her father had left when she was a child and her mother had brought up four children by herself. I liked her; she was an honest, hardworking woman. She reminded me of my mum, although she wasn't much different in age to me.

"Go back inside. I'll bring some tea in," I said.

She smiled and gave me a hug. I wanted a little more time alone to get myself together. I made a mental note to contact the doctor; perhaps I was heading for an early menopause.

Ben and Kerry left soon after I'd brought some tea in the room. Ben had an early start on a project he needed to get finished. Casey stretched and yawned, announcing she would get an early night. I had no doubt she wasn't tired, just wanting to get out of the way. I collected the mugs and took them to the kitchen.

"Perhaps we need to talk about this," I heard. Michael had followed me.

"I think it's a little too late for that."

"Will you at least sit down?" he snapped.

I tuned and raised my eyebrows at him. As I looked at him, I wondered how he could have spent all those years intimidating me. He was a bully, a childish bully who only ever wanted life his way.

"You've changed," he said as he took a seat.

"You've noticed? Wow."

"I don't like the red, a little too tarty," he said as he looked at my hands.

"You'd know about tarts, obviously," I answered with a smile.

"Let's not make this personal, shall we?"

"You don't like my nail varnish, not that I give a shit, and we're not to make it personal? Okay."

"I have been given a fantastic opportunity, one I can't turn down. I'd have hoped you would be supportive."

"Maybe if I'd have known, maybe if I hadn't found out from my daughter, I would have. When do you leave?"

"In a month. I thought I would put the house on the market; I'll need an apartment in London. I have use of a company one in Japan, but I'll be back in the UK for a month twice a year."

"Well, you thought wrong. I'm not moving from this house. While you're back in the UK, you can either buy yourself a flat or stay with her."

"Why do you always bring her into our problems?"

I stood and slammed my hands down on the table. "You have to be kidding me, right? She *is* the fucking problem."

"She understands me..." I cut him off with a bitter laugh.

"Please tell me you are not going to use that old cliché? Michael, I don't care. I don't love you, I haven't for a long time, and you know why? Because you never loved me. Not once have you cared about my life, not once have you appreciated what I do for you. Not once have you put me first, complimented me, taken me to dinner even. You go. I wish you well, Michael, I really do. We should have ended this farce many years ago."

I fought to catch my breath, stunned at the words that had left my mouth. Stunned that for the first time I'd spoken my mind, I'd stood up to him and judging by his slack jaw and wide eyes, made him finally hear me.

I didn't want him to see me cry so I turned and walked away. I took my laptop, my glass of wine and headed for my bedroom. I opened my emails and sadness crept over me when I noticed Stefan hadn't replied. Whether it was to cheer myself up or wallow further in self-pity, I wasn't sure, but I read through our exchanges from the beginning. Deep down, I knew what I was doing; I was escaping into my fantasy world for peace of mind and happiness.

Casey left the following morning; she had planned on staying for the whole weekend but a 'friend had called' she'd said. I suspected she wanted out of the house.

# Chapter Six

The following week dragged by. I hadn't heard from Stefan at all and began to get worried. I checked my emails daily, sometimes hourly. It wasn't unusual by that point to not hear from him for three or four days but it had been over a week. I sent him another.

*To: Stefan*
*From: Jayne*
*Date: 1 May 2014*
*Subject: Worried*
*Hey, S, how are you? I was getting a little worried that I hadn't heard from you. No need for a long reply, just let me know you're not ill. :)*
*J xx*

A thought had been bugging me. As far as I knew, no one knew I existed. If he were ill, I'd never be told. His silence worried me. I looked back at the last exchange and wondered if I'd gone over the top. Had I frightened him off by revealing my fantasy?

*To: Stefan*
*From: Jayne*

*Date: 4 May 2014*

*Subject: Concerned*

*Hey, S. Just send a word, let me know you're okay. I'm missing you and worried. I hope those silly emails haven't scared you off ha ha.*

*J xx*

*To: Stefan*

*From: Jayne*

*Date: 10 May 2014*

*Subject: Still worried.*

*Have I done something wrong? That sounds a little desperate, doesn't it? But if I have, please let me apologise. :(*

*J xx*

Michael and I seemed to have settled into a routine. He stayed out all day, although on 'garden leave' as he called it, from work, and we politely skirted around each other in the evenings. I'd told Carla about his job but no one else. My parents knew something was amiss. Whenever they visited, Michael was not around. I'd stopped going to see his in retaliation. My mum questioned me constantly, but for some reason, I didn't open up. I never told them what life was like because that would mean admitting I had been wrong from the day I married him. My dad had offered me a way out. He'd asked me on my wedding day if I was sure I was doing the right thing, and it was my own shame and embarrassment that forced me to walk the aisle to a man I already knew didn't love me.

I hid away; I avoided calls and only caught up with Carla when she pounded on my front door after days of not speaking.

"Right, what's going on?" she had asked.

"Nothing, I'm just miserable. I don't want to infect anyone with my misery," I said, forcing a chuckle.

"You've got the best thing going on. He's finally leaving."

How could I tell her that it wasn't Michael leaving that had me in a funk but the silence from Stefan?

"I know you're not going to like this but I've made an appointment for you to see my solicitor," she said.

"Whatever for? I'm staying in the house. It's a separation, Carla."

"You're staying in the house for how long? He said he wanted to buy an apartment, and I guarantee he can afford it without selling the house but you need to know your rights. This house is in his name, isn't it?"

"I think so. I don't know, to be honest. I don't see what that matters though."

"It means he can sell it from under you. He can turf you out whenever he wants, Jayne. You need to open your eyes now."

"He wouldn't do that, would he?"

"Maybe not, I don't know, but it won't hurt to know where you stand legally."

We were sitting in the garden while I finished my cigarette. My one a day that had turned to five had then increased to ten a day.

"How about lunch?" Carla said.

"I'm not hungry. I never seem to be hungry at the moment. Do you know I've gone down a dress size?"

"Did you call the doctor?"

"No, I'll do that tomorrow."

It was always 'tomorrow.' Everything I planned I seemed to put off and, of course, tomorrow never came. I had excuses for why I felt tired all the time. I just wasn't getting enough sleep, and I had too much on my mind. There had been days where I simply did not want to get out of bed. It was only the thought of Dini that had me struggle into clothes and drag myself with unbrushed hair downstairs to let him out.

"I'm worried about you. You seemed to pick up a month ago but now..."

"Carla, please. I'm fine. My husband is leaving me, I'm entitled to feel a little shit."

"Okay, but I still worry."

We finished our coffee and she rose to leave. She gave me a hug before departing. As she walked the path to her car, she passed the postman.

"Morning," he called out, and his gaze followed her arse. She chuckled.

Without a word, he handed me the mail. I closed the front door and looked through the letters. I held my breath as I saw a cream, slightly velvety envelope with an airmail sticker and a postmark from Denmark.

Stefan had never written to me before. My hands shook as I held the envelope, not daring to open it. I laid the mail on the hallway table and took the envelope to the kitchen. I sat and looked at it for ages. Eventually, I slid my finger under the flap and pulled out a plain white piece of paper. It had been folded into quarters. I opened it and read.

*Dear Jayne,*

*I'm getting a divorce, and I need some time to get my head straight. I'm living with my brother until I find an apartment, but I need some distance from everyone. Please understand.*

*Yours, Stefan*

It was a cold, emotionless, typed letter. No sign off with just his initial, no kisses, and the referral of me as 'everyone' stung.

I read the letter until the words blurred from my tears. I felt desolate and isolated. I felt as if my world was collapsing around me. My heart began to race, my palms sweated, and my stomach heaved. I rushed to the kitchen sink. I hadn't eaten, in fact, I didn't remember eating the previous day either. I dry heaved until a foul acid burnt my throat. With shaking hands I grabbed a glass from the drainer and ran the tap until the water was ice-cold. I took long gulps trying to rid my mouth of the taste.

I staggered up the stairs and threw myself on the unmade bed. I crumpled the letter then spent ages trying to straighten out the page. My tears dripped onto the paper, smudging the words. The ink ran further after I'd tried to dry it with the cuff of my sweater.

I looked at the white piece of paper, black words ran into each other, and I grieved. I grieved for the loss of a friend. I grieved for the pain he must be feeling. I grieved for the emptiness I felt. I closed my eyes, exhaustion took over, and I fell asleep.

It was dark when I woke. I heard shuffling from downstairs, the clatter of pans as Michael attempted to cook. I should get up. I should shower and brush my hair. My eyes stung, as did my cheeks from the salty tears that had dried.

I dragged myself from the bed and headed for the shower. As I stood under the warm jets of water, I cried again. I needed to get a grip and stop feeling sorry for myself. Stefan must have been going through immeasurable pain and I was the one crying over the loss of a friendship.

"Jesus, Jayne," Michael said as I walked into the kitchen. I had avoided looking in the mirror.

"I have a bug coming," I said.

For a moment I thought he was going to take a step towards me, offer me some form of comfort, but he didn't. He nodded his head and took his coffee to the study. I made my own tea.

It had taken two weeks for the crying to stop, two whole weeks of hiding away from the world. I'd read the letter over and over. I typed many emails in response and then deleted them. I wanted to just offer a few words of comfort and to let him know I was thinking of him. But in telling me he needed distance, he had, in effect, told me not to contact him.

Carla had rung, texted, and tried to visit over the previous two weeks. I'd fobbed her off, as I had Ben and Kerry, telling them all I had a bug. Michael had been able to verify that I was poorly, or so he thought.

"I think I'll leave a little earlier. I have some potential clients in London that I'd like to take over to the new company. I'm going to stay in town," Michael said one evening.

"When?"

"Tomorrow. I'll pack my things tonight."

I nodded and took another sip of my wine. I seemed to be surviving on wine and cigarettes. Michael headed upstairs and I was unsure of what to do. What was the etiquette when one's husband was preparing to leave? Did I help him pack? Exactly what did he want to take with him?

I moved to the living room and took a photograph from the mantel. It was one of him and the children—I doubted he'd want a family one—and then climbed the stairs.

"Let me help," I said, as I entered his bedroom and saw the pile of screwed up clothes.

He stepped back. For the first time ever, I thought I saw something in his eyes, a moment of sadness, or maybe it was pity.

I folded his shirts and suits; wrapped his shoes in tissue paper and packed two suitcases. Before I closed the last one, I laid the photograph on top. He stared at it.

"Thank you," he whispered.

I sat on the edge of his bed and gave him a small smile.

"I am pleased for you, Michael. It's your dream job and I know you'll ace it. But I ask one, no, make that two things. Keep in contact with *both* your children, not just Casey. And don't take my home away until I'm ready." My voice had dropped to a whisper.

"I'll pay the mortgage, I'll put an allowance each month in the joint account for the bills and things," he said.

I simply nodded and then rose. I placed my hand on his arm and squeezed a little before I walked away. He followed, carrying the two cases. I watched as he took a walk around the living room and the study. I hadn't noticed how tidy that room was. He'd obviously been 'clearing out' for some time.

We walked to the front door; he put on his coat and carried the cases to his car. I watched as he put them in the boot. He hesitated before opening the driver's door, not looking at me but at the house itself. I saw his shoulders rise as if he'd taken a deep breath, and then he climbed in and drove away.

I slowly shut the door, stepped back to the wall and slid down, a sobbing mess. I hugged my knees to my chest and Dini came and whimpered. He sat beside me with his head on my feet. His brown, sorrowful eyes looked up at me. I cried and cried. I cried until I had a sore throat, until my face hurt and my eyes were half shut. Then I curled where I lay and slept.

At some point I was woken by a shake to my arm. I'd felt like I'd been asleep for hours. I opened my eyes as much as they would to see Carla.

"Come on, let's get you up," she said.

"What are you doing here?" I asked.

"Michael called Charles to tell him he was in London, he called me. I guessed he'd left already."

I stood on shaky legs and let Carla lead me to the kitchen. She put the kettle on as I sat at the table.

"I think he's gone to her. He shouldn't be leaving for another week. I guess he didn't want to be around me for too much longer."

"He's a fuckwit, and I know you don't feel it right now, but in a couple of weeks, I guarantee you'll feel happy about it."

I accepted the tea Carla handed me before she tidied the kitchen. I winced a little at the clinking of glass as she lined up the many empty wine bottles. Even I was aware I'd drunk way too much over the past couple of weeks.

"You need a shower. When was the last time you washed your hair?" she gently said as she sat.

I thought hard. "I've had a bug," I said, defensively.

"Did you call the doctor?"

"Yes, there's not much anyone can do."

I could tell she hadn't believed me. I lowered my gaze and

studied the teacup in my hand.

"Why don't you go and have a nice bath. I'll finish clearing up."

I nodded and stood. I took a look around the kitchen. The bin was overflowing, the dog's water bowl needed changing and there were still dirty dishes in the sink from the previous day. I'd always been so house proud but lately, I just hadn't cared enough.

As I stood in the bathroom, I stripped off my clothes; my jeans were grubby and I wondered how many days I had been wearing them. I pulled the hairband holding up my ponytail and felt the tackiness of unwashed hair. While I waited for the bath to fill, I studied myself. My cheeks had hollowed and dark circles had formed under my eyes. The only thing that gave me a ghost of a smile was that, for the first time in a long time, I had collarbones visible ribs and protruding hipbones.

I chuckled bitterly. Nothing like a bit of desertion, of complete 'fuckedupness' to help with weight loss, I guessed. I sank into the bath and continued to sink until my head was under the water. I kept my eyes open, looking through the water. I could hear my pulse thump, getting faster the longer I held my breath. When I could hold my breath no more, when my body was screaming for air, I sat up and gasped.

A thought ran through my mind. How do people deliberately drown themselves? That instinct to survive must kick in at some point. I shook my head, washed my hair and body before climbing out. I didn't want to look at the grimy bath as the water drained away. I ignored it and made my way to the bedroom to find pyjamas.

I heard the Hoover running downstairs, I heard Carla calling for Dini after she'd let him out in the garden. I felt guilty. I always felt guilty. Maybe Michael hadn't loved me because I didn't clean the house well enough. Maybe Dini wouldn't love me because I hadn't walked him for a week. I needed to get my act together.

"Better?" Carla said as I walked into the kitchen.

"Much. I'm sorry. I fell apart a little there. And you're right, I'm glad he's gone."

I gave her a smile. It was a fake one, of course, but she'd never tell the difference.

"I thought I might stay tonight."

"There really is no need. Thank you, but seriously, Carla, you need to get home. I'm fine. I'm done with crying, and I'm going to look forward, to finally get my life on track. I'd like to get back to the gym. I can't believe how much weight I've lost." I smiled again.

She wasn't entirely convinced but accepted what I said, regardless. After one last cup of tea, she left. I bolted the front door behind her.

I stripped the bed of its dirty linen and remade it with fresh white sheets and pillowslips. I took the laundry down to the utility room and switched the washing machine on. Before I turned out the light, I noticed a white shirt in the laundry bin. It was one of Michael's. I pulled it out and held it to my face. It smelled of him, of his aftershave. It smelled of her perfume too.

I took the shirt into the garden and lifted the lid off the BBQ. I squirted lighter fuel over the top and with my lighter, watched it go up in flames. I laughed, puffing on a cigarette as I did. I rushed indoors, still carrying the cigarette in my hand and to my bedroom. I snatched Stefan's letter from the top of my bedside cabinet and ran back down. I threw that on the BBQ as well.

"Fuck you both," I said as I watched them burn.

When there was nothing left but ash, I closed the lid. Dini had sat beside me. He'd usually be off exploring the garden but instead he'd sat looking up at me.

I knelt down and cradled his head. "You know what, madness is quite fun."

Was I going mad? Some days it felt like it. Some days my head was full of noise but nothing distinguishable. Some days it was too much effort to move, I felt like I was wading through treacle. But then there were other days when I felt on top of the world, when the sun was shining and I walked Dini through the woods—I felt great.

I ran on autopilot most of the time. I took Mum and Dad shopping each Friday, I laughed and chatted to Ben and Kerry. I got excited with their baby news. I chatted to Casey when I'd managed to catch up with her, and I met Carla for coffee or shopping. I took each day as it came.

# Chapter Seven

Carla and I were in Bluewater Shopping Centre shopping for clothes. It had been three weeks since Michael had left and, as promised, he had deposited some money in our joint bank account, not before clearing out the balance, of course. It was just enough to cover the mortgage and bills, and left a little for living expenses.

"What do you think? This one or this one?" Carla held up two identical black dresses.

"The one on the left," I said, not seeing the difference.

"I'll try it on. Is there anything you've seen that you like?"

"Are you kidding? Tons, but I don't have the money."

"That offer of the solicitor is still available."

"For what? I can't make Michael give me money just because we've separated."

"No, but you can start divorce proceedings."

"I will, soon. I promise."

We had the same conversation every time we met. At that moment, I was keeping the house. I didn't want to antagonise him. I knew I needed a job. The car would need a service soon and I had no spare cash to pay for that.

Michael and I hadn't spoken since the day he'd left; I had no desire to talk to him. I heard, via Casey, that he was in Japan. She was eager to join him for a holiday. I suspected she was eager to see if she would get an internship with him. I envied her. I envied the fact that she could visit the countries that she did, that she travelled and had fun. Those were all the things I'd always wanted to do.

"How about a holiday? Maybe a weekend somewhere in the UK?"

"As I said, Michael doesn't exactly provide me with a great deal of money. I'll think about it. And before you say, no, you're not paying for it. Now go try on the dress."

She huffed as she headed to the changing room. A weekend away sounded ideal. I would have loved it and maybe, if I was careful, I could afford it. I'd work out a budget when I returned home.

With the dress purchased we headed for the car park. I hated shopping, any kind of shopping, and had started to use an online store for groceries. There was nothing worse than being surrounded by wonderful clothes, by necessities, and knowing I couldn't afford them.

I waved goodbye as Carla dropped me off at home and hurried indoors. Dini greeted me with his usual leap to my shoulders and a lick on my face. I grabbed his lead and we took a walk. It was as we walked that my phone beeped; I'd received a message. I dug the phone from my pocket and looked. An email had arrived. I opened the app and froze. My hand shook as I looked at the sender's name. I called for the dog and ran all the way home. I tripped as I tried to kick off my walking boots without undoing the laces. I let my coat fall to the floor as I rushed into the kitchen and opened my laptop. I closed my eyes tight while I waited for the email to load.

*To: Jayne*

*From: Stefan*

*Date: 4 June 2014*

*Subject: Hi*

*I'm so sorry. I'm not actually sure what to say. I have an apartment now; it overlooks the sea. I bought a motorbike too. I'd always wanted one. I've done a lot of thinking, some travelling the past weeks. If we can still be friends, I'd like that.*

*S xx*

I read, then again and smiled. I jumped from my chair and danced around the kitchen. All previous thoughts of what a shit he had been were gone in an instant. He wanted to be friends; I'd take that. I was quick to reply.

*To: Stefan*

*From: Jayne*

*Date: 4 June 2014*

*Subject: Hi yourself*

*Hey, it's so great to hear from you. The apartment sounds wonderful; I've always wanted to live near water. And a motorbike! Can you ride one? And, of course, I'll always be your friend.*

*J xx*

I sat and waited. He didn't reply immediately, and as time went on my disappointment rose. I needed to calm myself, needed to understand that he was probably busy, he couldn't respond immediately. I shut the laptop lid and decided to cook myself dinner. I hadn't cooked a proper meal since Michael had left. I opened the fridge to bare shelves.

Collecting my purse, I drove into the village. I could have walked but didn't want the struggle back with carrier bags of shopping. I went from the butcher's to the greengrocer's, to the pharmacy and the One-Stop shop. It surprised me to receive so many greetings. At first I'd tapped my foot impatiently as I waited at the counter to be served in the butcher's. He was having a chat with an elderly customer, explaining the best way to cook the meat she had just bought. But as I listened, as I was brought into their conversation, I relaxed. That was country living at its best.

I arrived home and set about to grill the steak and plate the salad I'd bought. I hadn't realised how hungry I was until I'd taken the last mouthful of food and pushed away an empty plate. I opened the backdoor slightly and didn't feel a shred of guilt as I sat at the kitchen table and had a cigarette.

The following morning I received his reply.

*To: Jayne*
*From: Stefan*
*Date: 5 June 2014*
*Subject: Of course I can ride*
*I've attached a photograph of the mean machine! I never asked, how are things with you? I missed talking to you. I buried my head in the sand for a while back there.*
*S xx*

Of course, I replied immediately.

*To: Stefan*

*From: Jayne*

*Date: 5 June 2014*

*Subject: Missed you too*

*Where to start? Like you, I'm single. I was sad for a while, although it had to happen. Michael took a job in Japan. I'm pleased for him but I'm not sure how long I'll keep the house. Burying your head is sometimes all you can do. My heart broke for you and I won't ask details. I'm just glad to have your friendship back. I love the bike. Please be careful though!*

*J xx*


*To: Jayne*

*From: Stefan*

*Date: 5 June 2014*

*Subject: I'm sorry :(*

*I'm sorry to hear that, my friend. I hope you'll keep your house, but you know what? Sometimes a complete break is the best thing. I was an ass; you're the only person I can be myself with. And yes, I'll be careful. I'll wear my leathers at all times.*

*S xx*


*To: Stefan*

*From: Jayne*

*Date: 5 June 2014*

*Subject: Leathers!*

*Pic please!! ;) Hugs and stuff.*

*J xx*

I was surprised at how quick we fell back into that comfortable friendship, how easy it was to flirt with him. My heart swelled a little at his words. I was the only person he could be himself with. I was curious, of course, about his break-up. I knew he had two sons but neither of us talked about our partners. In fact, I think that was the first time I'd mentioned Michael's name.

For some reason, I felt able to close the laptop, to not sit and anxiously await his response. Deep down I knew we'd fall back into our routine; a couple of emails a week was the fix I needed. All was right in the world if I had Stefan. Or so I thought.

I was due at my parent's house for the usual Friday afternoon trip to the supermarket. My parents lived a half hour drive away, and it was a shock to see my dad when he opened the front door. I'd missed our shopping trip the previous week; Mum had called and said that Dad had been poorly. She didn't give much detail, and I hadn't taken it seriously, however, looking at him wincing as he coughed and held his side, I was concerned.

"Have you phoned the doctor?" I asked as I removed my coat.

We always had a cup of tea and a sandwich before leaving to shop.

"No, it's just a cough."

"How long have you had it?"

"A week, I think," he replied.

"More like a couple of months now. Please tell him, Jayne, he needs to see the doctor," Mum said, bringing tea to the living room.

"You're kidding me? You've had the cough for a couple of months and not seen anyone?" I said.

Dad waved his hand in the air and raised a tissue to his mouth as another coughing fit wracked his body. I watched and knew I'd seen pink on that tissue when he'd removed it from his mouth and placed it back in his pocket.

"Dad, show me that tissue," I said, concern laced my voice.

"Will you stop your worrying, I'm fine. Now, tell me about my great grandchild."

My parents were as excited as I was about their first great grandchild.

"Don't change the subject. Show me or I'll call an ambulance. That was blood, Dad. That is serious."

"I've been telling him that for days," Mum said.

Dad had huffed and pulled out the tissue. Although tiny, there were spot of red on the tissue.

"I'm ringing the doctor now," I said.

Mum flicked through an old address book, it's pages held together with sticky tape, until she found the doctor's number. I dialled, pressed one for appointments and held. Ten or so minutes later; the call was finally answered. I explained that I wanted an emergency appointment, that my father had had a cough for months, and about the blood on the tissue. Her advice was to take him to Accident & Emergency, and immediately. I replaced the telephone slowly as her insistence dawned on me. I'd seen an advert on the television about prolonged coughs and what it could mean.

"Dad, the doctor said we should go to A&E."

"What? It's just a cough. It's that time of year. Everyone has one."

"Maybe they're so busy it's what they are recommending. You'll get a course of antibiotics and then we can come home." I hoped my words sounded convincing; they certainly didn't to my ears.

Dad had grumbled, mumbled, but eventually rose from his chair and pulled on his shoes. Mum grabbed their coats and we headed off to the local hospital. Thankfully Friday afternoon proved to be one of the best times to visit A&E. The wait was no more than two hours. Dad was seen by a nurse then shuffled off for an X-ray. Mum and I had waited outside the radiology department, sitting on hard plastic chairs. She wrung a tissue in her hand until her skirt was covered in white fluff.

I took her hand in mine. "Don't worry, I'm sure it's nothing more than a cough."

I hadn't believed what I'd said but wanted to offer something to calm her a little.

When Dad was done we were asked to wait until a doctor could see us. It hadn't taken long. Perhaps that should have alarmed me.

"I think, Mr. Adams, I'd like for a consultant to see you," the doctor said.

"When will that be? We need to get to the supermarket before it closes," Dad had answered.

"I'm requesting an appointment for this coming week."

My heart pounded in my chest. The doctor chatted to Dad some more, I tuned out as one word, and a word I would not speak out loud, swam through my mind. After what could have been minutes or a half hour—I'd lost track of time—we were free to leave.

Dad insisted on us driving straight to the supermarket, despite my protests that we could always make the trip the following day. He hated shopping on a weekend, moaning that the supermarket was busier and convinced the out of date food was placed on the shelves to be sold to the masses.

I think I walked around in a daze; my shopping trolley was only half-full by the time I made it to the checkout. Dad chatted, or grumbled, as normal. As much as he always insisted on accompanying us, he hated food shopping.

I dropped them home, helped unload the shopping, before being ushered off. I had wanted to stay a little longer but Dad insisted I head off before it got dark; he worried about me driving at night.

As soon as I arrived home, I dialled Carla. Her phone went to voicemail. I didn't want to leave my news in a voicemail message, so simply said I'd call her the following day.

*To: Stefan*
*From: Jayne*
*Date: 10 June 2014*
*Subject: Bad day*
*Hi, S. I took my dad to the hospital today. I'm really worried about him. He's had a cough for a while and I think this might be serious. :( I'm sorry, I just had to tell someone.*
*J xx*

I sat in the garden with a cigarette and a glass of wine. Dini, perhaps sensing my upset, sat beside me. The sun was setting over the woods and I shivered a little. It wasn't particularly cold that evening but I pulled my cardigan around my shoulders. My phone lit up indicating a message. I opened my emails.

> *To: Jayne*
> *From: Stefan*
> *Date: 10 June 2014*
> *Subject: Fuck*
> *Baby, I'm so, so sorry. Ring me. I don't have your number. I* can save it.
> *S xx*

All his emails contained an automatic signature for his business and listed was a mobile number. My hands shook. I hadn't spoken to him since we'd met six months previous. I needed to hear his voice, though, so I dialled.

"Hi, thank you for ringing," he said once he'd answered.

His voice was smooth, soft, and brought tears to my eyes.

"Hello," I replied quietly.

"So, tell me what happened?" he asked.

I could hear voices in the background. It sounded as if he had company.

"You're busy, I can always call another time. I don't want to disturb you," I said.

"It's just friends, and talking to you is more important. Tell me what happened?"

Was it wrong of me to smile at his words? I was important to someone.

I told him about the hospital appointment and my fears.

"It may be nothing, the blood could be because he's ruptured some blood vessels with all the coughing. But you did the right thing. When will you get to see a consultant?"

"I guess they'll call on Monday. I hope so, anyway."

"How are you? It's so good to hear your voice."

"I'm scared, if I'm honest. I have to deal with this on my own, and I just don't know what the future holds either."

"You're not on your own. I'm here for you, Jayne. I know I was a shit. I panicked and ran from everyone. My wife, ex-wife, found our emails. I don't know how but things had not been good for a long time."

"Oh, God, oh no. I'm so sorry, Stefan. I feel just terrible. She must have been devastated and that's partly my fault."

"Oh, don't feel so bad. She had two affairs; I forgave her both times. But let's not talk about her. I want you to know that I'm here whenever you need to talk."

I choked up a little at his words. "Thank you," I said.

"Do you remember the sand bank? Let's think happy thoughts."

I smiled as I recalled our time in the Maldives. I listened as Stefan ran through our shared memories. His voice was hypnotic, soothing. I could visualise myself falling to sleep while listening to him.

After a half hour or so I could hear the voices of his friends rise in the background.

"I should let you get back to your friends. It was wonderful to talk to you," I said.

"And you. I have your number now; I'll call again. Please let me know what happens with your dad."

"I will. Good night, Stefan, and thank you."

"You sleep well. Naughty dreams." He chuckled as he

disconnected the call.

I sat for ages, long after the sun had set, feeling conflicted. I was thrilled to have spoken to Stefan, my smile had been broad, but I shouldn't be happy, I should be worried about my dad. Was I being selfish? It certainly felt like it, and another layer of guilt was added.

I decided not to tell the kids about their grandad. I wanted to see what the news would be first, but I did call Carla. She came over straight away.

"Tell me again what happened?" she said as she came through the front door.

I repeated what I'd already told her on the telephone as we sat, and she opened a bottle of wine.

"Did they say they'd call with an appointment?" she asked.

"I think so. To be honest, I kind of tuned out. I was too stunned. The fact they are rushing this through is not good, is it?"

"It's good and not good. If there is something wrong, at least they can act fast. Have you told anyone else?"

"No, I want to wait before I tell the kids. I don't even know what country Casey is in at the moment, and I don't want to worry Kerry."

"Have you heard from Michael?"

"Not a word. I have mail for him. I'm not sure what to do with it."

"Send it to his mother?"

"I could do that, I guess. I haven't heard from her either."

"Well, that's a blessing." Carla laughed.

"I was thinking... I know you said about a weekend away but if this is bad news, I want to take Mum and Dad down to Cornwall for a weekend break. You know how much they loved that place."

"That would be amazing. I'll come, if you want me to, of course."

"Of course I do. It will be like old times."

We reminisced for a while; recalling our Cornish holidays and laughed at the fact we had hated the thought of going with our parents when we'd hit our teens.

"What do they know about you and Michael?"

"They think he's just working away. I don't want to worry them with it all. I will tell them, though."

We chatted back and forth as we emptied the bottle and retrieved another. I'd enjoyed our evening together.

"You can't drive home. Why don't you stay here," I said.

"I was hoping you'd say that."

After a cup of tea, to hopefully stave off a headache in the morning, we headed upstairs. Carla took one of the spare bedrooms, and I headed to mine. I slept well that night. I didn't wake once.

"Good morning," I said as I walked into the kitchen from the garden. I'd been for an early walk with Dini.

"I have bacon on," Carla replied with a smile.

"I could smell it from outside."

"Guess what? I have a date tonight."

"You do? How, when, with whom, and why did you not tell me this last night?"

"I only just found out. He sent me a text this morning."

"Who? Who sent you a text?"

"His name is David, and can you believe, he owns the gym."

"How did you meet him?"

"I was chatting to him recently. He works out at the same time as us. You must have seen him. Tall, dark hair, muscles on muscles?"

I shook my head. When I worked out I mostly kept my face down and my eyes on my feet to make sure they stayed on the running machine.

"Anyway, I've chatted to him on and off, for a while. He asked me for my number and this morning, he texted. He wants to take me to dinner."

"Oh, sounds fun. Where will you go?"

"No idea."

As we spoke, I buttered some bread and laid the bacon over the slices for a sandwich. Carla made the tea and we sat. Dini drooled by my side.

"What will you wear?" I asked.

"I have no idea, and talking of clothes, please don't think this is charity, but I have a few items that I was going to throw. Do you want them? We must be nearly the same size now."

"Of course I want them." I was desperate for new clothes and had exhausted the local charity shop.

"Good, I'll drop them over in the week. Now, I must go. I have a hair appointment, nails, waxing...oh, the works planned."

I laughed as I walked her to the door. I was pleased for her.

She wasn't someone who needed a man, but I knew she missed dinner dates. Pizza Hut with me just wasn't the same.

I cleared the dishes, made the beds then called my parents. I spoke for a while to Dad, who insisted on ignoring all references to our hospital visit before he handed me over to Mum. She huffed a little as she talked and I guessed she was walking to somewhere more private.

"I didn't sleep one bit, Jayne. I'm so worried."

"I know. It's easy for me to say not to worry but we have to keep positive. We'll know more when we see the consultant. If you don't hear from the doctors on Monday, give them a call, or I can, if you want."

"I don't know what I'd do without your father," she said, her voice caught in her throat.

"You can't think that way, not yet. Let's see what happens."

My parents had been married for fifty years; they were childhood sweethearts and had hardly spent a day apart. From what I remembered being told, Mum had miscarried many times, and once she had resigned herself that she would never be a mother, she fell pregnant with me. I had a wonderful childhood, despite them being a little older than my friend's parents.

"I was thinking, how would you like a weekend away, in Cornwall?" I asked.

"That sounds wonderful but I guess we need to see what the doctors say first."

"We will, but I'll start to have a look around."

"Your dad loved Cornwall," she whispered.

I was determined, whatever the news, we were going to take a short break to his favourite place, to a place of such wonderful memories and happy times. Nearly every photograph of me as a child was taken on a beach or around a BBQ in Cornwall. It had a special place in my heart, yet I'd never taken my own children there.

Michael had always insisted on the Caribbean, the same resort where he could lounge by the pool, or on the beach, for two weeks doing nothing. I'd come home more exhausted than when we'd left after spending the time entertaining the children. Not that I minded but it would have been nice for him to have spent some quality time with them; they barely saw him when they were growing up.

I decided to email his personal account. I wasn't sure he would receive it, but I'd let him know he had mail and that I would forward it to his mother. Although they lived a five-minute drive away, I'd mail it. I had no intention of visiting.

*To: Michael*
*From: Jayne*
*Date: 12 June 2014*
*Subject: Mail*
*I have some post here for you. I thought I'd let you know that I'll mail it to your mother. I guess she'll have an address and she can forward it on.*
*Jayne*

While I had my email account open, I sent one to Stefan, knowing he wouldn't receive it until the Monday.

*To: Stefan*

*From: Jayne*

*Date: 12 June 2014*

*Subject: Thank you*

*I just wanted to thank you for the call. It was lovely to talk to you and to hear your voice. Take care if you're out on that bike.*

*J xx*

I closed my email account and Googled cottages for rent in Bude. I wanted to take Mum and Dad back to the beaches we'd spent most of my childhood on. I read through agencies, looking for something but not quite knowing what. I scrolled page after page until I found it. A small letting agency had a cottage right on a beach. I couldn't place it from my time there, but being as young as I was, I guessed I wouldn't have noticed it. It wasn't on one of the two main beaches but a couple of coves up. I read through the details; it sounded perfect and best of all, dogs were allowed. I bookmarked the page, not trusting myself to book it until we knew what was happening with Dad. I did, however, print off the details so I could show them.

I received a call from my mum; an appointment had been made for Dad to have some further tests, a scan of some sort. The doctor had called her that morning. I'd offered to visit but Dad wanted to go to his boules club, he wanted normality and no fussing. That was an impossible request for Mum and me.

I spent a week ferrying Mum and Dad from appointment to

appointment, scans and blood tests were done until eventually we were given a date to meet with a consultant. During that week, I hadn't spoken to or emailed Stefan; each day seemed to have flown past in a blur.

Dad, straight-backed and with his usual mistrust of anyone in the medical profession, sat opposite the consultant; Mum and I were to his side. I could see the consultant's mouth moving, I watched Dad lean forward and listen intently. I saw tears roll down my mum's cheeks, but all I could focus on was one word—cancer. My dad had cancer. It was such an ugly, dirty fucking word for an ugly, dirty fucking disease: Stage 3B lung cancer. I had no real idea what the 'B' was for but it wasn't good.

"I'll need to think about that," Dad said.

"Think about what?" I asked. I hadn't heard half of the conversation.

"I was explaining that we can offer chemotherapy. It's palliative care—" I cut the consultant off mid-sentence.

"What's there to think about? Of course you'll have it," I said, turning in my seat towards my dad.

"I'll think about it, Jayne. We need some time," Dad replied.

"I'll make an appointment for a week's time. My secrctary will call you. Take some time to think things over," the consultant said.

Mum hadn't spoken the whole time. She had just sat twisting that damned tissue in her hands. Dad stood; I sat open-mouthed. I wasn't ready to leave; I had a million questions. I needed the consultant to repeat the whole conversation because I hadn't heard, and it hadn't stuck in my brain. I was the last to leave my chair.

"Oh, I think we need to pay for car parking. I'm sure I saw a machine somewhere," Dad said.

"Huh? Car parking?"

"Yes, Jayne, car parking. You don't think the hospital let us park for free, do you?"

I shook my head. Why were we having a conversation about car parking? We should be talking about chemo and finding a cure. I opened my mouth to respond.

"Let's just get home," Mum said.

We drove home in silence, a surreal silence. In fact, I remembered leaving the hospital and the next thing I realised, we were pulling alongside the kerb outside the bungalow Mum and Dad lived in. I watched as a neighbour waved while mowing his lawn and Dad waved back.

"I think we all need a cup of tea," Dad said as he opened the front door.

Mum and I walked to the living room and slumped on the sofa. I took her hand in mine. She had silently cried the whole journey home.

"It will be fine. If Dad has the chemo, he could have years and they might be able to do something in the meantime," I said.

"Did you not hear what he said?"

"He offered chemo."

Mum just looked at me. "It's in the lymph thingy's."

"Maybe they can cut those out, maybe they can remove the lung. People live on one lung," I said.

"I'll not be having chemo," Dad said as he walked into the room. He was carrying a tray with three mugs of tea.

"What? Of course you will. Why would you not?" I asked.

"Because it's not going to cure me. I don't want to spend the next few months sick as a pig either."

"Dad, the chemo might work."

Dad sat on the edge of the sofa and wrapped his arm around my shoulders.

"Did you listen to the doctor? There's no cure, baby girl. I'm going to die."

"No," I whispered. My mother echoed my words.

"When?" I had sat in the consultant's room, yet my father's words felt like new news.

"Three, four months maybe."

"But you just have a cough, you're not sick. You don't look sick."

"I have advanced cancer, not just in the lungs, and no, I don't look sick. I don't feel sick, and that's the way I want it to stay."

"I don't understand..."

"Drink your tea. You too, Grace."

He moved to sit in his usual armchair and we drank tea. Fucking tea!

After an hour of silence, other than the conversations, words, snippets of what I had understood whirling around my brain, Mum let out a sob. She had been holding it in from the moment we'd left the hospital. I pulled her to my side as she wailed, cried out loud, and cursed.

Dad leapt from his chair and knelt in front of her. He took her hands in his.

"Gracie, come on now. We always knew I'd go first."

Watching my mother sob, watching my father on his knees comforting her, broke me. My stomach hurt, my chest constricted, and my heart shattered.

I don't know how long we'd sat crying together. I know the

cuffs of my shirt were sodden with my tears and black with mascara. I'd used them to continually wipe my eyes.

"I think your mum needs to have a lay down, it's been a shock for her."

Although he was the one with cancer, he thought only of his family. He led my mum to their bedroom. I could hear him talking to her, helping her out of her clothes and into bed before he returned to the living room.

"I need you to be strong for her, Jayne. There's a lot to do."

I nodded my head. "I need to tell the kids."

"I want what time I have left to be normal. Please, make that happen for me?"

I closed my eyes as I heard my dad choke on his words.

"Whatever you want, Dad, I'll do."

"You need to get home. That dog will be tearing your house up. Can you drive? Shall I call a taxi?"

"I can drive. I'll be fine." I stood. "I'll be back in the morning, okay?"

The drive home was pure torture. Every fucking tune on the radio was a heartache, heartbreak song. I screamed at the radio and bashed it with my fist to silence the noise. I didn't know how I made it home, but I did.

The house was in darkness when I arrived. I'd forgotten to leave the hallway light on, and for the first time, I realised I was lonely. Regardless of my relationship with Michael, at least I wasn't alone in the house. I left the hallway light off and made my way to the kitchen. Dini was scratching at the back door, desperate to get out. I sat at the table after letting him out to patrol and wept. I prayed; I hadn't prayed since I was a child. I wasn't particularly religious but I begged God to save my dad.

My phone lit up the kitchen and I picked it up. I'd forgotten to turn the ringtone back on. Through my tears, I smiled at the name on my caller display.

"Hey, how did today go?" Stefan asked.

I choked, not able to release the words.

"Baby, take a breath. It's bad, huh?"

"Yes," I said, my voice was croaky.

"Oh, shit. I wish I were there with you. I can get a flight."

"Thank you, but it's okay, don't worry. I'm going to have a lot to do over the next few weeks, I think."

Despite the situation, my heart missed a beat at his words.

"Is anyone with you?"

"Just me and the dog. I need to call the kids and tell them. I don't even know where Casey is. That's so bad, isn't it?"

"Not at all. You call Ben, I'm sure he'll know."

As children, Casey and Ben had been best friends. As adults, they probably saw each other no more than a couple of times a year and that saddened me. No matter that I loved her, my daughter was spoilt by her grandfather, indulged by her father, and not always a pleasant person to be around.

"I'll call him now. Dad doesn't want any treatment; he'll have about three months without it. Why? Why would he not want treatment?" I had started to cry again.

"Hey, please, don't cry. I'm too far away to hear you cry. I guess if I were in your dad's situation, I'd refuse too. Maybe he wants to live the next three months and not be tied to hospital appointments and the sickness that he might go through. Chemo is a shitty thing."

He sounded as if he was speaking from experience. Somewhere in the back of my mind I recalled an old email; he had told me both his parents had died some years ago.

"Maybe he's also scared," he added.

I nodded before remembering he wasn't sitting in front of me. "You might be right. I just feel so helpless."

"Be there for him, every day. Just be there."

"I need to call the kids. Thank you for calling. I can't tell you how much that means right now."

"You're welcome. I was thinking of you all day. You take care. Ring me later?"

We said our goodbyes and I laid the phone back on the table. Dini was whining, wanting to be let back in. I rose and opened the back door, noticing that he hadn't jumped up at me; maybe he sensed my sadness.

I called Ben. Before I'd had the chance to explain how bad his grandad was, he told me he was on his way over. While I waited, I rang Casey. As usual, it went to voicemail. I didn't want to leave that news as a message so simply asked her to return my call.

Ben and Kerry arrived. They sat either side of me and after I told them all the details I had, I sobbed on his shoulder. Kerry made tea, and it made me chuckle. Tea was the cure-all in our family.

"I should be comforting you," I said, blowing my nose of a piece of kitchen paper.

"He's your dad. It's okay to have a breakdown," Ben replied.

My son, my firstborn, and the one who seemed to have inherited all my genes, sat and hugged me. He'd grown into a wonderful man, compassionate, kind, and loving.

We sat for an hour talking, reminiscing on times he'd spent with his granddad. The shock of what I'd learnt that day had started to wear off. I needed to be strong for my mum. I needed to do as my dad asked and make the last of his time with us the best I possibly could.

A week had passed before I finally got the news to Casey. She was in Japan visiting Michael, and it annoyed me that neither had the decency to let me know. She wanted to fly home immediately but my dad told her not to, and I suspect that was exactly what she wanted to hear. She made a promise to come straight home when her holiday was over.

As much as Dad enjoyed the constant stream of visitors, I could see it was already taking its toll on him. By the second week, things had settled down somewhat. The façade I put on was wearing me down though. My saving grace was Stefan—always Stefan.

*To: Jayne*
*From: Stefan*
*Date: 8 July 2014*
*Subject: Checking in*
*Hi, J. How are you? How are your mum & dad? I know I always start with the same question! Talk if you want to. I'm taking a week's holiday with Morton. We have a plan to visit Egypt and do some diving. I made sure the hotel had Wi-Fi so I'm here if you need me.*

*Alec finishes uni soon. I think he will come and work with me. His mother is not pleased!*

*Hugs, S xx*


*To: Stefan*

*From: Jayne*

*Date: 8 July 2014*

*Subject: Holiday sounds good*

*I'm okay, keeping busy. Dad wants all his affairs in order so we've been to a solicitor to organise everything. He wants to make his own funeral arrangements. I can't bring myself to be involved in that and I feel so bad about it. Alec finishes uni? Wow, doesn't time fly. :) I bet you'll love working with him. It must be wonderful to have your child in the business you set up. I want to see if Dad will come to Cornwall with me. It's the place we always went to for our holidays when I was a child. I'll attach the details.*

*Hugs back to you, J xx*


I purposely avoided any comment with regard to his ex-wife.


*To: Jayne*

*From: Stefan*

*Date: 11 July 2014*

*Subject: Cornwall*

*Cornwall looks amazing. I'd love to visit that cottage; it looks wonderful—maybe one day. I was in the UK a couple of years ago, in London for meetings, but didn't get to see any more of the UK other than the inside of an office. I hope your dad agrees to your holiday but don't be too hard on him if he doesn't.*

   *S xx*


I wished that I had known Stefan when he'd visited London. In truth, I didn't believe we would ever meet again. We talked on the phone, we emailed, but I had resigned myself that that was all it was ever going to be. Over the months we had been friends, so much had happened and he had been the one I turned to. It used to be Carla, and although she was and would always be my best friend, Stefan gave me something she couldn't. He made me feel beautiful and special when he called me 'baby.' I fantasised about him all the time. Some nights the frustration and desire for him hurt. But I wouldn't jeopardise our friendship by confessing the one thing I'd continually pushed to the back of my mind—I was in love with him.

Stefan had given me back my confidence; he made me want to walk tall. He gave me reason to smile when I was at my lowest. I had a lot to thank him for. But sometimes, late at night when sleep eluded me, I wished for more.

I longed to feel his arms around me, his lips on mine. I longed to feel his breath on my skin and to see those dark blue eyes stare so intently it felt like he saw straight to my soul.

I was in love with someone I could never have, and that hurt.

# Chapter Eight

The summer wore on, and we never did get to Cornwall. Dad went downhill quickly. He couldn't leave his bed; the effort of even sitting up caused him too much pain. The cancer had spread rapidly to his spine, and no matter how hard he tried to not show us how excruciating it was, the beads of sweat on his brow and upper lip gave him away. Mum and I sat, day after day, rubbing his back and massaging his wasted muscles to help ease the constant aches. A nurse came daily to administer pain relief and eventually a pump was fitted so he could do that himself.

I was tired, so desperately tired. I was back to not sleeping and it was only because I was constantly on alert, waiting for that phone call. I'd wake in the middle of the night and check my phone, just in case I'd missed a call. I'd placed the phone on the pillow next to me so it would be close. And then one night, that call came.

"I think you should come over," my mum said. I looked at the clock on the bedside table and saw it was two in the morning.

"I'm on my way," I replied.

I had wanted to stay overnight but Mum had insisted I go home each evening and sleep in my own bed. So for the past couple of weeks, I'd had a small bag packed with some clothes and toiletries, prepared for that call. Once I'd thrown on a pair of jeans and a shirt, I grabbed the bag and ran down the stairs. I checked Dini had a bowl of dry food and water, grabbed my keys and handbag, and headed for the car.

As I drove, I prayed. Not for the salvation of my father but that the end would come quick and painless. My prayers were never answered.

I'd seen death scenes in movies, on TV programmes, but the reality was so far removed. Mum and I sat either side of Dad, the nurse kept her distance in another room. His breathing was raspy; he was struggling to get enough air into his lungs. Although his eyes were closed, he would squeeze my hand every now and again to let me know he was conscious. There were times when his face screwed up as a wave of pain washed over him, and there was fuck all I could do. I would have taken that pain for him if I could have.

As the hours wore on, his breathing became worse, until his body tensed as he fought for breath. His eyes flew open, wide with panic. His mouth opened and closed and Mum screamed for the nurse. He shook his head from side to side, and his hand closed so tight around mine I knew it would bruise. His legs kicked against the mattress. He was basically drowning. We'd been warned but when the end came, it was the biggest shock of all. And then he was gone. His eyes still wide, his mouth still open but there was no noise. There was no gasping for air and no tension in his body as it gently relaxed back into the bed.

Watching my dad die, witnessing the process of death, would live with me forever. As would the smell. There were no words to really describe the smell of death, but it permeated the air, my clothes, and my hair. It was acrid with hints of acetone.

I held his hand, rested my head on his knuckles, and cried

harder than I'd ever cried before.

I guessed there was selfishness among the bereaved. For what seemed an age, Mum and I sat either side of the bed, refusing to let him go; absorbed in our own grief without acknowledging each other's.

The nurse spoke quietly to my mother. I watched as she looked at me and, through her tears, gently spoke.

"We need to let him go now," she whispered.

People had arrived at the bedroom door. A doctor wanted to pronounce him dead and that angered me. I knew he was dead; I didn't need that confirmed to us.

"I have to call the kids," I told Mum. She nodded.

"Ben, I'm sorry to wake you. Grandad passed away," I said.

"Are you there? I'll come over now."

"No, don't worry right now. If you could sort out Dini for me… Then if you want to visit Nan later, I'm sure she'd love that."

"I'll take him home with me. Do you want me to call Casey?"

"If you can. I didn't bring a charger with me, I don't have much battery."

"I'll grab that for you as well. I'll ring when I'm on my way, in case you need anything."

"Thank you. I'll see you later."

I sent a text to Carla and then Mum and I sat on the sofa, not quite sure what to do.

Dad was taken away later that day. It was heartbreaking to watch. The undertakers exuded respect, were quiet and sombre.

But to see him being wheeled to the back of a van, and driven away, made his death feel much more real. Neighbours came to the house to offer their condolences, some brought food, others made endless cups of tea.

"Why don't you lie down, get some rest," I said. I'd watched Mum yawn.

"I don't want to close my eyes. I don't want to see him," she whispered.

I understood what she meant. Those last moments with Dad were not the memories either of us wanted as our lasting ones. I stood and walked to the old-fashioned oak wood dresser that had stood proudly in every house I'd known my parents to live in. In the cupboard were stacks of photo albums. I grabbed a couple.

Mum and I sat and looked through them, we even managed a chuckle as we relived the past. It did us both good to remember Dad in happier times. It wasn't long after we flicked through the last album that I noticed Mum's eyelids start to droop. She curled up on the sofa and dozed.

Ben arrived with a phone charger and a takeaway from a burger chain. I wasn't hungry but sat at the small kitchen table and ate with him. We spoke in hushed tones so as not to wake Mum.

"What happens next?" Ben asked.

"Dad made us visit the undertakers ages ago, he planned his own funeral. I guess we have to get that process started. He made a will; a local solicitor has that. I'll contact them tomorrow."

"You need to get the death certificate and contact his bank, pension people, and the council. I can do that for you," he said.

"Is it so bad that I want a cigarette?" I said.

"Well, I'd hoped you might want to quit, but perhaps today's not the day for that."

He smiled and squeezed my hand as I made my way through the patio door to the small back garden. It was just a square of grass and a few slabs laid as a patio. Neither Mum nor Dad was big on gardening. I sat on a plastic white chair that cracked with age and lit my cigarette.

My phone beeped to let me know I had a text.

*Mum, I'm on a train but I don't think I can come to Nana's. I'll go home and wait there. :(*

I replied. *That's okay. You do what you have to. I don't know when I'll be home, but I'll call you later.*

I knew she had texted rather than called for one reason only. Casey found it a struggle to deal with emotion, more so in public. She had a tough exterior, and she would need that for the world she wanted to work in, but inside she was as soft as butter. All I hoped was that hardness she had started to develop didn't, like her father's, penetrate too far.

"Aunty Margie is on her way," Mum said. She had startled me when she'd stepped through the patio doors.

"That's lovely. I haven't seen her in years. How is she making the journey?"

Aunty Margie was my mum's sister and lived in Scotland. I couldn't remember the last time I'd seen her. I know she had visited when my children were small and, of course, Mum kept in regular contact.

"She's booked a flight and then a taxi from the airport."

"I could have picked her up, Nan," Ben said.

She patted his arm.

"You don't want to be stuck in a car with that dotty old bat for an hour, darling. Thank you though."

Aunty Margie had been, and I guessed still was, a live wire. Older than my mum, she'd been a hippy, a rocker, and everything in between. She'd travelled and never married. She lived in one wing of a stately home, as she called it. I suspected it was an old people's home, but judging by the photographs I'd seen, a very plush and exclusive one.

Carla rang a couple of times. She wanted to visit but I think the amount of visitors had worn Mum out.

Margie arrived and Mum sent me home for a rest. I wanted to stay, I could have slept on the couch, but she was insistent. Like Dad, she thought of everyone else before herself.

Kerry dropped Dini back and sat for a cup of tea. She had started to develop a little bump, only noticeable because she was so slim.

"Have you told work yet?" I said, as I placed my hand on her tummy.

"Yes, I'll be taking maternity leave, but I'm not sure what I'll do after the baby comes. Ben doesn't want me to work but we need the money."

Kerry worked at the local beauty parlour. She was a therapist and I'd been on the receiving end of her massages many times.

"Maybe start up yourself, I'll babysit," I said.

"We'll see, and you know you can be as involved in the baby as you want," she said with a smile.

Some mothers lost their sons when they found a partner—I

hadn't. I'd gained a wonderful daughter-in-law. Despite the fact they weren't married, there was no doubt in my mind they would be at some point.

"Has Ben heard from Michael?"

A flash of anger crossed her face. "Not a word. He's hurt by that but he won't admit it."

I shook my head. Michael was a prick, the worst kind to think only of one of his children. Ben wasn't oblivious to it, but he chose to ignore it. It was a testament to the kind of father he was going to be.

Once Kerry had left, I opened my laptop.

*To: Stefan*

*From: Jayne*

*Date: 10 August 2014*

*Subject: Sad news*

*Dad died yesterday. Mum and I were with him, right to the end. It was awful, Stefan. I feel totally lost right now. Mum's sister flew down from Scotland so she's sent me home for a rest. I'll go back in the morning. I didn't want to call you. I'd cry if I heard your voice. Right now, I need some sleep. I've been awake for twenty-four hours, I think. Casey is on her way home, so I think I'll get a nap before she arrives.*

*Speak soon, hugs.*

*J xx*

I closed the laptop, not expecting a reply. It was early evening, and what with the time difference, I didn't expect him to pick up the message until the morning. I could have called. Over the previous week or so, he'd insisted. Whenever I wanted to talk, I could call him, but at that moment I'd cry if I did. I was tired, emotional, drained, and hollow. I curled up on the sofa, dragged a throw over me and closed my eyes.

Dini's growling woke me. The room was dark and I took a moment to let my eyes adjust. I heard a knock on the front door.

I peered through the window before I answered and saw Casey standing on the doorstep.

"Where's your key?" I asked as I pulled the door open.

"I left it at Dad's, I think."

She dropped her bag and shrugged off her coat, leaving them on the hallway floor before falling into my arms, sobbing.

I led her to the kitchen and helped her to a chair. I put the kettle on and made two cups of tea. As I sat next to her, I chuckled.

"Grandad's answer to everything—hot sweet tea," I said as I raised my mug.

"How's Nana? Or is that such a dumb question?"

"Aunty Margie is with her at the moment. I imagine she's tearing her hair out by now. If you'd have called, I could have collected you from the station."

"It's okay, Dad drove me."

"Your dad?"

"Erm, yes. He's staying at Grandma's. He's back for a month."

"Oh." I bit my tongue so as not to speak out loud the words I had in my head.

"He sends his condolences. I met him for dinner earlier, it's why I'm a little late."

I blinked a few times and clenched my teeth together, forcing a smile.

"I guess he's not coming home, is he?"

"No. It's for the best, Casey."

"Couldn't you have tried?"

My body tensed in shock at her words. *Tried?*

"I *tried* for years. It wasn't my decision to leave. It was your father's."

We sat in silence for a little while. I was angry. At her and at whatever Michael had said for her to come to that conclusion. He was no more than five miles away, yet he hadn't bothered to offer his *condolences* in person. He'd taken her for a meal, but ignored his son. I rubbed my temples, feeling a headache approaching.

"I think we need to get some sleep. I have a busy day tomorrow," I said.

Casey nodded, oblivious to how hurt I had been by her words. Once she had made her way up to bed, I let Dini out in the garden before locking up and heading up myself.

The next few days flew by in a blur. We met with the undertakers, the bank, sent letters, and contacted as many of Dad's old friends as possible. Ben was a godsend; he drove Mum around, and he made calls. Casey visited once. She spent her days with Michael at his parents', only returning to sleep. It was on the tip of my tongue to enquire why she even returned home in the evenings, why she didn't stay overnight.

Stefan emailed, he texted, and on the night before the funeral, he called. I sat in the garden with a glass of wine and a cigarette to chat with him.

"Hey, how are you?" he said once I'd answered his call.

"Coping. Better than I thought, to be honest. There's so much to do."

"How's your mum?"

"She has good moments, and then I'll catch her sitting on Dad's side of the bed in tears. Her sister is here and she's been wonderful. Not how I remember her at all. She asked Mum if she wants to go back with her for a week."

"Will she?"

"I think so. I think it might be good for her to get away for a bit. It's so claustrophobic at the bungalow. People are being helpful but there's never a moment of peace. I wanted Mum to come here but she won't."

"She needs to stay connected to him, I imagine."

"Maybe," I sighed.

"I hate that you're so sad," he said quietly.

"I miss him. I want my dad back." My voice broke on every word.

"I know, baby. I know."

"I'm going to book that cottage in Cornwall for later in the year. I don't know if Mum will come; it might be too painful. But I think it will help me to feel closer to him. I close my eyes and all I see is him, lying on that bed, moments before he died. I don't want those thoughts anymore."

"I think that's a great idea. Go back to the place that gave you the best memories."

"I need to go, I need to get some sleep. I think tomorrow is going to be the worst day of my life."

"I'll be thinking of you, every moment of the day," he said.

We said goodbye and I hung up. As much as I loved to hear his voice, our calls always left me downhearted. More so knowing how awful the following day was going to be. Stefan was always friendly, caring, but there was never a hint that he felt anything more for me. I'd built him up in my mind to be something that he wasn't. He'd been a crutch without knowing it. He'd got me through tough times without knowing it. I'd relied on him for my happiness, living a fantasy life, and he had no clue.

The house was a hub of noise and people the following morning. Carla, Casey, Ben, and Kerry had decided to use my house to prepare for the funeral. I appreciated them being with me. I didn't want to wake and have to dress for my father's funeral on my own. I needed their company.

"Mum, there's mail for you," Casey said. The postman had just deposited the mail.

She handed me a stack of letters. I flicked through, handing back the ones for Michael; she could give those to him.

At the bottom of the pile was a small padded envelope. My hands shook as I saw the handwriting and the postmark. I dropped the remaining envelopes on the kitchen table and walked out into the garden. I noticed Carla looking at me as I did.

I opened the envelope and sobbed as I drew out its contents. I held in my hand a small silver angel. He'd remembered. Stefan had remembered a conversation where I'd asked him to find the artist who made the angels, and he'd sent one to me on the one day I needed it.

There was no note, just the most delicate, intricately carved, beautiful angel. I held her in my palm and cried.

"What's that?" I heard.

Carla sat beside me. I opened my palm to show her.

"It's beautiful, who sent it?"

I looked up at her. It was a while before I could speak.

"The kindest man I know. A man I'm in love with, but he doesn't know."

She stared at me, not understanding. Ben, calling that it was time to go, interrupted us. I stood, Carla stood, and silently we walked back into the house. I left the envelope on the side but placed the angel in my bag. I wanted to take her with me.

Mum's house was a hive of activity. Carla's parents had driven up from their retirement home in France, and Margie was busy making tea and organising people. Mum had wanted for us to make sandwiches, to have the wake at home, but after much persuasion from Margie and me, their local pub had been booked. Dad enjoyed a pint or two in that pub on a regular basis, so it seemed fitting.

Carla hadn't said a word on the journey and once at the house, it was too busy. I heard tinkles of laughter from some of my parents' oldest friends as they reminisced. Despite the pain I felt, it pleased me. I didn't want the day to be sombre; I wanted a celebration of my dad's life.

The mood swiftly changed though when a hearse and a black limousine pulled up outside. The house quietened as people made their way outside. The undertakers took the flowers that had been delivered to lay out in the hearse. Dad hated flowers; he would have winced at the expense that adorned his oak coffin.

As we drove away from the house, I thought I saw a familiar car pull into the cavalcade that followed.

The crematorium was packed; some of Dad's old docker colleagues had turned up to see him off. As I scanned the crowd, I saw faces I hadn't seen since childhood. It was a shame that those guys only got together for a funeral. Ben stood and gave a reading. His words about his life with his grandad brought fresh tears to my eyes. I'd tried so hard not to cry, to keep my sorrow in so I could be strong for my mother and my children. But to hear my son's voice break, and to see tears stream down his cheeks, dissolved me.

All too soon the first cords of my parents' favourite song echoed around the hall. I heard Mum sob as Jim Reeves sang *I Won't Forget You.* As we filed past his coffin, I laid the white rose I'd been carrying, kissed my fingertips, and passed that kiss onto my dad. I then took my mum's arm and we made our way outside in the sunshine.

Through my tears, hidden behind dark glasses, I saw Michael. He stood slightly to one side with the tart on his arm, and Casey walked to stand beside her. I turned away and held my crying son. In that moment, I knew I hated him. I was also deeply hurt by what I saw as betrayal from my daughter.

"He has brought that slut to your dad's funeral?" I heard.

"Nan!" Ben said.

Turning, I saw my mum, eyes wide with anger. I opened my mouth to speak.

"Oh, darling. I knew things were bad, but I never believed he could stoop so low."

"How did you know?" I'd never recalled speaking about her to my parents.

"Your dad saw them one time. We never mentioned it because you never did, but we knew that you knew."

"How long has that been going on?" Ben asked. I felt his body tense as I held him.

"Years. But today isn't the day to deal with it," I said.

We walked to the waiting cars. As I passed him, he made to speak. I held my head up high and ignored him. My mother however, couldn't. She stopped and turned to him. I stood by her side.

"How dare you bring that woman, that slut, to my husband's funeral, to your wife's father's funeral. You are not welcome, Michael. Casey, get in the car and join your family, now!"

I tried hard to suppress the smile that twitched at the side of my mouth.

"Way to go, Gracie," Carla said as she caught up with us.

"We have a slut on the premises? Where? I haven't seen one of those for years," Margie said, as she pulled her glasses down from her eyes and peered at the woman clinging to Michael's arm.

At that point, we laughed. Four *ladies*, at what should have been the most inappropriate time and place, laughed. My dad would have loved that. The tart had the grace to keep her mouth shut and Michael looked embarrassed.

*Hell, yeah! That's gutter talk at it's best,* I thought.

The pub was full to the brim with mourners and locals, who wanted to pay their respects. The landlord had done us proud. He'd laid a table full of good old-fashioned East End food. There were bowls of jellied eels, cockles, prawns, and whelks. My stomach recoiled at the eels and whelks, but I remembered with fondness sitting outside a pub on a Sunday afternoon with a bag of Salt 'n' Shake crisps, a bottle of Coke, and a tub of cockles.

My hand was sore with the amount of times it was shaken, my shoulders bruised from all the hugs, and my cheek tacky from the kisses. So many people had come to pay their respects, and I was pleased for my mum. I'd lost Carla and her parents among the throng of people; they had all come from the same circle of friends. I had a glass of warm, cheap white wine shoved in my hand from a man probably not older than myself. He told me a story of being my dad's apprentice way back. When the docks had closed, engineering had been the next step on dad's career path. In fact, engineering was where he'd stayed until retirement.

I moved around the room accepting hugs and listening to stories, many of which I knew by heart. The times when dad and his friends had stolen lead from the church roof and got caught, they'd run but were more scared of getting caught by the local priest than the police. The time when, unloading a boat of bananas, they'd found tarantulas and boxed one up to leave in the boss's cabin. The time when they 'found' a refrigerated lorry of meat that had then been distributed to all the occupants of our street, the elderly and the ones with children first. My dad had a past, a colourful one, and I loved to listen to those stories.

I felt a hand rub my back. "How are you coping?" Carla asked.

I sighed. "I think today will hit tomorrow. I'm exhausted, to be honest. I think Mum is too. It might be time to take her home."

"I have the car ready and waiting. I'm coming back to yours."

"I'd like that."

"Let's say our goodbyes, shall we?"

It took a half hour before we finally managed to leave the pub. Mum slumped into the back of the car with Margie, who had taken two bottles of wine from the bar.

"How are the kids getting home?" Mum asked.

"Ben will drop Casey off to Michael's parents'. One of his friends dropped his car over."

I heard a huff from the rear seat. "Shame she couldn't spend the evening with you," Margie said.

I bristled until I caught a glance from Carla. Margie was right, of course, but I didn't like anyone criticising my children. We dropped Mum and Margie off home before heading back to the house.

"I need to get out of these clothes," I said, as I immediately climbed the stairs.

"Same. We'll take Dini for a walk, get some fresh air," Carla said as she followed me.

I sat on my bed for a while, thinking. I took the angel from my bag and hung her on the bedpost, letting my fingers trail over the filigree and the silk ribbon that allowed her to hang next to my pillow.

"It's so beautiful," I heard. Carla was standing at my door.

"It is."

"Want to tell me about it?" She sat on my bed.

"I'm sorry. I've kept him a secret from you. I know why. I guessed, in the beginning, I was doing something wrong, and I thought that might upset you."

"What were you doing?"

"I was having an affair, I think. A virtual affair."

144

She looked at me, her brow furrowed. "A virtual affair?"

"Emails mainly, although now we talk on the phone. He doesn't know how I feel about him; I don't think I'd ever tell him. I'm not sure he sees me as anything more than just a friend, and that hurts."

"Oh, Jayne." She placed her arm around my shoulder. "Let's take a walk and you can start at the beginning."

I stood and unzipped the dress, letting it fall in a heap on the floor. I didn't care to pick it up. I pulled on some jeans and a light sweater, grabbed my walking boots, and we headed downstairs.

Dini had been locked in the kitchen; the back of the door was scratched where he had shown his displeasure.

"Hey, baby. How about a walk?" I said. He ran to the back door with his tail wagging.

As we walked, I talked. I told Carla everything. How I felt about Stefan, even on our holiday, the letter he'd sent not wanting anymore contact, to the phone call the previous evening. She stayed silent the whole time, listening. After an hour, we had walked our circuit and had arrived back at my garden. I lifted an upturned flowerpot from the top of the garden table and pulled out my cigarettes.

"I think we need wine," she said.

As I smoked, she retrieved a bottle from the fridge and two glasses.

"I don't know what to say. I don't believe you were having an 'affair,' as such. You needed something, someone, and Stefan was your escape. I'm hurt, of course, that you didn't confide in me."

"I'm sorry. I thought you'd disapprove. I know I went totally over the top in the beginning, and it was as if someone else took

145

over me, someone else wrote the flirty emails. But it made me feel good about myself, especially when he responded."

"Please tell me Scarlet didn't make an appearance," she said as she poured the wine and giggled.

"She did. It was fun, for a while."

"Oh, God. She must have terrified the poor guy."

When we had been teenagers, I'd wanted to change my name to Scarlet. For a while it was the only name I responded to. My parents thought it was a phase and humoured me. Carla thought it hilarious. No one really understood what it meant though. I was shy, geeky with a much prettier friend, a more popular friend. Being Scarlet meant I could pretend, I could act and be someone totally different.

"I did notice all the bottles of wine," Carla added quietly.

Somewhere in my twenties, Scarlet had disappeared, only to be replaced by wine. I hadn't realised at first. The confidence, the snarky comments, came from one too many glasses of wine. I didn't have a drinking habit; I just used it as a confidence booster. In later years, whenever I was tipsy, Carla would joke that Scarlet had appeared.

"So what now?" she asked.

"I don't know. I need to thank him for the angel. I guess we just carry on being friends. I'd love for it to be more but that's not possible."

I watched her close her eyes and lean back in the chair, catching the last of the day's rays.

"I'm worried for you. You need to move on with your life, get the divorce. I'd love nothing more than for you to find a really nice man, but a real one, not a virtual one."

We sat and drank, chatted about old times until the sun set.

"You thank Stefan, tell him I said hi, and I'll grill some steaks. We need to eat," Carla said as we made our way indoors.

I opened my laptop and brought up my email account.

*To: Stefan*

*From: Jayne*

*Date: 25 August 2014*

*Subject: Thank you*

*Oh, Stefan, thank you so much for the angel. I can't tell you how much I needed that today. She's hanging on my bed, next to my pillow, and I'll treasure her, always. Carla is here with me. She's cooking dinner and said to say hi. It was a good day, as funerals go, I guess. I'm glad I'm not on my own tonight though. I don't want to sleep. I don't want to shut my eyes because I'm scared I'll see that coffin and the flowers. I don't want to think about him in that casket.*

*Ben gave a speech; it was beautiful. He talked about all the things he loved about his grandad. All the stories my dad had told me as a child, he'd then told my children. He cried, and it broke my heart to see my boy standing there, with tears running down his face.*

*Michael showed up, with his girlfriend, the one he's had for years. Casey stood with them. That hurt. I'm not sure you want to hear all this crap. I'm rambling, I guess. I'm sorry.*

*I just wanted to thank you. You don't know what that meant.*

*J xx*

I pressed send and closed the laptop lid. A tissue was handed to me; I hadn't realised I had been crying.

"Tell him," Carla whispered.

"I can't."

"What have you got to lose?"

"His friendship. If I can't have him, then at least I still have his friendship."

She took the laptop from the table and replaced it with a plate. She'd grilled steaks and made a salad. We raised a glass of wine to each other.

"To your dad, to fucked up lives, and arsehole husbands."

Carla could always, no matter what the situation, bring a smile to my face. We clinked glasses. We ate and drank then fell into bed, tipsy.

I was first up the following morning and, surprisingly, without a headache. I let the dog out, made tea, then called my mum. We spoke for an hour, with Margie continually interrupting, before Carla made her appearance.

"Ouch, Paracetamol?" she said. I pointed to a cupboard.

I made her a tea and we settled at the table. "Was that your mum? How was she?"

I recounted the conversation. Mum was keen to head to Scotland with Margie but worried about leaving me. I'd told her many times I thought it a good idea. A change of scenery would give her a boost. And I know Dad would have approved. I'd even offered to pop over and help her pack.

"I'll run them to the airport. I doubt your car would make it that far," Carla said.

"It does need a service, and its MOT is due soon. I don't think it will pass."

"Get rid of it, buy a new one."

"I don't have the money for a new car. I need to find a job. Michael deposits enough money in the account for the mortgage and the bills with a little over for food."

"While he's living the highlife, earning his millions with the slut."

"I doubt he earns that much," I said.

"Wanna bet? He earns more than Charles, and with bonuses he wasn't far off that figure."

"You're kidding me."

"No. Have you any idea what Michael earns?"

"No. We had a joint account but that was for household expenses. He had a separate account for his salary."

"Clever fucker, if you ask me."

"This house is in his name. Maybe I do need to speak to your solicitor."

"You do. I'll make an appointment."

Carla left an hour or so later. She hadn't wanted to but I wanted some time alone. I wanted to reflect and wallow in my sadness, without having to pretend or chat or smile.

My phone indicated I'd received an email. My heart leapt as I opened the laptop and saw that Stefan had replied.

*To: Jayne*

*From: Stefan*

*Date: 26 August 2014*

*Subject: You're welcome*

*I'm glad she arrived in time. I worried she wouldn't have. It took me months to track down that artist. I'm pleased you love her. Don't be scared to sleep, not now that there is a little piece of Denmark by your pillow and if you ever can't, ring me.*

*Your ex is a douche. I'm glad I wasn't there, I would have punched the fucker, sorry.*

*And Ben sounds just like his mother, kind and considerate. I'd like to meet him one day.*

*S xx*


I read, and, as usual, read again. He was right—there was a little piece of Denmark by my pillow and that thought soothed me.

I smiled at the very American 'douche' comment, but it was the '...meet him one day' that had me flustered. Did he mean that? Or was he just being kind?


*To: Stefan*

*From: Jayne*

*Date: 26 August 2014*

*Subject: Douche??*

*Your comment made me smile, and it's nice to know I have a knight in shining armour ready to defend me. Thank you.*

*And I'd like for you to meet Ben too.*

*I look forward to falling asleep with a little piece of Denmark beside me.*

*J xx*

I spent the day curled up on the sofa reading a book and taking calls. I'd tried to call Casey; I wanted to check on her. But as usual, her phone went to voicemail. Ben had wanted to visit but I wanted some time on my own. Mum had rung to let me know she had arranged transport to the airport with Carla and would be leaving in the morning. I made arrangements to pop over, before they left, to see her off.

# Chapter Nine

Two days later, two days of not hearing from Casey, she finally texted. I was upset that she hadn't taken the time to call, and her message was just to tell me that she was heading to London with Michael, she would catch up with me at some point over the next month. I couldn't reply. Something had changed between us, and I suspected Michael was the cause of that.

I decided to look at the cottage in Cornwall, initially just to cheer myself up a little. Carla needed to visit her parents for a few days. She hadn't wanted to, she wanted to be close to me, but they were getting on and the death of my dad had her worried that she didn't see hers enough.

I brought up the details that I'd saved and looked through the photos. It looked a little rundown but in a wonderful location. It was small, just the two bedrooms, and full of character. Before I'd realised, I found myself on the availability page. The cottage was booked out for most of the year, but there were two weeks available. The first was the following week and the second in November. I called the agent to be told the owners were using the cottage over the summer to do some modernisation. If I was interested in the first week, it would be discounted. Without thinking, I booked it. I sweated as I handed over Michael's credit card details, wondering if he'd cut me off from it.

"That's wonderful, Miss Adams. All booked and paid for. You'll receive an email with instructions and where to find the key," I was told.

I disconnected the call, mildly shocked that I had, for the first time ever, booked a holiday just for myself. Michael would probably throw a fit, but I hoped by the time he realised, I'd have visited and been home.

*To: Stefan*
*From: Jayne*
*Date: 29 August 2014*
*Subject: Cornwall!*
*I just book myself a week in that cottage I told you about. They have two weeks available, one for next week and one in November. I chose next week! I can't believe I've done that; I've never been away by myself before. I'm panicking because I don't know if my car will make it that far but I'm excited as well.*
*J xx*

I rang Ben; he'd know where I could get a cheap car service. He was excited for me, and although it felt strange to laugh so soon after my dad's funeral, I knew he'd be pleased for me. Ben offered to lend me his car, it was much more reliable that mine. He also offered to print off a map.

*To: Jayne*
*From: Stefan*

*Date: 29 August 2014*

*Subject: Worried!*

*Sounds exciting. :) Please do something with the car. I can send some money over for the service. I don't like the thought of you driving a dangerous vehicle.*

*S xx*

*To: Stefan*

*From: Jayne*

*Date: 29 August 2014*

*Subject: Oh no!*

*Thank you, that's really kind of you, but no. I have it sorted. Ben is going to lend me his car. And as for driving something dangerous… you're the one with a motorbike!*

*J xx*

His offer to help overwhelmed me a little; it brought tears to my eyes. There was no way I would accept.

The week dragged on, I'd seen Mum off. She was upset to leave me behind but happy that I'd booked a holiday. We needed to do something after the funeral. There had been lots of promises of help and companionship, none of it had materialised. As soon as the wake had finished, other than a few close friends, Mum hadn't heard from anyone and that included Casey.

The night before my trip, I decided to send Casey an email. There was no point in leaving yet another message, and I'm sure the last time I'd spoken to her, her excuse of a poor signal to cut short our conversation was a lie.

*To: Casey*

*From: Mum*

*Date: 4 September 2014*

*Subject: Please call*

*Hi, Casey, I'm emailing because I can't seem to get you on the phone. Nan has a mobile, Ben has the number, it might be nice if you could take a moment to phone her, ask her how she's doing. You haven't seen nor spoken to her since Grandad's funeral. I know it may be difficult for you but one day, it will be her funeral you're at. Harsh, I know, and I'm sorry. It's not nice having to make excuses as to why you've disappeared without a word. :(*

*I'm off for a break to Cornwall tomorrow. I'll have my phone and I'm taking the laptop. There's Wi-Fi in the cottage, so if want to call me, I'll be happy to hear from you.*

*Please, give Nan a call. Just a short conversation. She'd love to hear from you.*

*I love you.*

*Mum xx*

I had no idea when Casey would receive that email. I knew she was busy but she'd finished her last year at university. She had partied all summer, and I assumed Michael was sorting an internship for her somewhere. I prayed it was not in Japan. Initially the plan was that she'd join his company in London, but since he'd left, and possibly taken clients with him, I doubted she would be welcomed.

I'd given up wondering why my daughter was so distant. She'd grown, and I hated to acknowledge it, into a selfish young lady—that saddened me. I'd spent hours wondering where I'd gone wrong as a mother.

Ben brought the car round early. He spent ages showing me how to turn on the lights, the wipers, and all the things I knew perfectly well how to operate. It was on the tip of my tongue to tell him I'd been driving since before he was born. He helped me load the dog and my bags in the car, gave me the map and a hug, and then I was off.

I took the motorway, stopping at a service station for Dini to stretch his legs and for me to grab a coffee. I'd never driven so far before but I was enjoying the experience. After three hours, I found myself on the Atlantic Highway, the sea to one side and fields to the other. I wound down the window and breathed in the sea air. Dini stuck his head out and joined me. The sun was low in the sky and I pulled over to see the rays bounce off the water. I could make out the silhouettes of surfers catching the last of that day's waves. I felt a sense of joy wash over me.

"Thank you, Dad, for bringing me here," I whispered.

I found the cottage, after a few wrong turns, down a country lane. It was dusk by the time I'd arrived. I pulled up on a gravel drive and sat in wonder, looking at the cottage. It had whitewashed walls and roses growing around the door. It was the cottage of childhood dreams, and I already loved it. I opened the car door, squealing when Dini jumped over the seats, and exited before me. I grabbed my bags from the boot and locked the car.

I had been informed in an email that I'd find the key under a flowerpot beside the front door. I fumbled around until my fingers clasped around it and opened the door.

I stepped into a small hallway, with a staircase to one side and a door to the other. At the end of the hallway was another door left open. I could see straight through the kitchen and to the sea. I left my bag and explored.

The cottage had a lounge with an open fire, where logs were already stacked, waiting to be lit. There were two brown leather sofas set at angles in the fairly small room facing the fire. I smiled when I saw bookshelves full of paperbacks. A small wooden coffee table sat in the middle of the room, and on top I found a folder of things to do locally and information on the cottage. The living room had two wooden doors that opened up to a small dining area, which connected to the kitchen. I stood at the patio door and looked out to a garden and then the beach. It was heaven to me.

I walked back through the lounge and to the hallway; the door at the end was a toilet. I picked up my bag and headed upstairs. There were two bedrooms and a bathroom. I was surprised at the bathroom; it was modern with a bath and separate shower. I wondered what the agent meant when she'd said the owners wanted to modernise; the cottage was perfect.

I left my bag on the double bed in the larger of the two bedrooms; its windows looked directly out onto the beach, and made my way back downstairs. I'd brought some shopping; not knowing if I'd find somewhere to eat locally, and put away my groceries while Dini explored the garden.

I took my phone, noticing I had no signal until I was at the bottom of the garden, where I found a wooden gate that led directly down some steps and onto the sand. I sent a quick text to Mum, Ben, and Carla to let them know I'd arrived safely.

With a glass of wine, I settled at the kitchen table and opened my laptop. Once I'd connected to the Wi-Fi, I sent an email.

*To: Stefan*

*From: Jayne*

*Date: 5 September 2014*

*Subject: Arrived!*

*I'm here! The cottage is perfect, small but absolutely beautiful. There are roses, not in bloom now, over the front door, and it's right on the beach. I'll take some photos and mail them to you. I can't believe, even after that journey, how relaxed I feel. I love it here. Dini immediately took ownership of the garden. I can't wait to take him for a walk on the beach in the morning. There are walkers with dogs, so I guess it's allowed.*

*You know what's really strange? I feel at home here. I've only been here a half hour and already it feels right. I don't think I've seen this cottage before but it feels familiar, the beach and scenery feel familiar. I think my dad would be pleased.*

*Hugs and stuff, J xx*

I left the laptop and email open while I decided on something to eat. I plated some cheese and crackers, a small salad, and some pickles from the welcome basket that had been left.

*To: Jayne*

*From: Stefan*

*Date: 5 September 2014*

*Subject: Sounds great*

*I'm glad you arrived safely. :) I bet Dini will love that walk on the beach, and yes, send photos. I bet you feel at home because that part of the UK was your dad's favourite place. I imagine it makes you feel closer to him.*

*And stuff?? ;)*

*S xx*


I laughed. Our emails had initially been friendly, then downright dirty, back to friendly but with a little harmless flirting. I enjoyed the banter with Stefan.


*To: Stefan*

*From: Jayne*

*Date: 5 September 2014*

*Subject: Stuff*

*Use your imagination. ;)*

*J xx*


*To: Jayne*

*From: Stefan*

*Date: 5 September 2014*

*Subject: I am*

*And not just my imagination. ;)*

*S xx*

I laughed out loud at that response. Before I could respond, the sky darkened. I'd raced the storm clouds on the way, hoping they'd change direction. A streak of lightning lit up the sea and a clap of thunder rumbled above.

*To: Stefan*

*From: Jayne*

*Date: 5 September 2014*

*Subject: Hope you have an empty office!*

*I have an image in my mind that will no doubt help me have nice dreams now! There's a storm rolling in, so I might lose power. Have a nice time with your, err, imagination and your empty office. ;)*

*J xx*

I chuckled and sipped my wine. I wondered where plain Jayne had gone when I read back through our exchange. Face-to-face, I'd never be able to say those things without flaming cheeks and stammering.

As predicted, once the storm closed in the power went out. I used my phone for light and fumbled around in kitchen drawers for candles. I settled on a sofa, wrapped in a blanket that had been laid over one, and read by candlelight. It was chilly in the cottage; the wind had picked up and rattled the windows. Dini was a little unsettled and curled up around my feet on the end of the sofa. I should have made him get back down on the floor; he never climbed on furniture at home but I welcomed his warmth. I felt safe; rattling windows was a normal sound throughout winter back home so I wasn't troubled.

When I'd strained my eyes too much and they'd begun to hurt, I picked up the candle and headed for the kitchen. The rain was lashing against the side of the house. I watched angry waves crash against the shards of black rock that snaked into the sea and foamed on the sand. I opened the door slightly, calling to Dini. He came to the door, stood by my side and looked up at me. I could imagine him telling me 'not likely' and laughed.

I left him a bowl of water and food, and with the candle, made my way upstairs.

I undressed and threw on my PJs before climbing into bed. I left the curtains open, and once I'd blown out the candle, I watched the lightning and listened to the rain. The bed was so comfortable that I feel asleep quickly.

# Chapter Ten

It was a bright morning; the sun streaming in through the window woke me. All traces of the storm the previous evening was gone. I climbed from the bed and picked up my phone to check the time. It was early, just after seven, but I was up. I made my way downstairs to be greeted by Dini stretching his front legs. He looked like he'd had a comfortable night as well. I'd brought his bed, which had somehow managed to find itself at the other side of the room. Dini liked to drag it around until he was settled. Opening the back door, I let him out.

I took a cup of tea and sat at the small metal garden table just looking out to sea. An elderly couple walked along the beach holding hands and laughing. They looked over as they drew closer and waved. It took me a little by surprise at first. I tentatively waved back.

"Good morning. Jayne, isn't it?" the elderly lady asked as she climbed the steps to the gate.

"Yes, and good morning to you, too. It's a beautiful morning." I wanted to ask how she knew my name but didn't want to appear rude.

"I'm Nora, and this is Jim. Hello you," she said as she leaned over the gate to pet Dini.

I always believed my dog to be a great judge of character. He wagged his tail and jumped up, resting his front paws on the gate. I stood and walked over.

"He's adorable. What's his name?"

"Houdini, although we just call him Dini."

"How are you enjoying the cottage? I look after it for the owners," she said, answering my question on how she knew my name.

"I love it. Will you come in for a cup of tea?" I asked.

I opened the gate for Nora and Jim and headed for the kitchen.

"Must get that gate fixed," Jim said as he inspected a loose hinge.

"It's a shame the cottage isn't used that much. The family lives abroad, I think. They came on holiday and fell in love with the place," Nora said.

"Not enough to want to use it though," Jim added.

"The agent said it was booked out all summer, there's only one week left in November," I said.

"They had plans to do the place up, although nothing's changed. I think they may sell. Such a shame," Nora added.

I made the tea and we sat outside in the morning sun.

"Have you been to Cornwall before?" Nora asked. Jim was inspecting the flower border and pulling up a weed or two.

"I have. We used to come here every summer. I love it here. I just lost my dad and thought this might be a nice place to come and remember him. Is that odd?"

"I think that's a lovely idea. We moved here from London, years ago. I say London, the South East, really. We own the little convenience shop up the lane."

"I passed it on my way here. I got lost a couple of times. I was born in South East London, Woolwich to be exact. I live in Kent for the moment."

"For the moment?"

Perhaps she saw the cloud of sadness that descended on me. She covered my hand with hers.

"I'm a nosy old bat, ignore me. Now, what are your plans?"

I laughed off the sadness. "I'm newly separated, Nora. I don't know how long I'll be able to stay in my house. And as for plans? I just want to walk this beach every day, relax, read a little, and think."

"I'm sorry to hear that, and as for those plans? Make sure you include a cup of tea at the shop."

Nora drained her mug, despite the tea still being scalding hot, and stood.

"Look at him, he does love a garden, my Jim."

I laughed. I liked her immediately. She seemed genuine and friendly.

"That storm didn't scare you, did it?" Jim asked as he placed his empty mug on the table.

"No, I was glad I found some candles though."

"The power goes off all the time, something to do with old overhead cables," he said.

"I'll be prepared for that."

I walked them to the gate and watched them continue their stroll along the beach before they waved as they turned the corner and out of sight.

After rinsing the mugs, I grabbed my camera. I called Dini and we set off down the steps and onto the beach. I rolled my jeans up and walked just where the water met the sand. I loved the feel of the wet sand between my toes. Dini ran in and out of the sea, jumping where the waves broke. I took endless photographs. Halfway along I came to some huts; a group of guys were standing outside. One whistled and patted his leg, attracting Dini's attention. I followed the dog as he checked out the young guys.

"Hi. Great dog," one said. He had an Australian accent.

"Thank you. His name's Dini."

"Are you here on holiday?" he asked. "Oh, I'm Greg, by the way, and this is Tom and Scott."

"I am, arrived last night. I'm Jayne."

With introductions made, the guys told me about the surfing. They spend all summer in Cornwall surfing, lifeguarding on the beach and in the evenings, working at bars and restaurants.

"You have to come to Life's A Beach," Greg said. He pointed to a glass sided building just up from the beach.

"It's a café during the day and a great restaurant in the evenings."

"It sounds wonderful, although I don't know that I'd visit on my own."

"Sure you will, we'll sit with you," Tom said.

The boys reminded me of Ben. They were about the same age and had that wonderful carefree manner.

"Come on, Jayne. Tomorrow night, eight o'clock. It's not busy tomorrow. I'm the assistant manager, I'll look after you," Scott said with a laugh.

I wasn't entirely sure if he was the assistant manager or not, but they made me laugh.

"I'll think about it," I said.

"The offer's there."

"And if you fancy surfing, let me know," Greg said.

"You know what, I've always wanted to do that, but I think I'm a little too old now."

"No way! Got a wet suit?" I shook my head. "No problem, we have some here, I'm sure I can find one to fit."

"I'm only here for a week."

"Well, you can't spend a week walking up and down the beach, as beautiful as is it. Tomorrow morning, I'll give you a lesson, on the house."

Greg was probably the world's best salesman. I found myself nodding enthusiastically. Why not? It was on my list of things to do.

"Yes, definitely. I've always wanted to, so why not. What do I need to bring?"

"Be in your swimwear, and bring a towel."

I'd spent nearly an hour chatting to the guys. I enjoyed their company and it felt good to laugh with them. I'd have pangs of guilt that I wasn't crying. It had only been a short while since my dad had died but being on that beach, in Cornwall, it didn't feel wrong to laugh. Inside I'd grieve for years, no doubt, but with the sun shining, I felt more alive than I had in years.

*To: Stefan*

*From: Jayne*

*Date: 6 September 2014*

*Subject: Surfing!*

*Guess what? I'm going surfing tomorrow. I met three Aussie guys. They surf, work the bars and restaurants here all summer (their winter) then go home when the season is finished. I've always wanted to have a go. No idea whether I'll manage to actually stand up on the board, but I'll let you know. I met an elderly couple. They look after the cottage and are so lovely. I've attached some pics. :) I'm going to have dinner with the Aussies tomorrow night, if I survive the surfing, of course.*

*J xx*

I sat in the garden with my laptop and rang my mum; I detailed the cottage, the beach, and what my plans were. She remembered that her and Dad had sat on that very same beach when I was a baby. Maybe that's why I felt so comfortable, perhaps there was a connection.

*To: Jayne*
*From: Stefan*
*Date: 6 September 2014*
*Subject: Be careful!*
*Surfing! I used to do that when I was younger. I'm jealous, although the Danes are way better than the Aussies. ;)*
*Love the pics. I can see myself sitting on that beach, beats being in the office.*

*S xx*

Jealous of what, I wondered, jealous that I was surfing? Or was he jealous that I was having dinner with the Aussies? And what were the Danes better at? I didn't reply for fear of misunderstanding what he'd meant.

I was down at the beach early the following morning. I'd taken Dini with me, as he would have jumped the garden gate if I'd left him.

"Hey, Jayne. Great to see you. Come on in," Greg called out as I approached the hut.

Inside it was kitted out with surfboards, wet suits, and a curtained-off area to change. I wore my swimming costume under my shorts and t-shirt.

"Let's get you sized up," he said, as he held wetsuits against me.

"Okay, change into that, and me and Dini will meet you on the beach," he added.

I hid behind the curtain, making sure not to tangle my feet in the Neoprene and fall arse first through the makeshift changing room. Once I'd managed to slither into the tight material, I ventured out.

Greg and Dini were on the beach. I was disappointed to see three other students, all at least half my age. However, they greeted me with smiles. We learnt the basics, and for me, that was learning the string thing that connected me to the board attached to my ankle and not the wrist I had it wrapped around. The 'leash' was there so I didn't lose the board I was told. I wasn't sure if Greg was joking or not. By the third attempt of kneeling and then leaping to my feet, I knew my knees would give out by the end of the day and surfing was probably not for me. But I had fun. I took the board out, wading through the waves, and although I never actually got to stand more than a few seconds before falling off, it was exhilarating, and I could totally understand the attraction.

As my fellow classmates headed up the shore and back to the hut, I sat astride my surfboard, content with just bobbing on the water and watching the guys. They sat and waited, leapt to their feet with ease and cruised all the way into the shallows. It seemed so easy. I guess it would have been had I been twenty years younger.

"I'm not sure it's something I'm going to master," I said with a laugh as I walked to the hut.

Dini had been patiently waiting beside the door. I imagined the copious amounts of burgers and hot dogs probably enticed him to stay put. He wagged his tail as I leaned down to stroke his head.

"You will get fat," I said to him.

I peeled off the wetsuit and wrapped myself in a towel.

"Don't forget tonight. See you up there," Greg called out as I walked back to the cottage.

"I'll be there," I said.

It had been a warm morning, a day that reminded me of my childhood, as I tasted the dried sea salt on my lips and felt the grittiness on my skin. My hair was a tangled mess and I couldn't help but smile.

I took a hot shower, pulled on some jeans and a t-shirt, and sat in the garden with my laptop, a cigarette, and cup of tea.

*To: Stefan*

*From: Jayne*

*Date: 7 September 2014*

*Subject: Did it!*

*I did it. I surfed! :) Well, I sat on the board, fell off a few times then sat some more and just watched, but I'm sure that counts, doesn't it? I really enjoyed myself. I'm so glad I made the decision to come here. It's somewhere I'd love to come back to. I'm rambling, sorry. How has your day been?*

*J xx*

I didn't receive a reply that day and, although that itch to keep checking my laptop was still there, I made a point of taking a walk up to see Nora and Jim. With Dini on a lead, much to his disgust, we set off up the lane.

"Morning, Jayne. Bring him in," I heard Nora call out.

The front door to the shop was open to allow the summer breeze to waft through; she had seen me looking for a suitable place to tie his lead to, I imagined.

"Are you sure?"

"Of course, come on in. I'll put the kettle on."

The shop stocked everything from food to fuses—a complete general store. A few tourists were browsing the shelves and a couple of locals leaned against the counter, chatting. I was introduced to them.

With a cup of tea in hand, I joined the conversation.

"Are you here on your holidays?" I was asked.

"I am. I used to come here all the time as a child. I love the place."

"You're staying at the Turner's place? Shame that's closed up so much," another said.

I had been under the impression the locals were not overly fond of homes being bought up for holidays, but I guessed if the cottages were used, they would be happier.

I stayed and chatted for a half hour, even helping an elderly lady pack her bag, before heading back to the cottage and then took another walk along the beach. Dini bounded ahead jumping in and out of the waves as they broke on the sand.

It was with trepidation that I entered the restaurant. I'd never eaten out alone and took a book to occupy myself, in case I was sitting on my own. I needn't have worried though. A table had been laid towards the back and I was waved over. Within minutes, I fell in love with the place. The staff wore jeans and t-shirts, and there was casualness among the busyness. The restaurant was full of diners and I could appreciate the popularity. Two walls were glass and overlooked the beach. As I sat and the sun set, silhouettes of surfers could be seen.

"Hey, my favourite lady is here," I heard.

Scott stopped at my side and handed me a menu. The restaurant served a wonderful selection of fresh, local fish and meats.

"What do you fancy?" Scott asked, taking our orders himself.

I chose the restaurants 'famous' crab bisque to start, and then their equally famous, salt baked bream to follow. How famous the dishes were, I wasn't sure but that's what it said on the menu. At first I listened to the boys, their banter and laughter reminded me of times when Ben would bring friends home. It hit me with a jolt that in latter years that had stopped. Neither Ben or Casey brought anyone to visit, and I wondered if the tension in the house had been that noticeable.

"Greg tells me you did good today," Scott said, when he'd

returned with our drinks.

"Then I think he was being very kind," I said with a laugh.

"No, seriously, most people can't even sit on the board. At least you managed that for an hour," Greg said with a wink.

I loved that they felt comfortable enough to tease, and I found it really easy to have a conversation with them. It seemed strange. I was twice their age and had only met them for a brief time but felt like I'd known them for ages.

We talked about everything; their lives back in Australia, my reason for being in Cornwall, my kids, my separation, the dog, their girlfriends—of which there were many—and life in general. We laughed, we drank beer, and ate the wonderful food. I thoroughly enjoyed myself.

With the evening over, I planned to make the walk back along the beach. Greg had other ideas.

"No way, it's too dark," he said. "I have the truck."

We piled out and into the back of the red lifeguard's truck, sitting on the metal floor and holding on as he roared back along the beach. I was sure it shouldn't have been allowed and wondered if the misuse of the truck would land him in trouble. But with the wind whipping my hair across my face, the warm night air rushing around us, I felt wonderful. I felt young, I wanted to stand at the cab and have my *Titanic* moment but my forty-five-year-old brain urged me to hold on to the sides of the truck tighter.

I was dropped off at the bottom of the cottage garden, and with a wave I climbed the steps to the back door.

"Tomorrow, eight o'clock," Greg shouted as they drove away.

I shook my head and laughed. Opening the back door, I let Dini join me as I sat in the garden. I sent a text to Ben to tell him about the guys and how much he would love being here.

A wave of tiredness washed over me. I guessed the surfing, the sea air, the beer, and a stomach full of food had caught up with me. I made a cup of tea, took my book and laptop up to bed for an early night.

As I lay under the covers, I rested the laptop on my thighs and opened a blank document. I wanted to type up my thoughts and experiences so I could remember when I got home. I added some of the photographs I'd taken, creating a pictorial diary, and when I was done, I shut it down and turned off the bedside lamp.

Dini barking and a banging on the back door woke me the following morning. I threw on my shorts and a t-shirt before rushing downstairs. Greg was standing at the back door. He smiled when he saw me through the glass.

"Are you okay?" I asked as I opened the back door.

"No, I need your help. Can you spare a couple of hours? Trish has upped and left the shop. I need someone to cover while I'm teaching. Please? I'll buy you lunch?" He held his hands together in prayer, tilted his head to one side, and gave me a goofy grin.

"I'm not even dressed," I said, laughing but panicking.

"You'll do. Come on, I have coffee and cake."

"I don't know anything about surfing."

"Neither does anyone who comes in, remember?"

I laughed. "Okay, let me get my bag at least."

I grabbed my bag, phone and keys, a bowl and some food for Dini, and then we set off.

"What do I have to do?" I asked as we walked along the beach.

"Just answer the phone, book people in for lessons, that kind of stuff."

"What if someone asks a question?"

"Tell them I'll call them back or make it up," he added with a laugh.

As we approached the surf school, which was an oversized beach hut, Tom was waiting with arms outstretched.

"Man, you're late," he said.

"I know. Jayne's gonna step in. Trish has left."

"Cool, now help me get this open."

The guys unlocked the padlocks on either side of a large wooden shutter, which they then raised and propped open. I set down Dini's bowl so he at least got breakfast. The door was pinned open and we walked inside. At one end was a counter; I stepped around it and placed my bag on a shelf underneath. I took a look around to familiarise myself. It was a mess of paperwork, pieces of equipment, and food of a questionable date.

Immediately we had three people arrive for the first surf lesson of the day. I stood with Greg and listened, watched as he booked them in. It was simple enough; take their details and payment, size them up for a wetsuit if they didn't have their own, then send them outside to wait. Greg would hand over their boards from a selection he'd lined up outside against the hut wall.

With the first group gone and Tom already surfing, I set about to tidy up and create some order. I found a couple of old box files and separated up the paperwork into receipts and invoices, filing them in date order. I cleaned the counter, the shelving, and then found a mop and bucket to wash the sandy floor.

"Wow, looks like a new place," I heard.

I hadn't realised the time I'd spent cleaning. Greg stepped back in, ignoring the scowl I gave as his wet sandy feet left a trail across the newly washed floor.

"No phone calls, but as you can see, I've tidied up."

"Scott is bringing breakfast and coffee. We have a kitchen of sorts. I forgot to show you."

"I found it. I have all the cups in soak at the moment. I don't believe they've been washed up for a while."

He laughed. "I'm gonna call you mum while you're here."

I showed him what I'd done with the paperwork, and he showed me how the till worked. Scott arrived with bacon rolls and cardboard cups of coffee. I sat with the guys outside in the rickety plastic chairs around a couple of tables, desperately in need of a clean.

Before he'd finished his coffee, Greg was off again with the second class of the day. I carried on with the cleaning, took a couple of calls, and quoted from a brochure I'd found before booking them in. I enjoyed myself; it was fun watching the guys come and go.

"Mum, want some lunch?" I heard. I was rehanging the wetsuits in size order, shorties on one rail and long on another.

"Yes, please. Let me grab my purse."

"On me. Be back in a minute."

I chuckled at the 'Mum.'

By the end of the day, all the guys were calling me Mum, some of the customers were calling me Mum and I was exhausted. I helped Greg cash out and as we locked up, he handed over some cash.

"Wages," he said with a smile.

"I don't want your money. I was just helping out."

"Ah, but can you help out tomorrow?"

"I can but I don't want paying. I'm enjoying myself."

I walked back to the cottage, thinking. I had intended to just have a holiday, not spend each day doing chores, but I realised I was doing something I actually enjoyed for people that appreciated it.

After a quick shower I settled at the kitchen table with a salad and opened my laptop. I'd received a couple of emails.

*To: Jayne*

*From: Stefan*

*Date: 9 September 2014*

*Subject: Go you!*

*Way to go! You'll be a surf dude, or should that be dudette, before you know it. I'm sorry I didn't reply yesterday, been in meetings for two days. I'm exhausted and in need of a break.*

*S xx*

*To: Stefan*

*From: Jayne*

*Date: 9 September 2014*

*Subject: :(*

*Don't apologise for not replying, I know you're busy. I hope the meetings were productive but maybe you do need to think of having a day or so off. Take that bike out for a road trip. :)*

*J xx*

The second email I opened spoilt my day.

*To: Jayne*

*From: Michael*

*Date: 9 September 2014*

*Subject: Credit Card*

*I noticed that you were able to take a holiday. I trust you'll make arrangements to pay the fee from the credit card.*

*Regards, Michael*

"Prick!" I shouted to the screen.

He could more than afford the few hundred pounds I'd spent on the cottage rental. He thought nothing of spending twice that on a meal out with his friends once a month, playing the big 'I am.' I slammed the laptop shut without responding. I'd pay that off. I wouldn't give him the satisfaction of thinking he'd provided a holiday for me while he lived it up in Japan or London, or wherever the fuck he was.

The rest of the week passed by too quickly. I spent another day helping the boys, an afternoon chatting with Nora and even serving an elderly customer when Nora made yet more tea, and plenty of walks on the beach. My last night was spent having dinner at Life's A Beach with them all.

I reluctantly packed the car up; Jim unpacked and repacked it to ensure everything was safely loaded. It was with sadness that I drove away with promises to return and a list of email addresses in my purse so we could keep in contact. Nora had offered to put me up and insisted I visit again. I felt like I'd made some firm friends in just that one week. The boys would be heading back to Australia at the end of the month, the season over, and I was looking forward to hearing of their adventures white-water rafting back home.

The house felt empty and cold when I'd finally arrived back home. Although still September, the weather in Kent had taken a dramatic turn for the worse. Once I'd unpacked the car, I opened the fridge and smiled. Someone had stocked it for my return. I sent a text to both Ben and Carla, letting them know that I had arrived home safely and then decided to email Casey. It seemed to be the easiest way to contact her.

*To: Casey*

*From: Mum*

*Date: 13 September 2014*

*Subject: I'm home*

*Hi, darling. I'm home from Cornwall. Had a lovely time and guess what? I learnt to surf, sort of! When you're home next, I'd love for you to come back with me. It was a wonderful cottage and I spent most of my time with the surf instructors and an elderly couple who owned the local shop. I even manned the surf school for a couple of days. Let me know you're okay. I miss talking to you.*

*Love, Mum xx*

I settled down with my phone and decided to call mum. Although we had chatted a couple of times during the week, our calls had always been brief. Once I'd managed to get past the gatekeeper that was Aunt Margie, I had a long conversation with Mum. She chuckled when I explained that Margie seemed reluctant to hand the phone over.

"I think she's probably bored of listening to me. I imagine she enjoyed a change of voice," she said.

"I'd really love for you to come to Cornwall with me, the cottage was amazing. I have some great photographs to show you."

"We'll see. I'm not sure I can without your dad, but let me think on it."

I hadn't thought Mum might struggle to revisit the place that held so many memories of Dad for her. I'd felt closer to him during my time there, I had a sense of 'approval' from him. He'd be turning in his grave if he thought we'd stopped living just because he had.

Once our conversation was over, I headed to bed. It was as I climbed under the covers that the loneliness hit. I'd escaped for a week, been living a fantasy, and now that I was home, reality hit. I needed to find work and make some decisions on my future. It was with a heavy heart that I fell asleep.

# Chapter Eleven

September turned into October and with it the weather became decidedly autumnal. Winds blew, rattling the windowpanes and brought heavy rain. Stefan and I emailed maybe once a week, and I missed the frequency of the previous months. He'd told me he was pitching for a really large project. It would take him out of the office a lot and if they got the contract, he'd be working seven days a week for a month or so. I didn't want to keep disturbing him but I missed our chats.

I tried to call and email Casey a few times; I never received a reply. In the end, I resorted to the one thing I didn't want to do. I asked Ben to intervene. He sent her a text message, which resulted in a rather snotty reply.

*Mother, I'm working 18 hours a day right now. I'm sorry I'm not able to keep answering your messages. Dad and I will be back in the UK mid-November, and I'll be sure to make some time to visit.*

My heart broke a little at her message. I wasn't sure what I'd done to deserve that response. I'd only wanted to keep in contact with my daughter. As the winter drew in, so my moods started to fall. Ben was my godsend.

"Hi, Mum. Thought I'd pop in for a coffee," he called out one morning, as he walked through the front door.

"Hey, it's great to see you. How's Kerry?"

"Moaning that she's getting fat," he replied with a laugh.

I didn't want to rely on my son and Carla for company all the time, but they seemed to be all I had.

"We have a problem. Our landlord wants to increase the rent, and we can't afford it."

"That's not fair. Can you appeal?"

"We tried, but according to the agent, what he's asking for is market value. We need to find somewhere to move to and pretty soon."

"Why don't you move back in here? I have all this space."

"I was kind of hoping you'd suggest that," he said with a laugh.

"Well, why not just say in the first place? This is your home whenever you want it."

"What do you think 'he who must be obeyed' will say?"

"I don't care what he says. This is my house as much as his. If I want you to stay, then you will."

"That's brilliant, thanks, Mum. Kerry has been in pieces over it all."

"Tell her not to worry. We can turn the small room into a nursery; you and Kerry can take the other one. It will be exciting," I said.

"Here's the other thing: we need to move next week."

"Okay, we best get cracking then. What do you need me to do?"

"Nothing really. We have some friends who will help us move."

We made plans for furniture storage and clearing out the bedrooms, getting ready for their things. Once Ben had left, I decided to email Michael.

*To: Michael*

*From: Jayne*

*Date: 10 October 2014*

*Subject: Holiday and house*

*Just to let you know I saw your email. I didn't respond because, quite frankly, I couldn't be arsed to. Ben and Kerry are moving into the house. Not that I need your permission, just letting you know in case you wish to actually get in touch with him.*

*Jayne*


I bit my nails after I'd pressed send. He'd be pissed off with my email but he hadn't spoken to Ben in months, and he never enquired about Kerry or his impending grandchild.

It was as I was about to close down my laptop that I received another email.


*To: Jayne*

*From: Stefan*

*Date: 10 October 2014*

*Subject: Got the contract and a holiday!*

*Hey, J. Guess what? I got the contract. It took months of negotiations but it's a huge deal for me. And I booked a holiday. I'll have this project wrapped up end of November, or at least in a position where I can take a week off, so I booked a week in a wonderful cottage on a beach. ;) Say that you'll join me…*

*S xx*


I reread, my jaw fell open, and I grabbed my phone.

"Guess what?" I said before Carla had even finished her 'hello.'

"You're pregnant? Michael was killed in a tragic rafting accident?"

"Pregnant! And sadly not. Stefan wants me to join him for a week's holiday."

"What?" She screeched so loud I had to remove the phone from my ear.

"Stefan wants me…"

"Yes, I heard. When? Where? Oh my God, Jayne, what did you say?"

"When, I don't know. Where, I don't know either, although I suspect the cottage in Cornwall, and I haven't replied."

"You haven't replied? Get the fuck off the phone and answer him."

"He emailed, I can talk to you while I reply. What shall I say?"

"You say, 'No, I'm sorry, I can't possibly spend time with the man I've been fantasising over for nearly a year'."

"Huh?"

"You say, 'Yes, when and where?' obviously."

I didn't answer.

"Are you still there?" she asked.

"Yes. I don't know what to do, Carla. I mean, what if he doesn't like me in real life, what if he's changed? So much has happened over the year. What if we don't get on?"

"You're kidding me, right? Of course you'll get on, but if you don't, you come home. What do you have to lose? Please, Jayne, do it. I'm coming over tomorrow and we are going to plan."

"Okay, I'll see you tomorrow."

"I'm not going now. I'm hanging on the line until you reply."

"I need to think. Ben and Kerry are moving in next week, did I tell you?"

"Don't change the subject, type."

"Oh, for Christ's sake. Hold on."

I spoke as I typed a reply.

*To: Stefan*

*From: Jayne*

*Date: 10 October 2014*

*Subject: Wow!*

*Congratulations on the contract! I know you've worked so hard for that. I'm thrilled for you. And a cottage on a beach? I'd love to, thank you for inviting me. When? Where? Or can I guess? :) Are you sure?*

*J xx*

"Did that sound okay? Not too desperate?" I asked Carla.

"No, perfect. You make sure you let me know what he says. This is so exciting!"

"It's fucking terrifying. Please don't tell anyone. I feel sick at the thought now. Oh, God, I wish there was a way of retracting emails. I need to think about this."

"There's nothing to think about. I'll be over in the morning."

We said goodbye and I sat and looked at the email I'd sent. Holy fuck, he wanted to meet! After nearly a year, he still wanted to meet. I was stunned. No—I was scared, terrified.

I drummed my fingers on the table, unsure if I wanted him to reply immediately or not.

*To: Jayne*

*From: Stefan*

*Date: 10 October 2014*

*Subject: Cornwall*

*You sent me the details; I went online and booked. The week in November was still available. Can you make that date?*

*S xx*

I didn't reply immediately. My heart was hammering in my chest. A hundred questions ran through my mind. What if he didn't like me? I wasn't as confident in real life as I was in our emails. I thought back on some then let my head fall into my hands. Oh God! I'd sent some smutty comments over the past year. What if... No, I wasn't going to go there.

Carla was at the front door before I'd even finished dressing the following morning. She walked through to the kitchen, shouting up the stairs that she'd brought breakfast. I joined her just a few minutes later.

"Well?" she said, as I grabbed the mug of tea she'd placed on the table.

"Well, what?"

"What did he say?"

"He's booked a week in November. I need to check because he didn't specify a date but it's mid-month, I think."

"And?"

"And he wants me to join him."

Her face broke out into a wide smile. "This is so exciting."

"This is so terrifying."

"We need to get you pampered, get your hair done. When was the last time you had your hair done?"

"Months ago. I can't afford those luxuries."

"I can. I'll book the appointments. We have much to do, my friend," she said with a laugh.

"I don't know that I can do this." I couldn't drum up the level of excitement Carla felt.

"Why?"

"What if...? What if he wants, you know. I can't do this." I was getting upset.

"If he wants sex? Is that what you're worried about?"

I nodded my head.

"First, you don't know that he isn't just looking at this as two friends on holiday, and second, if he does, why not? Don't you think you deserve some affection?"

"Carla, I haven't had sex for years, and I mean, *years*! I doubt any of it works."

"But you've..."

"No!" I cut her off before she could finish her sentence.

I could see she was trying not to laugh, until she realised I was serious. Tears formed in my eyes.

"I've acted like a slut online, what if that's what he's expecting?" I whispered.

"You haven't. Jesus, Jayne. It was a little flirty. If you think what you wrote was raunchy, you really have led a sheltered life."

She took hold of my hands.

"Just go with the flow. Don't have anything in mind, and if it

186

happens, it was meant to be. Just be prepared, that's all. And you know what? You do all this 'Scarlet did it' crap, but that's you. Maybe that glass of wine was the confidence booster that allows you to be you."

"I've lied, though."

"No, you haven't. You haven't told him anything that isn't true. So you were braver online, maybe he's done the same. Don't overthink this."

"I told him my fantasy." I cringed as I spoke.

"Then let's hope you get to play that out. Unless it was the one where you get locked in the basement after being kidnapped and tied to a bedpost for days. You didn't tell him that one, did you?"

"Oh, fuck off." I laughed, although being tied to the bedpost sounded appealing.

"Seriously, don't overthink it. What will be, will be."

Carla left after devouring the pastries she'd brought. I envied the fact she could eat like a horse and not put on weight. One sniff of a pastry and my hips expanded. We made plans to meet up the following week for a little shopping and 'pampering', as she called it. Maybe she thought I needed more 'work' on me than I'd realised. The holiday was two months away; I couldn't think about it. I had Ben and Kerry to worry about first.

I spent the rest of the week clearing out and cleaning the two bedrooms. They were full of memories. Casey's old bedroom had boxes of schoolbooks, toys from when she was a child, and photograph albums. I sat on the floor flicking through one. I came across a photograph of her; it wasn't in an album and was taken maybe just a few years ago. I didn't recognise the photo as one I'd taken. She sat on a wall, a sea defence wall I imagined, and looking out to sea. It was a side profile of her and she appeared to be unaware the picture had been taken. She looked so sad. I touched the picture and wondered what had made her look so pensive.

I turned the photograph over. Written on the back in black ink and in handwriting I didn't recognised was a date and place.

'*Broadstairs, 2012 – Think of me sometimes, and soften your heart. Too soon your life will be over and you'll have missed it. I can't love you all the while you hate the world.*'

Broadstairs was a beach town not far from where we lived, and I wracked my brain to remember a time in 2012 we'd been there. The sky was grey, the sea angry, so I guessed it to be winter. I read the inscription again. Who wrote that? Was it a quote from a book or a personal message? I placed the photo to one side and continued to box up her things.

I was unsure what to do with Michael's things. He had left some clothes that I folded into a suitcase. When I sat and thought, other than the winter clothes, there was nothing of Michael anywhere in the house. He'd been moving out for a long while before he actually did.

Ben would put the boxes in the loft and move any furniture they didn't need to the garage when they moved in.

I decided to take a walk into the village. As usual, Dini protested about being on the lead, but over time the village had grown, there were more cars speeding through the country lanes than ever. I passed what used to be a hairdresser and noticed a new sign, black and silver, advertising a beauty parlour. A young girl was standing outside, she handed me a leaflet. Perhaps I looked like I needed their help, as she seemed to ignore other people passing by.

I read as I walked. Waxing, massage, pedicures and manicures, and make-up lessons were just some of the treatments on offer.

I heard my name being called from across the road. Carla came power walking towards me.

"What on earth are you doing?" I asked.

"Exercising, obviously. What's that?" she said as she looked at the leaflet.

"A new beauty parlour. The girl forced it on me as I walked by."

She took the leaflet and scanned. "You might want to book some treatments before your holiday," she said.

"I was thinking that. What do you suggest?"

"How about a little waxing? When was the last time you had a trim up?"

"I shave my legs and armpits, of course."

"I'm talking down below. They do a Brazilian."

"A what?"

"A tidy up, that's all you need to know. Want to book in?"

"No. I'm not having my ninny waxed!"

She spluttered a little, I wondered whether her power walking had affected her lungs.

"Go in there and book some treatments, and don't, whatever you do, ask for a ninny wax."

"I'm not having my ninny waxed," I said, raising my voice then glowing red with embarrassment.

"You want him to go down on you and get a mouthful of

pubes?"

My mouth fell open. I spun on my heels and 'power walked' in the opposite direction, desperately trying to avoid the glare from old Mrs. Jones, the florist.

Carla's laughter followed me and I was nearly at a jog to keep some distance. She'd closed the gap with her silly walking thing.

"I'm kidding. Well, actually, I'm not, but you know I'm just teasing. How about a coffee?"

"I can't, I doubt they'd let Dini in."

"They do in the pub. Come on." She grabbed my arm and ushered me across the street.

I hadn't visited the village pub for a long time. In fact, the last time it had been a dingy, brown painted ceiling, smoking den. It was a surprise to walk into a bright room, one end housed tables and chairs for diners and the other comfortable looking leather sofas.

I pointed to Dini when the bar lady looked over. She nodded and told us to take a seat; she'd be right over.

"So I need waxing. I've never been waxed before. Why can't I just shave or trim with scissors?" I asked.

"You can shave, if you want to end up looking like you have a nasty rash. And do you trust yourself down there with a pair of scissors?"

"I doubt very much we're going to have sex, let alone...*that*!"

She smirked at me. I hated when she smirked at me because that usually meant I was totally out of the park on my thoughts. The bar lady brought over some cups and a jug of coffee. We hadn't asked for them but I thought it a nice touch. She laid a couple of lunch menus on the table.

"Why don't we start with a pedicure at least? He may want to suck on your toes."

I spurted the coffee I had just taken a sip of across the table. Carla squealed as the hot liquid hit her designer power walking outfit, and Dini jumped to his feet, assuming I was being attacked.

I stared at her. "I'm not going."

"You are, I'm kidding," she said between fits of laughter.

"I'm not. Seriously, Carla, this is terrifying me. I might have it all wrong, and I just know I'm going to make a complete fool of myself."

She rested back on the sofa and sipped her coffee.

"How do you feel about him?" she asked.

"I like him, probably more than I should. I know I use him as an escape but there is a friendship there too."

"Then don't blow this chance. It might be the only one you get to meet up."

"What will people think?" I whispered.

"Is that what's really bothering you? You're separated, Jayne. You're cheating husband left you for a job thousands of miles away."

"I know but not that long ago."

"Is there a time limit then? We're not talking about being bereaved here; you're single, not legally, but still single. No one needs to know, Jayne. We'll keep it just between us."

We finished our coffee and decided to skip the lunch. Carla had another mile of power walking she'd told me, and I didn't relish the idea of eating beside Dini. His drool at one sniff of food was enough to put anyone off a meal.

"When are the kids moving in?" Carla asked, as we made our

way back out.

"Next couple of days, I think. I'm looking forward to it. I'm painting the nursery this afternoon."

"I'll pop round in a couple of days and give you a hand."

We said our goodbyes and I watched her backside sway vigorously from side to side as she walked off. Dini and I casually strolled back home.

A week later the nursery was finished. Ben and I painted the walls a soft cream and I surprised myself with my artistry skills. I'd taken lots of photos over the years of animals while on my walks, and I created a woodland theme on one of the walls.

"It looks amazing," Kerry said. She had been ferrying items from their house in the car, much to Ben's annoyance.

"I wish you'd sit down," he said.

"I'm pregnant, Ben, not disabled," she replied.

After some shelves had been fixed, I placed a photograph of my dad on one. We stood and remembered him in silence. I wanted to have him in the room; he would look after the baby when the time came for him, or her, to share the room.

"He would have been here nagging us," I said.

"I know, but I bet he's smiling now," Kerry answered.

A day later the rooms were furnished. Ben and Kerry had stored most of their things in a friend's garage, only bringing bedroom items, the baby's things, and some small kitchen appliances.

"I have an idea. How about we clear out the study? No one uses it, and you can put your sofa, TV, whatnot in there. It will give you your own space, some privacy," I said.

A second day of moving furniture was arranged.

Ben had driven to the fish and chip shop. We were all exhausted and I sat with Kerry at the kitchen table.

"I'm going back down to Cornwall in November, so you'll have the house to yourself for a week," I said.

"Oh, sounds lovely. I've always preferred the beach in the winter."

She didn't push on who I was going with, and I was glad; I'd hate to have lied to her.

"Ben did tell you he was picking Nan up from the airport tomorrow, didn't he?"

"Yes, he's leaving early to avoid the traffic."

"I've missed her. I'll be glad to see her home."

Mum's stay in Scotland had extended way beyond the week she'd originally planned. I'd popped round to her bungalow on occasions to make sure everything was okay, and I'd organised for some shopping to be delivered. We also had the dreaded task of packing up my dad's clothes.

Mum had mentioned in our last phone call that she wanted to take his things to the charity shop. I'd told her there was no rush but there was no right time to do that, I guessed.

# Chapter Twelve

October made way for November, and as the weeks wore on, so my nerves began to fray. Both Ben and Kerry constantly asked what was wrong, Mum would look at me with a brow furrowed in question, and Carla's smile got broader.

"You booked the appointment?" Carla asked, as we sat with a glass of wine.

"Yes, in the morning. I can't fucking believe I'm doing this," I replied.

"You'll probably need to do it again before the holiday."

"Well, let's see how this goes first."

"Can I come and watch?"

"No, you bloody can't. Now go home, I need to have a bath, apparently."

Carla laughed as she collected her coat and bag and made her way out the front door. I had already bitten my newly manicured nails down to the quick in panic.

I took a long bath, shaved my legs and armpits, plucked a stray hair from my chin and then panicked more would grow as its replacement. Once done, I climbed out and wrapped myself in a towel. I attempted to shape my eyebrows while I waited for the bath water to drain away. I laughed as I looked in the bath; it resembled a sheep-shearing marathon.

I entered the beauty parlour and immediately wanted to step back outside. The reception resembled the waiting room at the doctors, except most of the patients looked healthier than the three women who turned to look at me. I smiled at the receptionist, gave my name, and took a seat next to a small coffee table. I picked up an out of date copy of *Hello* magazine and flicked through. Victoria and David Beckham's wedding was being covered that week. I closed the magazine to check the date. 1999!

As I looked around the room, I swallowed down a chuckle. One of the occupants would have been better off at the local hardware shop with a hedge trimmer; such was the length of hair on her legs. Even in the depths of winter, when I preferred to grow a fur coat, I'd never had hair that long.

Perhaps it was nerves, but the chuckle turned into a stifled laughter as I saw the moustache on lady number two. Then I remembered why I was there. I looked towards the door. I could make it out unnoticed if I crept, or I could pretend to have left my purse in a car somewhere and promise to return, then run. Before I could make my mind up on what exit strategy to use, my name was called.

"Miss Adams?" I heard.

A young girl stood just outside an open door along the corridor. I was too late. I rose and smiled at her.

"My name's Andi. Have you visited us before?" she asked.

"I haven't, I assumed you had only just opened."

"Oh, we've been here a couple of months now," she said with a smile. "So what can I offer you today?"

I swallowed and felt the colour rise to my cheeks. "I'd like a tidy up, erm, you know, down there." I couldn't stop the stage whisper or my fingers pointing to the top of my thighs. I cringed.

"Have you had a bikini wax before?"

"No, I'm a waxing virgin," I said, adding an embarrassed chuckle.

"If you'd like to remove your clothes, you can leave them there," she pointed to a closet.

"All of them?"

"No, just your trousers and pants," she said with a chuckle.

*Pants?* It seemed a strange choice of word but I undressed and grabbed a towel to wrap around my waist.

"Now, let's get you settled, shall we? Did you decide on what you wanted?"

I climbed onto the bed then had to raise my backside in the air so Andi could whip the towel away. She placed another over my waist, keeping me partially covered.

"I don't know what you mean, I just want a tidy up," I replied, as I watched her snap on rubber gloves. The image of a farmer about to shove his arms up a cow's vagina to aid birth sprang to mind.

"Leave it to me." She held her hands in the air, like a surgeon would before performing an operation.

She scared me. She was constantly smiling and inspecting my 'bits.' I wondered what on earth went through her mind every time she did a 'tidy up.' She reminded me of the gynaecologist, who always smiled as if he had some secret joke running through his

196

mind. Or both found my ninny amusing.

I watched as she snapped off the top of an applicator and placed a hand on my thigh, gently moving it away. I wanted to fling my arm over my eyes at the thought of her staring. I felt a warm liquid make a trail around an area of my body that hadn't been viewed by a stranger for many years. I didn't class the gynae as a stranger; we seemed to be on first name terms.

Andi placed some material over the warm wax and used her other hand to stretch the skin. She smiled over at me.

"Do you live locally?" she asked.

I opened my mouth to speak. Instead of words, the sound that left resembled a scream as she theatrically pulled the material from my skin.

"What the…"

I tried to sit up, but the bitch was relentless. As quick as flash, she placed the strip elsewhere and ripped it off.

"Any pets?" she asked.

*Pets? Was she fucking mad?* I thought.

I clenched my jaw, bit my lip and gripped the sides of the couch as my poor hairs, hairs that hadn't seen the light of day, were mercilessly ripped from their safe place. Those hairs had done no harm to man or beast, I could hear their screams; they mirrored mine.

"Any kids?"

*Shut the fuck up, bitch!* I screamed, in my head, of course. My mouth was closed so tight the only sound I could make was grunts.

I breathed in through my nose, trying to absorb the pain. Giving birth hadn't hurt that much, or maybe I'd just forgotten.

"All done, now that wasn't too bad, was it?"

*Are you fucking insane?*

"No," I whimpered.

Andi smoothed on some very cold lotion. The heat of being partially flayed wasn't doused by the icing of the aloe vera in the least. I tried not to pant as the sting intensified.

"You can get up now. I'll let you get dressed while I wash these bowls, then I'll be in reception."

Get up? My body was in shock—it was trembling. Or at least my legs were. I swung them from the bed, not daring to look, and stumbled to the closet. I dressed as quickly as I could, wincing as my knickers elastic pinged against my poor, sore ninny. I cursed myself for wearing jeans. I should have worn a skirt. I could have walked home commando and let some cool air soothe me.

With as much dignity as I could muster, I walked to reception.

"Miss Adams, one Brazilian, that will be £25, please," the receptionist said.

My face coloured with the same heat that was coursing over my ninny. Why did she have to do that? I didn't need the sniggering Mrs. Amazonian to know what I'd had done. And fuck her luck, having those legs waxed!

I paid and left. I tried my hardest not to walk like John Wayne after a twenty-four hour horse ride through the Rockies, or wherever he rode.

As soon as I arrived home, I made a call.

"You nasty, horrible, bitch, cow sucking, nasty... Give me a minute, I'll come up with more," I said to Carla as she answered her phone.

"Cow sucking?"

"Yeah, cow sucking, shit face."

She laughed so hard down the phone I had no choice but to join in.

"I take it you're in pain?" she said.

"Yes, I'm in fucking pain, pain like I've never felt before. You should have warned me."

"Take a hot bath," she said.

"A hot bath! I'm on fire here already!" I screeched, actually screeched.

"Take a cold bath then."

"I'm that hot, I'd turn a cold bath into a Jacuzzi."

"Oh, you do exaggerate, Jayne."

"Okay, so not quite that hot but you know what I mean."

"It will settle down in a couple of hours. Put a packet of frozen peas on your fanny."

"I hate you," I said with a laugh.

"You'll love me when he goes down on you and..."

I cut the call before she could finish her sentence. I wasn't a prude; I'd had sex. Okay, boring sex, and not for a long time, but I wasn't about to be given a sex education lesson from my best friend.

I walked upstairs and into my bedroom. Gently peeling off my jeans then *pants,* I stared. Oh my! It wasn't often that I took a good look at my ninny. In fact, I couldn't recall a time I had, but there it was, all pink and practically bare. A small line of black hair was all that was left. Andi should have put a V on the end to create an arrow! I looked ridiculous. What was I thinking?

I rifled through my knickers drawer and found some old period pants, as Carla would call them, big knickers that would leave a little breathing space. I then slipped on my pyjama bottoms.

"Are you okay?" I heard as I walked down the stairs.

"I'm fine," I said through partially gritted teeth.

"You sure?" Kerry asked.

"No, actually I feel like I've just been assaulted."

"Assaulted?"

"I had a bikini wax. Why? I have no idea, well, Carla had the idea."

I watched her bite her lip to stifle the giggle. "I could have done that for you."

"Kerry, it was embarrassing enough with a stranger, let alone family."

"What did they do?"

"They plastered me in hot wax and tortured me with material strips."

"Oh, that doesn't sound good. Did they soften the hairs first?"

"I have no idea."

"Next time, let me do it. It's no different to your doctor looking at you. I see body parts all the time."

"Darling, I haven't seen that particular body part for many years. I have no intention of showing it again."

She laughed as we walked to the kitchen.

"I'll make you a cup of tea," she said.

As she sat opposite she smiled. "I like the new you. Not that I didn't like the old you."

"I don't understand."

"You're happier. I don't think I've ever heard you joke or laugh as much."

"I guess being single suits me."

"Ben says that you should have left him years ago. I never liked him; he always made me feel inferior. Sorry if I'm talking out of turn."

"You're not. He made me feel inferior too."

"I'm going to take a nap. This baby is exhausting me," she said.

I patted her belly as she walked past and settled down to check my emails.

*To: Jayne*
*From: Stefan*
*Date: 1 November 2014*
*Subject: Brrrr!*
*Snowing here and my apartment is freezing. I need warming up. ;) Flights are booked and I've rented a car. I know you offered to pick me up from the airport but I don't want to trouble you. I'm flying into Exeter, so I'll meet you at the cottage. I'll email times later. Have Ben & Kerry moved in yet? I bet you're excited. Can't be long now before the baby arrives.*
*S xx*

*To: Stefan*
*From: Jayne*
*Date: 1 November 2014*
*Subject: I have ideas for warming up ;)*
*I am excited, although still in denial that I'm about to be a grandmother. Did you print off directions? I can send them, if you want. Do you know that if you're ever stranded in a snowstorm the best way to warm up is get naked? I saw it on a survival programme once. Spoon naked! ;)*
*J xx*

*To: Jayne*

*From: Stefan*

*Date: 1 November 2014*

*Subject: Spoon!*

*Sounds good. I have a nice mental picture now. ;) Will there be snow in Cornwall?*

*S xx*


*To: Stefan*

*From: Jayne*

*Date: 1 November 2014*

*Subject: Snow in Cornwall!*

*Sadly, no. I don't think our coastal towns get much snow. You'd need the highlands for that. We are scheduled for a terrible winter though. Wind and rain will probably be the norm. Huddled in front of the fire, listening to the storms—my idea of bliss.*

*J xx*


I smiled as I read back. I'd questioned myself many times as to why we emailed when we could speak on the telephone. Our emails were always more fun, more flirtatious than our calls, and it worried me a little. Would there be that fun and banter when we met? I hoped so.

With just a few days before my holiday, I was frantic. I had no real winter clothes other than jeans and the odd sweater. Carla had loaned me a couple of items, but I was too much of a klutz to be allowed her designer wear. I'd be mortified to find I'd dripped red wine down the front of her cream cashmere cardigan. I sat on my bed, looking at a pile of clothes. There was little to do in Cornwall except walk so I'd made sure to add some jeans, socks and my walking boots. I'd telephoned Nora to ask what the weather was like. We'd stayed in contact, perhaps speaking once a month, and I filled her on what the boys were up to. Both Greg and Scott emailed periodically, often with tales of adventures or wanting girlfriend advice. I was hoping that Ben and Kerry would join me next year in Cornwall so they could all meet.

"I need to go into the village, want to meet for a coffee?" I asked Carla.

I'd telephoned her with my clothes woe.

"Sure, give me ten minutes?"

"I'll meet you there. I'm going to walk."

I wrapped up warm and headed out. The cold air stung my face but it felt invigorating. I pulled my scarf tighter around my neck and stuck my gloved hands in my coat pocket.

The warmth and steamy atmosphere of the coffee shop was welcome. I took a seat by the window and was immediately reminded of the time I'd sat there and Carla had mentioned our holiday. It was nearly a year to the day. So much had happened in the previous year. I watched Carla as she walked across the green. She had a military-style red coat with brass buttons, a black fur hat, all Russian-style, and black gloves. I knew those gloves would be kid leather and Burberry. Carla had a thing for leather gloves; I think she must have owned at least five pairs. They were all the same colour and all the same brand.

"Hello, my friend," she said as she approached.

"I just ordered you a coffee, good timing."

"So tell me about the clothes woe, or whatever you called it."

"I have jeans, t-shirts, a couple of sweaters and what you've loaned me. I need something to wear if we go out for dinner."

"I know it sounds odd but that black dress you wore at your dad's..." She hadn't wanted to say the word.

"Oh, yes. Good idea. I have a red silk scarf somewhere that will jazz it up."

"So check list. Manicure? Pedicure? Waxing? Condoms?"

"Done, done, not doing, and what?"

"Condoms, Jayne. You need to be prepared."

"For what? I'm not having sex with him, and I'm beyond getting pregnant, I think. Anyway, I'm on the pill."

"You might, and it's to prevent disease," she said, just as Jo, the coffee shop owner, placed our coffees on the table.

"Cake, dears? We don't sell condoms here," Jo asked.

Both Carla and I looked at her. I turned beetroot, Carla laughed.

"Oh, in my day, we had to reuse them. Washed them out in the sink, we did."

I wanted to die. I wanted to swallow my tongue and choke but then my ears would still be active. I needed to find a way to die instantly at that table. I was mortified.

"Oh, recycling at it's best, I guess," Carla said.

"We have coffee and walnut on offer today."

"Huh?" I asked, still in shock.

"Cake, dear. We have coffee and walnut."

"Erm, yes, thank you," I said.

204

Jo walked away; I stared at Carla.

"You can take that smile off your face. You know what will happen now, don't you? Every-fucking-one in the village will think I'm a raving slut."

"No one thinks that. Maybe that you're about to have rampant sex with a hot Danish guy, but that's all."

"No Danish, just cake," I heard.

"Jo, do you have your hearing aid in today?" Carla asked.

"I hear perfectly well. Now, did you want a Danish?"

"Oh, for fuck's sake," I whispered.

"I think Jayne wants a Danish, shame you don't have one here. The cake will do."

Jo placed two plates of cake on the table and winked at me as she walked away.

"I think a little bit of Danish won't hurt. Beats that twit of a husband of yours," she said over her shoulder.

"That's it, I'm out of here," I said.

Carla was still laughing; I was trying very hard to stay mortified. Jo was a clever old bird. She'd pretend to be deaf but she knew everything that went on in the village. The coffee shop was the hub; I guess she got to hear a lot of gossip.

"Kerry said something interesting today. She said she liked the 'new me.'"

"You can't see how much you've changed since Michael left. You're nearly back to the Jayne I knew pre-prick."

"Pre-prick? And nearly?"

"Pre-Michael. You've blossomed. When was the last time you rang me and invited me out for coffee? A long time ago, Jayne. I always had to nag you to leave the house."

"Really?"

"Yes. Now, can we get back to the condoms? This is a serious discussion."

"I doubt anything will happen. I'm not sure I want anything to happen, and shouldn't it be up to him to sort that type of thing out?"

"Maybe it will, maybe you will, and perhaps back in the fifties."

"I don't have time to drive into town anyway," I said.

"Then it's lucky we have a chemist here," she said with a smile.

"I'm not buying condoms from *our* chemist! I've known Mr. Harris since the kids were little."

"Drink up," she said.

"I'm not..."

"We are. I'll hold your hand."

We finished our coffees, ate the cake, and left our payment on the table. I wrapped my scarf around my neck as we stepped from the warmth of the coffee shop into the biting cold.

"I'm not buying them," I said, pouting as I did.

"Think of it as part of your liberation."

We pushed through the chemist's door, the bell tinkled to alert Mr. Harris he had a customer.

"Oh, God! It's her," I whispered.

Leaning on the counter was the gum-chewing, sullen assistant. Thankfully, she hadn't bothered to look up, she was too engrossed in her trash mag.

"Even better, that one won't bat an eyelash at you buying condoms."

"Stop saying the word and keep your voice down."

"Okay, keep your knickers on. Now, down that aisle."

As I started to walk, Sullen Girl looked up. I gulped; she'd seen me. I stopped to look at the row of shampoo and selected one, not that I needed shampoo. I began to read the label. I glanced, as subtly as I could, towards her. She stared back. I turned to speak to Carla; she wasn't there. The bitch had deserted me.

"Liberated," I whispered to myself. I took two sideways steps while still holding the bottle of shampoo.

Trying to appear as if I wasn't looking, I scanned the shelf in front of me. I gasped. I could hear the clip clop of high-heeled boots and knew Carla was somewhere in the shop. She had to be ducking down so I couldn't see her. I cursed her under my breath. Fishing in my pocket for my phone, I sent her a text.

*There are three fucking sizes!! Small, medium and large!!* I wanted to overdo the exclamation marks so she knew I was in a serious dilemma.

*Pick one.* Came the reply.

I studied the shelves, squinting to read the small text.

I furiously typed. *How the fuck do I know what size to pick! I might be insulting him, not that I'm going to use them.*

*Ha ha ha, go for safe, medium.*

"Medium," I whispered. I gasped again.

My fingers fumbled over my phone as I tried to text.

*They are flavoured! This is not good.*

*Strawberry medium then.*

*Why are they flavoured?*

*So they taste nice when you blow him?*

I dropped the shampoo, the bottle exploded, and a creamy liquid pooled over the grimy tiled floor.

I heard a tut and looked over in time to see Sullen Girl slam her trash mag on the counter.

"I'm sorry, I seem to have dropped this," I called out. I could hear snickering from the next aisle.

I grabbed a box from the shelf without looking and rushed to the counter. Sullen Girl picked up the box, studied it for way too long before raising her clearly painted on eyebrows at me. I raised my chin. Thank God the counter was high enough for her not to see my shaking legs. She scanned the box, slower than I imagined she normally would, and grunted something inaudible.

I opened my purse; my hands shook as I extracted a five-pound note. She raised her painted eyebrows even further. I looked at the register. Trying to disguise the shock I felt at the price, I fished around for a twenty. She handed me back the five-pound and a couple of coins as change.

"Want lube with that?" she said.

I blinked, probably the most I'd blinked in one go all day.

"No, I don't want lube with that."

Laughter coming from behind echoed around the thankfully empty shop. Sullen Girl slid the box towards me. I stared at it; she stared at me.

"Do you have a bag?"

She sighed, snapped her gum, then produced a virtually see through small plastic bag.

I placed the box in the bag, wrapping the excess plastic around it as a disguise then shoved it in my pocket. I walked, no, power walked, back out the shop.

I slumped against the wall, drained at the experience when Carla caught up with me.

"Don't. Do not speak," I said.

She slid her arm through mine. "I think we need wine," she

said.

I slumped into the sofa in the pub, beside a roaring fire, as Carla stood at the bar. She came back to two large glasses of red wine.

"I..." She started to speak.

I shook my head and raised my hand to halt her sentence.

I took one, and then two, large gulps of wine before letting my head fall back against the sofa and closed my eyes.

"Don't ever make me do that again," I said.

"You can buy them online next time," Carla replied.

My eyes snapped open, I growled at her. "You mean I just went through the most humiliating experience to learn I didn't have to?"

"Ah, but we had fun, didn't we?"

My head jolted forwards slightly and my eyes widened.

"Okay, maybe it wasn't fun for you. But you got them, so it's done. Drink your wine and relax. You're a modern woman, Jayne. We take responsibility for our sexual health."

"If you say the S word, the C word, or any other fucking word relating to fucking, this wine will go all over that nice Prada, or whatever it is, coat."

"You're very aggressive today."

Then she laughed, and I laughed. Tears rolled down my cheeks and my stomach ached. I clamped a hand over my mouth to quieten the sound. It took forever for us to calm down.

"Oh God, my sides hurt," I said with a groan.

"When was the last time you laughed like that?"

Her statement sobered me somewhat. "I don't know, years ago."

"You've changed so much over the past few months, I might

start calling you butterfly," she said with a laugh.

I wanted to laugh but didn't. Her statement made me realise how much of my life I'd missed, how miserable I'd been, and how I'd let that happen.

The house was quiet when I returned home. Ben's car was missing from the drive so I assumed he and Kerry were out. I unwrapped the scarf and shrugged off my coat.

"Hello, baby," I said to the dog. He looked up from his warm spot by the Aga.

I placed the carrier bag of shame, as I'd called it, on the counter while I waiting for the kettle to boil. I was so deep in thought I hadn't heard Kerry approach until she was next to me.

"Hi," she said.

I startled, as I did I spun around and my arm swiped the bag of shame to the floor. Dini jumped up, expecting it to be a bonus meal and grabbed it in his teeth. Both Kerry and I bent at the same time to retrieve the bag, which split in a tug of war, and the condoms bounced across the floor.

Before Dini could grab the box, Kerry had them in her hand. She looked at them, then at me. My cheeks flamed.

I watched as she slowly put them back on the counter. "Shall I make some tea?" she asked. All I could do was nod.

I slumped into a chair at the table, and she placed two mugs before taking a seat opposite.

"Not my business, Jayne," she said, as she dived into the biscuit barrel.

"Oh, fuck it. I'm meeting someone in Cornwall. Carla made me buy those but nothing is going to happen."

I took a deep breath, not sure of her response. "That's great news. I'd avoid the strawberry if I were you, though. Yucky taste."

I choked on the mouthful of tea I had just taken. "I didn't get strawberry."

She leaned back in her chair and reached for the box. "Multi-flavours."

"Chuck them in the bin. I guess you don't need them."

"I've embarrassed you, I'm sorry."

"Oh, don't be. I'm just not used to this dating lark. I have no idea what I'm doing. I really shouldn't go." I could feel tears brimming in my eyes.

"Do you want to talk about it?"

I took a deep breath. "I think you might dislike me after."

"Try me."

"I met him at the beginning of the year, on that holiday with Carla, and we kept in touch by email. He lives in Denmark. We've spoken a few times on the phone but I find it easier to email. I just…" I could feel myself getting choked up. "I just really like him, and I know this is wrong, he helped me."

"Helped you? How?"

"He doesn't know he did but I hated my life, Kerry. I was so miserable and when I wanted to escape, I emailed him. I feel guilty for that. I used him, his marriage broke up because of those emails, and I kept him a secret for a long time, but I don't know what I am to him."

"First, his marriage couldn't have been strong if he was emailing back. Maybe you both used each other for a release. I don't think you've anything to feel guilty about. Whatever it is, it's obviously a strong friendship, at least."

"But I was having an affair," I said quietly.

"Not sure I agree with you there. If you had a great marriage, would you have been emailing him? If Ben did the same, I'd be upset, for sure, but come on Jayne. Everyone knows Michael was screwing around. So good for you."

"Everyone knew?"

"Everyone. Why do you think Ben doesn't give a shit about him? We argued about it recently, he doesn't want him at this little one's christening."

"Oh."

"I thought he was being mean, this is Michael's grandchild, but I totally see where he's coming from. Ben, and me, have watched you get more and more sad over the past couple of years. So if you've met someone and you're going to meet up, I'm over the moon for you. And I know Ben will be, too."

I smiled at her. "We're just friends. I don't think anything will happen. This is just Carla being silly, and to be honest, Kerry, I wouldn't even know how to use one."

"Then best you learn." She opened the box and pulled out a foil packet.

"Don't use your teeth, you see that in the movies but you'll tear the condom." As she spoke she pointed to her belly and winked.

Then she did something I don't think I'll ever forget. She reached over to the kitchen counter and grabbed a courgette from the veg rack.

"Oh no, no, no, no. I get it. Should it happen, I'll figure it out. And I need that for a stir fry later."

"I'm teasing, anyway the courgette is too small."

"Can you keep all this to yourself? Carla knows, but I don't really want anyone else to. It might be nothing more than just a holiday between two friends."

"My lips are sealed."

*To: Jayne*

*From: Stefan*

*Date: 17 November 2014*

*Subject: Packed*

*Hey, J. All packed and ready for my flight tomorrow. I estimate I'll be at the cottage about eight in the evening. Looking forward to seeing you again. ;)*

*S xx*


*To: Stefan*

*From: Jayne*

*Date: 17 November 2014*

*Subject: Not packed!*

*Hi, I have a bunch of clothes piled on the bed, just need to decide how many coats, gloves and scarves to pack. It's cold here, although we don't have any snow. I'll have the kettle on. :)*

*J xx*


My nerves were shot. So many scenarios had run through my mind over the past couple of months. What if he didn't like me? What if I didn't like him? We would be stuck together for a week. I guessed I could always leave but how terrible would I look? I had made a backup plan with Kerry. If I texted her that things were not going well, she would ring me to say she thought she was in early labour and could I come home. I also kept my fingers crossed that would not be the case.

"Will you stop panicking?" Carla said.

We sat in the kitchen with a bottle of wine the night before my departure.

"I'm trying. It's okay for you, you've got the confidence of the population in your little finger."

"Have I? Or am I just pretending, like you?"

I looked at her. "My husband betrayed me, too. He had a child, the one thing I can never give someone. Believe me, Jayne, some days are a struggle to even get out of bed."

"Oh, I'm sorry. You just..."

"I know, I just get on with it. You'll be fine. He obviously likes you to arrange this trip, and after this week, you'll know if there's any future in it."

"I don't think there's a future. We live in two different countries."

"Then just have fun for this week, promise me that, at least."

After giving me a hug, Carla left and I locked up the house. I'd already packed the car with my case, some shopping, and Dini's things.

I left early the following morning. Kerry saw me off and made me promise to text as soon as I'd arrived. I knew I would reach the cottage before the allotted check-in time, but I planned to stop for a cup of tea with Nora and Jim. She had the cottage key and she'd let me in early if I wanted.

The traffic was light, and I soon found myself on that Atlantic Highway. It was a different view I encountered on that journey. The sky was grey and the sea angry. I loved it. I loved being by the sea in the summer and I loved it more in the winter. There was something beautiful about seeing Mother Nature at her fiercest.

"Come on in. Oh, it's so good to see you," Nora said as I opened the car door. "And bring that beautiful hound of yours, too," she added.

Nora pulled me into a hug; she squeezed me hard.

"So tell me all. What have you been up to? Any babies yet? And who is this friend you're meeting?"

So many questions! I laughed as I answered. I told her Stefan was just a friend who wanted to explore Cornwall. It wasn't a lie, as such. It was how I'd rationalised the holiday in my mind.

We had a cup of tea and I warmed myself in front of her little electric fire. I'd need to get the heating fixed in the car when I returned. It had blasted lukewarm air through its vents the whole journey.

After an hour, she handed me the key and I drove down the lane to the cottage. I smiled; it was like visiting it for the first time. The roses had died around the front door, and in their place was a tangle of woody stems.

Nothing had changed when I walked through the front door. Although the cottage was slightly warmer, I imagined Nora had been down in the morning to turn the heating on. I unpacked the shopping, settled the dog, and took my case upstairs. I hesitated in the double bedroom, unsure whether to unpack or not. What if Stefan wanted this room? Would it be more polite to wait and ask which room he wanted to sleep in?

"Liberated," I whispered to myself.

I placed the case on the bed and opened it. Sitting on top was the box of condoms. I really panicked then. What do I do with them? I could've put them in one of the bedside cabinets but what if he looked? For the umpteenth time, I wished I hadn't bought them. I stuffed them back in the case once I'd unpacked my clothes and stashed it in the bottom of the wardrobe. I hadn't made it out the bedroom door before I rushed back in and repacked the case. I didn't want Stefan to think I was being presumptuous or greedy that I wanted the double room.

I sat heavily on the bed; I simply wasn't cut out for this kind of thing. I had no idea what I was doing. I lugged the case to the hallway and left it there.

I decided to open a bottle of wine; a large glass of red was needed to calm my nerves and the anxiety that was building. I checked my watch and wished I hadn't. Stefan wouldn't arrive for another four hours. That was four hours of overthinking, of building nerves, and panic.

I tried to read; I looked at the clock. I paced the house; I looked at the clock. I took a walk along the beach with Dini; I looked at my watch.

It grew dark quickly, and as the night drew in, so the temperature fell. I lit the fire, already stacked with logs, and connected my phone to a docking station. I found a playlist and let the music calm me as I curled on the sofa.

A bright light swept across the living room. I held my breath

216

as I heard the crunch of tyres on the gravel outside, and Dini ran to the front door.

I slowly slid from the sofa and tiptoed to the hallway. A car door slammed, then another. I heard footsteps make their way to the front door and then a knock. I was frozen to the spot, I couldn't breathe and my chest constricted. A second knock came and I forced one foot in front of the other until my shaking hand reached for the door latch. I took a deep breath before opening the front door.

He stood there, all tousled-haired with piercing blue eyes. The man I hadn't seen in a year was standing, smiling back at me, on the front door step.

"Hey," he said, and that soft voice melted my insides.

"Hey, yourself."

"Are you going to let me in?" The skin around his eyes creased, as his smile grew broader.

"Oh, yes, sorry." I laughed as I opened the door wide and stood to one side.

I was unsure how to act. Any decision I should have made was taken from me when he stepped forwards and wrapped his arms around me. He kissed my cheek, just shy of my mouth, and I swear I heard him sigh.

"It's so good to see you again," he whispered into my hair. My heart hammered in my chest. "And this is Dini, I take it."

Dini butted his head between us, wanting attention. Stefan laughed as he leaned down to pet him. Dini gave his seal of approval by licking his face.

"Let me get you a glass of wine," I said, finally pulling myself together.

Stefan grabbed the bag he had left at the front door and moved it to the bottom of the stairs, so I could shut the door. I shivered at the drop in temperature in the hallway.

"Did you have a good flight?" I asked.

"It was okay. This is an amazing place, show me around?"

We headed to the kitchen, and he took a look out the back door as I poured him a glass of wine. As I handed him the wine and our hands brushed against each other's, a spark of static prickled my skin.

I led him to the living room. The fire crackled in the hearth and cast an orange glow over the room. Stefan placed his wine on the coffee table next to my half-drunk glass. From there, we headed back to the hallway; he collected his bag before we made our way up the stairs.

"There's two bedrooms, one double and a twin, and a bathroom with a shower. It's not very big and cold at night," I said with a laugh.

"I like cold at night," he replied.

I stood to one side outside the double bedroom and he walked in. As he did, he picked up my case and carried it with him. He placed both his holdall and my case on the bed.

"We can unpack later. How about food? I'm starving," he said.

My earlier reservations, the unease and anxiety, disappeared at the sight of his lopsided cheeky grin. It took a few minutes more for us to fall straight back into that easy way we'd experienced one-year prior.

"I take it you're expecting me to cook?" I teased.

"Baby, you do not want to experience my culinary skills, although washing up is something I am ace at."

My skin tingled at the 'baby.' "Come on then."

We headed back downstairs, and I was more than aware of the proximity of his body so close to mine as he descended behind me.

As I stood at the counter to slice some vegetables for a stir-fry, Stefan asked where the plates were. I looked up to the cupboard above my head. He stood behind me, closer than necessary, and with his hand on my hip, he reached over my shoulder to open the door.

I held the knife steady in my hand as static coursed through me from his touch. The chuckle under his breath had me thinking that he knew exactly what he was doing. I shook my head and smiled.

We sat at the kitchen table and ate. All the while, he told me of his new contract and how it had elevated his company within the marketing world. We talked about our children, the impending birth of my first grandchild, and made plans of what to do during our week in Cornwall.

I stood to clear the plates. "Let me do it, go and sit."

"We only have to stack the dishwasher."

"So I'll stack the dishwasher. Grab that wine, and go and sit."

I quite liked the forcefulness of his tone. I laughed, picked up the wine, and headed to the living room. The fire was still roaring, and I turned off the main light, opting for the subtle wall lights instead.

I winced at the crashing and banging and smiled at the conversation Stefan was having with Dini; those two would get along just fine.

I settled on the sofa and it wasn't long before he joined me. He sat beside me and placed his arm along the back.

"This really is a beautiful place. I miss an open fire. I like my apartment but it's not a home." He had shuffled closer as he spoke.

"I'm sorry you had to go through that. I feel partly responsible."

"It would have ended anyway. She had an affair, with my best friend of all people. I stuck in there because our sons were young. For some reason, she wanted to spend the next few years punishing me for that, so don't feel guilty. She went through my work emails one night when I wasn't there, saw our conversations and flipped. You know what, I was glad, really. It gave me the push I needed to finally leave."

"I'm so sorry to hear that."

"Stop saying sorry," he said with a laugh.

We fell into a comfortable silence, watching the fire and drinking our wine. I twirled the stem of mine in my fingers until I saw him place his on the coffee table then reach for mine. He took the glass from my hand and placed it next to his.

Stefan shuffled himself until he was facing me, his legs curled under him. His fingers twisted a strand of my hair.

"I'm so glad to be here," he said.

"So am I."

"Are you nervous? You're shaking, and you can't be cold."

I smiled. "I am."

He leaned closer. "So am I."

His soft lips found mine, and his hand snaked around my head, pulling me closer to him. I parted my lips as his tongue swiped across. As his kiss deepened, I placed my hand on the back of his head; my fingers gripped his hair. If I was shaking with nerves before, I was trembling with desire then.

My stomach flipped and I felt a heat creep over my body. Stefan slid down the sofa, pulling me on top of him. As I rested one hand on his chest, I could feel the muscles ripple under his shirt as he moved.

He held my head, his fingers dug into my scalp as his kiss became more desperate. He moaned and the sound reverberated through his chest and into mine. I felt him pull back as he moaned again.

"Ouch."

"Huh?"

"Cramp," he said then laughed.

"Oh shit, sorry."

I sat up, and as I did, he stood to stretch out his legs, I guessed.

"Great start, huh?"

I bit down on my lower lip to contain the laughter. He reached out for my hand and pulled me to my feet. Silently, he led me from the room and up the stairs. I stood in the middle of the bedroom, while he moved the case and his holdall from the bed. My legs shook and my skin puckered with goose bumps. I was verging on the edge of panic. I could feel my heart race and my breathing became shallow. Tears started to build in my eyes.

Stefan walked towards me. He ran his fingers down my cheek.

"Hey, what's wrong? We don't have to do this. Have I made a mistake here?"

I shook my head and took a deep breath.

"No, you haven't made a mistake. I just...I haven't done this for a while, a long while." I stammered over the words.

"We'll go slow. You call the shots, okay? If you want to stop, just say the word."

I nodded. He ran his hands down my sides to the hem of my t-shirt before lifting it over my head. I made to cross my arms over my side. He took my wrists and placed my arms back down.

"I've seen you in less clothes than you're in now," he said with a wink.

He lowered his head; I was expecting him to kiss my lips. Instead, he aimed for my shoulder, pushing my bra strap to one side. He kissed up the side of my neck as his hands roamed around my back to the clasp. He had it undone in seconds. His fingers trailed up and down my spine, sending shivers through me. I gripped the front of his shirt, more so to hold me up.

Stefan stepped away and looked at me. His eyes roamed my body and he smiled. He reached forwards to the waist of my jeans, popping the button then lowering the zip. He ran his hand around my waist under the jeans and slowly slid them down to my thighs. As he lowered to his knees, he kissed his way down my stomach. I gripped his hair and the most unbelievable feelings coursed through my body.

I felt on fire, my body was a mass of static and electrical currents, nerve endings sparked where his lips touched my skin. He reached up and grabbed the sides of my knickers as I stepped out of my jeans. With a painful slowness, he slid them to my ankles and I stepped out of those, too. I really panicked then. I crossed my legs and held my hands in front of me.

"Oh God, I haven't showered," I said.

He looked up at me, his head right at *that* place.

"Good, I don't like the taste of soap."

I didn't think my face could have gotten any redder. He laughed at my embarrassment but not in an unkind way. I let my arms relax down by my side as his lips kissed my navel.

Stefan stood and smiled at me. "Relax," he whispered.

He started to undo the buttons on his shirt. I reached forwards and gently knocked his hands away. He'd undressed me; I wanted to do the same to him. My hands shook a little as I popped open the buttons. I eased his shirt off his shoulders and down his arms, distracted by a tattoo across his ribs. Words I hadn't noticed when we had been in the Maldives.

"It's new," he said, noticing me studying it.

"I like it."

I continued to peel the shirt down his body and then encountered a problem. He wore cufflinks, I hadn't thought to remove them; his arms were trapped by his side.

"Oh for fuck's sake," I said, before letting my head fall to his chest and laughing.

"How about we give up on the sexy stripping, but you're going to have to undo those cufflinks. I can't reach now."

I undid the cufflinks while both of us laughed. It certainly broke the ice. He removed his shirt then wrapped his arms around me. I could feel the heat of his skin on mine and the hardness of his cock as he pressed against me.

I was determined to get it right. I undid his jeans and they fell to his ankles. He stepped out of them and as he did, somehow and only using his feet, he peeled off his socks. I tried my hardest not to look down. He hadn't worn pants; I felt his cock against my body as he pulled me back into his arms. He just held me; his arms were so tight around me I could feel his heart beating in his chest.

"I've waited a long time to do this," he whispered.

I could have cried. I was wrapped in the arms of a man who

wanted me.

Stefan pulled away, he picked me up and I squealed in surprise. He gently laid me on the bed and climbed on beside. At first, we lay facing each other; nothing was said as he ran his fingers down my side.

"Tell me what you like," he said quietly.

"I don't know what I like. I'm not very good at this."

"I want to punch that fucker you married. You're so beautiful. I can't believe he wouldn't want to spend every minute in bed with you."

Those words were my undoing, my unleashing, I guessed. I reached for his head, pulling him towards me. I wanted him, desperately. Our kiss was bruising; a clashing of teeth, nipping of lips kiss. I rolled to my back, Stefan rolled on top of me without breaking our kiss. His hands held my face and I wrapped my arms around his neck.

His lips moved from mine, kissing across my jaw and down the side of my neck. He slid down my body, propping himself on his elbows. My body convulsed as his tongue circled a nipple. I cried out as his teeth closed around it and he sucked. My stomach quivered with desire, and at that point, I got exactly what Carla meant by the 'fanny tingle.' A throbbing escalated between my thighs, and I could feel the wetness. He moved further down my stomach and I gripped the bed sheets beside me. As his tongue ran over my hipbone, I moaned. I raised my hips, wanting him. I felt his chuckle against my skin, skin so sensitive even the gentle brush of his hair as he moved left heat in its wake.

His nose ran over my clitoris, and he inhaled my scent before his tongue swiped. I clamped my jaw closed for fear of screaming out. His hands held my thighs, gently pushing them apart. I was totally exposed to him and when he pushed his tongue inside me, when his fingers dug into my skin and he moaned; I came for the first time—ever.

My stomach was a mass of quivers, my breath was laboured and I writhed under him. Wave after wave of pleasure washed over me. Sweat beaded on my upper lip and my mouth was dry. He was relentless, licking, sucking, and biting. He pushed my thighs up until my heels were near my backside, exposing me further. I raised my hips, wanting his tongue deeper.

I felt a sense of disappointment when he raised his head. His chin was smeared with my cum, and I watched as he licked his lips.

"You have any idea how good you taste?" he said.

I shook my head. He crawled up my body and when his face was close to mine, close enough for me to smell my arousal on him, he whispered.

"Lick."

I closed my eyes, partly from embarrassment, and let my tongue run over his jaw. I tasted myself, metallic, sharp yet strangely sweet. I licked his lips, they parted slightly and I bit down on the lower one. He moaned.

"I need to fuck you, so bad," he said, once he'd pulled his head away.

"I need you to fuck me," I replied, surprised that I'd spoken those words out loud.

He ground against me, and I raked my nails down his back. "We need a conversation first," he whispered.

I didn't want a conversation; I wanted him inside me. My body was screaming for his touch. I could feel his cock pressed into my stomach, throbbing as he moved.

"I'm on the pill," I blurted out.

He stilled before raising his hips. His hand trailed down my side and then he reached between us. His fingers teased my clitoris, spreading my juices before he guided his cock inside me.

He propped himself up on his elbows and moved so slowly it was agonising. I wrapped my legs around his waist, forcing him deeper. Then he kissed me hard and he fucked me fast.

Sweat dripped from his brow; I imagined it sizzling as it hit the heat of my skin. I'd never felt so much want, so much desire, as I dug my nails in his back and as I kissed and nipped his shoulder.

Butterflies partied in my stomach and my heart hammered in my chest as another orgasm raced over me. My body went rigid and I tightened my legs around his waist. I screamed out his name as I came.

Before I'd come down, Stefan tensed, his biceps shook and he came himself. He cried out words I didn't understand. His body relaxed on mine, his head rested in the crook of my neck, and for a few minutes, we were silent.

He rolled off me and lay on his side, facing me. I turned to face him. He smiled and gave me a wink.

"Wow," I said, not entirely sure how I should have reacted.

"It will be better next time. I waited too long to do that."

I heard Dini whine from downstairs. "I think he needs to go out," Stefan said.

I froze. I could feel wetness between my thighs, a lot of wetness. The first thought that ran through my mind was concern for the duvet we were lying on. The second thought was how to get up without it running down my legs. I closed my eyes and started to giggle.

"What?"

"I...I need to clean to up," I said, covering my eyes with my hand as if that would hide my embarrassment.

He laughed before rolling from the bed. From between parted fingers, I watched him stride naked to the bathroom. He returned with a box of tissues that he placed on my stomach. As he extracted one, I grabbed it from him.

"I think I can manage," I said.

"By the end of this week, you won't care," he said.

"Is that a promise?"

"Oh, yeah."

I cleaned up, slid from the bed and tried to be confident as I walked, naked, to the bathroom to grab a towel. I hadn't unpacked and had no pyjamas to wear. I'd never slept naked before. I had that silly thought instilled from childhood—never sleep naked in case the house caught fire. I had a fear of the fireman having to help me down a ladder with my bare arse on show.

While I stood shivering in the kitchen and Dini did his thing in the garden, I heard the shower. The thought of a naked Stefan under the jets of water made my stomach flip. Despite the lateness, I grabbed my phone and sent a quick text to Carla.

*We did IT.*

I turned off my phone. She was the kind of person to ring and want the full details.

Stefan was propped up against pillows and under the duvet when I returned to the bedroom.

"I'm going to take a quick shower," I said.

"Shame I've just had one, I would have joined you," he replied.

I took the quickest shower in history, making sure not to wet my hair and headed back the bedroom, still wrapped in a towel. Before I'd made a decision to rifle through my case for PJs, Stefan pulled back the duvet for me to climb under.

I snuggled into his side as he slid further down the bed and wrapped an arm around me. As he stifled a yawn, I turned off the bedside lamp. We'd left the blind open and the moon gave an eerie glow over the room.

"How do you feel?" he asked.

"Truthfully? Strange, but in a good way, and sleepy."

His arm tightened around my shoulders and I placed one hand on his chest. He turned his head to kiss me gently on the forehead.

# Chapter Thirteen

I woke but kept my eyes closed. I wanted to wallow in the warmth of being wrapped in his arms. I couldn't remember a time I'd ever felt so comfortable. When Michael and I had shared the same bed, we'd lay back-to-back with as much space between us as possible.

I felt Stefan shift position; he turned on his side to face me. I also felt his fingers push a strand of hair behind my ear and his breath as his face came closer. With my eyes still closed, I smiled.

"Good morning," he whispered before he kissed me.

I was conscious that I hadn't cleaned my teeth. I tried to keep my mouth closed but his tongue was persistent. I gave in to a sensuous kiss that had my stomach in knots.

As he pulled away, I finally opened my eyes. Piercing blue ones stared back at me.

"Did you sleep well?" I asked.

"I think that was the best night's sleep I've had in a long time."

I sighed as his fingers slid up and down my side.

"What would you like for breakfast?" I asked, then immediately realised it probably wasn't the most appropriate time to ask that question.

He smirked. "You."

My cheeks reddened, I could feel the heat as they flamed.

"I love it when you blush," he said as he ran his fingers down my cheek.

I blushed further.

He pushed himself up on one elbow and gently pushed at my hip so I lay on my back. His fingers trailed up and down my thigh.

"Do you like this?" he whispered. I nodded. "How about this?" His fingers circled my clitoris.

I gasped and parted my legs slightly. He hooked his ankle over mine; sliding my legs towards him and parting them further. I shivered and not with cold as he threw the duvet to the floor.

"I want to see all of you," he said.

He pushed one, then two, fingers inside me and his thumb caressed. I moaned as the pleasure intensified. I could feel his cock pressed against my hip and I reached for it. As his fingers brought me to an orgasm, I slid my hand up and down his cock, feeling the silkiness of his skin in my palm. I watched with utter fascination when he'd removed his fingers and placed them in his mouth. He sucked before rolling to his back and allowing me to pleasure him.

I gently scraped my fingernails against his balls. I tightened my grip on his cock as my hand moved, adjusting the pressure and speed according to his moans.

"Ride me," he said between gritted teeth.

I knelt up and swung one leg over his. I'd never done that before but instinctively lowered, guiding him in, and he held my hips as I did. I felt him at my very core. I placed my hands on his chest, the muscles tensed under my touch before I moved, slowly at first until I found my rhythm. As I lowered, he raised his hips, meeting me halfway. I curled my fingers and my nails dug into his skin each time he did.

I loved watching him. He kept his eyes open, watching me, and I could see the emotion flood his face. When he parted his lips, when his tongue ran gently over the lower one, I wanted to take that lip between my teeth. His chest expanded under my touch as he took deep breaths. He reached up and cupped my breasts in his hands, his palms roughly brushed over my nipples. I leaned down to kiss him and his moan filled my mouth. I felt his arms snake around me and squealed as he rolled me on my back.

I hooked my feet inside his thighs as he took over. He grabbed one wrist, then the other and raised my hands above my head. He kept his gaze on me as he fucked me, hard and fast. His face was close; I could feel his breath as he gasped and moaned. I mirrored him. My cries seemed to echo around the room. Blood rushed through my ears, the sound resembled the waves crashing on the shore and my body shook. A heat crept from my core to my neck as my orgasm built.

"Come for me, baby," he whispered.

It was as if on command my body obeyed. I dissolved around him, tears ran down my cheeks as waves of static, heat, and chill rolled over me. His stomach tensed, he shuddered, and threw back his head as he came. His body convulsed before he finally lowered his head, his body, and rested on me.

"Fuck," he whispered into my neck a minute later.

"Fuck, indeed," I replied before laughing.

He released my wrists from his grip; such was the firmness I was sure I'd have bruises. I wrapped my arms around him.

The sweat that had formed on his back had chilled, and as I ran my fingers over his spine, he shivered. Neither of us wanted to move. I had felt his cock soften inside me but I didn't want him to move. However, Dini had other ideas.

"I guess we have to get up," I said, after the persistent whining echoed up the stairs.

"We should be lucky he hasn't found his way up here."

I laughed as he rolled to one side. I didn't care about his cum running down my thigh as I walked to the bathroom. It was part of him, of us, of that magical hour we'd shared.

I smiled as I stood in the shower. I had no idea what *this* all meant, what would happen at the end of our week, but for the first time in forever, I didn't care about the future. I only wanted the *now*.

With a towel around me, I walked back into the bedroom. Stefan had made the bed and had placed my case and his holdall on it. He had started to unpack for me. I covered my eyes with my hands, allowing the towel to drop to the floor as he turned and held up that damned box of condoms.

"Medium? And flavoured," he teased.

I reached to grab the box from him, but he held his hand up high.

"Uh ah. I'm intrigued."

He opened the box whilst still holding it too high for me to grab. The packets spilled to the floor but he'd caught one. I watched as he used his teeth to tear one open. That 'fanny tingle' returned at the sight. There was something very raw and sexual about the way he was staring at me as he did. I took a deep breath.

"So," he said as he unrolled the condom over two fingers. "A medium," he added.

"How the heck was I supposed to know what size? And as for

flavoured...I was mortified, Carla made me buy those. I grabbed the first box that came to hand."

"I'm flattered that you even thought to, but..." He stalked towards me, peeling the condom off his fingers and dropping it to the floor.

I backed up until the back of my legs hit the bed. He reached forwards and placed both his hands on my hips. He turned me away from him.

"Am I just a medium?" he whispered into my back.

"No," I squeaked, inwardly cursing myself for fucking squeaking.

"Shall we see?"

He placed his hand between my shoulder blades and pushed the top half of my body down towards the bed. I had no idea what he was doing, but my body was telling me I was going to like it. I felt a pulsing between my thighs; my clitoris throbbed just at his words.

Using his foot, he kicked my legs apart. I had leaned on my forearms and my hands gripped the bedding. Before I could take a breath, he slammed into me. I cried out his name. He stilled.

"How long can Dini wait?" he whispered. The blond stubble on his chin scraped over my back.

"I don't care," I replied.

"Right answer."

I had never been fucked that way before. In fact, I'd never been fucked, full stop. Whatever it was that Michael had done bore no resemblance to what had happened that night, and what was happening that morning.

It was short, sharp, and deliciously erotic, especially when he called out words in his own language as he came.

I collapsed on the bed, landing on the edge of his holdall and laughed.

"Oh my God," I said.

"He won't save you from me," Stefan said as he took a step away.

I stood and faced him; laughing at the wicked grin he gave me.

"I could fuck you all day," he said.

"I think my body may protest at that. I've gone from nothing to...well, this."

"You must have been very frustrated. You'll need to show me what..."

I cut him off with a raise of my hand and headed from the room, back to the bathroom.

"Not going there," I called over my shoulder.

"Oh, you will. I want to see you make yourself come."

I laughed as I cleaned up. I was cleaning my teeth when he came into the bathroom and gave a brief kiss to my shoulder before climbing in the shower. He was so confident in his own skin, so brazen with his words—maybe it was a Danish thing. Maybe there was that British reserve, that stiff upper lip the world talked about.

I looked into the mirror, partly to watch him but I caught sight of myself. My eyes shone, my hair was a tangled mess, that 'just fucked' look women paid a fortune at the hairdressers for. Who was the woman looking back me? That woman had a smile from ear-to-ear, pink cheeks, and sparkling eyes.

I dressed in jeans and a sweater, pulled on some socks and rushed downstairs, worried about the dog. He was standing by the back door and if a dog could cross his legs, he would have. I hadn't

234

got the handle all the way open before he barged out.

I put the kettle on to boil and picked up my phone. I switched it on to see five messages from Carla, each one getting more demanding for information.

I laughed as I replied.

*Let's just say, I'll need treatment for thrush at this rate.*

I switched the phone off again and set about to grill some bacon. I could hear Stefan moving around in the room above me and smiled as I thought about the previous night and that morning. I'd surprised myself with how much I'd wanted his touch. I giggled as a thought crossed my mind. As gross as it sounded, the dam had been opened.

"Is he happy now?" I heard. Stefan strode into the room in jeans and a t-shirt.

"Yep. I'm grilling some bacon."

He stood behind me, wrapping his arms around my waist as I reboiled the kettle.

"Mmm, smells good. So does the bacon." He nipped the side of my neck before heading for the back garden.

I chuckled at his response and smiled further when I saw him throw a ball for Dini. I took a cup of coffee to the back door.

"You'll freeze out here," I said.

He smiled as he came towards me and took the cup from my hands. Dini bounded in and fussed around his bowl. I fed him, made bacon sandwiches and tea, then joined Stefan at the kitchen table.

"What do you want to do today?" I asked.

He raised his eyebrows and smirked.

"We can go for a walk along the beach," I said.

"Sure, sounds good. We should book that restaurant, the one you told me about."

We ate our breakfast, and I left him to clear the dishes, while I found my walking boots and coat.

Hand in hand, we walked the beach. We passed other dog walkers and bade a good morning. Using his phone, Stefan took pictures; he threw his arm around my shoulders for a selfie. I protested; I had no make-up on.

"I want to send that to my kids," he said as he fiddled with his phone.

I couldn't imagine he would realise how profound that statement was. I wasn't a secret in his life, and I felt a little guilty that it was only Carla and Kerry that knew about him.

He showed me the photo. My hair was streaming behind me, still a tangled mess, and we were laughing. It was a beautiful photograph, and I was surprised at the quality, bearing in mind he'd used his phone.

"You'll have to send that to me as well," I said.

Stefan picked up a stick that he threw to entertain Dini while we walked. We talked the whole length of the beach and up to the restaurant. I waited outside while he went in to book a table for the following evening.

He came out with two coffees and we sat on a bench, warming our hands with the mugs.

"I love it here. I can't believe I've never visited before," he said.

"I used to come here all the time as a child. See those huts over there?" I pointed along the road. "We used to stay in similar ones, they're gone now but all we did was spend every day on the beach."

After we'd drunk our coffee, we made the walk back. The cold air stung my face and brought colour to my cheeks. The sea pounded the centuries-old cliffs and we climbed over the shards of black rock that snaked their way out to sea. We must have walked for a couple of hours.

The kitchen was warm as we stepped in; it was welcoming. We left our boots just at the back door and Stefan took my coat to hang in the hallway.

He retrieved his laptop from his holdall, while I made more tea. He sat at the kitchen table to answer some emails he'd told me he needed to reply to, and I sat and watched. His brow furrowed in concentration and I watched his fingers fly over the keyboard. Fingers that had, only a few hours prior, brought such pleasure to me. I blushed.

"What are you thinking?" he asked without looking up. I guessed he'd seen me watching from the corner of his eye.

"Nothing. I'm going to grab my Kindle and read while you work."

I wasn't about to tell him what I was thinking. I walked to the living room and plugged my phone in the docking station. The wind had picked up, the window frames rattled and the room chilled. I decided to light the fire. Once it was lit, I curled on the sofa and read.

An hour or maybe two had passed before Stefan joined me. He gently pushed me to one side, so he could sit in the corner of the sofa with his legs outstretched, then pulled me between them. I rested with my back to his chest and his arms around me. He nuzzled my neck.

"Do you remember you asked me what my fantasy was?" he said.

"Oh, God, I do. Sorry, that was rather embarrassing."

He laughed before replying. "This is partly it. A fire roaring on a winter's day and you in my arms. It's been a lonely year, and your emails kept me going."

"Do you want to talk about it?"

He sighed. "I met Tasha in university. She was very driven, very educated. We dated on and off, we graduated then married, and she was awarded a position in a medical research facility to complete her PhD. She worked long hours and we didn't see each other that much. I started my business and I guess she looked down on marketing. She thought I could have done so much better for myself. Anyway, she fell pregnant and was furious about it. She wanted an abortion, and whether I was right or wrong, I wouldn't allow it. I'd have given up work and cared for our son myself."

Stefan paused, he shifted position; I wondered if he was uncomfortable in telling me his story.

"You don't have to tell me," I said quietly.

"I want to. She went through the pregnancy, blamed me for all the sickness, the clothes that didn't fit, but she carried on working, right up to the week before her due date. Alec was born and she was back at work within two weeks. We had a nanny and I worked from home most of the time. She never bonded with him, and even today, he finds it difficult to spend time with her. A couple of years went by, she fell pregnant again but that time seemed happier about it. It was while she was pregnant that I discovered she'd been sleeping with my best friend. Because of the baby, because of Alec, I forgave her and we limped on."

"Is he...?" I didn't finish my sentence, realising too late it was intrusive.

"My son? Biologically I don't know, to be honest. I don't know why we stayed together for as long as we did. There was no love between us. I could forgive the affair, but I could never forgive her favouring Eric. Alec lives with me now."

"I'm so sorry to hear that. Do you speak now?"

"Not unless we have to. You know, you're the only person I've told this to. Tasha knows I've questioned Eric's paternity but we've never really spoken about it."

"I'm glad you can talk to me."

"So am I."

We settled into a comfortable silence. The fire crackled in the hearth and the sun began to set. We had dozed on and off, chatted some more about our friends, our lives, and our children. My stomach grumbled, reminding me that we had missed lunch.

"How about I make us dinner?" I said, reluctant to leave the warmth of his embrace.

I slid my legs from the sofa and stood, stretching my arms over my head. As I walked around the sofa and to the door, Stefan reached out and his fingers trailed down my arm.

He stood and followed me.

"What do you want me to do?" he asked.

"You can let Dini out and then lay the table."

"I know what I'd like to lay on the table," he replied with a laugh.

"Is it normal for the Danes to think about sex all the time?" I teased.

"I can't help it if I find you desirable."

"I find it strange, that someone wants me," I said, my voice lowered to a whisper.

He stopped in his tracks, his hand hovered over the door handle, and he turned his head to look at me. I stared at him, at the sadness I was convinced I'd seen in his eyes.

He opened the door and Dini bounded out, once he'd closed it, he walked towards me.

"I wanted you from the moment you stumbled on a speed boat. I don't know what it is about you, but I need you. I've never connected with someone the way I connect with you. You pull me, all the time. I got scared about that, and I still kick myself for sending that fucking letter."

He was close; his hands were either side of me on the countertop. I looked up at him.

"I know you feel the same," he whispered.

I reached up and cupped his face with my hands, he lowered his head so his mouth was just millimetres from mine. His body pressed me on to the cupboards, and I could feel his erection against my stomach.

"I don't know how this is going to work," I said.

"We'll figure it out, we have to. For now, I'll fly back and forth, but I want you to visit me as well."

His kiss was gentle at first, deepening as his want for me grew. I moaned and gripped the hair at the nape of his neck. His stubble scratched against my face as he devoured my mouth. My legs grew weak; never had I been kissed with such passion. The dog whining to be let back in broke the moment.

He chuckled and rested his forehead against mine.

"I don't know what it is about you, Jayne, I just know I don't want to let you go."

He stepped away and walked to the back door. I scowled at

Dini as he sat, wagged his tail, and looked between us.

"I'll feed the dog, you feed me," Stefan said.

I laughed as I raided the fridge. I placed some cheeses, meats and breads on the table. Stefan opened a bottle of red wine.

"How about we take this into the living room?" he suggested.

We carried the plates and wine, set them on the coffee table, and picnicked in front of the fire as the evening drew in.

Once we had eaten, I sat on the floor between Stefan's legs as he rested his back against the sofa. His hands were on my thighs, gently caressing until he moved them up to my waist. As he kissed my neck, he undid my jeans. I gripped his thighs as he slid his hand inside.

"This is the second part of my fantasy," he whispered.

His fingers teased my clitoris. Just the slightest touch from him had me moaning. I slid my jeans down my thighs, I drew my knees towards me, and they fell to my ankles. I kicked them off. I leaned forwards slightly and pulled my t-shirt over my head, I unclasped my bra, and threw the clothes to one side.

I pushed myself from the floor, turning to straddle his lap. I took hold of the hem of his t-shirt and lifted it over his head.

With just the flickering flames for light, I explored his body. I kissed his neck, letting my tongue run along his collarbone. I kissed his throat and up his chin. I held his head in my hands and kissed his mouth.

I raised my body slightly so he could remove his jeans and pants, all without breaking that kiss. There was something I wanted to do for him, something I'd never done before. I lowered my head, gently licking then nipping his nipple. I shuffled back slightly as I lowered further. My heart hammered in my chest as my tongue gently touched the tip of his hard cock. I heard his sharp intake of breath as my lips closed around him.

I could feel my body shaking with nerves. I held his hips as I dipped my head lower, taking him further into my mouth and sucked as I released. His hands fisted in my hair, gripping and pulling. When I heard him moan, I smiled. Perhaps I wasn't doing such a bad job after all.

Encouraged by his moans, by the tightening of his hands in my hair, I took him further. I sucked harder and let my tongue swirl around the tip before I lowered again.

"Fuck," he said, as I took him to the back of my throat.

I reached below him to cup his balls with one of my hands. I gently rolled them in my palm.

"Jayne, shit, you're going to have to stop," he growled.

I didn't want to stop; I wanted to bring him to his release. It wasn't something I was prepared for though. He tried to warn me, he pulled my hair to encourage me to release him. I felt his cock pulse, warm liquid shot to the back of my throat. I tried to swallow but his cum filled my mouth quicker than I could. I raised my head holding it in my mouth. My eyes were wide with, well, shock, I guessed.

He laughed when he saw me. I tried not to smile and covered my mouth with one hand. I looked around the room, not sure what I was looking for. Stefan handed me his t-shirt and I deposited the contents of my mouth into it.

"Oh my God, I'm so sorry," I said.

"First time, huh?"

"Can you guess?" My face burned.

"I'm sorry for laughing, but your face," he continued to laugh.

Tears formed in my eyes. "Hey, come here," he said.

I shuffled on my knees and he held my head in his hands.

"That was an amazing blow job. I'm sorry for laughing."

"I'm just crap at all this," I said.

"No you're not. Jesus, Jayne, if you were crap, I wouldn't have come."

I chuckled. I don't think I'd ever had a conversation with as many sex terms before.

He kissed me, tenderly. It concerned me that he would taste himself on my tongue. He held the back of my head and twisted his body. He gently laid me down on the rug and lay beside me.

"I want to make love to you," he whispered.

There was something in the way he said those words that had tears roll down my cheeks. He kissed my eyelids; his lips followed the path the tears had left. He kissed every part of my body.

He was gentle, he took his time and did as he said—he made love to me like no man has ever done before.

# Chapter Fourteen

Stefan and I spent the following day driving along the coast, stopping to take pictures and walk along the many beaches we found. We found a little pub and sat in front of the fire to eat lunch. Most of all, we didn't stop talking or laughing.

"We're going to have to get ready," I said.

We had been back at the cottage for a couple of hours and I'd taken a nap on the sofa. The sea air and the walking had worn me out.

"You go shower first, I'll be up in a minute," he said.

Stefan had been sitting beside me, with his laptop resting on his thighs. He closed the lid and picked up his phone.

"I'll just give Alec a call," he said with a smile.

I headed upstairs and stripped off before stepping under the warms jets of the shower. The only thing the cottage lacked was a power shower, but the gentle fall of water was enough to wash my hair and clean my body.

I was partially dressed and blow-drying my hair when Stefan stepped into the bedroom with a towel around his waist, having just showered himself. He kissed my shoulder as he passed to take a clean shirt from the wardrobe.

"Alec asked me to say hi," he said.

"How is he?"

"Good, probably partying all week." Stefan chuckled at the thought.

It was nice that he'd spoken about me to his children. I made a plan that I would do the same. Not that I was sure how our 'relationship' was going to work, but I wanted to be open to everyone.

His stomach muscles flexed as he shrugged on the shirt, his biceps bulged as he bent his arms to do the buttons. The tight pants he wore showed off his glorious backside.

"Checking me out?" he asked, catching me staring at him.

"Always."

He came to stand behind me as I sat at the dressing table. He reached over my shoulder and slid his hand inside the cup of my bra. My nipple instantly hardened.

"Yep, thought so," he said with a wink.

"You are so conceited." I laughed as he retracted his hand.

"Ah, but you love me anyway."

I stilled at his words; he stilled at his words. I watched him watching me in the mirror. He leaned down to kiss my neck.

"Jeg elsker dig," he whispered and then he walked away.

I hadn't understood what he'd said. I'd heard him say it the previous evening when we'd made love in front of the fire, and it had slipped my mind to ask for a translation.

I finished my hair, applied my make-up, all the while thinking. I loved him, there was no doubt about that; I'd loved him for a while. I needed to understand what was happening between us, and I needed to make our relationship public.

I chose the black dress and slipped the red silk scarf around my neck to hide my cleavage. I grabbed my shoes from under the dresser and made my way downstairs.

I heard Stefan wolf-whistle as I walked into the kitchen. He had fed Dini and was standing by the back door, waiting for him to return.

"Oh, stop it," I said.

"You look sexy as fuck."

I laughed. I grabbed my bag and the car keys. I had opted to drive since Stefan had been driving all day. We locked up the cottage and headed for the restaurant.

We were seated immediately, the restaurant was only half-full, and judging by the accents I heard, I assumed most were locals. The lighting was low and a candle burned in the centre of each wooden table. As a beach café in the evenings, Life's A Beach was unrecognisable from its daytime job.

Menus were placed in front of us and I noticed the waitress focussing her attention on Stefan. He was a good-looking man. Those piercing blue eyes mesmerised, his messy blond hair looked like he'd just got out of bed, and his athletic fit body attracted women. I think I fell a little more in love with him when he took my hand in his across the table.

"Baby, what do you want to eat?" he said in a seductive voice.

I placed my order and without looking at the waitress, he told her what he wanted and she left.

He made no mention of the salivating waitress, perhaps he hadn't noticed. His attention was focused on me. He ran his thumb across my knuckles as he stared at me. I watched as he slowly ran his tongue over his lower lip.

"I have a plan for that scarf later," he whispered.

I frowned, my hand instinctively played with the silk material. His gaze was intense. I wanted to draw my eyes from his but found it impossible. The chatter of patrons, the smells of cooking, all seemed to disappear. In their place was just him. A cough interrupted us; he sat back in his chair and slowly looked up to the waitress, who was holding the wine.

"Do you want to taste it?" she asked.

"Always." Stefan slid his glass towards her but kept his lust-filled eyes on me.

Her hands shook a little as she poured. I wanted to comfort her, to tell her he had the same effect on me, and I stifled a giggle at the thought.

I watched as he swirled the wine, slowly sipped before, again, running his tongue over his lip. It was a display of pure sexual teasing. He nodded and she poured two glasses.

When she left, he raised his glass to me. "To us," he said.

I clinked my glass against his before taking a sip of the rich red wine.

Our meals were placed on the table and our chat returned to safe ground. Until I watched him use his fingers to peel a prawn that he then held out to me.

"Taste," he said.

I reached forward with my fork. He shook his head. I leaned slightly across the table and opened my lips. He placed the prawn in my mouth, leaving his fingers resting on my tongue a little too long. As I closed my lips, he slowly pulled them out.

"Mmm, that was nice," I said. I could play his game.

We never made it to dessert. Stefan asked for the bill, and without taking his eyes from mine, he laid his credit card on the small leather folder when it arrived. Once he had paid, he took my hand and led me from the restaurant. As we reached the car, thankfully parked in the darkest corner of the car park, he pushed me against the door.

"Feel what you do to me," he said, as he took my hand and placed it over his cock.

I gently squeezed the bulge straining against the front of his jeans. He pressed his body against mine, trapping my hand. With two hands on either side of my face, he kissed me. It was a kiss filled with desperation, with longing, and one that left me breathless.

A sweep of light across the car park startled me. A car was approaching. I giggled as Stefan took a step back. I saw him take a deep breath before he reached around me to open my door.

As I drove, he ran his hand up my thigh. I lifted slightly off the seat so my dress would rise with his touch until it was nearly around my waist. When his fingers trailed over my knickers, I pushed my foot harder on the accelerator.

"I'm going to drive into that bush if you keep doing that," I said, my voice rose on each word.

"I'm going to drive my fingers into that..."

"Oh no, don't tell me that. Not now."

His laughter had a wicked edge to it. Somehow, we made it back. I fumbled with my seat belt to release myself from the car, and then fumbled some more trying to find the cottage keys in my bag. He took them from me and unlocked the door. I hadn't taken more than a couple of steps into the hallway before he grabbed my waist and pushed me roughly against the wall.

His mouth crashed down on mine, his hands ran up my thighs, dragging my dress to my waist, and I heard the rip of lace as he tore the knickers from my body. My stomach knotted at the sound and my body shook.

I grabbed the top of his jeans, desperate to get them undone, and as they fell, I released his cock from his pants. He groaned as he lifted first one thigh and then the other. His body held me against the wall as I wrapped my legs around his waist. Without a word he pushed into me. I placed my arms around his neck and held on.

My back scraped against the stone wall as he fucked me. His head was in the crook of my neck and he said those words, over and over.

"Jeg elsker dig."

I cried out as my stomach convulsed, as my body became a mass of static and as heat coursed over my skin. My orgasm hit me hard and fast. I gasped for breath, and my fingers dug into his back.

I saw him throw back his head, his jaw was clenched, and he cried out through gritted teeth as he came.

"Fuck," he said.

My legs had started to quiver. I let my forehead fall to his shoulder and felt the sting across my shoulder blades from the bare brick they had been rubbing against.

He slowly released my legs but kept hold of my waist. I was thankful; I didn't think they would hold me up. When he finally looked at me, he smiled as he bit down on his lower lip.

"Fuck," he whispered.

Before I could reply, he stepped out of his jeans, readjusted his cock back in his pants and scooped me up. I laughed as he carried me up the stairs.

"Do you remember your fantasy?" he whispered.

The bedroom was dark but the sky outside clear. The moon lit the room as he placed me in front of the full-length mirror that stood in one corner.

He moved behind me, unzipped my dress, and it pooled around my feet. He reached around and gently untied the scarf, sliding it slowly from my neck. I stood in just my bra, watching as he lifted the scarf and placed it over my eyes. He tied it at the back of my head.

"Trust me," he whispered.

I felt him unclasp my bra and slide the straps from my shoulders. I felt his hot breath and his soft lips as they trailed down my back. I gasped as his tongue circled over my arse.

"Kneel down," he said. I complied; my legs were struggling to hold me up.

"Part your legs," he whispered.

I felt him kneel behind me, his already hard cock rested against my arse.

"Touch yourself," he said. I hesitated. "Don't think about it, just picture in your mind what I do to you."

My hand shook as I tentatively placed my fingers just above my clitoris. I leaned back into him. His arms snaked around my chest, each hand cupping a breast, and I could feel his breath on my neck as he looked over my shoulder.

My heart hammered as I slowly touched. The wetness surprised me.

"That's me, my cum. Now spread it," he said. His voice was so quiet I strained to hear.

The stickiness coated my fingers as I explored myself. My flesh burned at my touch. When I ran the tip of my fingers over my clitoris, it was as if an electrical current had shot through me. I moaned.

"Fuck yourself."

I pushed two fingers inside me. I was wet, very wet, and hot.

"I want my tongue in you, I want to taste you and drink in your cum. Can you feel my tongue?" In my mind I could see and feel him. I nodded.

"And then I'm going to slam my cock inside you so hard you'll feel it here." He placed his hand on my lower stomach.

"You'll feel me fuck you hard because I can't get deep enough, I can't get fast enough. I can't get enough of you."

His voice was raspy, his breathing accelerated.

"I can *never* get enough of you," he whispered.

I moaned. I struggled to breathe as my fingers moved faster at his words and at the images I had in my head.

"Now watch," he said. He whipped the scarf from my face and my jaw fell open in shock.

I didn't recognise the person in front of me, the reflection in the mirror wasn't mine. My eyes were hooded; the normally brilliant green was dark as my pupils dilated. My hair was a mess, a sexy mess. My nipples were so hard the skin around them had puckered, but it was my fingers I watched. They stroked, they teased, they were coated in juices, white sticky cum.

Stefan moved slightly to one side. I watched as he gripped his cock with one hand and the other wrapped in my hair. I stared with total fascination as he pleasured himself. His hand slid effortlessly up his cock, his thumb ran over the tip before lowering. Unconsciously I matched his speed. The faster he stroked, the faster I fucked myself. I'd never seen a man masturbate before, never seen the emotions that crossed his face, or the vein that bulged on his bicep and forehead as he gritted his teeth.

"I need to be inside you," he growled.

He moved behind me, pushing my shoulder blades so I fell forwards onto my palms. Before I had a chance to take a breath, he pushed into me so hard I jolted forward, and my knees slid on the carpet. He gripped my hair and raised my head.

"Watch us," he said, his voice was harsh.

I watched. I watched him kneeling behind me, I watched him pound in and out while I was on all fours. I watched him pull my hair to keep my head up, and he watched me.

Sweat rolled down his forehead and dripped onto my arse. I dug my fingers into the carpet as pure carnal desire washed over me. I forced myself back onto every thrust he gave, needing him deeper. I screamed out his name as I watched his cum drip down my inner thigh.

My vision blurred, a noise filled my head, just white noise. A pulse throbbed in my neck as blood pumped hard around my body. I wanted to tear at his skin, I wanted to bite and kiss and taste. I lowered to my elbows as my arms shook, loving the tighter pulls on my hair, and then I came. A freight train hit me right at my core. I couldn't control the muscle contractions and I had no desire to. Stefan collapsed on top of me; his shaking arms landed either side of my head. He rested his forehead on my back, and as my legs gave out and I slid to the floor, he lay on top of me.

I couldn't speak, I couldn't catch my breath but I cried. Sobs wracked my body. Stefan rolled to one side and cradled me to his chest. We were a mess of sweat that had started to chill on our bodies, of cum that had started to dry on our skin.

"Tell me. Please, tell me," he said. When I looked at him, tears had formed in his eyes.

"Jeg elsker dig," I whispered.

I'd known what that meant without the need for a translation. *I love you.*

He closed his eyes. As he rested his back against the bed and pulled me into his lap, tears rolled down his face.

"I can't let go of you," he said.

"Don't ever let go of me," I whispered.

My body was stiff and cold when I opened my eyes. It couldn't have been more than an hour that had passed.

I had to move, my legs were cramping. I slowly stood and held out my hands to help him. He pulled me to his chest and kissed the top of my head.

"I need to shower," I said.

"How disgusting would you think I was if I told you I loved the smell of us on your skin?"

"Oh...I might have to think on that one."

He laughed as he took my hand and we walked to the bathroom. He turned on the shower and led me in. I stood as he poured gel onto the sponge and ran it over my body. He washed me, and in return, I washed him.

Wrapped in towels, we headed back to the bedroom. I dried my body and my hair as best as I could before climbing under the duvet.

"I'll let Dini out then be back up," he said. He strode with his towel around his waist from the room.

I lay thinking on what had happened. There had always been a connection but something had changed. Our souls had merged, we'd become one. I tried to fight the heaviness in my eyelids, tried to stay awake. I felt the bed dip as he climbed in and wrapped his arms around me. I heard him whisper that he loved me. I think I said it back. I know it ran through my mind over and over.

I woke with a start, the room was dark and I lay still, listening. A few seconds later I heard it again—a knocking on wood.

"Stefan, wake up," I said.

I climbed from the bed and grabbed my dressing gown. I wrapped it around me as I walked from the bedroom.

"Wait. Don't go down, stay here," I heard but was already halfway down the stairs.

I heard him curse and stumble across the floor above me. Urgent, rapid knocking came from the front door. I reached out to open it as Stefan bounded down the stairs. I had the door open as he reached the last step.

Carla stood under the porch light and as I looked at her, I knew.

I don't know when, but I know I had taken a step back. I know I had fallen to my knees, but what I couldn't figure out was where the noise was coming from. The sound was like an animal being tortured, being mutilated. It echoed around the room, and I searched frantically for its origins. I felt arms around me but I fought. I needed to save the animal; maybe it was Dini. It was only when I had no breath left that I realised the sound had come from within me.

I stilled, confused. My eyes wouldn't focus. I knew Stefan had knelt in front of me; I could feel his chest under my fingers. I could also feel stickiness. I brought my fingers close to my eyes and saw blood. Whose blood was on my fingers?

I looked up, and as my vision came into focus, I saw Carla. Her hands covered her mouth and she sobbed. Why was she here? Why was she crying?

And then I remembered her words. I opened my mouth and screamed again.

My world dissolved, imploded. Pain ripped over me like a knife through soft butter. I hurt like I'd never hurt before. I wrapped my arms around myself and rocked, trying to lessen the pain, trying to stop the words I'd heard from rushing around my brain. I wanted to sing—loudly—to drown out those words. But no matter how loudly I screamed, and I think that was in my head, those words were still there.

My son was dead.

# Chapter Fifteen

I was sat on the sofa; I had no recollection of getting there. Stefan was kneeling in front of me and was lifting a foot to place it in the leg of my jeans.

"Why are you dressing me?" I asked, my voice was hoarse.

"We need to go," I heard.

Carla had sat beside me. She took one of my hands in hers.

"Go where?"

"We need to go home," she said.

I watched her look towards Stefan, and when I followed her gaze I saw the gouges down his chest. I held my fingers to them. I had done that.

"Baby, look at me. Can you hear me?" he said.

I looked up into his eyes. "Yes," I said.

"Carla will take you home. I'll pack up here and bring your car back to you, okay?"

"Pack up," I said with a nod.

He held my hands and pulled me to my feet. I felt him raise my jeans to my waist and then a sweater was placed over my head. I sat back down on the sofa. Stefan and Carla talked, they made plans but I wasn't interested.

I didn't care about my things. I just wanted to get my dog and go. I wanted to see that it was a terrible mistake. It wasn't my son; it was someone else's. I would laugh and then feel terrible guilt when I told them they had it wrong.

Ben would come rushing home and I'd hold him in my arms, maybe cry with relief.

I stood and strode to the front door. I heard my name being called. Stefan wrapped me in his arms.

"I'll be there as quick as I can, okay?" he said. I couldn't answer. I just nodded.

I climbed in the passenger seat of Carla's car, Dini was settled in the back and she backed out of the drive. I was silent until we hit the Atlantic Highway.

"Tell me again," I whispered.

"Oh, Jayne. I can't."

"Please, tell me again."

I hadn't looked at her. I knew she was crying; I could hear it in her voice.

"Ben was driving home, they think his car skidded on some ice. I don't know all the details. He hit his head."

"And you think he's dead?"

"He's... He didn't make it. They got him to the hospital but he didn't make it."

"Who was with him?"

She didn't answer me. I sank in my seat and cradled my legs to my chest. Reality was starting to creep into my thoughts. My son was dead. I cried. I cried so hard my stomach hurt.

"He died alone, didn't he?" I said between sobs.

Again, she didn't answer and I knew then. While I'd been having the most amazing time of my life, while I'd been in the arms of a man only two people knew about, while I'd been brought to orgasm after orgasm, my son had died alone. The guilt consumed me. I heaved.

Carla screeched to a halt on the hard shoulder of the motorway, just in time for me to open the door and throw up over the tarmac. Exhausted, I slumped back into the car seat and we continued the journey in silence.

My nerves were jangling as we pulled up onto my drive. Every light in the house was blazing. The front door opened as I exited the car. My mum stood on the doorstep with tears streaming down her face. I ran to her and she wrapped her arms around me. She led me into the living room. Kerry sat on the sofa with her mum. She stood. I walked towards her and she sobbed into my chest. I sat her down and took the seat vacated by her mother.

"What happened?" I asked.

"I don't know. A policeman knocked on the door. I panicked and called Carla." She was inconsolable.

While we sat, a policewoman walked from the kitchen carrying a tray of mugs. It irked me that she had been helping herself in my house. She placed the tray on the coffee table then introduced herself as a family liaison officer. I nodded at her.

"I want to see my son," I said.

"I'll make some calls," she replied.

I had no idea what to do. I kept my arm around Kerry's shoulder and watched people make calls, bustle around as if they knew what to do.

"Has anyone contacted Michael?" I asked.

"He's on his way," Carla replied.

"From Japan?"

"No, he's at his mother's."

"Casey!"

"She's with Michael," my mum answered.

"Why? Why is she not here?"

No one answered me. I was numb. I was cold, so cold that I couldn't stop shivering. I wouldn't believe it until I'd seen my son.

The policewoman spoke to Carla and I was told that I could see Ben.

"Do you want to come?" I asked Kerry.

She nodded and I asked Carla to let Michael know. I needed to go, I needed to see for myself. I refused to allow myself to believe what I'd been told, and I refused to cry anymore until the nightmare was over.

Kerry and I were taken by police car to the hospital. When we arrived I saw Michael pacing. We walked towards him.

"Where the fuck have you been?" he shouted.

His vicious tone halted me in my tracks.

"My son died alone. Where have you been?" he asked again.

The policewoman stepped between us.

"Why don't we find out where Ben is? You can discuss this later," she said. I grew to like her then.

We were taken to a room and asked to wait. Michael continued to pace while ignoring us, and my blood started to boil. It could have only been minutes, but sitting in the confines of that room with the anger radiating from Michael and suffocating me had me lose track of time.

"We're ready for you now," I heard. A doctor had walked into the room.

We followed. I wasn't ready. My head pounded, my palms

sweated, and my chest hurt. The door was opened and I hesitated. I could see him. I could see my son lying on a bed with a sheet covering him, leaving only his head exposed.

They had shaved his hair. Why had they shaved his hair?

I sobbed as I walked forward. I wasn't aware of anyone else in the room; it was just Ben and me. I closed my eyes as I reached out to touch his cheek.

"He's cold. He needs a blanket," I whispered.

I could hear someone talking; a clinical description was being given as to what had happened to my son. I didn't want to listen; I didn't want to know. My son was dead.

I ran from the room, passing a sobbing Kerry on the way. I couldn't stop; I couldn't help her. I needed air. I felt as if I was suffocating, couldn't drag enough oxygen into my lungs. In my head, or maybe it was real, I screamed until I reached the front door and ran out into the early morning. I slid down a wall onto the dirty pavement and let my head fall to my knees.

"Shall I take you home?"

I looked up and into the eyes of the liaison officer. Kerry stood beside her and I forced myself to my feet. I pulled Kerry into my arms but I had no words of comfort.

Michael strode past and climbed into his car. He roared away without a word to us. When we arrived home, I noticed his car parked outside my house. I also saw my own car parked on the drive.

As I walked into the living room, I felt the hostility. My in-laws stood with Casey between them. Carla stood next to Stefan. Michael stood with his arms folded over his chest and leaned against the window.

"Where were you, and who is this?" Michael asked.

"I don't think that's any of your business," Carla answered.

I walked towards Casey with outstretched arms; I expected her to run to me. Instead, I watched her take a step back, shielding herself behind her grandfather.

"So while my brother died, alone, you were on holiday fucking this man?" She spat the words at me.

I was stunned into silence.

"Casey!" For the first time Kerry had spoken.

"Don't you 'Casey' me. My brother died and she should have been there!"

"How about you? Or him? Either of you could have gotten there. You knew, Michael. They told you but not me. I'm carrying his child and you didn't think to tell me. You sent a policeman here," Kerry said.

"Is that true?" I asked. The room quietened. "You knew and you didn't get to our son? You fucking coward."

I flew at him. Years of frustration, of watching him neglect his only son exploded from me. I punch, kicked, scratched, but before I'd managed to do any real damage, I felt two arms wrap around me. I screamed and kicked out as I was pulled away.

"Baby, shush. Calm down," Stefan said.

I heard a bitter laugh. Casey and the in-laws walked towards me; I was still trapped in Stefan's arms.

"You're a slut," my daughter said before she slapped my face.

I looked at her. "Get out of my house!" I screamed at them all.

"Get out of my fucking house!"

As they walked away, I collapsed to the floor, a sobbing mess. The only noise in the room was tears and heartbreak.

"I should have been there," I whispered.

Stefan knelt beside me; I scrambled back. I felt dirty. I felt like the slut my daughter had called me. I was fucking a man in secret while my son lay dying. I knew I couldn't have saved him, but I should have held his hand. I should have whispered words of comfort as he took his last breaths. I should have been the one to tell Kerry and not a stranger.

"You need to go," I said. I couldn't look at him.

"Don't do this," he whispered.

"Please, leave me alone, just for a while. I should have been here, Casey is right."

"Casey is not right, Jayne," Carla said.

I stood and walked out of the room, covering my ears with my hands. I needed to be alone, and I headed for my bedroom. I locked the door and threw myself on the bed. As I buried my head in my pillow, I cried. Every fibre of my being hurt. I cursed and begged God in equal measure. I wanted to scream, I wanted to wake up and it all have been a dream.

I don't know how long I'd been on my bed, but the room had darkened. My throat was sore, my eyes so puffy they hardly opened, and the skin on my face was chapped from my salty tears. I heard a gentle knock on the door.

"Please let me in," my mum said.

I slid my aching body from the bed and crossed the room. As I opened the door, fresh tears fell.

"Oh, Mum," I said.

She led me back to the bed and sat beside me, cradling me in her arms. She rocked me like she had when I'd been a child.

"I don't know what to do," I whispered.

"I know, darling."

There were really no words, what did one say?

"Will you come downstairs? Maybe get a drink of something?"

I stood. Every step I took caused my muscles to throb and my head to spin. Exhaustion had crept into every bone.

Kerry was curled up on the sofa, her mum sat beside her with her hand resting on her thigh. Carla rushed over to me.

"Come and sit down," she said.

I looked around the room. "He's gone to my house," she said.

There was a little part of me disappointed but I nodded anyway.

# Chapter Sixteen

It was the guilt that consumed me. It ate away at me like a cancer. My stomach was a cauldron of acid that burned, but I welcomed the pain. It was my punishment for what I'd done.

As the days wore on, I sank more and more into a world of my own. I stopped speaking, I hadn't showered, and I couldn't eat. I slept a lot, totally exhausted all the time. I found it hard to walk even, every step was as arduous as running through treacle.

Carla, my mum, and even Kerry in the end, badgered me to speak to Stefan. He called, he texted, he'd even turned up at the house but I couldn't see him. As inexplicable as it was, I didn't want him to see me in the state I was. Yet I made no effort to change that. Nothing made sense. I would look at the people in the room and knew they were talking, but I didn't hear them. All I heard were four words swimming around my head.

*Shut the fuck up.*

Meal after meal congealed on plates that had been placed in front of me. I had no desire to eat. It was enough to sip at the glass of water that was constantly refreshed.

I would look at the worried expressions on Carla and my mum's faces and a layer of guilt was added. It weighed so heavily on my heart that I willed it to stop beating. I didn't want to live. I would wake each morning and cry that I hadn't died in the night. I didn't want to live in a world where I was thought of as a slut, where such hostility was thrown my way, and where my precious son was dead.

"He's going to leave today. Please, see him before he goes," I heard Carla say.

I furrowed my brow. Who was leaving?

"Ben's leaving?" I said.

I watched her look towards my mum. Tears rolled down her cheeks and I shut down before she answered.

"You need to shower. I want you up. Now, young lady."

I looked at my mum. The person I saw was the mum I'd had thirty years ago. She stood with her hands on her hips. I stood, although the effort made me wince. I hadn't left the sofa in days.

I followed her up the stairs and into the bathroom. She stripped me of my clothes; my arms were too weak to help. I stepped under the shower and waited for her to turn the dial. Not even the shock of the cold before the water warmed roused me. I stood with my arms hanging by my side and let the water run over me. Through the haze, the blurred vision, I saw a nailbrush. I reached for it. In my foggy brain, I had the idea that it would clean the 'slut' from me.

I scrubbed my skin until it was red raw, until it bled in places. I continued to scrub until it was snatched from my hand. I cried; I wanted it back. If I bled, I would be cleansed. I wanted to bleed. I needed to bleed.

Mum turned off the shower and wrapped a towel around my body. I stared at my arms, at the raw skin and at small dots of blood gently oozing to the surface. It comforted me. The sight of my blood quietened the screaming in my head, its metallic smell overpowered the scent of the slut on my skin. I smeared it up my arm.

"What have you done?" she whispered. I felt the anguish in her voice like a punch to my gut, and another layer of guilt was added.

A pair of fresh pyjamas was laid out on the bed. I was helped into them before I collapsed under a clean duvet. I needed to sleep. It was only during sleep that my brain stilled enough for me to remember my son, and I wanted to remember him, every minute of the day.

I was woken the following day, or it could have been days later, I had no idea, by Carla and my mum. A woman accompanied them. She sat on the edge of my bed and had kind eyes; I distinctly remembered her kind eyes.

"Jayne, I'm Dr. Hogan. Do you think we can have a chat?"

I looked at her. "The weather is kind of mild right now, don't you think?"

She smiled. I didn't want her to smile. I felt mean that I had been so rude, and yet another layer of guilt was added.

I closed my eyes. "My son died. I wasn't there holding his hand like a mother should have been. Instead, do you want to know where I was?" My voice was challenging.

"I was having the best sex I've ever had in my life. A man, a man no one knows, was fucking my brains out. I've been having an affair; I caused the break up of his marriage. My family hates me, my daughter thinks I'm a slut, and she'd be right if she knew what I'd actually done."

The words spewed from my mouth, and I couldn't stop them.

"I've been selfish, self-absorbed, and right now, Dr. Hogan, I just want to die. I want to close my eyes and never wake up. I get angry every time I do. How's that for fucking starters?" The anger in my voice made my mouth acidic.

"I think that's a great start. How do we progress from here?" she asked.

"How do *we* progress? I have no fucking idea."

"You need help to process this."

"I *need* to close my eyes and for it all to be a dream. I *need* to turn back the clock. I *need* for my son to walk through that door and it all be a terrible joke."

I shut down, conversation over. I turned on my side and closed my eyes.

I felt the bed move as she stood. The bedroom door closed and I heard whispered voices from beyond. I had no inclination to know what the conversation was about.

An hour or so later, the bedroom door opened again. I sighed, irritated by the disturbance.

"Jayne, I've brought you tea," I heard. I sat up at the sound of Kerry's voice.

"Oh, baby. Come here," I said.

She shuffled across the bed to sit beside me. She looked shocking; she'd lost so much weight. I should have been looking after her.

"Michael is arranging the funeral, Jayne. We need to stop that. Ben wouldn't want to be buried. Please help me. I have no say here."

I looked at her, at the pleading in her eyes. I lowered my gaze to her hand, laid protectively over her stomach, over her child. "I need my phone."

She eased herself from the bed and I noticed how large her bump had become. The baby was due in a little over a month and I closed my eyes against yet more tears.

It wasn't Kerry that returned to the bedroom but Carla. She sat next to me and took my hand in hers.

"I've spoken to Michael. You can't ring him, Jayne."

"Why?"

She took a deep breath. "He wanted to report you for assault. I've got my lawyer involved because things are going to get nasty. He's filing for divorce on the grounds of adultery."

I was too stunned to speak at first. "He's the one who had an affair, we're separated," I said.

"It's one of those quirks, but it doesn't matter who files for what. I'm going to fight tooth and nail for you."

"What do I do?"

"You need to get up, you need to help me fight."

"I don't have the energy. I think I have flu."

"You've lost your son. You're spiralling into depression and no one can blame you for that. But I need you to help us. Stefan calls every day, will you speak to him?"

"I can't. I just...can't."

"But why?"

How could I explain how I felt? I didn't know myself. I just knew there was blackness in my mind and it was comforting. The screaming, the crying, the thinking had all stopped. I was in a black hole and I wanted to stay there. The darkness surrounded me; I didn't have to feel. I didn't have to remember or take responsibility for anything. If I spoke to Stefan, it would all come back, and I was scared. I was terrified I'd do the one thing that I actually wanted to do—kill myself.

I'd thought of dying over the past few days. I would lay at night, wide awake, and know, if I had the energy, I could walk downstairs and swallow enough pills to stop the hurt—forever. Something always pinned me to the bed, something that shimmered in the moonlight and hung on my bedpost. I just needed a few more days.

"Please, help Kerry," I whispered.

"I will, believe me, I will. I have some medication for you, something for your *flu*."

She held in her hand a small white tablet. I eyed it suspiciously.

"I don't need anything for the flu."

"It's an anti-depressant, just to get you over the next couple of days."

"Who's idea was that?"

"Dr. Hogan thought you needed something just to help with the grief."

"I just need help with the funeral. I'll be fine. I can deal with my grief. Surely I'm allowed to grieve?"

She sighed and left the tablet on the bedside cabinet.

"I don't know what to do, to help." Her voice sounded small.

"I just need someone to stop this funeral. Ben can't be buried."

I was desperate.

"I'll try."

Carla stood, and before she left the room she bent down and kissed my forehead. She was another one that had lost weight and her normal immaculate attire was crumpled.

When I was alone, I reached for my phone and switched it on. I deleted the unanswered texts from Stefan, scrolled past the missed calls and searched my contacts for Casey's number. I held the phone with a shaky hand to my ear and listened to it ring. It rang and rang. Her usual voicemail failed to kick in and after a couple of minutes, the call cut off. I sent a text.

*Darling, can you call me.*

I slid my legs to the side of the bed and sat. Kerry needed my help. I had to move my body, regardless of the ache. I picked up the little white pill and rolled it in my fingers. I closed my eyes as I popped it in my mouth and took a sip of water.

"You are one nasty bastard. Believe me when I say we will fight you on this," I heard Carla say into her phone.

I hesitated by the living room door, hoping I wouldn't be noticed.

"He is her son too," she said.

Who was she talking to? Carla turned and saw me. She gave me a sad smile.

"I mean it, Michael, we will be there and you will be civil or all hell is going to break loose." She cut off her call.

"What was that about?" I asked. I noticed the change in pitch in my voice.

"Come and sit down. Let me get you some soup."

I sat on the sofa while she rushed to the kitchen. A minute later mum returned with a tray.

"Where's Kerry?" I asked.

"She's sleeping. The doctor saw her too, gave her a check up. She needs lots of rest, like you do, and to eat."

Carla returned to the room with another tray for herself. She sat beside me and encouraged me to eat. I wasn't hungry but I took a couple of mouthfuls, more to please and stop the nagging.

When I was done I placed the tray on the coffee table.

"What was that call about?" I asked.

I saw the look that passed between my mum and Carla.

"Michael won't change any of the funeral details and he asked that you don't attend. He doesn't think you are *well* enough."

"He doesn't think I'm well enough? What the fuck does that mean, and how does he know anything about me?"

"He's being a prick, and I won't stand for it," Mum said. "In fact, I'm going over there."

She bustled from the room and grabbed her coat.

"Mum, don't. I'm going. He can't stop me. When and where is it?"

I didn't think I had any tears left but fresh ones rolled down my cheeks. How could he try to keep me away from my son's funeral? What kind of a man does that?

"Why would he do that?" I whispered.

Mum came back into the room, sat beside me, and placed her arm around my shoulders.

"Because he is a nasty prick wracked with guilt."

If the situation wasn't so dire, I'd have found the use of the word 'prick' funny coming from my mother's mouth. She never swore normally.

"Darling, we need to get you fit enough. You need to walk in that church with your head held high and take your place at the front. Will you help us do that for you?"

I nodded. I needed to find enough strength to get through that one day. I could collapse back into my world after.

There was no black hearse for us on the day of the funeral. No visitors to our house, no flowers lay at our gate. But we dressed, four women in mourning, and we headed out to a waiting car. Carla had arranged for a black car with a driver to collect us. We arrived at the church at the same time as the hearse and the one black limousine. Carla instructed our driver to pull up behind them. We exited the car at the same time and I held my head high. Casey didn't look over. Michael kept his head low but his mother, Francis, walked over.

She placed her gloved hand on my arm. "I'm so sorry. I've argued with him over this," she said.

She was another one that had aged. "It's not your fault, Francis. To keep me away from my own son's funeral is about the lowest thing your son has done, and he's done some pretty shitty things. Is his tart here with him? The woman he has had an affair with for years?"

Her face blanched. "Oh, you didn't know about her? I'm sorry," I added.

I patted her hand and started to walk towards the church. I was stopped by many of Ben's friends, and it pleased me to see not one person speak to Michael.

I held on to the arm of my mother and we filed into the church. I took a seat in the front pew with Kerry, my mum, and Carla; Michael sat the other side of the aisle. I refused to look over. I refused to acknowledge him at all.

One of Ben's friends stood and gave the eulogy. It was a touching speech from someone who had known him since childhood. He talked about the fun they had, he mentioned me many times and spoke fondly of Kerry and the baby. Again, Michael wasn't mentioned. How could he think he could organise a funeral for someone he didn't even know?

The longer the service went on, the angrier I became. I sat rigid and found I was struggling to breathe. Mum placed her hand on my arm and I looked down. I hadn't realised I had been holding her hand and was squeezing tighter the more my anxiety rose.

"Just breathe," she whispered.

The room swam, the echo around the stone interior hurt my ears, and my vision blurred. I could feel my heart racing, it pounded so hard in my chest I felt physical pain. My legs shook and at that point, I wanted to run. I wanted to leave the church and keep on running. I focused on the dark wood, grotesque coffin with the ridiculous array of roses on the top. Ben hated roses. Why did Michael not know that?

Thankfully, before I got to point of passing out, the service was over. Carla stood; my mum stood and held out her hand to me. I was unsure if my legs would hold me up as I gingerly got to my feet.

The pallbearers carried Ben's coffin down the aisle, and Carla made a point of blocking Michael's exit so we could follow first. I shuffled behind my son.

Four chairs were laid out beside a hole in the ground; Carla led me to one. I sat and patted the seat next to me for Kerry. I looked up as Casey appeared.

"Sit with us," I said quietly. She ignored me and that hurt.

Her refusal to acknowledge me must have been witnessed by all. I bowed my head, not wanting to see if their brows furrowed in question. I didn't hear the priest; I didn't watch my son being lowered to the ground. I kept my gaze on my feet. It was a tug on my arm that alerted me to the fact it was over.

"Do you want to stay?" Mum asked. I shook my head.

Michael was talking to the priest. He showed no emotion, and I doubted he had even cried. I was led to our car and we drove home. There was no invitation to join the wake; I wasn't even sure if there was one.

We arrived home and I climbed the stairs, ripping at my tights as I did, tearing them from my body. I wanted rid of the sombre clothing. I wanted to climb in bed in my pyjamas and shut the world out.

I woke, not realising I had fallen asleep and looked at the bedside clock. It was early hours of the morning. I wasn't sure of the day. Had I been to Ben's funeral, or had that been a dream? I struggled to understand what was real and what wasn't.

I needed fresh air. I staggered down the stairs with tears blinding me. I reached the kitchen more by instinct than anything else. As I headed to the sink, I noticed a bottle. Somewhere in my frazzled brain the idea that alcohol would dull the pain emerged. I drank straight from the bottle. It spilled down my chin and puddled on the floor at my feet. I needed to be numb, needed the noises in my head to stop. I needed to sleep, the sleep of the dead.

I shook the bottle, not understanding why all of sudden it was empty. It had been heavy when I'd first lifted it to my lips. And then I spotted them. A white box sat on the counter top. I lifted it, intending to read, but as if they had a will of their own, my hands opened the packet. I stared at them. Tranquillity wrapped its arms around me. I knew what I needed to do.

One pill, two pills, three pills—how many did I need?

Four pills, five pills, six pills—I lost count after that.

I know I placed them on my tongue; the chalkiness dried my mouth as I tried to swallow. I cupped a hand under the running tap and drank from it. Washing the solution to my nightmare down my throat.

More pills—more water.

I heard a whining, something wet nudged at my face. I couldn't open my eyes and I couldn't move my body. I wasn't sure where I was, other than it was quiet: it was peaceful. There was no screaming in my head. I floated, I felt light, and without pain. A warm body lay beside me. I blocked out the sound of the whines that grew louder.

There was so much noise and light, I was angry. I didn't want to wake. I was happy in my black hole; the darkness comforted me. I didn't feel. I didn't hurt. Hands pulled and tugged and prodded. Lights flashed in my eyes. Voices drifted in and out. All I wanted to do was sleep.

# Chapter Seventeen

I woke in a strange room. The soft cream-coloured walls were bare of any pictures, but a TV was mounted up high. A wooden wardrobe stood alongside a matching dressing table. To one side was a large sash window with tapestry curtains, and I found it peculiar for them not to have tiebacks. It spoilt the look of the obviously expensive drapes. I lay in an unfamiliar double bed, cocooned in a floral covered duvet; the pattern matched the curtains.

My head thumped, my throat was sore, and my body felt heavy. A young man walked into the room. He wore a uniform of blue trousers and a white polo shirt. He smiled and spoke; I didn't hear his words. I drifted back into sleep.

I woke periodically, the man—or maybe it was another—would be there. The time between waking seemed to lessen.

"Where am I?" I asked.

Memories popped in and out of my head: Dini lying on the floor next to me, a scream from someone, being woken to take medication. Crying.

"Morning, Jayne. How are you feeling today?"

The man sat beside my bed. He smiled at me.

"Who are you?"

"My name's Glenn, and I'm your nurse. How about we sit you up a little, and maybe you'd like a drink?"

"Where am I?" I repeated.

"You're in the hospital."

He fussed around, arranging pillows behind my back. I couldn't think straight. I felt like I'd woken from the longest sleep. My body ached and my mind was hazy.

"Why?"

"Let's get you comfortable first."

I didn't have the energy to question any further. I dozed on and off throughout the day. Glenn would leave and return on a regular basis. When I woke, I could see out into the corridor. People walked up and down, some stopped and gave me a smile; one called out hello. I wondered what kind of a hospital I was in. No one wore nightclothes or gowns.

I needed to pee and I was hungry. I swung my legs from the bed and was surprised to feel how weak they felt. I sat to allow my head time to stop swimming. I didn't like the feeling, I didn't like that I couldn't concentrate.

"Shall I help you?" I heard. I looked up to see Glenn stride into the room.

"I need the bathroom."

"Okay, how about you take my arm. You've slept on and off for a while, you might feel a little weak."

"How long have I been here?"

"A week now."

I stopped mid-stand. "A week?"

"Louise is coming to see you in a minute. She'll be able to explain everything to you."

278

I finally stood and was helped to the bathroom. I paused at the door. Surely he wasn't going to accompany me in?

"I'll stand here, don't worry," he said with a chuckle, perhaps noticing my hesitation.

I closed the bathroom door behind me and realised there was no lock. I wore unfamiliar pyjamas. I pulled down the grey flannel trousers and sat. The bathroom housed a bath, a sink, and a separate shower. White fluffy towels were placed on a rail above a small radiator and I noticed toiletries on a shelf. They were the same as the toiletries I'd used at home.

"A week?" I whispered to myself.

It frightened me to realise that I had no memory of being in that place for a week. Flashbacks filled my mind. I was at home. I'd been to my son's funeral. I'd been excluded from his wake and my family hated me. Tears rolled down my cheeks.

I stood and washed my hands; there was no mirror in the bathroom and I know I thought that strange.

I wanted to shower, wanted to wash my greasy hair, but I just didn't have the energy to do that. Without bothering to dry my tears, I left the room.

"Hello, Jayne. My name is Louise White. Are you hungry?" A woman sat on the edge of my bed.

I paused before answering. "Yes."

"Glenn, perhaps you can organise some dinner for Jayne. Would you like to get back into bed or sit by the window for a while?"

I looked over to the large bay sash windows. Two armchairs partly facing each other and a small table were placed in the bay.

"Bed. Who are you?"

I felt panic rising in my chest. My breath started to quicken and my legs shook. Louise stood and held out her hand. I ignored it and made my way to the bed. For some strange reason, I felt safe under the duvet. It was like a shield between reality and me.

"I'm your therapist, Jayne. Do you remember coming here?"

I shook my head. "I was at my son's funeral." I choked a little on the words.

"We know. You tried to end your life. You were taken to your local hospital and then transferred here. Can you remember any of that?"

I looked at her as the flashbacks continued. Although she smiled and seemed a kind person, her words were blunt, to the point, and cut like a knife.

"Why can't I remember it all?" I whispered.

"You've been heavily medicated. We believe sleep is needed after such trauma, so we help with that for the first week of your stay. Now it's time to start your recovery."

"You kept me asleep?"

"Yes, on and off. You've woken many times. We've chatted but I doubt you'll remember that."

"I want my mum."

"You'll be able to have visitors in a few days."

Her words were firm but her voice soft. As I continued to cry, she reached over for some tissues that she placed in my lap.

"Where am I?"

"This is a private mental health hospital in Sevenoaks, Jayne. Your family arranged for you to be here."

"My family?"

I had so many thoughts running through my mind but nothing

seemed to make sense.

"Tomorrow morning, I'd like to go through the schedule with you. I'm going to leave this here if you feel up to reading. I know you're anxious right now and probably very confused. We're here to help you, Jayne."

Glenn arrived with a tray of food and Louise stood to leave.

"I'll let you eat, and if you need anything, just use the call button." She smiled as she left.

Louise had said one thing that resonated with me. I was confused, very confused. I knew what I'd done; I remembered that part. I wasn't sure it was a conscious decision to take those pills or a spur of the moment thing. I just wanted the pain to end and to feel the numbness. I wanted to stay in my black hole, and I wasn't convinced I wanted to 'recover.' Part of me needed the pain; part of me hated it. Part of me wanted to remember, part of me needed to forget.

I ate the meal, and although I'd never spent time in a hospital before, I was surprised at the quality. I was given soup to start, with a bread roll, and then roast chicken and vegetables. Glenn came in with a cup of tea, a plastic glass of water and some pills.

I didn't ask what the pills were for. I swallowed them with a sip of water and then picked up the tea.

I didn't sleep well that night. The light from the corridor, people walking, however quietly they tried, kept disturbing me. I'd asked for the door to be closed to be told it wasn't allowed.

I watched the sun rise on a cold morning. The trees outside the window were bare of leaves and their branches covered in frost. I tried to remember what day of the week it was.

"Good morning. How would you like to join me for breakfast?" Glenn asked as he strode into the room.

I shuffled up the bed.

"What day of the week is it?"

"Thursday, all day," he said with a smile. "I'm starving, and I think it's time you visited our award-winning restaurant," he added.

"Restaurant?"

"Patients have to eat, Jayne. So, up you get."

He walked over to the wardrobe. "You have a choice of yoga pants, is that what they're called now? Oh, I like these ones, what about these ones?"

He held up some unfamiliar 'yoga pants.' "They're not mine," I said.

My heart sped up a little. Maybe they had me confused with someone else. Perhaps I shouldn't be there.

"They're new. Look, there's a tag." He laid them on the foot of the bed with a black t-shirt. "How about a shower?"

I eyed him suspiciously. People jolly in the morning always made me suspicious. I climbed from the under the duvet and made my way to the bathroom.

I winced as I saw the grey water swirl around the plughole. My hair must have been filthy. I scrubbed my skin until it was red; I wanted to wash the dirt, the grime, and the guilt away.

"Time for breakfast," Glenn called from the room.

I switched the shower off and wrapped myself in a towel. I sat on the edge of the bath, swallowing down the panic. I wasn't sure I was capable of leaving the room.

"You need to leave the room so I can dress," I said.

"Okay, I'll be right outside the door."

I peeked out and noticed the bedroom empty. Dressing as quickly as I could, I then dragged a brush through my tangled hair and tied it up.

"Are we ready?" Glenn said as he came back into the room.

"No."

"You've had breakfast in your room for over a week now. It will be nice to meet a few people and see the facilities."

We had gotten halfway along the corridor when I came to a halt.

"I don't want to meet people."

They'd all know. They'd know what a slut I'd been; fucking a man while my son lay dying. Casey's words swam around my head.

"Then we can sit on our own," he said with a smile.

I wanted to punch the fucking smile from his face. My anxiety levels rose as we descended a sweeping staircase, something that would look better in a stately home. A receptionist looked up from behind her desk and smiled. We continued along a corridor. My palms started to sweat and my legs shook the closer to the double doors I got. I should have stopped walking, I could have turned and walked away. No one could force me to eat, or sit in a room full of nutters.

The restaurant was large, bright with floor-to-ceiling windows along one side. Tables with occupants were dotted around. I sat at the closest unoccupied table and made sure not to make eye contact.

I could feel my heart racing and I breathed in deep through my nose to control it.

"Good morning. Tea or coffee?" I heard. I looked up to a smiling waitress holding a jug.

"Tea," I managed through my clenched jaw.

"Lovely, I'll be right back with a pot for you. In the meantime, here's the menu," she said, still smiling.

I scanned the room as subtly as I could. There was a mix of people, male and female, young and old. One table housed a group of teenagers and a burly man who wouldn't look out of place on a nightclub door.

"Have you decided what to eat?" Glenn said, bringing my attention back to the menu.

"I'm not hungry."

"How about some toast, or there are pastries on the counter?"

The waitress returned with two pots of tea and stood waiting to take an order. Glenn placed his and I just asked for some toast.

"It's not so bad, is it?" he said as he watched me looking around.

"Most people look, well, normal," I said.

He chuckled. "First thing on the agenda today is to meet with your doctor. She'll go through the programme with you."

"Didn't I meet her yesterday?"

"That was Louise. She's your therapist for one-to-one sessions, but you'll see a doctor as well."

Our breakfast arrived and we ate in silence. I wasn't in the mood for conversation. I was scared, anxious, and felt very alone.

I was shown to a room and introduced to Doctor Tanner. She was my psychiatrist; I truly had to be nuts to warrant her. However, I liked her. I didn't like the forms and the silly questions I had to answer. *On a scale of one to ten, do I want to kill myself?* Or words to that affect. How the fuck does one answer that? I didn't know if I had intended to kill myself or just numb the pain. As my anxiety increased so my skin itched. It felt like a million ants were crawling over me. I scratched my arm, not realising I was until she pointed it out to me. I'd left track marks; big red angry lines ran down my forearm.

Without knowing what we spoke about, our meeting was over.

Glenn appeared from nowhere and we headed back to my room. Louise was waiting to go through my programme. I felt exhausted and all I wanted to do was to climb back into bed. I was given a timetable, as if I were back in school. A daily schedule of therapy to attend was explained to me.

"When can I see my family?" I asked.

"You have visitors this evening. Maybe they'd like to join you for dinner?"

"No, I want to stay in here."

I had no intention of sitting with whoever planned on visiting me in the restaurant.

I didn't attend any therapy sessions until late that afternoon. I refused to go until my head was a little clearer. I struggled to piece together the past couple of weeks. It was all just a mess of flashbacks and blurred memories. Glenn managed to coerce me, or maybe it was pure manipulation, into attending a group session.

I followed him to the basement and into a room. A semi-circle of chairs was laid out and Stephen, the therapist, greeted me. I sat on one closest to the door and kept my head down as the chairs started to fill with people. I refused to speak. I didn't look up but I did listen.

Some people spoke about what had brought them to the hospital, some cried. I cringed as I listened to the whining of one and shed a tear as I witnessed the pain of another. I was invited to speak; I shook my head.

I had nothing to say in front of those people. I'd have to confess my secrets, and I wasn't ready for that.

When the session was over I walked back to my room and collapsed on the bed. I didn't want to be surrounded by other people's misery and I felt terribly guilty about that. I just wanted to wallow in my own.

"Jayne, you have visitors," I heard.

I had been lying on my side, facing the window. A meal had been brought to me and I'd picked at it with no appetite. I sat up and immediately the tears started to fall.

Carla and my mum stood in the doorway. I looked at the anguish and sadness on their faces and knew I'd done that.

"Oh, my baby," mum said as she sat beside me. She wrapped her arm around my shoulders.

"I'm so sorry," I said.

"Hush now, nothing to be sorry about."

"How did I get here?"

I saw Carla look towards the open door.

"Let's not worry about that now. How are you?" she said.

"I feel strange. My brain is fuzzy, I can't think straight. I don't want to be here. Please, Mum, take me home?"

I heard her sob. "You need to be here. You'll get well here."

"I'll get well at home. Please, I'm begging you, take me home."

My voice rose, I scratched my skin until it bled, and I watched the two most important women in my life cry. I fucking hated myself. I dug my nails into my skin, dragging them down my arm, punishing, hurting, bleeding.

"How about a cup of tea?" Glenn said, as he strode into the room with a tray.

"I don't want a cup of tea, I want to go home," I was on the verge of shouting.

Carla sobbed as she watched me dissolve. I curled on the bed and cried.

"Please, take me home. Don't leave me here," I whispered over and over.

My mum brushed the sodden hair from my forehead.

"It was a mistake. I didn't want to kill myself. I won't do it again," I said.

"You have to stay here," she said, her voice was gentle and soft.

"Why don't we have some tea? I know I'm thirsty," Carla said with a forced cheerfulness in her voice.

Had I embarrassed her? I'd cried in front of her before. Why was she more interested in a cup of fucking tea?

It was as she handed Mum a cup and it rattled in the saucer that I realised how upset she was.

We sat for a little while in silence, not knowing what to say to each other. How did I explain myself to them? I had no idea what was going on in my head.

"How's Kerry?" I asked, finally remembering she would still be at home.

"She's okay, getting bigger. The baby is due soon," mum said.

"And Casey, have you heard from Casey?"

Mum looked towards Carla. "She headed back to Japan with Michael."

"Do they know?"

Carla nodded her head. "Yes. Jayne, I need you sign this form. I need to be able to look after things."

Glenn appeared in the room at that point and I wondered if he'd been listening outside. He sat at the end of the bed and I stared at him.

"What form?"

"It just means I can take care of things on your behalf."

"I can take care of things myself. What's happening?"

"Please, darling, just sign the form then concentrate on getting well. I want you home as soon as possible," Mum said.

A piece of paper and a pen were placed on the bed beside me.

I held it in my hands but the tears in my eyes blurred the words. I didn't understand what I was signing but I did it anyway. I thought I heard a sigh of relief from Carla.

"It's time for you to leave now, visiting hours are up," Glenn said.

I turned sharply to face him.

"What? They've only just got here."

"We have to be strict, Jayne, because of the other patients. I'm sure they'll come back soon, won't you?" He looked at my mum.

"Of course we will, darling." She patted my hand.

"I'll walk down with you," I said.

"I'm afraid that's not possible," Glenn said. No matter what he said he had a smile on his face and it irritated me.

"I can walk where I bloody well want."

I began to get agitated.

"Please, Jayne, stay here. I don't want you to walk down with us. I want you to get better and come home." My mum's voice had taken on a pleading tone.

"You could have died had Dini not barked. Yes, he barked. I can't live through that again. You have to stay here and get better," she added.

I saw the tears roll down her face but her words paralysed me. I nodded and watched as they walked away. Carla had her arm around her and I saw her shoulders shaking as she sobbed.

"What have I done?" I whispered.

"You're ill, Jayne. Depression is a real illness that most don't understand. People can't see it, it's not a broken leg, and only you can feel it. It's unique to every sufferer. I can assure you of one thing though, you're in the best place to conquer it."

I lay back on the bed as a wave of exhaustion washed over me. Every bone hurt, every muscle felt fatigued. I wanted to sleep, I wanted my brain to not be so cloudy, but I didn't want to think either. I guessed I had no idea what I wanted.

I took my medication and changed into my pyjamas. It wasn't long before I felt my eyelids grow heavy and I drifted into a dreamless sleep.

# Chapter Eighteen

Each day was the same. I rose, showered, and made my way down to breakfast. For the first few days, Glenn accompanied me, but it soon became time for me to do it alone. I sat on my own at first, but as I started the therapy session so some of the 'inmates' joined me at mealtimes. Lilian was one lady I grew close to. She shared part of her story with me. We were each encouraged to talk about what had brought us to the hospital, but other than saying I'd lost my son, I never expanded.

Lilian had been referred because she'd finally escaped an abusive marriage. But by doing so, she found herself alone and unable to cope without the level of control that had been exerted over her for so many years.

Our rooms were next to each other and on occasions we'd sit in the TV room and chat. We would walk to therapy together, and she'd give me a hug when things got too much after my one-to-one sessions or my weekly meeting with Dr. Tanner. She was a kind woman who didn't deserve the life she'd had.

I followed the programme, I took my pills, and I talked. I saw Louise for an hour every day and we talked about anything and everything. By the end of a week, I had a clearer understanding of what was wrong with me.

Art Therapy was something I had no desire to participate in. The session was taken by a student but with a trained therapist overseeing. I remembered one day we were sat in a row along a wall and asked to act a colour. I stared at the therapist in total bemusement. I didn't like her. I got the impression she was some arty farty do-gooder who, in actual fact, wasn't very tolerant of her patients.

"Jayne, I'd like you to act a colour, a colour that best represents you right now," she'd said. There was no asking, no gentleness in her voice.

"I'd rather not, thank you."

"The rest of the group are participating," she said.

"Good for them."

"I think it would be nice if you joined in."

I shrugged my shoulders. How the fuck does one 'act a colour'? I watched the rest of the class struggling and generally taking the piss. Not one person in that room was taking it seriously yet she didn't appear to be aware of that.

"Jayne?"

"I'm doing it. Can't you guess what colour I am?"

She made notes. That was something that irritated me; whenever I spoke, she made notes.

"I think, class, Jayne would like us to guess what colour she is."

Class? I wanted to remind her that it wasn't primary school. She was in a room of people clinically depressed, nuts, barmy, off their rocker, highly medicated, and fucked up. Her condescending manner annoyed most of us.

"I'm fluorescence," I said to the 'class' standing before me.

Lilian sniggered, she'd been prancing around and waving her arms shouting that she'd give us a clue and think 'daffodil.'

"Fluorescence?"

"Yes, it's perfect. We're both chemically induced."

With that, I stood and left the room. Beyond the restaurant was another art room, that one was for painting, which led to a conservatory then the garden. I headed that way and pulled a packet of cigarettes from my pocket. Lilian, bless her, had her son bring some in for me.

"Fluorescence. That was funny, not that I should say so," I heard.

I turned to see Louise walking towards me.

"How did you know? I've been out of that room for no more than a couple of minutes. Are the rooms bugged?"

"Of course not. Stephen just told me. I was walking past to grab a coffee. I've got one for you too."

She placed two plastic cups on the metal garden table.

"It's cold out here," she added, as she pulled her cardigan around her.

"Yes."

"How about you finish your cigarette and we find somewhere warm to talk?"

"I don't need to talk, thank you though. I truly don't get the art therapy. I can't draw, I'm not interested in playing with figures in a sand box, and as for acting a colour, that's about as barmy as we all are."

For the first time in weeks, I laughed. I stubbed out my cigarette and picked up the coffee. It was too cold to sit outside for any length of time.

"It's Christmas next week, isn't it? What do I do?"

"You'll be here. I hear Christmas lunch is something not to be missed. Your family can join you."

"But I can't go home?"

She shook her head slowly. "Why?"

"There are too many triggers at home. We need to ensure that you are in a position to deal with those. That you are stable enough to function in an environment that is going to upset you."

Sadness washed over me. I used to love Christmas. I doubted I ever would again.

Mum and Carla visited often; they joined me for meals and met with Louise for 'family therapy.' Mum set up a small tabletop Christmas tree in my room as a surprise. She laid a couple of presents underneath and was upset when I told them not to come on Christmas Day. The hospital wasn't the place I wanted her to spend that day at, especially since it would be the first without Dad. I wanted them to have a proper family meal at home, with Kerry and the bump. I wanted them to walk to the church for midnight Mass and to say a prayer for Dad and Ben. It took some convincing to explain I would be okay. I felt safe in that hospital. I felt calm.

Christmas came and went. I stayed in my room most of the time, despite Lillian's constant interruptions. I read, I slept, I watched programmes on the TV that I had seen twenty years prior, and I cried. Christmas had been Ben's and my favourite time of the year. We'd sit in front of the fire for hours wrapping presents, decorating the tree, and laughing. It was a tradition; a tradition that would have been broken with the birth of the baby, but it was wrenched from me before I was ready.

I knew the *calmness* I felt was medically induced and I willingly took the pills. I also knew that at some point I'd need to come off them. I didn't want them long-term, but through the therapy sessions I came to realise I'd suffered with depression for many years. It would take time for me to come to terms with that and to change a lifetime of behaviour so as not to sink so low in the future.

"You have visitors," Glenn said, when he walked in to the room.

I looked up to see Kerry, Carla, and my mum, but it was the bundle hidden beneath a blanket that Kerry held in her arms that caused me to cry.

"Surprise," she said, as she stepped closer and handed me her baby.

"Oh my God. When? Oh, Kerry," I struggled to get the words out.

"Boxing Day. Say hello to your grandson, Benjamin."

"Boxing Day! Should you be out of the house?" I asked.

"I'm fine, Benjamin is fine. It was an easy birth and I really wanted you to meet him."

I peeled back the blanket so I could get a proper look. Blue eyes stared back at me. He had blond hair and was most definitely his father's son. A tear dripped from my cheek and landed on his forehead. I used my thumb to wipe it away.

"I should have been at home," I whispered.

"No, you should be here because, Jayne, I need you. Benjamin needs you, and we want you well enough for that."

"I'll be home soon, I promise you that."

Benjamin pulled a face. I knew it wasn't a smile, and I wasn't sure my empty stomach was up for dealing with the alternative. I laughed as I handed him back.

Mum smiled at me. "You look well," she said.

"I feel better. I'm having one-to-one sessions every day and I see Dr. Tanner every week. Of course, Glenn watches me like a hawk."

"Heard that," he called from the corridor.

He no longer stood outside and I'd learnt why that was. If my visitors stressed me, he was immediately on hand to calm the situation but that day he was just passing. I didn't need him as much.

"So tell me about this place," Kerry asked as she changed the baby.

I told her about the therapy sessions, how each day I attended four. I explained about the art therapy and we laughed at my refusal to participate in that. I showed them the notebook I'd already filled after learning about the mechanics of depression, how the brain works, and why I was depressed. I also showed them my journal.

"I'm keeping a diary. I write every day and I've gone back and wrote things from the past. Sometimes it's so I don't forget, my brain isn't so good anymore, but also as a way to discharging the memories."

"You used to write all the time when you were a child. I have a bundle of little stories you and your dad made up," Mum said.

We chatted about their Christmas and New Year and I asked whether anyone had heard from Casey. I had written her a letter, I'd poured my heart onto paper, and I handed it to Carla for posting. It was my last attempt to contact her.

"Stefan calls, every week. He wants to visit," Carla said.

I didn't answer immediately. Slowly, I shook my head.

"He's better off without me and my issues. I'm not that person anymore, Carla. I don't know what I have to offer. I don't want to burden him."

"I'm not sure he'd see it that way. Maybe we'll chat about it when you're home," she replied.

I'd thought of Stefan a lot. His face was something I conjured in my mind frequently when I needed comfort. But I meant what I said. I wasn't the same person to the Jayne of just two months previous. Part of me was still numb, and part of me was terrified of seeing him again, of wanting him, and then not being able to have him because the memory of our last day together was so painful.

I didn't know what I had left in me to offer. My heart was still so very bruised.

We chatted for a half hour but I noticed Carla become nervous. She pulled some papers from her bag and set them on her lap. I looked at her.

"Tell me," I said quietly.

"I have some papers for you to sign. Michael put the house up for sale, I'm sorry, Jayne. I fought him hard but it's his name on the mortgage. Your solicitor has managed to secure half of the proceeds, and we should be able to get a small settlement in the divorce, but he's hidden everything."

"Tea anyone?" Glenn strode into the room holding a tray.

"Do you time exactly when I'm going to get shit news?"

"Yep," he said, and then smiled.

I reached for the papers. "Where do I sign?"

I scribbled my signature where indicated then handed them back to Carla.

"Thank you, for all you've done. I think I need some time on my own right now."

Kerry handed Benjamin back to me for one last cuddle. I kissed his forehead as his fingers curled around one of mine. "Nanny will see you soon," I said.

I stood and hugged each of the women and ushered them from the room before they saw my tears. They'd seen me break down enough in the past; I wanted them to finally walk from that hospital with the memory of my smile.

"You up for your tea?" I heard. Lilian always knew when to make an appearance.

"They bloody forgot me," she added as she poured herself a cup.

She sat on the end of the bed holding her mug. "So?"

I told her what Michael had done. "You know we could probably kill him and get away with it. Play the insanity card."

Through my tears, I laughed. "Karma, my friend. He'll grow to be a lonely old man," I said.

"How's your dog?" she asked.

"Kerry is still at the house until it's sold, I guess. She'll be looking after him but I need to get home and get this sorted."

That day I made a pledge to myself. I'd attend the daft art classes, and I'd work hard to beat that illness. I was needed at home and Michael selling up had spurred me on.

Lilian and I walked to relaxation together. I never quite got the class, other than it was an excuse to lie on a hard yoga mat on an equally hard floor and listen to sounds of the sea. Jenn, the therapist and about the only one I actually liked, smiled as we entered the room. Another patient, Karen, or KL as she wanted to be known, sat beside me.

"Evening, Jayne, I am so ready for this. I'm exhausted," she said with a yawn.

Relaxation class was just everyone's excuse for an hour's nap. Or it would have been had KL not chatted the whole way through. I often wondered if they had her meds mixed up; she literally bounced everywhere.

Carla came frequently; she brought more papers and eventually told me the house had been sold. The first people that viewed it had put in an offer way below the asking price, but Michael had accepted it. My belongings had been packed up and were to be placed in storage, and Dini was staying with Mum. The divorce was quick to follow. I didn't contest the adultery charge. I didn't care what reason was given, just as long as it was done and finished with. The solicitor had done well. My marriage ended with half the equity from the sale of the property and a lump sum of money. It wouldn't make a dent in what Michael had hidden away but I didn't care.

"I need to find somewhere and quick. I have Kerry to think about," I said, as we completed the last of paperwork.

"Well, I have news on that as well. Francis, and you're not going to believe this, has handed over the trust that was set up for Ben. Kerry has enough to buy a small house."

"You're kidding me?"

"No, seriously. She came to see me. I can't tell you how fucking surprised I was to see the old bat on my doorstep. Anyway, the Colonel had wanted the money to be left in trust for Benjamin but she overruled. Can you imagine that?" Carla laughed at the thought.

"I'm so pleased. So what's Kerry doing?"

"She wants to stay on that little estate they lived on before. She's made friends and her mum and baby groups are there. I'm going with her tomorrow to look at a couple and, she doesn't know this, but if she's short, I'll make up the difference. My investments are doing quite well and I don't need all that money."

"Just need to sort me out now," I said with a sigh.

"When you leave here, you come back with me for a while. Give yourself some time to think about things. And you know, he keeps calling."

I didn't have to ask who the 'he' was.

"I can't, not yet. I'm too embarrassed. Why would he want to be tangled up in my mess?"

"Maybe just email? He either calls or emails everyday, Jayne. If he didn't want to be 'tangled up in your mess,' he wouldn't do that, would he?"

"I just don't know what I can offer him right now. I need time."

What she didn't understand was, although I accepted my depression, it was under control because I was medicated and working through my issues. It was hard work. I was exhausted all the time with the internal battles that waged. I didn't have the energy to give to another.

# Chapter Nineteen

I had been at the hospital for three months and it was time for me to go home. As much as I'd begged for that, when the day came, I was terrified. I spent ages packing up my room, folding the new clothes that Carla had bought me. I hugged Glenn and Lilian; we made promises to keep in touch, promises we knew we'd never keep.

We were stripped bare in that facility, raw and exposed for all to see. Deep down we knew we'd never keep in touch because that would be a reminder of the worst time of our lives. But it was nice to walk out that front door on the arm of my best friend and my mum and know I'd made a lifelong friend in Lilian, but one that would stay in my heart only.

It had been decided that I would go back to Carla's but I wanted to collect Dini on the way. He'd saved my life, whether he was aware of that or not, and I'd missed him. Carla had agreed that Dini would stay with us; she knew I'd keep him under control and away from her large collection of handbags.

As Mum opened the front door, he ran at me. He leapt, nearly knocking me to my feet. I don't think he'd ever licked or whined as much. If there was ever a way of communicating with him, I'd want to thank him.

Going home, wherever that was, wasn't as easy as I had hoped. For a while Carla walked on eggshells around me. There was a forced cheerfulness, an awkwardness that made me sad. I tried to fit back in to some sort of life, but knowing I'd lived just a short distance away in my dream house made me not want to be in the village. We'd driven past one day while a removal lorry unloaded the furniture of its new occupants. That had hurt.

Kerry and I decided to visit the storage facility that was the temporary home for all my furniture. She needed some pieces for her new house.

"Can we go in your car? Mine needs a service," she'd said on the phone.

When I'd first left the hospital, Kerry always drove. She didn't seem comfortable with me driving and with Benjamin in the back. It was those little things that I noticed, that lack of trust in me and my mental state. I had a lot of repairing to do, but asking me to drive was a step in the right direction.

I picked her up from her little house and we made our way out of the village. It would be the first time I'd 'visited' my belongings. We were given a key and a number of a storage box. By 'box' I meant something the size of a shipping container in a warehouse that could have housed a jumbo jet.

Each box was labelled and neatly stacked. My furniture was wrapped in protective material. We made a note of what she needed; the delivery company would transport it over to her.

I paused by a stack of boxes with Ben's name on them. It actually saddened me to see that Casey had far more in her name.

She'd obviously taken nothing when the house had been packed up.

"You need to send those to Francis," Kerry said as she patted one.

"I might have to. I can't keep the cost of this going each month. I haven't told Carla, but I need to find somewhere to live soon. I can't stay with her indefinitely, and I know everyone is worried about me, but I can't be myself with her anymore."

"What do you mean?" Kerry asked, as we sat on the sofa and pulled a box with Ben's name on it towards us.

"She's not 'normal' around me, no one is. I feel like everyone is being too happy, no one wants to share bad news or have a bad day even when I'm around."

She looked at me. "I guess we're all scared it might cause you to...you know."

"I get that, but that's not the case. I just need everyone to be normal. I'll never go back to the person I was before, but this is hard work for me."

"I guess it's just going to take us all a little time," she said gently.

I watched her hands shake as she opened the box and pulled out a shirt. She held it to her face and closed her eyes.

"I miss him so much," she whispered.

I placed my arm around her shoulder as she cried. She was the first to 'let go' in front of me. I wondered how hard it was for everyone to hold in their grief.

"Tomorrow, let's go to the cemetery, take Benjamin," I said.

It would be the first time I'd visited since his burial. I didn't feel guilty about that; Ben would not want us wailing at his graveside.

I rifled around in the box and found a smaller one. Inside the white cardboard was a blue velvet box. I held it up in my hand to examine the intricate clasp.

"Do you know what this is?" I asked.

"No, I don't think I've seen that before."

"Shall I open it?"

"Yes."

I slowly opened the lid and what I saw brought tears to my eyes. A slim gold wedding band sat on the velvet cushion. I gently picked it up. Inside it was engraved.

KG & BA

"I think this is for you," I said.

We all believed Kerry and Ben would marry at some point, perhaps Ben had plans for that sooner than we thought. Kerry's hands shook as she slowly slipped the ring on her finger.

She picked her baby up from his car seat and cradled him to her chest. She laid her cheek on the top of his head and cried.

We sat for a while before Kerry wiped her tears on the sleeve of her jacket. She smiled sadly at me before putting a sleeping Benjamin back in his car seat.

"Shall we go?" I asked. She nodded.

We locked the container and made arrangements for furniture to be delivered before handing back the keys, then made our way back to Carla's. Kerry was going to stay for dinner and Carla had decided on Chinese takeaway.

"I'm going to start looking for somewhere to live tomorrow," I said as we sat around the table.

"Are you sure you're ready? You don't have to, you know," Carla answered.

"I am and I know. But I have to start getting on with my life. Tomorrow we're going to the cemetery if you want to come with us. I need to say goodbye, and then I'll never visit that place again."

Carla looked at me; I guessed she was unsure what I'd meant.

"I don't need to be by a grave, Carla, to remember my son, and he'd hate for us to do that," I added.

We ate, I even had a glass of wine, my first in months, and we pretended we were happy and life was dandy.

I think that was the hardest thing about the previous few weeks—the pretence.

I might not be mad, I might be medicated to even out my moods, but that didn't mean I wasn't sad. But the slightest downturn from the corners of my lips caused Carla and my mum to give each other sly looks, shifting eyes, and the wringing of hands. I wasn't going to fall apart, and it was exhausting having to hide how I felt all the time. I needed my own place; I needed somewhere I could cry if I wanted to, without everyone assuming I was about to slit my wrists.

It was a bright spring morning when we set off for the cemetery. Piled into Carla's car, we drove with a forced cheerfulness out of the village and to the small church. My stomached was knotted as we parked the car and walked across the dewy grass to Ben's grave. Nothing looked familiar and it dawned on me that I was seeing his final resting place through fresh eyes and a calm mind.

Benjamin gurgled in his carry seat, oblivious to the mounting emotion as I laid a blanket on the ground and we sat.

"At least this is a beautiful place," Kerry said. She laid a single white rose under his headstone.

I didn't hold back the tear that leaked from one eye. I didn't bother to dab it away before anyone saw. I reached forwards and traced his name, engraved in the granite. My boy, my firstborn, lay forever underground and in the last place he'd want to be.

We sat for an hour, or so, reminiscing and found plenty to chuckle about. Recalling some of Ben's childhood escapades weren't as painful as I thought they might have been. As the clock in the church bell tower chimed midday, we packed up to leave. It was as we were leaving that a car pulled alongside ours.

I came to a halt as Francis wrapped a woollen shawl around her shoulders and locked her car. She stumbled a little, in shock at the sight of us, I guessed.

"Jayne, I didn't realise you would be here today," she said.

She had aged, dramatically. Gone was the perfect hair, styled and sprayed within an inch of its life. Gone was the perfect made-up eyes; in their place I saw wrinkles and sadness.

"I'd rather not be, Francis. I'd rather Ben be where he wanted to be and not stuck six foot underground but, as you know, I didn't get a choice in that."

I tried really hard to keep the bitterness from my voice.

She had the grace to lower her eyes. "I'm sorry, I truly am. Can we talk for a while?"

I looked to Carla and Kerry. Francis smiled when she noticed Benjamin. She crouched down and held out her hand. He grabbed her finger.

"He looks so much like Ben, and you, of course, Kerry," she

said.

"If Jayne is happy about this, why not join us for a cup of tea at my house?" Carla said.

"That would be lovely, thank you."

I nodded my consent and we headed for our respective cars. Francis followed us the short distance back to Carla's.

I had been silent on the way back, watching the village through the side window and thinking. I'd never had a great relationship with Francis, in fact; I remembered our first meeting.

It was just after I'd found out I was pregnant with Ben when Michael decided to introduce me to his family. We'd driven to a house that sprawled across the countryside, one I was sure I'd seen in a fancy magazine. I noticed the lack of affection from his parents. A handshake from his dad and an air kiss from his mother was all Michael received as the front door was opened for us. I was granted a cursory look. I'd perched on the edge of a hard floral sofa in a 'drawing room,' reserved for afternoon tea with the ladies, and interrogated.

"So which university did you attend, Jayne?" Francis had asked.

"I didn't. I left school and went straight to work."

"And your parents? Where do they come from?"

Her nose had delicately wrinkled when I'd said South East London.

I wasn't good enough for their son. I wasn't from the county set, my parents didn't play golf or have a drawing room for afternoon tea. Over the years, we'd been polite to each other, formal and distant.

"Earth to Jayne," I heard.

I snapped out of my thoughts and realised we had arrived; the car was idling on the driveway of Carla's house.

"How about that cup of tea?" Carla said as we walked through her front door.

"That would be lovely, thank you," Francis replied.

We made our way to the large kitchen and sat at the table. Per square foot, I imagined Carla's house was larger than Francis' and I watched as she scanned the room and it's high tech appliances.

I held back the smirk as four mugs were placed in the centre of the table with a bottle of milk, a teaspoon, and bag of sugar. I knew she had a jug, a bowl, but I guessed she was making a point.

"I feel terrible. I should have stepped up, Jayne. I've wanted to speak to you for weeks but I just didn't know how. We've never been the best of friends and I regret that."

Francis' confession surprised me. I watched her take a cotton, neatly-pressed, handkerchief from her purse to dab her eye.

"I'm glad for you, I'm glad you found the courage to pursue happiness. If I'm honest, I'm jealous."

Not a sound could be heard, other than the click of my jaw as it fell open.

"I don't imagine you're jealous of my situation right now," I said, and added a chuckle to be sure she realised I wasn't serious.

"You're free of Michael, how ever hard that has been for you. I only wish I'd had your courage when I was younger."

"Oh, it's been hard. I've lost my son, I've lost my house, my daughter, and I've lost my friend. Whether I deserve that or not, I'm not sure, but Michael has never been faithful to me our entire marriage. I find it unbelievable how heartless he is. He buried our son knowing that wasn't his wishes. He tried to keep me, his

307

mother, from his funeral."

I had to check myself; my voice was starting to rise in anger. It wasn't her fault per se, but she sure hadn't made much effort to defend me, or Ben's wishes, in my mind.

"We argued, Jayne. And whether you'll believe me or not, Albert fought for a cremation as well. Do you want the truth? I dislike my son, and that's a hard thing to not only admit, but deal with."

I reached forwards and took one of her hands in mine. She felt fragile under my touch. I'd never seen her so vulnerable.

"Then we welcome you to our club," I said then laughed.

She smiled at me. "How is your friend? Stefan, isn't it?"

I ignored the raised eyebrow glare from Carla.

"I haven't spoken to him since...well, since that day. I'm too broken, Francis."

I watched her finish her tea. She patted my hand and then stood.

"Don't lose that chance at love, Jayne. One day, you'll wake up as old as me and bitterly regret your life. I know I do. I loved once, a long time ago, and I let him go. It was the worst thing I ever did."

With that, she gave Carla a smile, ran her hand over Benjamin's head, and shrugged on her coat.

"Can we stay in touch?" she asked.

"Of course, I'd like that."

"And you, young man, I'll be seeing you soon," she said to Benjamin.

"Thank you for the tea. I'll bring a cup and saucer next time. Kerry, may I visit you soon?"

She'd given Carla a wink when she'd spoken, and it was

laughter that followed us as I walked her to the front door.

As she opened her car door, she turned to me. She placed her hand on my arm—the first act of affection I'd ever received from her.

"Ring him. I saw the way he looked at you that night. Don't lose that. It's never too late."

Francis climbed into her immaculate, vintage Jaguar and reversed from the drive.

"Well, fuck that," Carla said when I'd returned to the kitchen.

"I know. That is about the most surprised I've ever been," I said. "What a wily old bird she is."

"Do you think we could have the milk jug and the sugar bowl now she's gone?" Kerry said.

For the first time in a long while, we laughed, really laughed, and I didn't feel guilty about that. Ben would have found that hilarious himself.

The house hunting started in earnest and soon turned into despair. There was no way I could afford to stay local, and I didn't relish the thought of the boxes masquerading as houses on the new estate. Spring edged its way into summer and I grew restless. Carla's life had been on hold for far too long and the persistent references to Stefan were upsetting me.

I knew he still called her, although not as frequently, and his last email to me had been months back. A part of me regretted my decision to fight my depression alone, yet another knew that it would have been impossible, for Stefan and for me, had we stayed in contact. He would fret while he was home, I'd miss him, and he would end up having to choose from his life in Denmark or his life with me. That was a decision I'd never want him to have to make.

It was an email from Tom, letting me know the boys were back and they were badgering Nanna Nora, as they'd nicknamed her, into learning to surf that had a thought run through my mind.

I'd missed Nora and Jim, I missed the boys, and I sure as hell missed the cottage. I wondered...

While I had the laptop opened I searched for the website. I could have checked my emails but that would mean seeing Stefan's name. Although I'd never opened them, I hadn't deleted them either. It was comforting to know they were there, and selfishly I missed them when they'd dried up.

I fired off an email without telling Carla what I'd done. I wanted to check availability before I told her I was heading for the cottage, alone.

That place was the last hurdle in my mind. It was where I'd had the best and worst experiences of my life. I wanted to walk in the front door and remember both Stefan and Ben.

# Chapter Twenty

I packed up the car after having it serviced, with some shopping and the dog, a week after deciding I needed to visit Cornwall. Carla had been upset. Memories of her having to make that drive to collect me and then, miraculously, getting us home under such terrible circumstances must have been whirling around her mind. Mum thought it was a good idea. "Laying the last of my ghosts to rest," she'd said.

"I'll be fine, Carla. We need some space. I know that sounds terrible, but your life is on hold with me being here, and I'm not about to break down. What I did wasn't planned. I don't think I ever wanted to die. It won't happen again."

"You'll ring as soon as you get there, though, and you've left Nora's number in case of...well, you know, emergencies?"

"In case you want to check up on me, you mean?"

"I can't help it, Jayne. You scared me, and that's not something I'll get over anytime soon."

"I know, and I'll always be sorry about that. But I need to do this. I won't have any spare money once I've found somewhere to live, so this is my last chance."

We hugged and I climbed in the car. It saddened me to realise there was a crack in our friendship, one that may or may not ever be repaired, and I believed some time apart would do us the world of good. I had to prove to her that I was capable of being on my own. I had a lot to prove to a lot of people.

I took the journey from memory, passing Stonehenge on the A303 and eventually, as the sun was setting, found myself on the Atlantic Highway. I did the thing I'd done on all the other times I'd driven that road—I unwound the window and breathed in the sea air. Immediately, I felt my shoulders relax and a smile form on my lips. As I drove the last few miles, I knew I'd done the right thing. I felt like I was going home.

"Helloooooo," I heard echo down the lane.

A flashlight zigzagged from side to side.

"Nora, is that you?" I called out.

"Of course it's me. Who else is mad enough to walk down here at night just to see my favourite girl?"

She pulled me into a hug, petting Dini at the same time. I hadn't got through the front door of the cottage.

"Oh, it's so good to see you. Now, you unpack, I'll make tea and you can tell me all that's happened."

I nodded and turned my head; I didn't want her to see the tears that had formed in my eyes. I realised how much I'd come to love her as a friend and I'd missed her.

By the time I'd taken a bag upstairs, sorted the dog out, she had the tea on the table and my shopping unpacked.

"Now, what the frig has been happening? You've had us all so worried here. Jim was in a mind to drive up to Kent to see you, you know?"

"Oh, Nora. I don't know where to start."

"The beginning would be good, and I've got all night."

312

I did what she asked; I started at the beginning, right at the beginning. I totally unloaded on her; from the time I met Michael to that morning.

I was drained. I'd cried and she'd held my hand but hadn't said a word for the two or three hours I'd spoken. Other than to refresh our tea, and to make us both a sandwich, she'd stayed with me. It felt cathartic, I felt cleansed and lighter in my body. I hadn't realised how much I needed to let that out. I'd told her things I hadn't told my therapist.

I chuckled. "Carla would be pissed off at the amount of money she paid for my therapy and all I needed to do was come to you."

"Ah, there's a place for shrinks and there's place for friends. Now, Stefan. I imagine everyone has told you what a fool you've been, but you know what? I think you made the right decision for you, not that I agree with it, of course," she said with a chuckle.

"I can't message him now, Nora. It's been too long, and I don't know what to say. I feel like I threw him to the wolves that day. He loved me and I pushed him away. I was scared to be honest, scared that if I had kept in contact, at some point he would have had to make a choice—be with me or with his family. Because I think I would have been too needy of him."

"And now?"

"And now, I don't know just yet. I'll never stop loving him, but I need to recover fully, and I haven't yet."

"There's nothing stopping you from contacting him though, getting that friendship back. You forgave him for running away. I'm sure he'll do the same."

I hadn't thought about it that way. I still had some bridges to repair and I had to start with my daughter first.

Nora left with a promise that we'd catch up the following day. I worried about her walking back up the lane in the dark, but she'd waved my concern away. She'd been doing it for years but she would call to say she was safely home.

After she called, I opened the back door and sat in the garden with a cigarette. The smell and sound of the sea soothed me. Dini walked around the garden, claiming it by cocking his leg on every plant; while I sat and felt the world that had been carried on my shoulders slowly roll away.

I'd already texted Carla, Kerry, and my mum to say I had arrived safely, so I turned off my phone, called the dog in, and headed to bed.

I climbed the stairs and hesitated at the bedroom door. Although I'd taken my bag up earlier, I'd dumped it outside the room. I stood and looked at the bed. Stefan had told me he'd loved me in that bed. Memories flooded my mind. Perhaps if the bedding had been different I wouldn't have grown so upset, but I cried as I stripped my clothing and cried even more as I climbed under the duvet.

I hugged the pillow he had laid his head on and whispered into it.

"Jeg elsker dig."

Did I feel terrible I was crying for him and not Ben? Yes and no.

Mourning for my son went beyond tears. I'd sobbed for days initially, and I still shed tears for him, but I was hollow inside. A part of me was missing and that would never change, never grow back, and never mend. I'd live on, obviously, but I'd never have the child I made, I'd given life to, given my own blood to, and I'd come to accept that. If I hadn't, I'd be dead.

I slept in late the following morning. It was the sound of Dini whining and a bashing on the back door that woke me. I struggled out of bed and pulled on some clothes before looking out the bedroom window.

The boys stood in the garden. I opened it to call down. Tom waved a bag of something at me.

I unlocked the door and received hugs and a bag of pastries.

"So, before we come in, are you still mad?" Greg said.

I laughed at his openness. "No, and thank you for your emails. I want to hear all your adventures."

The boys sat at the table and I made tea to go with the pastries. They filled me in on their time back in Australia. I loved talking with them, listening to their antics, and at no time did I feel they were judging me on my depression. It was refreshing to have such banter about it.

"So what are your plans?" Tom asked.

"I'm just going to relax this week, read, chill out on the beach, and sleep a lot."

"Surf?"

"Maybe, we'll see."

The boys left soon after to open up the surf shop and get in the water. I was left with a smile on my face. I hadn't genuinely smiled in a long time.

For most of the morning, I sat in the garden with my notebook and wrote. I watched holidaymakers set up, sunbathe, and paddle in the sea. I watched people laughing, playing ball and children rock pooling. I wrote those people into my notebook, creating short stories around them. I had a box full of notebooks and I'd decided, as part of my week away, I'd transfer them to the laptop, make some kind of story from them all. It would be a project I could be proud of. I also decided I was going to write another letter to Casey. Now that Francis seemed to be on my side, I hoped she might be able to pass it on.

I sat in the garden every morning and typed my stories into one. It was my life in fiction. There were parts that brought fresh tears to my eyes and parts that had me chuckling out loud. In that one week, I'd written over forty thousand words. Something happened to me in the process. I fell in love with me again. I read about me, and my life, in a totally objective way, and I became addicted to writing. I'd wake in the night with an idea and scribble it down on my notepad. I walked the beach and dictated thoughts into my phone. I wondered what people thought of me as I paced, getting excited by my plots.

As the week wore on, and after spending my afternoons either catching up with the boys or Nora and Jim, I'd made a decision. I called the travel agent and asked if I could extend my holiday. As much as I didn't want to leave the cottage, if it wasn't available, I'd take another. Thankfully it was available, in fact, it would be the last week the agents were responsible for the cottage. It was coming off their books and that saddened me a little.

"Did you know the cottage is coming off the travel agents'

books?" I said to Nora over a cup of tea.

"No, I wonder why. I know the owners are never here. I have their phone number. I could give them a ring and see if they're placing it elsewhere."

"That would be great. I called Carla earlier. I think she's a little worried as to why I'm extending my stay. Did she call you?"

"She did. I told her you were happy, getting a tan, and not killing yourself."

I chuckled. "Did she believe you?"

"She said she might pop down for a *surprise* visit. I took that as code to check up on you. Maybe I should take a photo and send it to her, show her that you are indeed alive and kicking."

I laughed some more. "I don't want to leave here. I don't know why, but I feel totally at home. I feel like I belong and I can be myself. I know that sounds terrible, bearing in mind what she, and my mum and Kerry, have done for me but..."

"I know what you mean. There's something about this place that just captures your heart and holds on. When Jim and me came, that first time just for a holiday, I felt the same. It took a lot of persuasion to convince him to pack up and move, but we've never looked back and regretted our move."

Nora left to head back to her shop and I continued to write. I wrote until my hands ached, until my shoulders and back were screaming at me to change my posture. And I loved every second of it. I poured myself onto the pages and it felt cleansing. I had no idea what I was doing, of course. I hadn't even bothered to Google structure or punctuation and flicked back and forth to the dictionary many times.

It was the following day that my life was to take a dramatic change of route.

"Guess what?" Nora said as she huffed and puffed up the garden path.

"Why didn't you come in the front door?" I asked.

"I don't know really, but I'm here now, and guess what?"

I shook my head a little and smiled. Nora had a key; she normally let herself in the front door. That day she'd walked a little further down the lane to the beach entrance, along and up the little steps to the back garden. I sat, as usual, writing at the metal garden table with Dini lying by my feet, soaking up the morning sun.

"What?" I asked, knowing I'd never guess.

"The cottage is up for sale."

I looked sharply over at her as she sat opposite me.

"Oh!"

My heart sunk a little. "Do you think the new owner will keep it as a holiday cottage?"

"I don't know, no one's bought it yet. They want me and Jim to still caretake."

I made my way to the kitchen and put the kettle on for a cup of tea. While I waited for it to boil, I looked around. The whitewashed walls needed a coat of paint, some of the windows needed replacing and, of course, the heating system was non-existent. Outside, it was weather beaten. The West Coast could be brutal in the winter; the trees along the lane grew at an angle due to the strength of the wind. The furniture was dated and, although I loved the cottage, it did have an unloved feel about it. I wondered what it would be worth.

"Who are they selling it with?" I asked as I took the tea outside.

"I didn't ask. I could," she said. I saw the twinkle in her eye as she caught my line of thought. "And I imagine they would do a deal if there were no estate agents involved," she added.

We drank our tea, chatted about the shop and my writing. Nora was excited to read what I'd written. It hadn't crossed my mind to show it to anyone, it was just my way of getting all the crap out of my head. I let her have a look at a couple of paragraphs while we sat. She chuckled and laughed at a couple of scenes.

"I love it. You should write it up properly. And you should correct some of that punctuation. I might be able to help with that."

"Oh, I don't know. It's not going anywhere once it's finished," I replied with a laugh.

"Why not? Who knows, you could be the next book of the week on *Richard and Judy*."

Richard and Judy were daytime television show hosts and had recently started a book club. I'd found out they actually lived not a million miles away as well.

"Now that I doubt. But thank you for the vote of confidence. I'll keep it in mind."

"Well, I best be off, and I want to read some more. Interweb it to me."

It took me a moment to understand what she'd meant. As she closed the gate behind her and started down the steps, I called out.

"Do you mean email it?"

"That's the word."

"I don't have your email address."

"Oh, do I need one?"

She laughed as she tottered off. I didn't think Nora had a computer; she'd only recently joined the masses with a mobile phone. And even then, I was constantly reminding her to turn it on.

I closed down the file with my writing and started another—a letter to Casey. I'd given up emailing; they seemed to constantly bounce back. At first I started at a blank page, thinking of what to write. How to put my life in way she would understand. I was beyond begging for her forgiveness, and if I'd learnt one thing over the past few months, it was that I hadn't done anything wrong. I just wanted her to understand.

I wrote the first words that came into my head, and before I knew it, an hour had passed and I'd written ten pages, most of which was babble.

I had no way of printing the letter off and maybe I would never send it. It said nothing more than I'd already tried to say in multiple emails and previous letters, but in my mind I was communicating with her.

"Jayne, guess what?" I heard.

"Nora, why don't you telephone me instead of running up and down that lane?"

She chuckled. "It gets me out of the shop. Now do you want this news or not?"

"Go on."

"The Turners want to talk to you."

"Who are the Turners?"

"The owners of this," she said, as she waved her hand at the cottage.

"Oh, about what?"

"I don't know. Well, I think I do, but call them."

She thrust a piece of a paper towards me. Written in pencil was a telephone number.

I held the piece of paper in my hand for what seemed like an age before picking up my mobile.

"I don't know if I need to think about this."

"You're only asking questions, nothing more. You can't make any decisions without knowing the asking price."

I dialled. The dial tone suggested I was calling abroad and I cringed at the thought of, one, if there was a time difference, and two, the cost.

"Hello?"

"Oh, Mrs. Turner? My names Jayne, I'm staying at the cottage in Bude. Nora gave me your telephone number. I wondered if you had time to chat?"

"Oh, yes. Thanks for calling, Jayne. She said you might be interested in purchasing the cottage."

"I might be. I don't want to waste your time if the cottage is out of my price range, and I haven't spoken to my family about this yet."

"I understand. I'll be honest with you; my husband has a terminal illness. We live most of the time in Portugal, he loved his golf, and to be honest, I'd rather settle things before..."

She couldn't finish her sentence. I could hear how choked her words had made her, and I swallowed back the lump that had formed in my throat.

"I'm sorry to hear that. I lost my son recently, so I know how hard it must be for you."

"Nora said. I hope you don't feel she was gossiping. We fell in love with that cottage when we first visited. I know it will sound strange but we want someone to live in it, someone who will love it as much as we did. Bob has been ill for so long, and it's a shame that we haven't gotten to visit in such a long a time. We haven't put it with an agent yet so, if you're interested, how about making an offer?"

"I have no idea what it's worth, Mrs. Turner, to be honest. I don't have a great deal of money, and I don't want to insult you with a low offer."

I had no idea how to go about buying a house. Michael had dealt with the purchase of the one in Kent, and he already owned the apartment in London we'd first lived in.

"Have a think. Maybe I shouldn't say this, but the value isn't important right now. I just want to settle everything."

I said that I'd call again in a few days, once I'd looked at my finances.

"Well?"

"She asked me to make an offer. I have no idea what to do."

"Is this somewhere you can live? You'll need to think about your family."

And therein lay the problem. I would be five hours away from Benjamin, from my mum, Carla, and Kerry. Maybe if I could find a job, I'd be able to rent a little place in Kent and commute. But then I wasn't sure how practical that would be, and I didn't want to purchase the cottage and have it standing empty for weeks on end.

Nora left and I sat in the garden, looking out over the calm sea. The sunlight bounced off the water, making it hard to see the surfers. I could hear the tinkle of laughter from children making sandcastles and paddling. I could feel the sun on my shoulders and the slightly salty breeze ruffle my hair. It was my dream cottage, the cottage I'd drawn as a child. It was the one place I'd felt the most relaxed and seemed to run to, although I'd only visited three times. But could I live there?

I took a walk along the beach. I thought of Ben. He would have loved the area. I pictured him sitting on a surfboard and waiting for the next wave to hit. I sat facing the sea and in my mind I saw him. He was laughing, enjoying his life.

I remembered Stefan and I sitting in the exact same spot, our backs to the cliff and taking selfies. I hadn't looked at those pictures for a long time. I took my phone from my pocket and scrolled through my contacts. I thought for a while, before I sent a text.

*Hi, I'm not sure what to say other than I'm sorry. J xx*

My finger hovered over the send button. It would be a text out of the blue and I wondered how Stefan would feel when he saw it. I closed my eyes against the tears and pressed send. My hands shook as I turned off the phone and placed it back in my pocket. It was time to make some changes, time to start a new life. I could never go back to the old me; I couldn't return to Kent, I had to start afresh.

I practically jogged back to the cottage. There was a bubbling of excitement in my stomach. I grabbed my laptop and went to my online bank. Could I afford the cottage and have some left over for the repairs? Could I live after I'd spent the money? I sat with a pad and pen and worked out my finances. I then Googled cottages for sale in the area. Hardly any came up, which didn't surprise me but it didn't help in determining a fair value. All I could do was offer what I could afford and see what happened.

I called my mum first.

"Hi, Mum. How are you?"

"Hello, darling. I wanted to talk to you today, how strange that you should call first. I've had a good day, actually. Mabel and Eric took me shopping and we are off to Scrabble at the community hall in a minute. I've decided to join some of the local clubs."

"That sounds like a great idea. I have an idea to run past you. The cottage I'm in is up for sale and I have an opportunity to put in an offer. I don't know what to do."

"Are you happy there?"

"Yes. I'll be honest, I don't know if I want to stay in the village. There are just too many horrible memories, and I can't walk past my house without it affecting me. But I don't want to be so far away from you, either."

"Jayne, the one thing I do not want you to do is hang around because of me. If you have this opportunity, then go for it. Imagine if you didn't, imagine if you saddled yourself with a house here that you don't love and I die. You're stuck."

"Oh, don't say that..."

"It's true. I'm not going to be around forever. How much is it?"

"Well, that's the thing...I don't know. They asked me to put in an offer. The owner, Mrs. Turner, said her husband was dying and she wanted to settle everything before he did. I'd feel I was cheating her out of a fair value if I don't do some research, but there's nothing for sale to compare it with."

"I'm going to say something you might think is mean. You don't know these people. She's giving you an opportunity to put in an offer. If she wanted a fair price, she'd be going to an estate agent, who'll have the same trouble as you in coming up with a value. Offer

324

what you can afford. And if it's not enough, I have savings."

"I don't want your money, Mum."

"You'll be getting it anyway, less what the tax man wants, so why not have it now?"

"What do you think Carla would say?"

"Carla is your best friend. If she's not happy for you, then I'll kick her backside. Ring them, then call me back and let me know what they say."

"I want to speak to Kerry first. I won't be able to see my grandson so frequently and that's going to be hard."

"Think about all those summers where he can grow up on a beach. What child wouldn't want that?"

I hadn't thought about that. As we said our goodbyes, I was already planning on summer holidays and Christmas around the fire. I took a walk around the cottage, making my mind up. It had two bedrooms; enough space for me and only a five-hour drive back to Kent. It wasn't the end of the world.

The ping of my phone alerting me to a text had my heart stop. Could that be Stefan had replied? I walked back the kitchen and picked it up, holding my breath as I did. I scrolled my finger across the screen and breathed out sharply. It wasn't him. In fact, it was a pizza company offering me a discount on my next purchase. I felt a sense of disappointment that it wasn't Stefan replying then chastised myself. I wasn't going down that road again. I wasn't going to hang onto the phone or the laptop hoping for a response, and I had no right to expect one.

I decided to call Kerry next. She was thrilled and urged me to do the same as Mum had, to call and make an offer. She assured me she had a support network around her that she could call on if necessary. Francis had been to see her a couple of times, she had my mum, her own, and Carla. She'd miss me, of course, but looked forward to spending time at the cottage. And like mum had said, she was thrilled that Benjamin would have somewhere to grow and play in the summer months.

Calling Carla was the hardest. I felt like I was letting her down. She'd cared for me, paid for my hospital treatment, although I'd offered to pay her back, she'd refused. I felt like I had taken her generosity and was walking away.

Nerves got the better of me, I'd think for another hour or so before I decided on what to do.

Mrs. Turner called me before I had a chance to get back to her.

"Jayne, I know we said we'd leave it a few days but I've been talking to Nora. She explained your situation, all of it, and I know asking for an offer might be awkward. I've talked to my husband, and we would be more than happy to accept two hundred thousand pounds. We know the cottage needs some work, we don't have a mortgage, and to be honest, no one to leave the money to. If that's agreeable with you, and I don't expect an answer today, we can get cracking with the sale."

"Wow, I think that's way under value. Are you sure about that?"

Two hundred thousand pounds wouldn't buy a starter home in Kent, nor would it buy a two-bedroom cottage on a beach in one of the most popular places in Cornwall. I'd expect the cottage to be double that, even in its current condition. The view and location was worth another hundred thousand on it's own.

"It may be, but I want to be able to enjoy some time with Bob and not worry."

"Then yes, I'd love to buy the cottage."

Was I being impulsive? Maybe, but I could afford the two hundred thousand pounds from my divorce settlement and that would leave some to renovate and live on for a while. I wouldn't have enough forever, but I'd certainly not have to worry for a couple of years.

"That's great news. How about I get our solicitor to contact you?"

"Thank you, yes, that would be good."

We finished our call and I sat stunned that I had just bought a house. Not only a house, but one at a fraction of its value. I grabbed my pad and pen and made some lists. New heating system, new windows, a lick of paint, upgrade the bathroom and new flooring. I would need to speak to the solicitor about the furniture. I imagined Mrs. Turner wouldn't be worrying about collecting it, which meant I would either have to dispose of it, or keep it and sell my own.

Another thought ran through my mind. I called Carla.

"Hey you, I was just thinking of you," she said after she'd answered.

"I have some news, I'm not sure how you'll take it, though."

"Oh, I don't think I like the sound of that."

"I might have just invested in property."

"You found somewhere? Oh, that's great! In the village?"

I paused. "No, here in Cornwall. The cottage I'm in is up for sale and at a ridiculously low price."

"Really?" She didn't seem overly upset.

"Yeah. I just spoke to the owner. They want two hundred thousand and it's right on the beach. I showed you the pictures from last time, didn't I?"

"You did, that's seriously cheap. Are you sure you heard them right?"

"Yes, her solicitor is contacting me. I can afford to buy this outright, have some money for repairs, and still some left over to live on."

"So you won't be looking back here, then?"

I was dreading that part of the conversation.

"No. Other than you, mum, Kerry, and Benjamin, there's nothing there for me. I feel terrible in leaving you, especially after what you've done for me, but I love it here. And when is an opportunity to buy a beachfront cottage at that price ever going to come along again?"

"So you're not coming back?" The tone of her voice had changed; I detected sadness.

"Of course I am, in a couple of days. Until the sale is sorted, I guess."

"Oh, that's good then. At least we can have a proper goodbye."

"It's not goodbye, though, it's only five hours away. Think of summer holidays on the patio with a Pimm's and watching the surfers," I said.

"Mmm, carry on, I'm warming to the idea."

"Sinking our toes into the warm sand and walking along the beach. There are some amazing restaurants locally and as I said, surfers to ogle."

Carla laughed. "Your mum told me earlier. I'm thrilled for you, Jayne, I really am. I'm going to miss you like mad, of course, and no doubt we'll be putting some miles on the car, but go for it."

"You bloody tease! I was terrified in telling you."

"Why?"

"Because of everything you've done. I feel like I'm just walking away."

"Do you know something? That's about the best thing you could have said. I've loved having you here but if you're able to walk away, start again on your own; then my work is done. And I'll be glad to get rid of that stinking dog."

We both laughed, harder when I explained Dini had perked up his ears as if he'd heard her comment.

"Seriously, Jayne, for that price, you can't not do it. That will double in value overnight."

"I'll be back in a couple of days. Will you help me with the solicitors?"

"Of course I will. Now, drink that Pimm's and say hello to those dishy surfers. I'll see you in a couple of days."

We said goodbye and I danced around the kitchen. I felt totally stupid and I didn't care. I was about to buy my own home, all by myself.

I packed up the cottage with a slight hangover, after spending the previous evening drinking wine with the boys. I'd made them dinner, the first proper meal they'd eaten in ages, they'd said, although I suspected that was a lie. I knew they ate at Life's A Beach once the diners had all left, but it was nice to have their company. I told them about buying the cottage and that I hoped to get back within a couple of weeks. I was hoping I could pay rent until the sale went through.

Dini and I made the journey home, and whether it was subconscious or not, I felt the tension return the closer I got to the M25 motorway. I passed my in-laws and noticed Michael's car on the driveway. I thought back to that letter I'd typed and decided I would print it off and leave it with Francis to give to Casey.

I was welcomed with a big hug from Carla, who immediately wanted to show me her research. She'd been Googling Bude and was excited that I was, indeed, getting a bargain with my cottage. A one-bedroom apartment with a sea view started at more than I was paying.

That evening, I babysat; Kerry had a couple of friends who wanted to take her out for a meal. It was to be the first time she'd left Benjamin and the first time she'd been out since Ben's death. Carla was over the moon to play Great Aunty, although not so keen on the title she'd been given.

"I'm not old enough to be an aunty, let alone a great one," she complained.

Benjamin was a delight; he slept most of the evening, waking only for a cuddle, to give a smile, and a feed. Kerry called constantly until I reminded her that I had fairly successfully brought up two children of my own.

"You know, I've been looking at you. You look so different. Two weeks in the sun has done you wonders," Carla said.

"I feel good. Not great, but good. I don't know what it is about the place; I love it there. And I'm sure the Victorians had it right when they said the sea air was healing."

"Have you heard from Casey?"

"Not a word. I've got a letter to print off and I'll give it to Francis, but other than that, I don't know what else to do. I've called, I've emailed, and whether this is right or wrong, but I don't know for how much longer I can do that. It kills me every time she ignores me."

"I'm stunned by her, to be honest. I know she was angry, she had no right to be, but this is way beyond reasonable."

We fell silent for a while, sipping on our wine. I didn't want to dwell on her.

"Have you heard from him?" I asked, not wanting to use his name.

"Not for a while. I can email him, if you want me to. You..."

She paused, staring into her wine glass.

"I what? Come on, I need to hear it."

"You broke his heart. I think he needs to cut all ties so he can move on."

I sighed. "I know I did, and I regret that."

I didn't tell Carla that I'd texted him, or that he hadn't replied. I wasn't entirely sure why. I would have thought she'd been delighted, but I needed him to make the decision whether to contact me back. If she knew, I believed she would email or call him and want to know why the silence.

It saddened me that he'd given up, and I really shouldn't have expected him not to. I'd treated him abysmally, and it was something I regretted. I wished I could turn back the clock, I wished I'd done things differently, but I couldn't dwell on that. I had to move on as well.

I received a call from the Turner's solicitor with details of the cottage. I forwarded details of a solicitor Carla had recommended and waited anxiously for them to do whatever it was they did. In the meantime, Carla and I went through the boxes at the storage facility. There was a lot of junk to dispose of; boxes to deposit to Francis' for Michael and Casey, and Ben's things went to Kerry. I made a list of what furniture I wanted to keep and we sent the rest to an auction.

It didn't fetch much, enough to buy some new tyres for the car and a haircut for me. My hair had grown so long it neared my waist, and despite the medication and abuse it had received over the past few months, it looked healthy.

I took a couple of boxes back to Carla's and we sat in the lounge and went through them. They contained my personal things, some old letters that went in the bin, birthday cards from my parents from when I was a child, and towards the bottom of one, I found a tissue wrapped small object. I pulled it out and just by the feel knew what it was. I sighed as I unwrapped it.

I held the silver angel in my hands, my finger traced the delicate filigree before I closed my hand around it and held her to my heart.

"You miss him, don't you?" Carla said quietly.

I didn't answer. We'd had the same conversation many times. Yes, I missed him, a lot. I loved him. But he'd moved on, he'd given up, and I didn't blame him. The last thing I wanted was to have him hanging by a thread, waiting on me. I wasn't ready for a relationship.

"Will you do me a favour?" I asked.

"Sure."

"Give this letter to Francis, ask her if she'll hand it to Casey when she sees her next."

Carla took the envelope from me. She held it in her hands without speaking for a while.

"Are you sure you don't want to hand it to Francis yourself?"

"No, I think that's another area of my life I have to let go. As much as I appreciated her coming to talk to me, she will always be a reminder of Michael, and I want to forget."

"You'll never forget your marriage, as much as I'd love you to."

"Forget is the wrong word. I just want to move on now. I want to get back to Cornwall and start to live the life I've always dreamed of. Can you understand that?"

She hugged me. "I do."

# Chapter Twenty One

A month passed and I finally headed back to Cornwall. Although I didn't own the property, the Turners had agreed I could rent the cottage directly from them until the sale was complete.

I stopped at Nora's on the way, to stock up on some essential items, before I could get to the supermarket the following day. I opened the door to the cottage and Dini rushed in before me. He'd made it his home as well.

I decided to make some notes of what work was required before the winter arrived. It was already September, and I wanted certainly for some of the windows to be replaced before the howling winds arrived.

Jim had decided he was the one to negotiate with tradesmen on my behalf. I could have done it, I was more than capable of negotiation, but I was informed that as a newbie, it was likely I'd be taken advantage of. I smiled and gave Jim a free rein. I'd call him the following morning with the dimensions and he could get to work.

The following week was a whirlwind. The boys wanted to help paint the outside with me. We started at the back, and after scouring the local hardware stores; I found a masonry paint that I hoped would withstand the sea spray and the harsh winters. A window company came to measure for a quote and my furniture arrived.

Nora was concerned that I was being a little premature. If the sale fell through, I'd have to pack it all up again. I had no doubt the sale would proceed as expected and after some grumbling, she helped me load most of the contents and take it to the local charity shop. Mrs. Turner had told me the cottage had been furnished from charity buys so I didn't feel bad in returning it.

Greg took some of the furniture; he had taken over fully as manager at the restaurant and would be staying on once the others left for the winter. There was a small flat attached so I was glad to hand over some of the older things, the double bed, and bedroom furniture to him.

A week later the cottage was starting to feel like home.

I'd set up a small home office in the corner of the living room. I'd found a rather nice antique, ornate desk in the charity shop, small enough to house my laptop and a printer without taking up too much space. It blended in well with my brown leather sofa that was arranged in front of the fire.

September ended and with it the last of the tourists. It had been a busy past couple of months; the lane outside was often congested with cars heading for the small beach car park.

"Phew! I'm glad the season is over," Nora said, as she took a seat at my kitchen table.

"How's business over the winter?" I asked.

"Slow, mainly locals, but we earn enough over the summer to

keep us afloat."

"I got the contracts on the house. I think we complete in a couple of days. I want to get the window company in as soon as."

"That's great news. When is your family coming to visit?"

"Christmas. I wanted to get the work done first."

"If you need a bedroom, you know we have spare."

Nora visited frequently and I enjoyed the friendship we had developed. Maybe what I enjoyed more was that she hadn't seen me at my worst. I had a sense of embarrassment towards those that knew what I'd done. The boys, Nora, and Jim, they made light of my depression. It wasn't an issue for them, and I appreciated that.

Once Nora had left, I took Dini for a walk. He'd not been himself the past couple of weeks and I'd taken him to the local vet. Nothing was found to be wrong with him, but I'd made the requested appointment to take him back should he not improve. He didn't run off to greet Tom as usual but stayed by my side.

"Hey, Mum. How is he?" he asked as he bent to pet Dini.

I smiled at the 'mum.' "I don't know. I might insist on a blood test."

"You know he has a lump, here? He might have got something stuck in his throat."

Dini was forever chewing up sticks or other objects he'd brought home from the beach. I bent to feel his neck. There was a lump just to one side of his throat that hadn't been noticeable the previous day.

"I'll ring the vet today. I bet he chewed on a stick and part of it is stuck."

It might account for why he hadn't wanted to eat as much.

"I would."

Tom stood and opened the shutters to the surf school. He had a couple of weeks before heading back to Australia for the winter. I would miss the boys when they left.

Dini and I started the walk back to the cottage. We'd normally walk the length of the beach but he wasn't up for it. As soon as I got in signal range, I called the vet and made an appointment to take him back that afternoon.

When it came time to leave for our appointment, Dini was about as enthusiastic as I was visiting the dentist. He didn't bound into the car, jump over the seat and press his nose to the window, waiting for it to be wound down. I began to worry.

He didn't care about the cat in the box that sat on the floor next to him in the waiting room. Normally I'd keep Dini outside until it was his turn to be seen, such was his dislike of cats. Fran, the vet, wanted to do some tests; I couldn't fail to notice her creased brow.

"What do you think it is?" I pressed her for an answer.

"That lump is a lymph gland. Both sides are enlarged. I think we can rule out that he has something stuck in his throat, and I'd like to get some blood work done before I make assumptions."

I left Dini with Fran and headed home. I sat in the garden and remembered. He'd been part of my family for seven years, which was pretty good going for a dog of his breed. He'd been my constant companion, the one I unloaded my thoughts and upset to, the one that cheered me up when sadness threatened to overwhelm.

It was late that evening when the vet called and asked me to visit. I drove with a sinking feeling in my stomach at the tone of her voice.

"I'm sorry, Jayne, but Houdini has cancer. It's in the lymph glands and its official name is Multi Centric Lymphoma. We've done a scan and there are signs of an enlarged liver and spleen."

"What does that all mean?"

"We can offer chemotherapy, but in this case, I don't think it's going to help."

"How long does he have?"

"Four, maybe five weeks. It's hard to be accurate. I'm sorry, Jayne, I wish I could have given better news."

"What's your recommendation?"

She sighed. "If he were my dog, I'd take him home until he got poorly and then I'd bring him back."

She didn't need to explain what 'bring him back' meant. I nodded, clipped the lead to Dini's collar, and led him back to the car.

Tears blurred my eyes and I blinked repeatedly to clear my vision as I drove home. My heart ached, more so when he leaned over the seat and licked the salty tears from my cheek.

Two weeks later, I was making that fateful journey back to the vet's. I'd made a promise to Dini that he wouldn't suffer, I remembered seeing my dad and the agony he'd endured. The boys, Nora, and Jim waited at the cottage for me. He was buried in the garden close to the gate, and I sobbed when Tom presented a plaque. A piece of driftwood with Houdini carved into it. Jim anchored the plaque in the ground and I said goodbye to one of my most faithful friends.

# Chapter Twenty Two

The end of October was approaching. I was walking back from lunch with Greg when I saw a figure standing in my garden. I shielded my eyes from the low-lying sun to get a better view. I couldn't make out the face but I knew. Instantly, or instinctively, I knew my daughter was standing in my garden. I ran, my feet stuck in the damp sand and my calves ached from the exertion. I watched her stumble down the steps and run towards me. She hesitated when she got close, not knowing what to do, I guessed. I wrapped her in my arms as she sobbed into my chest.

"I'm sorry, I'm sorry," she said over and over.

"Hush now. It's okay," I whispered into her hair.

Casey looked up at me and I noticed how gaunt she'd become. Dark circles framed her dull blue eyes. I cupped her face with my hands and kissed her forehead before placing my arm around her shoulders and walking her back to the cottage. She sobbed all the way.

"When did you get here?" I asked as I led her into the kitchen.

"A half hour ago, I think. Grandma gave me your letter. I got the train. I don't know what to say. I'm so sorry, Mum. I can't believe what an utter bitch I've been." Her words tumbled from her lips as the tears continued to fall.

"Sit down, let me make a cup of tea. You're here now, so no more apologies." I smiled at her.

I watched as she hugged herself, and I also noticed her wince. I placed the tea in front of her and watched her hands shake as she cupped them around the mug.

"Tell me, darling. Tell me what's wrong."

She looked up at me, and my heart broke at her tear-stained face and the haunted look in her eyes. She opened her mouth as if to speak, then closed it quickly.

"There is nothing you can't tell me. I'm your mum; I love you. Always have and always will."

"I just had an abortion. But that's not why I came," she blurted out.

I wasn't expecting that and tried hard not to show any emotion.

"Okay, where?"

"In Japan..."

"Was it a proper clinic?" I asked, interrupting her.

"Oh, yes. I'm just a little uncomfortable right now."

"When did this happen?"

"A couple of days ago, and please, Mum, I don't want you to think I came here just for sympathy. I..." She sighed. "I wanted to come months ago, I wanted to come the day after Ben... But Michael wouldn't let me."

I noticed the use of his name instead of her usual 'Dad'.

"Start at the beginning, and tell me everything," I said.

Inside I was fuming. Anger was bubbling away in my stomach and I tried my hardest not to let that show.

"I can't excuse my behaviour in the beginning. I didn't know about dad's other woman until Ben told me. I...I'm just going to say this. I was angry that you didn't do anything about it, about her. But that was before, before I did what I did."

She was choking on her words, I could see how hard it was for her to be honest with me and I stayed quiet.

"I met someone, he was married, and I knew that from the beginning. We had an affair, and I got pregnant. I didn't mean to, I'm on the pill. He freaked, Dad freaked, and I was dumped outside the clinic. I had to get a taxi home the next day."

My body shook with anger, with sadness, and with a desperate need to comfort her. I stood from my chair and sat beside her. I wanted to pull her into my lap and hold her tight, take her pain away. I placed my arm around her shoulder and she cried.

Casey was exhausted. I led her upstairs and helped her into a bath. I sat on the edge and sponged warm water over her, like I had when she'd been a child. I closed my eyes to the skeletal body that sat broken in front of me. When she was clean, I dried her, helped her into a pair of my pyjamas then put her to bed in the spare room. I lay next to her holding her in my arms until she fell asleep.

It was only when I'd returned to the kitchen that I cried. My baby was hurting and nothing that had happened in the past meant a thing at that point. I fired up my laptop.

*To: Michael*

*From: Jayne*

*Date: 10 October 2015*

*Subject: My daughter*

*You absolute fucking nasty piece of shit! How could you? How could you keep my daughter from me? How could you dump her outside an abortion clinic, and let her get a taxi home! You are despicable. You're a sorry excuse for a man. She's your flesh and blood, we made her, we brought her into the world, and no matter what she's done: You do not abandon her. She had you on a pedestal and you've destroyed her. You are about the poorest excuse for a father I've ever seen. She's here with me, in case you're interested, and part of me wants to tell you to stay away, don't ever contact her again but unlike you, I can't do that.*

*You can be the prick all you want to me, but let me tell you this, you treat my child this way and I will come after you.*

*You, Michael, will end up a very lonely old man, and one day all I can hope is that you will look back at your life and realise you were fortunate, but you threw it all away with your selfishness.*

I didn't sign off the email, and I pressed send long before I thought about the words I'd written. I didn't care about any repercussions, I doubted he would even reply, but I needed to say that. I meant every word. He could do and say what he wanted to me but to my child? I'd rip him to pieces.

I opened the back door and pulled my cardigan around me as I sat. There was a chill in the air but it was still a bright day. I called Carla and relayed the morning's events to her. She wanted to jump in her car and drive straight down. I asked her to wait a day or so, give me some time with Casey to find out all the details.

It was an hour or so that Casey surfaced. I'd heard her moving about upstairs, the floorboards had creaked as she made her way to the bathroom. I put the kettle on and then chuckled. That was the thing my dad had always done when there was a crisis.

I had a mug of tea ready on the table for her when she walked into the kitchen.

"I've missed this," she said.

"What, being waited on hand and foot?" I replied. I regretted my words as soon as I saw the anguish on her face. "I was joking, darling."

"But that's the thing, we all took you for granted. Okay, maybe not Ben but certainly me and..."

"Let's call him fucktard for now, shall we?"

Casey spat the mouthful of tea she'd just taken across the table before we both dissolved into a fit of giggles.

"Twat features? How about prick? That's my favourite word for him," I said.

"Do you hate him?" she asked quietly.

No matter what had happened, he was still her father.

"No, I dislike him immensely though. I don't hate anyone, Casey. I don't have it in me to do that. I hate situations that I can't control. I hate what I did to my family. But as for people? No."

"Will you tell me about that?"

"Absolutely. I can do better than that. How would you like to read about my life? And I warn you; some of it will be uncomfortable. When I was in the nuthouse..."

"Mum! You can't call it that."

"I can, and I do," I said with a laugh. "Anyway, when I was in the *hospital*, I was encouraged to write a journal. That journal has morphed into a book. It's not very good, it won't ever see the light of day, and I wrote it for two reasons only. I needed to, and I wanted for you to be the only one to ever read it."

"You wrote a book?"

"I wrote a lot of words, whether that can be classed as a book, I have no idea."

"Can I start now?"

"Only if you're up to it. But before you do, will you answer me one thing?"

"Yes."

"Who was the father? And did his wife know?"

"Technically, that's two questions. But he was a colleague of Dad's. I'm not sure I want to share his name right now. He doesn't deserve any protection, but I don't know that he deserves your wrath either. I went into that relationship with open eyes, knowing full well what I was doing. And no, his wife doesn't know."

"He most certainly does deserve my wrath. Someone as old as your father should know better. Make sure his wife never knows."

"I think I was just so lonely. I've lied about my life for years. It was never the fun that I made it out to be, and I think he took advantage of that. I certainly fell for his bullshit and that egotistical side of me, the side I hate, lapped up all the attention. You know what else? I was punishing myself, and Dad, by doing what I did."

I wasn't sure how to respond so said nothing at all.

"Can I ask you a question?" she said.

"Of course."

"Stefan. Are you still seeing him?"

"I haven't seen nor spoken to him since that day. I pushed him away because, at the time, I believed that was the right thing to do. I believed what you said, what your father said, and I blamed myself for not being around when Ben died. I felt I'd failed everyone. I regret that. Every day I sit here, or I walk the beach and do things Stefan and I did and my heart breaks a little more. I loved him,

344

Casey, like I've never loved—my children excluded—another human being before."

She sat staring at me for a while. I watched her wipe the tear from her eye with the back of her hand before staring out the window to sea.

"Did Dini love it here? I saw his grave."

"He did, and everyone loved him. I miss him."

"Do you wish so hard that God would turn back time? I pray, Mum, and I'm not even sure I believe, but I pray for forgiveness and to go back in time."

"I used to, but I learnt that's not possible, not probable, and not practical either. We go through shit and we learn from it. It's who we are after that counts. I'm not the same person you knew prior to my breakdown, and when you read my story, you're going to be hurt. I've been brutally honest with my words but know one thing: I love you, I always have, and I always will."

I pushed the laptop towards her after having located the file and opening it. It was over one hundred thousand words long, and by that point, at least in chapters and with some structure. She stood and took the laptop with her to the leather chair in the corner of the room. She curled up, wrapped a comforter around her shoulders to protect her from the chill from the panes of glass behind her, and started to read.

Casey read all that day and the following, and the one after. She stopped only to eat, wipe her tears away, or sleep. Even then I heard the creak of floorboards as she made her way downstairs in the early hours of the morning and I'd find her, head down on the kitchen table, with the laptop open when I rose.

I sat and anxiously awaited her verdict. On day four she closed the laptop and joined me in the garden. She picked up my packet of cigarettes and opened it.

"May I?" she asked.

"I can hardly say no but I'd rather it wasn't a big habit."

I smoked about ten a day, but that would be the first cigarette I'd ever seen her smoke. By the way she expertly inhaled and exhaled a smoke ring, I knew it wasn't her first.

"I found a photograph when I was clearing out one of the bedrooms at the house. It was of you in Broadstairs, 2012, I think. It's a beautiful photograph. I have it here."

Casey didn't meet my gaze but I heard her sigh.

"I'd forgotten about that."

"Who was he?"

I saw the tears that had formed in her eyes. "Someone I fell in love with, a forbidden love, a lecturer. Which is why I know I had no right to judge you."

"Was he married?"

"No, but it was that student—teacher thing. He wanted to love me back, but I was angry back then."

"At what?"

"You know, I don't actually know. He wanted to quit his job so we could be together, and I didn't want that. I guessed, and you'll hate me for this, I liked the forbidden part of our relationship. When he wanted it to be real, when he quit, I left. I've done a lot of bad things, I've ruined a lot of lives."

We sat in silence and looked out to sea. The sun was low on the horizon and the surfers were silhouetted as they waited for the last of that day's waves.

"It needs an edit," she said quietly, referring to the book.

"I'm sure it does."

"It needs to be published."

"I'm sure it does not," I chuckled.

"Have you read it?"

"I wrote it, of course I've read it."

"No, have you really read it? Taken yourself outside of the author and read it as a reader?"

"No, I guess I haven't."

"It's heartbreaking. It's funny and thought provoking, and with some tweaks to really make it fiction, it should be available for others. Someone might take comfort from that book, might stop just one person from doing what you did."

"You're just saying that because you're my daughter."

"No, I'm saying it because it's true. It was hard to read how you felt about me, and yet I feel...does cleansed sound right? I can't explain it. I know how I behaved and I guess I hadn't thought how you felt at all. I know you now, and never did before. I know you, the woman. Not the mum, not the cleaner or the cook, but the person you hid inside for all those years."

"Then it's served its purpose. I just wanted you to know the whys."

"Please, let's put it into print, just for us. We must be able to do that."

"I don't know. I haven't looked into it."

"I know I have no right to ask anything of you, but will you do me one thing?"

"Depends what it is," I said with a smile.

"Contact Stefan."

My smile slipped. "He doesn't want to know, Casey. I broke his heart and he's moved on. I texted him, he never replied."

"Try again."

I placed my hand on the side of her face. She leaned into it and covered my hand with hers.

"How about you edit my book, and then we'll find out how to make a cover or whatever we have to do."

I had no desire to print my book but I did have a desire to give her a project, to take her mind off her situation for a little while, and to distract her from more chat about Stefan.

"Aunty Carla is due today. Don't let her catch you smoking," I said as I rose and headed back inside.

Carla spent a long weekend with us and it was great to catch up. She loved my little cottage and the area. She fell in love with Nora and Jim, too. It felt great just to chat for hours on end with a glass of wine and laugh again.

Casey had told her about my book and they both nagged me to do something with it. Casey was spending hours a day correcting my poor spelling and grammar, restructuring and if anything, just the change in her was enough to satisfy me. In the few days she'd been at the cottage, like I had, she'd started to heal. I'd wanted her to visit the local doctor but she wasn't having any of it. I'd kept a close eye on her, watching for any wincing and even checking her clothing when I collected it for washing for signs of bleeding.

"So how are you?" Carla asked.

We sat in the garden, wrapped up and enjoying a glass of wine, before she headed back the following morning.

"Good. I'm feeling good. I emailed Michael, tore him off a strip. He never replied, of course."

"Did you expect him to?"

"No, not really. But I'm doing fine, you don't need to worry about me. I love it here. I'm feeling sad because, well, you know…but I made the right decision in buying this place."

In a little over a month, it would be the first anniversary of Ben's death and a subject we'd been skirting around. I'd made a decision not to return to Kent, although Casey wanted to. She wanted to lay some flowers on his grave and I'd told her she could take my car.

"I can see that. I just wish you could have been here with Stefan. That would have been your happy ever after."

"I texted him, a couple of months ago. He never replied."

She looked sharply at me.

"You never said."

"I wanted to see if he would before I said anything. And I didn't want you to badger him to reply." I smiled over at her.

"I can't believe he didn't reply. His last email to me was that he would always love you."

"I hurt him, Carla. I sent him away and basically humiliated him in front of my family."

"And he never mentioned that once in all the time I was speaking to him. If he felt humiliated, I'm sure he would have said."

"Well, it's done now. I have fond memories of him. I'll always treasure our time together, but I need to just let him go."

"Part of me wants to shake the living daylights out of you, Jayne. What harm can it do to contact him one last time?"

"His rejection, Carla, isn't something I could take twice. I know

I snubbed him, I ignored all his messages, his calls, but then I wasn't in a place, mentally, to deal with it. When I was, and rightly so, it was too late."

We fell silent other than our simultaneous sighs.

Casey and I linked arms as we waved Carla off the following morning. She'd be back for New Year's, heading over from France after spending Christmas with her parents.

Casey wanted to head into Bude for some shopping; I lent her the car and waved her off. With the cottage to myself, I sat at the desk and flicked through the book Casey had printed off and was working on. I noticed all her pencil scribbling; I also noticed the tearstains. I flicked through the pages and came to rest on one that had a small Post-It attached. It was the part where I'd described my feelings for my daughter after that fateful night. How I loved and disliked her in equal portions. I held the page up. In the light I could see words that had been rubbed out.

*I'm sorry.*

I replaced the page and tidied the desk. We hadn't spoken about the actual content of the book and I wondered if we ever would.

I pottered around the cottage, changing the bedding and generally tidying up. I had a box of clothing stored at the bottom of the wardrobe I was yet to unpack because of lack of space. I decided to go through it. I sat on the floor with my back to the bed and opened the lid. The clothes had been neatly folded and from memory, were last worn on the trip to the cottage with Stefan. I pulled out the black dress that still had white marks from the hallway wall on the back. I closed my eyes as the image of him holding me against that wall flooded my mind. I placed it to one side. Next, I pulled out the red silk scarf and a white shirt. I held the shirt to my face, inhaling the scent of his aftershave. After all that time, there was still a trace of Stefan.

Maybe it was the conversation with Carla, maybe it was the reality of knowing I'd written about him in a book Casey wanted in print, maybe it was the realisation that I'd lost the best thing that had ever happened to me—whatever it was, I broke down.

I'd tried my hardest not to cry over him, but at that moment, with those memories around me, I gave in to the sadness.

"Mum?"

I looked up and saw Casey in the doorway. She rushed over and crouched down beside me.

"I'm sorry, I just found these and..."

I wasn't about to explain their significance but I was holding his shirt in my hands.

"Oh, Mum."

It was her turn to comfort me. She sat beside me with her arms around my shoulder.

"I was doing okay, for months I've been doing okay," I said.

"It's okay to have a flip out every now and again. Something reminded you of him and now you're upset."

I wiped my eyes with the back of my hand.

"What do you have there?" I asked.

Casey held a plastic bag in her hand.

"Oh, it's nothing. Something I picked up today."

I wasn't convinced by her false smile, but it was her business so I said nothing.

"Oh, fuck it. If we're going to cry, might as well do it all in one go."

She handed me the bag. I opened it and pulled out a picture frame. As I turned it over, fresh tears pooled in my eyes.

"I'm sorry. I was going to give it to you for Christmas, but then I thought you'd be crying all day."

Staring back at me was the most wonderful photograph of Stefan and me. One of the many selfies he'd taken as we'd walked the beach.

"Where did you get it?"

"It was on the laptop. I'm sorry; I was snooping. I wanted to see what he looked like, I couldn't remember."

I looked at him, my fingers traced over his face. His piercing blue eyes stared back at me and that lopsided wicked grin had me smiling.

"Look at you though, Mum. Look at that smile. I haven't seen you smile like that for years."

"He made me happy."

I stood before we could continue the conversation. I folded the dress and scarf and placed them back in the box. The shirt I laid on the bed.

"Come on, help me get dinner on," I said.

I took the photograph downstairs and placed it on the mantel over the fire. It stood next to one of Ben and Kerry, another of Kerry and Benjamin, and one of Casey at her graduation.

We ate together and chatted about her plans. She couldn't return to Japan and doubted she would get a reference, bearing in mind she'd been on an internship and had walked out. I had enough to support us both but it wouldn't last forever.

After dinner, Casey settled herself at the desk to continue with her editing. She chatted about punctuation, or lack of, and offered alternatives for some of the strange wording that had found its way in my writing. She was animated when she worked.

Two weeks later, we had a manuscript. We just needed a title and then half an idea of what to do after. Casey spent all her time on Facebook, Google and other Internet sites until she eventually announced we could publish it ourselves on Amazon.

"Whoa, no. I can't have that up for everyone to read. What if he sees it? He might not agree. What if Grandma sees it?"

"It's written as if it's fiction, Mum. Just deny it's real if anyone asks."

"Those that know me know it's real."

"And they're unlikely to read it. We'll come up with a pen name."

We sat for an hour, drinking wine and laughing at some of the most ridiculous pen names she'd thought up. Eventually we settled on one. *Charley Williams.* My dad's first and middle names.

"We need a cover," Casey announced.

I had no idea how to go about that. But like the diligent daughter she was, she already had it in hand. She'd found a designer in Canada, Margareet, who had agreed to help. A few emails later, we had an idea.

Within that week, *A Virtual Affair* was born.

It was an exciting time and a project that brought Casey and me closer together. We'd sat side by side, hour after hour looking at marketing, setting up a Facebook account and making teasers. I was stunned at how quickly she'd grasped the concept of self-publishing. Now all we had to do was actually publish it.

The night we pushed that publish button, we celebrated with a glass of champagne. I had no idea what was to happen, and I was under no illusion that the book would actually sell. It wasn't meant to. It was just a project that healed both of us.

The following morning I woke to a squeal.

"Mum, we sold three books!" Casey said with excitement.

"Really? Let me see."

There was a little red line on a graph that showed three sales. We danced around the living room at the thought three people would read our story. I classed it as our story because she'd done all the hard work. Little was I to know the hard work was actually about to begin.

Margareet was amazing. She guided us through the world of indie publishing, arranged for some bloggers to talk about our book, and by the end of week one; we'd sold ten.

We'd ordered some paperbacks, just enough for our family and a few friends. Nora wanted one, as did Mum, Carla, and to my amazement, Francis. Francis was the one I was most concerned about. Those people knew what I'd written wasn't fiction. But in one way, they'd get to see the real me, the person I'd hidden from them for years.

November seemed to have snuck up on us and with it the rain

and winds. I was thankful for the new windows, which kept most of it at bay. The new heating system didn't appear to work and we spent many an hour on the phone to plumbers and engineers, arguing for a return visit. Again, Casey came into her forte. She was the ultimate professional, until it got to the point of threatening to splash their poor service and thievery all over the local press! Needless to say, two engineers arrived and the heating was up and running.

Our books arrived, and the day we opened the cardboard box and held one in our hands was one of the proudest of my life. Other than producing two wonderful children, I'd done nothing else. My dreams of building homes for the poor so I could leave a legacy paled into insignificance when Casey pointed out that no matter what I did with the book, whether I pulled it from publication or not, it was out there—forever.

We spent some time wrapping and sending the ones out to family. It was with reluctance that I personalised a message inside the front cover. That was for two reasons; first, I didn't want to spoil it, and second, it just felt a little vain. Each week we saw an increase in sales. It wasn't enough to live on, of course, but enough to cover our costs. Casey became a social media addict and would regularly post about the book, tweet or whatever it was called. She would report to me with excitement in her voice when a review came in or when someone talked about it. And, of course, we sobbed and plotted the death of the lady who left a scathing one star review. Nothing was realistic for her and it was on the tip of my fingertips to give her my phone number, and I'd tell her how realistic the book was.

Three things happened that month. Nora informed me that

she had customers who wanted to buy the book and the local press picked up the story. But the most surprising was that Francis had called. The Women's Institute wanted to have it as book of the month. I was pretty sure they were terrified of her, so no doubt hadn't done that because they felt the book was worthy, but I didn't care. More books were ordered and Casey set up a web page for me. I decided to share the profits with her. She was the one doing all the work, after all.

Karen and Alison were two girls that regularly chatted with Casey online; they had become fans of the book and wanted to help. I spent many an hour messaging with them and we soon became firm friends. They got together a team, Elaine, Kerry-Ann, and Ann. My Angels, as I called them, spent all their time 'pimping' the book. It totally baffled me, but somehow whatever it was they did, it seemed to be working.

*A Virtual Affair* became a bestseller, and I think the night we found that out was the night I nearly died of fright. Shit just got real, as Casey was prone to saying.

"Mum, look," Casey said, as she bounded through the front door one morning.

She opened the local newspaper to an article on me. We sat at the kitchen table and read, squealed, winced, threw in a few 'holy fucks,' and then read it again. I was being branded as a new bestselling local author in Bude. Not that any of it was a lie, but I certainly wasn't as grand as they made me out to be. They had a photograph of me sitting at the garden table and looking wistfully out to sea. The wind had caught my hair and it fanned out behind me. Despite being very critical of myself, even I agreed the photo was a great one. Casey ordered a copy; it could be my profile picture she'd said. I had no idea what she was talking about, of course. Marina, the reporter, had done a wonderful job of detailing the book, keeping my life fairly private, and even read and left a glowing review.

# Chapter Twenty Three

As November wore on, so our excitement of the book and its progress became tempered with the impending anniversary of Ben's death.

"He would have been so proud of you," Kerry said, during one of our weekly conversations.

"I know he would have. I dedicated the book to him, but I just wish he were here with us. I'd give up everything for one more conversation with him, one hold of his hand, and I can't help that feeling of letting him down returning."

No matter how hard I tried, anxiety started to build. That feeling of guilt and regret crept over me until it took a hold. When it got to the point that I didn't want to get out of bed a couple of days before the actual anniversary, I made a call.

"Louise, it's Jayne. I think I need to talk today."

I had her number on speed dial, with permission to call should I need to chat. I'd informed the hospital that I had moved, and although I didn't the need to visit for therapy, it was nice to know someone was on the end of the phone if I needed to talk. That day, I needed her.

We chatted about how I was feeling. She reassured me that it was to be expected and reminded me of some coping techniques.

Although not entirely happy, by the end of our call I had accepted that how I felt was normal. Jenn called me an hour or so later. I guessed Louise had informed her I was in need of a chat and she talked me through some relaxation.

It had been quite a few months since my stay at the hospital and I'd forgotten a lot. In fact, my memory of that whole period in time was hazy, so it was nice to have some reminders.

I woke the morning of Ben's anniversary and lay in bed, listening to the rain battering the back of the house. The bedroom door opened and Casey silently walked in. Her eyes were red-rimmed. I lifted the duvet and she climbed in beside me. She snuggled into my side, like she had as a child, and we lay in silence for a while just remembering.

She had initially wanted to travel back to Kent but, although she hadn't said so, I imagined she wanted to stay with me. Either for comfort or to ensure I would be okay. I didn't mind either way; I was happy to have her.

"I'd like to go for a walk," I said.

We climbed from the bed and dressed in wet weather gear, walking boots, jackets with hoods, and gloves. It felt invigorating to walk the beach; we had the whole place to ourselves. The rain lashed, it was cold and our cheeks burned, but God did we feel good when we returned. We'd stood at the bottom of the grassy steps and watched the sea rage against the shore and the rocks. White angry foam roared up the beach, bringing with it driftwood and seaweed. It completely mirrored our mood. It was as if Mother Nature was agreeing with me and complaining about the injustice of life.

As I always did, I touched my lips and placed that kiss on Dini's plaque as we passed. We stripped off our wet clothing and made tea.

"I don't want sadness today, I want to remember him and laugh. Let me tell you some funny memories."

We sat for a couple of hours as I recalled memories from their childhood. Casey remembered some, not others. We laughed, we shed some tears, and we took calls. Each time the phone rang; Casey asked if it was Michael. And each time I shook my head.

He wouldn't call to speak to me, I knew that, but I hoped he might at least have rung his daughter. I watched as the day drew to a close and the disappointment showed on her face.

That evening, we snuggled on the sofa in front of the fire and raised a glass of wine to Ben. I was glad I wasn't alone that day. I was also glad when we headed to bed and it was over. I'd dreaded that day for a year.

It was the week before Christmas and still with a heavy heart, Casey and I went in search of a Christmas tree. I'd found the box of decorations stored in the cupboard under the stairs and together we decorated it. It had been something Ben and I had done each year, and although it wasn't intentional to exclude Casey, I felt a little sad that she hadn't been involved. I enjoyed our day, we chatted, and we rearranged each other's baubles and laughed. We wrapped presents and placed them under the tree, and once done, we sat and looked at the little white lights, reflecting off the windowpane. Kerry was due to arrive with Benjamin and Mum the day before Christmas Eve. I'd managed to purchase a travel cot from the local charity shop and a new mattress from a store in town.

I had a little panic about where everyone was to sleep until Nora brought down an inflatable bed. Casey offered to take the blow up bed and we stored it behind the sofa. Mum would take my room and I offered to share with Kerry in the twin bedroom. I didn't want Mum to be disturbed should Benjamin wake in the night. She didn't want to disturb Kerry with her many trips to the bathroom either. We'd sort Carla's sleeping arrangements out when she arrived.

Nora and Jim joined us for Christmas lunch and it was the most raucous, wonderful Christmas I'd had since childhood. We laughed non-stop, opened presents, and drank wine. Poor Jim was well out of his comfort zone being surrounded by women, tipsy women at that. That evening, we settled in the living room with full bellies and chatted.

"He didn't even send me a card," I heard Casey whisper.

I'd watched her during the day check her phone repeatedly.

"Maybe he left one at Grandma's," I offered, knowing full well he hadn't.

She shrugged her shoulders then raised her glass.

"Let's kill him off in the next book," she said with a glint in her eye.

"I don't know that there will be another book."

"There has to be, you can't leave it at one," Kerry said.

"Well, I did have an idea a couple of days ago."

"Tell us then," Mum said.

I sat back on the sofa and looked at them. Then I shook my head. "No."

I laughed. I had a good plot line, for sure. But how my family would take the romance I wanted to write with the steamy sex scenes I had imagined, I had no idea.

It was early hours of the morning that I woke to gentle sobs. I slid from my bed, cradled Kerry in my arms and rocked her.

"I miss him so much," she whispered as she drifted back into sleep.

"I know, darling, I know."

Boxing Day was much the same as the previous. We ate, we took a walk along the beach, and we sat in front of the fire, revisiting our gifts from the previous day. Carla had brought me an e-reader and loaded it with money, or whatever one did with an e-reader. I could buy books and I took delight in browsing and downloading. Kerry had had some professional photographs done of Benjamin and her. They were framed and as soon as Jim could, he'd hang them on the wall for me. Casey gave me the most precious gift. She'd taken a selfie of us at the computer some time ago; she framed it with a cover from the book. She'd duplicated that little orange bestseller badge on the white card surround and added the poem that was featured at the front of the book. It was a poem I'd learnt in the hospital and one I looked back on when I needed to find some strength—an adaptation of The Serenity Prayer.

I whispered the words. It was something Jenn would whisper in relaxation class. In the beginning the words meant nothing to me. As time went on, it became important and I understood.

The following day, Kerry and Casey took themselves into town for a couple of hours; I babysat Benjamin while Mum took a walk up to see Nora. Being the same age, and from the same area as children, they had a lot in common and I was pleased that they seemed to have become friends already. I sat with Benjamin and showed him a photo album I'd found in one of the storage boxes. Not that Benjamin understood but I showed him pictures of his dad. His little fingers would grab at the page, pulled the clear plastic cover as if he wanted to hold the photographs himself. I vowed that he would, when he was older, own those albums.

When I looked at him and he stared back with the same eyes his father had, I felt closer to Ben. I wasn't religious, I wasn't superstitious, but I could have sworn I heard Ben's voice.

Tears rolled down my face as, and I was sure it was just a figment of my imagination, I heard, "It's all right, Mum."

Benjamin reached up, his hand touched my cheek, and I smiled at him. He was the spit of his father at that age. The same blond hair, blue eyes, the same nose but with Kerry's dimple on one cheek. He was going to be a nightmare where the girls were concerned when he grew up. I chuckled at the thought.

# Chapter Twenty Four

New Year's Eve arrived and with it, Carla. She'd driven from France, after visiting her parents, and arrived with yet another armful of gifts. Benjamin had been thoroughly spoilt. She brought cheeses, wine, olives, pate, and the most delicate and delicious Parisian macaroons. We devoured the lot and as the evening drew in, we headed for the beach. People had gathered, bonfires were lit and parties were underway. We picked a spot outside the gate, laid a blanket on the damp sand, and dragged the garden chairs and table to set up camp. We opened champagne and as midnight struck, so the boats moored out to sea sounded their foghorns. Fireworks could be seen from every direction, their brilliant display reflected on the sea. When the displays had calmed down, we lit the Chinese lanterns I'd bought. I whispered words to Ben and then let mine float up.

We were five women that had had a terrible time with loss, divorce, and change. It felt cathartic to watch five lanterns float away, as if we were letting go of the past, of our upset and sadness.

We headed inside and while Mum, Kerry, and Casey went to bed; Carla and I sat while I had a cigarette.

"I have something to tell you," Carla said. She had poured us another glass of wine.

"Oh, do tell."

"I've met someone, someone I think I can really grow to like."

"And you kept this a secret?"

"Well, I didn't think the timing was appropriate."

"Fuck the timing, tell me," I said with a laugh.

She told me of Mason, a business man she'd met initially in a coffeehouse in Bluewater Shopping Centre, of all places. He'd backed into her, causing her to spill her coffee. He'd replaced it; they got chatting and eventually ended up going out for dinner. I was a little upset that she hadn't told me at the beginning but understood her hesitance in sharing good news at a time when it was all about Ben.

We chatted for a while, she showed me a photo she had on her phone and I was pleased for her. It had taken her a long time to get over Charles, and I really hoped Mason was someone she could settle with.

Casey and I waved Kerry, Benjamin, Mum, and Carla off the following day. It had been wonderful to have them stay, and we made a plan that Casey and I would visit in a couple of weeks. I looked forward to that and realised I didn't feel the dread I had in returning to the village.

We sat in the living room to plot out the new book; I was excited to start writing again. Casey opened the laptop.

"Mum, you have an email," she said.

It had become commonplace to receive messages and emails from readers who had loved my book, and I took the time to reply to every one. I took the laptop from her and without looking, opened the page. My fingers froze over the keyboard and my breath caught in my throat. I heard a strangled sob, and it took a moment to realise it was from me.

"Mum?"

"It's from him," I whispered.

"From who?"

"Stefan."

In front of me was an email with one word in the subject line. Casey sat beside me.

"Please read it, Mum, I'm begging you."

I closed my eyes as my finger hovered over the email, and then clicked. It took an age to load.

*To: Jayne*

*From: Stefan*

*Date: 28 December 2015*

*Subject: Please!*

*I know I'm a little late, and I'm so sorry about that, but I just wanted to let you know I was thinking of you right now. I haven't stopped thinking of you, in fact. I kept in touch with Carla, she told me about Cornwall and I'm pleased you are there. I loved that cottage, and I know you did too. I don't know if you'll read this, I don't know if you read any of my emails. I'm struggling with what to say except...*

*I miss you – Jeg elsker dig.*

*S xx*

The words blurred. I pushed the laptop away and Casey caught it before it crashed to the floor. I curled my legs under me on the sofa and wept. My heart hurt so badly.

"Answer him."

"I can't."

"You can. Do not let this opportunity slide past, Mum. Please, what do I have to do here? Beg? I sent him your book; he knows it all. This is him reaching out to you. Please." Her voice caught in her throat and tears pooled in her eyes.

"What do I say?"

"The first thing that comes in your mind." She handed me back the laptop.

*To: Stefan*

*From: Jayne*

*Date: 1 January 2016*

*Stefan, I am so, so, sorry. The past year has been pure hell and I've missed you so much. I'm at the cottage and I'm healing. I think about you a lot and our time here. Sometimes I think I can still smell you in the bed. I hope so, anyway. I have your shirt and I sleep in it each night. It makes me feel closer to you. I still picture us on the beach and have such wonderful memories; it helps me to deal with the pain of what has happened. I miss Ben dreadfully but as each day passes, I don't hurt so much.*

*I know I have treated you badly and I can't say sorry enough for that. But please understand, I had to go through this alone. I really thought what I was doing was for the best, but now? I wish you had been here with me. Can you ever forgive me? I want you in my life; I just hope I'm not too late. If I am, please, just don't answer, don't reply. I will understand.*

*Jeg elsker dig, always.*

*J xx*

I closed the lid and stood. "Darling, I need to be alone right now."

I grabbed my coat and left the house. I walked down the garden path to the gate at the end, the gate that still needed one hinge fixed, and then down the grassy steps to the beach. I kicked off my shoes and walked barefoot in the cold damp sand to the water's edge. I breathed in deep. I closed my eyes and let the tears fall one last time. Whatever the outcome of that email, I needed to move on with my life.

I walked, lost in my thoughts and memories. I cried, I chuckled; I let the wind blow my hair until it was wild. My feet were cold but I still walked barefoot, letting the sand slip between my toes. I circled back to the cottage and saw Casey standing in the garden; she waved to me, calling me back.

I breathed in the smell of the salty air and seaweed, and I hoped.

"He replied," she said, as I closed the gate behind me.

I didn't speak. I wasn't sure what to say as I followed her to the kitchen. The laptop was on the table, open.

*To: Jayne*

*From: Stefan*

*Date: 1 January 2016*

*Subject: Jeg elsker dig*

*I'm on my way.*

TRACIE PODGER
*The End*

# Letter from Tracie

I want to tell you a little about how this book became.

For those that don't know me personally, some time ago I had a breakdown, a breakdown that resulted in me spending some time in the 'nuthouse.' All the scenes where Jayne spends time in the nuthouse are real. They are my experiences. Art therapy was something I never quite got the hang of!

This isn't the original version of *A Virtual Affair* that I wrote, that version is too personal. There are, however, many truths and a lot of made up stuff! I'll leave you to decide what is real and what isn't. I'm putting something out there that is painful to remember, but it's something only now I feel brave enough to do.

I started writing a journal as part of my therapy, that journal ended up a story of over one hundred thousand words. I wrote all day, every day when I came home from hospital. I got lost in the words, I forgot my troubles and I fell in love with writing.

So let's talk about depression—It's real, friends. It's a terrible illness that a lot don't understand. It isn't a broken leg; you can't see it. Unless it's something you have suffered from, you'll never understand the pain, the frustration, and the hurt to those surrounding someone with depression. I never believed in depression until it hit me like a freight train. I'd suffered for years before I understood what was wrong with me. I urge anyone in the same situation to get help. Speak, initially, to your doctor and be open and honest with your nearest and dearest. Seek counselling and if you're in the UK, fight for it.

There are charities than can help, I won't list them because it will depend on your country of residence, but use Google and make that call. Admitting you have a problem is the first step on your road to recovery.

I will always be a depressive; I just don't always suffer with depression. It's there, in the background and sometimes I fall a little but I'm able to pick myself up and carry on. It's hard for my family; I'm often under constant watch because times are not easy for hubby and me right now. But I'm able to cope far better than I've ever been and that's partly because I'm also surrounded by some wonderful friends.

*You can live, you can survive depression, and you will become stronger.*

# Acknowledgements

I could never have written *A Virtual Affair* without the support of my family. My husband has been my rock, without him, I wouldn't be here.

My heartfelt thanks to the best beta readers a girl could want, Karen Shenton. Alison Parkins and Lilian Flesher - your input is invaluable.

Thank you to Margreet Asslebergs of Rebel Edit & Design for yet another wonderful cover.

I'd also like to give a huge thank you to my editor - Megan Gunter with Indie Solutions by Murphy Rae. Please check out their web site - www.murphyrae.net

A big hug goes to the ladies in my team. These ladies give up their time to support and promote my books. Alison 'Awesome' Parkins, Karen Shenton, Karen Atkinson-Lingham, Marina Marinova, Lilian Flesher, Ann Batty, Fran Brisland, Jennifer Teasley, Elaine Turner, Kerry-Ann Bell and Louise White — otherwise known as the Twisted Angels.

To all the wonderful bloggers that have been involved in promoting my books and joining tours, thank you. I appreciate your support. There are too many to name individually – you know who you are.

The cottage in this book is real; it's not in Bude. I've used a little artistic licence to move it from its real location in Woolacombe. Life's a Beach is a real café come restaurant and is located on Summerleaze Beach, Bude. If you are ever in the area, visit, it's one of my favourite places. The Blue Cow is real, located in Meopham, Kent and owned by my friend, Jo Emery. She's not a barmy old woman but a wonderful supporter of my books.

If you wish to keep up to date with information on this series and future releases - and have the chance to enter monthly competitions, feel free to sign up for my newsletter. You can find the details on my web site:

*www.TraciePodger.com*

*Life is not about the destination but the journey.*

# About the Author

Tracie Podger currently lives in Kent, UK with her husband and a rather obnoxious cat called George. She's a Padi Scuba Diving Instructor with a passion for writing. Tracie has been fortunate to have dived some of the wonderful oceans of the world where she can indulge in another hobby, underwater photography. She likes getting up close and personal with sharks.

## Available from Amazon, iBooks, Kobo & Nook

*Fallen Angel, Part 1*

*Fallen Angel, Part 2*

*Fallen Angel, Part 3*

*Fallen Angel, Part 4*

*The Fallen Angel Boxset*

*Evelyn - A Novella*

*Rocco – A Novella*

*Robert*

*Travis*

*A Virtual Affair*

*The Facilitator*

*Gabriel*

*A Deadly Sin*

*Harlot*

*Letters to Lincoln*

## Coming soon

*The Passion Series – Jackson*

*Rocco: The Missing Years*

*Allana*

*A Deadly Mission*

## Stalker Links

*https://www.TraciePodger.com*

*https://www.facebook.com/TraciePodgerAuthor/*

*https://twitter.com/TRACIEPODGER*

*Amazon Author Page – http://author.to/TraciePodger*

# Recommended Reads

If you enjoyed *A Virtual Affair* then you might also enjoy *Letters to Lincoln*.

### *Description:*

What do you do when your husband dies unexpectedly?
You write him a letter, of course.
What do you do when someone answers that letter?

Dani was mid-thirties when she found herself alone and without her soulmate.
Coming to terms with her loss took all her strength and her voice.

If Dani thought she'd experienced the worst life could throw at her, she was wrong.

Lies, deceit, confusion surround her.
A stranger, a builder, and a priest, comfort her.

Letters to Lincoln is a contemporary romance about

overcoming loss, finding the strength to rebuild a life, and learning to forgive.

You can find *Letters to Lincoln* on all retail sites.